Why him?

What was wrong with her that she was so irrationally attracted to such an unsuitable man? She suddenly realized she was staring and jerked her gaze up to find him watching her.

Those dark eyes held secrets that called to the depths of everything female within her. As if he had seen everything there was to see in the world, knew everything there was to know.

Could do . . . *anything.*

Her pulse skittered and she sucked in a slow breath, willing her body to calm. She had seen his like before. He reminded her of Edward, with his untamed good looks and dangerous allure. But where Edward had been a charismatic man who used his gift for words as a way to entice people into doing what he wanted, Captain Breedlove wore danger as well-fitted as his elegant evening clothes. Edward had charmed, but Samuel Breedlove demanded.

And somehow, to her horror, some part of her responded to that subtle summons and longed to meet the challenge.

By Debra Mullins

Debra Mullins

Tempting
A Proper Lady

AVON
An Imprint of HarperCollinsPublishers

This is a work of fiction. Names, characters, places, and incidents are products of the author's imagination or are used fictitiously and are not to be construed as real. Any resemblance to actual events, locales, organizations, or persons, living or dead, is entirely coincidental.

AVON BOOKS
An Imprint of HarperCollins*Publishers*
10 East 53rd Street
New York, New York 10022-5299

Copyright © 2010 by Debra Mullins Welch
ISBN 978-0-06-188249-4
www.avonromance.com

First Avon Books paperback printing: June 2010

Avon Trademark Reg. U.S. Pat. Off. and in Other Countries, Marca Registrada, Hecho en U.S.A.
HarperCollins® is a registered trademark of HarperCollins Publishers.

Printed in the U.S.A.

10 9 8 7 6 5 4 3 2 1

For my awesome agent,
Lucienne Diver.
This is just the beginning.

Chapter 1

May 1876

Within the hour he would reclaim what was his.

Samuel Breedlove fisted his hands in impatience as the coach crept along behind the long line of vehicles waiting to reach the door of the country manor. Nineteen months he had waited, interminable nights when he had not expected to live through the next day. The goal to return to the life he had begun to build, and the fiancée who would help him do it, had kept him alive when he had been tempted to give up.

That, and the determination to thwart his enemy by surviving what should have been his murder.

The lights of the house beckoned; there was a celebration going on tonight. Would the lamps burn as brightly when Samuel darkened the doorway? Would Annabelle throw herself into his arms, blue eyes flooding with tears of joy? Or would Annabelle's father order the footmen to toss him out the door for disrupting the party?

He was betting on the first outcome. He and Annabelle had pledged to wed almost two years ago. She had wanted a husband, and he had needed a wife to help him realize his dreams of children and family. He was certain that once he explained where he had been all this time, she would be more than happy to acknowledge his prior claim for her hand. And certainly her parents, the closest thing he had ever known to family, would support him in the endeavor.

The coach came to a stop, and a glance out the window confirmed they were close enough for him to traverse the rest of the drive on foot. He jerked open the door and climbed out, the rasp of his shoe soles on the hard dirt grating against the edginess that had plagued him since he had made this decision.

"Are you certain about this, Samuel?"

He glanced up at his friend and ally, John Ready, who served as coachman tonight. "I made a promise, John. And you know I always keep my word."

The great hall of Nevarton Chase had never looked more spectacular.

Cilla Burke allowed herself a small smile of satisfaction as she surveyed the ambience she and twenty servants had created. The polished wooden floor gleamed beneath the light of the crystal chandelier, and cheerful garlands of flowers wrapped around the columns that encircled the room. The doors to the terrace had been left open so that the cool evening breeze could alleviate the heat from the crush of bodies. At the moment the musicians played a lively country dance, and peals of laughter overrode the murmur of conversation as young ladies promenaded with their partners.

Once she, too, had been one of those carefree misses, fresh and innocent and longing for the day she would be married. Bittersweet regret seasoned the memories. If she had only known . . .

Rather than being the belle of the ball, she was now in charge of arranging the affair—a paid employee whose future depended on whether society considered Annabelle Bailey's wedding the ultimate social event of the Season. It was no longer shameful for a woman to earn a day's wage for a day's work, and her husband's death had left her with very few choices. Anyway, she had no desire to return to the life of a debutante whose survival depended on ensnaring the right husband. How could she possibly, when the disaster of her own marriage had proven her instincts to be flawed?

Sensing the imminent melancholy lurking behind her thoughts, she forced herself to focus on the present. She was determined that Annabelle's wedding would be a stunning success—both for the bride and for Cilla's business reputation. Tonight's engagement party should set the tone.

"There you are, Cilla." Dolly Bailey, her employer, huffed to a stop beside her. Dolly's buxom figure had been squeezed into a dress of creamy azure, showing off her blond hair, blue eyes, and generous bosom. Matching blue diamonds sparkled at her ears and throat, glittering with every breath she took. "The butler has informed me that we may not have enough champagne for all the guests."

Cilla frowned. "How can that be? I made certain that we had enough for fifty people—"

"Fifty? No, no, dear. Seventy. I told you I sent out a few invitations of my own."

Cold dread seeped into her stomach. "No, you did not tell me that."

"Of course I did." Dolly smiled, her dimples flashing as her gaze followed the dancers. "I remember discussing the matter with you yesterday while we were at the Archer picnic."

Cilla let out a slow, quiet breath. "Dolly, I did not attend the Archer picnic. I stayed behind, do you not recall? To help the housekeeper count the linens that had just arrived."

"Oh." Dolly's brows beetled. "Then who did I tell? Oh, perhaps it was Annabelle."

"Perhaps it was." Cilla made herself smile with calm assurance even while a voice inside her head screamed in frustration. Annabelle would never have thought to pass on the message—not unless it affected herself, that is. "I will go discuss the matter with Evers."

"Bless you, Cilla. That's a wonderful idea." Dolly's eyes grew misty as Annabelle danced by in the arms of her fiancé, the Earl of Raventhorpe. "My baby is getting married, and to an earl of all things. She's going to be a countess." Dolly withdrew a delicate lace handkerchief from inside her sleeve and dabbed at her eyes. "Who could have imagined such a thing when I gave birth to her so many years ago in a one-room farmhouse in Virginia?"

"You can be very proud of your daughter." Cilla patted Dolly's arm. "No mother could ask for more."

"If her pa hadn't discovered that huge coal mine under the south field, none of this would have happened." Dolly sniffed into the hankie, then blew her nose rather loudly.

Cilla managed to keep her polite smile in place. No amount of lessons about English society had succeeded in tempering the Baileys' casual comportment.

The orchestra came to the end of a waltz. Then instead of continuing, the musicians remained silent as Virgil Bailey climbed the two steps leading to the terrace and stood on the landing before the open doors. He held up his hands to silence the buzz of conversation.

"Good evening, my friends, and welcome." He sent a genial smile around the room. "Tonight we celebrate a very special occasion. If my dear wife would come up here, and my daughter, Annabelle? And you too, Lord Raventhorpe."

"It's time!" Dolly fluffed her hair and tugged at her dress. "Do I look all right?"

"You look wonderful."

Dolly's radiant smile faded. "Oh, dear. The champagne . . ."

"We will use wine if necessary and tell everyone it is an American custom." Cilla shooed Dolly toward the steps where her husband awaited. "Go on now. They're waiting for you."

"Thank you," Dolly whispered, gratitude shining

in her eyes. Then she hurried across the expanse of the hall.

Cilla quickly turned away and headed for the double doors leading to the hallway. She had worked so hard to make Annabelle's engagement party the premier event of the Season. Nothing could ruin it, not if she hoped to earn the reputation she craved. She had no idea if there was enough wine in the cellar for twenty additional people, but she would consult with Evers and come up with a solution. Efficiency was what the Baileys paid her for, and she always made certain they got their money's worth.

Servants balancing trays with glasses of champagne streamed into the great hall from the servants' stairs as Cilla headed for the main doors. She started to step out into the hallway and found her path blocked by a stranger.

Though he wore sophisticated evening black, something about him read *untamed*. Was it his ink black hair, slightly too long for fashion? The sun-browned skin of his face and hands? His powerful build, made more impressive by the elegant cut of his clothing? Or maybe it was the go-to-the-devil look in his dark eyes?

A dart of pure feminine appreciation shot through her. Thrilled her. Annoyed her.

"Pardon me." He brushed past her with a brusque nod of his head, the contact brief but potent. She could not look away as he swept a glass of champagne from the tray of a nearby servant and continued to make his way to the front of the crowd.

Who was he? The accent might have been American. A friend of the Baileys?

Evers appeared in the doorway, two footmen at his side, breaking her focus on the mysterious man.

"Ah, Evers, Mrs. Bailey is concerned about the champagne."

"Where is he?" the butler asked, scanning the room.

"Who?"

"The American. He pushed past Thomas before we could stop him. Knocked the poor boy down."

"What?" She whipped her head around, searching for that tall, dark form. Men clad in evening black thronged the room from wall to wall, making it impossible to spot just one.

"He has no invitation," Thomas said, rubbing his swollen lip.

"He demanded to see Miss Annabelle," Evers added. "He was most adamant on the matter."

"Find him," she snapped at Thomas. The young man nodded and plunged into the morass of people. She looked at the butler. "Send for more help. The more people we have looking for this interloper, the more likely we are to find him. But for heaven's sake, keep it quiet. We do not want to ruin Annabelle's night."

"I will rally the footmen belowstairs."

A servant with an empty tray passed by them, reminding her of why she had come seeking him to begin with. "Also, Evers, send someone to see if we have enough wine in the cellar for twenty people. Apparently we will not have enough champagne."

He gave a nod. "We will begin serving champagne, and if that runs out, we will begin serving white wine."

"Yes." With the matter delegated, Cilla turned her attention to this new crisis. Her blood ran cold at the notion of a man breaking into the Bailey household on such an important night. Not only was Annabelle Bailey beautiful, but she was the heiress to her parents' substantial coal mining fortune. What could this man want? Did he intend to abduct the girl? Something worse?

Whatever his nefarious plans, he must be stopped. It was not often an American with Annabelle's humble beginnings married a peer of the realm. Nothing must interfere with the girl's triumph.

She worked her way through the crush, nearly invisible in the plain gray satin that marked her as beneath notice. Though she had known some of these people since childhood, she was only a paid employee now. Those who did not know her looked right past her. Those who did politely glanced away, as if sparing her the embarrassment of acknowledging her fall from social grace.

Once their remoteness would have stung. Now she simply did not have time for such nonsense. If this wedding came off as the social success she anticipated, she would have the reputation to build a business assisting debutantes in planning their wedding celebrations. She would be financially independent, never again reliant on a man to provide for her welfare. Her late husband had taught her that harsh lesson.

And she certainly would not allow a *man* to ruin the engagement party she had so painstakingly planned.

Thomas said the trespasser had demanded to see Annabelle. The Baileys were even now standing before the garden doors, waiting for the servants to finish distributing the champagne. If she were the intruder, where would be the best possible spot to get near the prospective bride?

She directed her gaze toward the columns on either side of the steps. Ah, there he was, beside the left one—hidden from some of the crowd but with a clear view of Annabelle. He watched the lovely blond with ferocious intensity, his fingers clenched around the delicate wineglass. He definitely looked like trouble.

But trouble was Cilla's specialty.

She headed toward the interloper, catching the eye of Thomas across the room. With a jerk of her head she indicated the stranger's hiding spot. Thomas nodded and signaled to another footman as he headed in the same direction.

Cilla was closer and got there first. She could tell her sudden appearance had startled the stranger, so intent had he been on Annabelle. Though he topped her height by more than a head, she stood in his path, folded her arms, and met his gaze squarely. "Good evening, sir. May I see your invitation?"

"I don't have it with me."

American. She had been right. She would know the accent anywhere. "Perhaps you might tell me your name then? I will check it against the guest list."

He scowled down at her, then leaned forward with graceful menace. "I don't think you want to do this."

"Indeed?" From the corner of her eye, Cilla observed the two footmen closing in. "You forced your way in here. Why?"

"That is my concern."

"No, it is *my* concern when you strike one of the servants and attempt to disrupt the evening." She signaled to the footmen, who aligned themselves behind her.

His eyes narrowed. "Listen, Miss—"

"*Mrs.* Burke."

"Mrs. Burke then." He smiled at her—much, she thought, as a shark might smile at a floundering fish. "I've come a long way to see Annabelle, and nothing is going to stop me. Not these fellows and certainly not a pint-sized lady like yourself, no matter how much gumption you've got to stand on."

Cilla narrowed her eyes, both flattered by his assessment of her and infuriated by it at the same time. "What do you want with Annabelle?"

Nearby, Virgil Bailey cleared his throat, preparing to make his toast. She was running out of time.

The intruder shot a hard look at the group on the steps. "Annabelle and I go way back."

"What do you mean?" Cilla persisted. "Who are you?"

"Samuel Breedlove."

"Am I supposed to know that name?"

His lips thinned. "Guess not."

Virgil's voice rang out across the spacious room.

"If you would all quiet down now . . . My wife and I have waited for this day ever since our little girl was born." Dolly sniffed loudly, and Virgil patted her arm in comfort without looking away from his audience. "So raise your glasses, everyone, and join me in offering best wishes to my daughter, Annabelle, on her engagement to the Earl of Raventhorpe."

"I do not care who you are or why you are here," Cilla hissed. "I demand you leave the premises immediately—or I will have you removed."

The banked rage in the look he gave her nearly made her draw back. "I don't mind fighting for what's mine. And Annabelle *is* mine. I'm her fiancé." And before she could stop him, he stepped from behind the column into sight of the entire assembly.

Samuel expected the footmen to come after him. But it came down to what mattered more to the little firebrand who had tried to eject him from the party— the scandal of an uninvited guest causing a scene or a brawl in the middle of the party. He was banking on scandal being the lesser of two evils.

At first the group on the steps didn't notice him. He took in the scene like a thirsty man sighting water, more moved at seeing them than he liked to admit. Virgil and Dolly, who had welcomed him into their home like a son, allowing him to escape the misery of his own childhood for their warm hearth many a time. Virgil had taught him how to be a man, and Dolly had held him when his mother died. Annabelle, pretty and sweet, his constant companion in youth, who had become his fiancée in adulthood. She stood proudly beside her parents now. And on her other side . . .

Raventhorpe.

Rage roared through him as he watched the wily snake smile with smug possessiveness at Annabelle. First the bastard had left him to die on that deserted rock in the middle of the Caribbean, and now he thought to steal Samuel's bride. Samuel clenched his jaw, his body vibrating with the force of anger almost too volatile to control.

But control it he did. There was no way he could bring Raventhorpe to justice on the marooning. He had no evidence, no clout in the British justice system—not when pitted against an earl's influence. But he could spoil Raventhorpe's little engagement. He could get Annabelle back and prevent an innocent girl from marrying the man who had tried to murder him.

This time Raventhorpe would *not* win.

Murmurs of congratulations accompanied the raised glasses as the guests joined in the toast. Annabelle pinkened, her blue eyes sparkling as she shyly smiled at Raventhorpe, touching her glass to his.

And Raventhorpe smiled back.

Triumphantly.

Samuel took another step forward, but someone grabbed his arm. He looked down into the earnest face of the redoubtable Mrs. Burke.

"Do not do this," she hissed. "Have some respect for Annabelle. Spare her this scandal."

"She accepted me first. Any damage I do to her

reputation, I will repair." He shook her hand off his arm and came to the base of the steps, raising his glass high. "A toast! To the engagement of Annabelle Bailey—*to Captain Samuel Breedlove.*" He drank deeply as gasps echoed around him.

Annabelle paled when she saw him. The glass slipped from her fingers and shattered on the steps. "Samuel!"

Astonishment flickered across Raventhorpe's face, but then he quickly recovered and narrowed his eyes.

"Samuel!" Dolly gasped. "What—"

"Samuel Breedlove." Virgil's fingers tightened around his glass as his expression darkened. "What in God's name do you think you are doing?"

"I told Annabelle I would return for her." Samuel met Annabelle's gaze, her blue eyes so familiar after so long apart. "And so I have."

"So you have," Annabelle whispered, her expression shocked. She took a step forward, crushing the broken glass with her delicate slippers. The earl caught her arm, bringing her to a halt.

"Have a care, my dear, lest you injure yourself." Raventhorpe pulled her back to his side and met Samuel's gaze with the cool deliberation of a coiled rattler. "Have you no shame, Breedlove? How dare you show yourself here!"

Samuel indicated Annabelle as a servant scurried forward to collect the pieces of broken glass on the floor. "I must thank you for watching over my fiancée for me, Raventhorpe. As you well know, I have been indisposed these past two years."

"You sound as if you are making an accusation, Captain."

"Maybe I am."

Fervent whispers rippled through the crowd, though their audience did not appear to bother Raventhorpe a whit. "Be on your way," the earl demanded. "You are disturbing a private party."

"I came for Annabelle."

"You abandoned her," Raventhorpe said.

"I did not abandon her."

"You were betrothed to a poor farmer's daughter, but you came back when you heard about her change in fortunes."

Gasps. More whispers.

"That's a lie." The servant finished clearing the glass and hurried away, allowing Samuel to put his foot on the first stair toward Annabelle. "Shall I tell the lady what really happened?"

Raventhorpe shifted Annabelle behind him and came down a step to block Samuel's way. The crowd shuffled, murmured. "Save your falsehoods for some other maid, Breedlove. You have lost her. Accept it."

Samuel leaned closer to the earl's face. "Never."

Raventhorpe shoved at his shoulder, pushing him back a pace. "Leave. Or shall we have the footmen escort you?"

Samuel shoved back. "You first."

Ladies cried out, and gentlemen moved protectively in front of them.

Mrs. Burke rushed forward but then stopped as Virgil cut bodily between the two men, putting an end to the scuffle. "Enough of this foolishness. Haven't the two of you given these folks enough to chew on?"

"I must speak to you, sir," Samuel said. "I suspect you have been told lies about me."

"Lies, is it?" Virgil looked him long and hard in the eye. "I reckon we've all got something to say about this. Best get it done since you already wrecked the party."

"Throw him out," Raventhorpe hissed. "Has he not done enough damage to your family, Bailey?"

"My family, my decision," Virgil said. "Mrs. Burke, you take Samuel and wait for us in the library. Lord Raventhorpe and I will be along once we've said good night to the guests."

"Me?" Mrs. Burke protested.

"Please, Mrs. Burke." The tension lines around Virgil's mouth indicated the strain he battled. "You're so good at handling these sorts of things."

"Very well," she conceded.

"And Annabelle?" Samuel asked.

"She's none of your concern," Raventhorpe said.

"She is my fiancée. That makes her my concern."

"My ring on her finger says otherwise."

Behind them, Annabelle stood pale and silent, lips quivering.

"Enough!" Virgil scowled as the crowd's low murmur of speculation became a dull roar. "Samuel, to the library. Raventhorpe, with me."

Samuel glared at the earl. "I would prefer that Lord Raventhorpe adjourn to the library as well."

"Some of the guests are friends of Lord Raven-thorpe's," Virgil replied. "He has to say his fancy good-byes. It's what they do here in England."

"Then I will wait here."

"No." Virgil leaned closer to Samuel and lowered his voice. "You're on thin ice, my boy. Lucky for you I'm curious enough to hear your side of the story before I toss you out of my house."

Samuel had expected more sympathy from his surrogate father. He opened his mouth to speak, but Virgil continued, "This is England, not America, and these folks use gossip like a weapon. I reckon you've given them enough to jabber about tonight, don't you? If you still care for Annabelle like you claim, you'll do what I ask."

Samuel glanced at Annabelle, her face bleak and stark with shock. Then he looked at the crowd around them. The bright eyes, the snickers, the derisive grins hurriedly hidden behind hands and fans. Like a pack of wild dogs, they scented blood in the air.

Virgil was right. Best they handle the rest of this behind closed doors.

Ignoring Raventhorpe's glittering gaze, he gave a respectful nod to Virgil and then turned to look at the woman appointed his keeper. "Mrs. Burke, kindly lead the way to the library."

Her mouth a thin line of disapproval, she gave a curt nod. "This way, Captain Breedlove." The crowd parted before her as she led him back toward the double doors, her spine rigid, her skirts swaying with simmering temper.

Virgil raised his voice to the crowd. "As you can

see, an urgent family matter has arisen, so I regret that we will have to cut the evening short. Thank you all for coming."

The clank of glasses being collected by the servants and the rising volume of excited voices filled the great hall as the guests began to organize their exit. Samuel paused in the doorway to look back at Annabelle. Dolly held her distraught daughter in a protective embrace and tried to urge her toward the terrace doors, away from curious eyes.

He'd hated to hurt her, but there had been no other way.

"Captain?" Mrs. Burke waited several paces down the hall, her expression one of impatience.

The Baileys had not ejected him from the house. If he had any hope of breaking Annabelle's engagement to Raventhorpe, better he continue to play according to their rules. Slowly he moved to join her as the rest of the crowd wedged themselves through the great hall doors and then flowed toward the cloakroom.

She waited until he had reached her before she turned to continue with her duty. He glanced back to see Raventhorpe and Virgil standing just outside the great hall, bidding their guests good-bye. Raventhorpe took the hand of an ancient dowager and bent over it, then looked up and met Samuel's gaze. The fury and hatred there reaffirmed that Raventhorpe was the same merciless snake who had tried to kill him on that tiny island in the Caribbean.

All the more reason to wrest Annabelle from his clutches.

Chapter 2

C illa opened the door to Virgil Bailey's study and waited for Samuel to precede her. After a momentary hesitation that made her believe he had at some point in his life been taught proper manners, he walked into the room. Cilla followed behind him and shut the door to block any curiosity seekers from seeing inside.

Only after she turned back to face him did she consider that leaving the door open might have been a wiser choice. The brief twinge about propriety was easily dismissed; she was not only a widow but a paid employee. There would be no gossip.

But she would be a fool if she did not admit her misgivings about being shut away in a room with him. After his scandalous behavior this evening, who knew what he might do or say next? She took comfort in the fact that Virgil Bailey knew this man, and he would not have left Cilla alone with Captain Breedlove if there was any chance of danger to her person. However, there was more to her apprehension than that.

The other half of it was much more perilous, much

more personal, and shook her even under these extraordinary circumstances. She had sensed it the moment she had set eyes on the brash American.

She noticed him as a man, reacted to him as a woman in a physical manner that seemed beyond her control. She did not like it, had not sought it. But there it was, like an elephant in the middle of the drawing room, daring her to ignore it.

She tried, certainly she did. But the richness of the clearly masculine study with its floor-to-ceiling carved bookshelves, massive mahogany desk, and huge marble fireplace only emphasized the sheer size of the man she wanted to dismiss. She knew she was not a tall woman, but closeted away with him, she became more aware of how much space he claimed, even outside of the physical.

He was tall, certainly, and broad in the shoulders. His hands looked strong and tanned, so different from the pale, pampered hands of the gentlemen she knew. These were hands that had performed the manual labor necessary for sailing a ship, hands that looked rough with calluses and nicked with scars. Could hands like that be gentle? Hold a butterfly or a flower or a woman? Even as the thought crossed her mind, he reached out to the unusual clock sitting on the desk, that of a standing Greek Muse balancing the clock face beneath one arm and holding up a clear crystal globe with her other hand. He stroked his finger over the curve of the Muse's hip.

The lazy motion made her breath catch. Why him? What was wrong with her that she was so irrationally attracted to such an unsuitable man? She suddenly realized she was staring and jerked her gaze up to find him watching her.

Those dark eyes held secrets that called to the depths of everything female within her. As if he had seen everything there was to see in the world, knew everything there was to know.

Could do . . . anything.

Her pulse skittered, and she sucked in a slow breath, willing her body to calm. She had seen his like before. He reminded her of her late husband with his untamed good looks and dangerous allure. But where Edward had been a charismatic man who used his gift for words to entice people into doing what he wanted, Captain Breedlove was a man who wore danger as easily as he wore his well-fitted evening clothes. Edward had charmed, but Samuel Breedlove demanded.

And somehow, to her horror, some part of her responded to that subtle summons and longed to meet the challenge.

"Shall we sit down?" he asked.

His voice made her aware that she continued to gape at him like a ninny. Putting forth her most dignified bearing, she perched on the edge of one of the chairs in front of the massive desk. Then he seated himself quite properly in the chair beside her.

Too close. She could practically feel the heat from his body across the few inches that separated them. What was the matter with her? How was it this rough American with his indifferent boldness could so completely take her outside herself, make her forget the disaster that loomed before her?

"You don't like me much, do you?"

His question surprised her. "It hardly matters how I feel."

"Maybe." He leaned back in the chair, stretching his legs out as much as he could with the desk so close. "So who are you, some kind of cousin?"

"No." He continued to regard her expectantly, and she let out a huff of impatience. "I am Mrs. Bailey's assistant."

His brows shot up. "Assistant? I thought for sure you were some married relative of Raventhorpe's come to help with the wedding."

Her spine stiffened the slightest bit more. "I am simply an employee, nothing more."

He shrugged. "I'm just saying, you strike me as a woman born and raised in an English drawing room."

"Who and what I am is no concern of yours."

"See? That's what makes me think I'm right. You tell me to mind my own business with the prim and proper words, but that go-to-hell look in your eye tells me how you're really feeling."

"I will thank you to not use profanity in my presence."

"Sorry, ma'am." Silence stretched between them. "What do you suppose is taking so long?"

"There were seventy guests. It takes time to summon that many carriages, though I imagine Mr. Bailey will make short work of it."

"All that for an engagement party? Seems a waste."

His careless tone rankled. "Thanks to you, sir, it *was* wasted. All that planning, all that expense. Poor Annabelle must be devastated."

"It's just a party. When we get married, I'll throw her a jamboree fit for a queen."

She clenched her teeth with an audible click. "Why do you persist with this ridiculous charade? She has accepted Lord Raventhorpe. It is unreasonable for you to continue to press your suit."

"*Unreasonable?*" His low snarl set her nerves humming in warning. "I'll tell you what's unreasonable, Mrs. Burke. Annabelle is engaged to *me*. That scurvy bilge rat is trying to steal her away."

"If you cared at all for her, you would not put her through such an ordeal as you have enacted tonight," she snapped. "I do not know what misunderstanding has brought on such dramatics—"

"Misunderstanding? Dramatics?" He leaned toward her. "The drama has not yet begun, I assure you."

"Annabelle is happy, or she was until tonight. She will be marrying a man with an old and respected title. Do you really expect her to jilt His Lordship to be the wife of a . . . what is it? Sea captain?"

"Yes, I expect exactly that."

"And what would compel her to do such a foolish thing?"

Before he could respond, the door to the office opened. The three Baileys and Raventhorpe entered.

Samuel stood and offered his seat to Dolly. Cilla

rose as well and started to leave the room, attempting to give them privacy.

"Stay, Mrs. Burke," Virgil said as he took his chair behind his desk.

Cilla paused, then took up a post near the door. Raventhorpe escorted Annabelle to Cilla's vacated chair, then stood behind it. Samuel lingered beside Dolly's chair, though he noticed she would not look at him.

"We have a problem," Virgil said, glancing from Samuel to Raventhorpe. "Both of you claim the right to marry my girl."

"Surely you will not entertain this madness," the earl said.

Samuel ignored Raventhorpe. Instead he kept his gaze on the man he had thought would be his father-in-law. The steady gray eyes that had always looked at him with such understanding, now reflected the hard steel of displeasure.

"Madness or not, she did accept me first," Samuel said.

"That she did," Virgil agreed. "But then you left on that sea voyage and never came back to her. You ran off to live a new life, free of responsibility."

"That's a lie!" Samuel took a step forward. "You know me. You know that once I make a promise, I keep it."

Virgil's expression did not soften. "Then where the hell were you, boy?"

"Marooned on an island in the Caribbean."

"Marooned!" Dolly exclaimed, glancing at him with astonishment.

"You expect us to believe that?" Virgil said.

"It's the truth." Samuel jerked his head at Raventhorpe. "Ask him. He's the one who left me there."

"Lord Raventhorpe already told us what happened," Virgil said. "You left the ship in the middle of the voyage because the two of you argued. And we all know what your temper's like."

Samuel looked from one face to the other, his gut knotting at the lack of forgiveness in their eyes. "In all the years you've known me, you honestly believe I would abandon ship over a quarrel?"

"The rest of the crew backs up his story. Like I said, we do know you, and you can be a real hothead sometimes."

"If only you'd written or come home to us to tell us what had happened," Dolly said. "We would have understood. We knew you took the job on Lord Raventhorpe's ship to earn some money to start your life together. Annabelle would have waited for you if you'd just told us the truth. But disappearing like that . . ." She shook her head. "Shameful."

"And cowardly."

Samuel shot his gaze to Virgil's. "I am no coward, sir."

"You never used to be." The older man narrowed his eyes. "We loved you like you were one of ours, boy, but what you did to our baby is not the act of any man I want for a son."

"Why did you wait so long to come home to us?" Dolly asked. "We waited for you. Especially Annabelle."

"The timing is obvious to me," Raventhorpe said.

"Clearly it was your change in financial circumstances that brought him back."

"Is that it, son?" Virgil asked. "Is it about the money?"

"Of course it is," Raventhorpe insisted. "Annabelle was a poor farmer's daughter when he left, but now she is an heiress. It all makes perfect sense."

Samuel fought to speak past the pain burning in his chest. "It's not about the money. I don't care if she's rich now. None of you are hearing what I'm saying."

"We hear you," Virgil said. "But you're telling us that Lord Raventhorpe, an English lord with blood bluer than the sky, left you stranded on some deserted island just so he could marry Annabelle. Aside from the fact that that's just crazy since he didn't even know Annabelle at the time, you've got to agree that it's a far-fetched story."

"As soon as I was able, I came back to Annabelle. And that's the truth."

"The truth? I sure would have liked to hear the truth. To hear you admit your mistake like a man. Like I taught you." Virgil's voice caught, and he cleared his throat. "Yes, I sure would have liked that. But now . . . well, Annabelle's already announced her engagement to Lord Raventhorpe."

"The banns were read this week," Raventhorpe said, "and a notice was sent to the *Times*. You are too late, Breedlove."

Samuel whirled on the earl. "I'd like to remind you, Raventhorpe, that you tried to get rid of me once and it didn't work."

The earl raised his brows. "Are you making these wild accusations as an excuse for abandoning your lady? Good God, Breedlove. You will say anything to save face."

"Get rid of you?" Annabelle broke her silence and looked at Raventhorpe. "What does he mean, Richard?"

"He has made a muck of things," the earl replied, laying a possessive hand on her shoulder. "Captain Breedlove underestimated the consequences of his abandonment of you and now he is trying to make *me* look the villain."

"Don't listen to him, Annabelle. This man is not the saint he pretends to be."

"Saint? Goodness, no." Raventhorpe chuckled, casting a glance at the others to encourage them to share in his amusement. "No man is a saint. But you have some gall coming here uninvited and abusing us with your unfounded accusations. You say I marooned you on a deserted island . . . ?"

"You know the truth." Samuel's hands fisted. "And now you figure to steal my bride."

"And yet you stand here before us. Clearly you escaped this mythical captivity." Raventhorpe shook his head, his expression tinged with pity. "Poor man. You must have loved Annabelle very much for your mind to have become so unhinged."

"You know what you did."

"I know what you are claiming I did. Where is your proof?"

"Good question," Virgil said. "It's your word against his. You got any proof or witnesses? Because

Lord Raventhorpe has a boat full of people who back what he says."

Samuel remained silent. He could see the gleam of triumph in Raventhorpe's eyes behind the mien of benevolence. It took every fiber of control not to reach out and choke the man with his bare hands.

"So, you have no proof." Raventhorpe cast a meaningful look at the Baileys.

There was no way to win, not without evidence. Samuel turned his attention to his fiancée. "Annabelle, you are still my betrothed. Surely you believe me." He held out a hand to her, then dropped it when she didn't take it. "We had plans. Dreams."

"We did." She fixed him with a deadened stare, spearing him with disappointment from that too-somber gaze. "But you disappeared with no word that you ever intended to come back. Not so much as a letter." Annabelle glanced up and laid her hand over Raventhorpe's on her shoulder, eyeing the earl with devotion. "Richard was there. He comforted me in my heartbreak and my humiliation. That is why I chose him for my husband."

"I see." Samuel looked at Virgil.

The older man nodded. "That's how it is. I want my gal to be happy."

"I could make her happy."

"Oh, leave off, Breedlove!" Raventhorpe snapped. "You have lost. Accept it like a man."

Samuel glanced back at Annabelle.

"You should leave now, Samuel," she said.

"Why him?" Samuel asked, the words jerking from him like a tightly leashed beast fighting to escape.

"His title? Social prestige? I never knew you to be a social climber, Annabelle."

"Here now!" Virgil surged to his feet.

"There's no need to be hurtful," Dolly hissed with a glare at Samuel. She patted her daughter's hand.

Samuel kept his gaze on the woman he had once thought would be the mother of his children. "Once upon a time you wouldn't have doubted me for an instant. None of you would have. But now . . ." He shook his head. "How in God's name can you let your head be turned by wealth and status? What's happened to you?"

"Don't try and make this about me," Annabelle said, lifting her chin. Tears slipped down her cheeks, but her eyes burned with fury. "You were the one who left me, who never sent word of the state of our engagement. You were the one who made a fool of me. Don't come back here with some wild story and expect everything to be as it was."

Raventhorpe took a step toward him. "I think you've upset my betrothed quite enough, Breedlove."

"I regret that." Samuel meant those words, though he did not back down. "None of you are the people I thought I knew."

"I'm asking you again to leave now," Virgil said. "Annabelle has made her decision, and I've already asked the servants to summon your carriage."

"Yes, Breedlove, run along," Raventhorpe said. "If you go quietly perhaps we will not have the footmen throw your miserable carcass into the gutter."

Annabelle stood. "Our engagement is over, Samuel.

I am marrying Richard, and that's the end of it. I can't say it more plainly than that."

Samuel looked from one familiar face to the other. All the Baileys—these people he had once embraced as family—looked at him with disapproval and disappointment. They did not believe his tale. They sided with Raventhorpe, the man who had tried to kill him.

The warmth of hope faded from his heart to be replaced by ice. "Very well. But this is not over." He turned on his heel and left the room.

Behind him, Annabelle softly began to weep.

Captain Breedlove strode past Cilla like a thunderstorm, his mouth tight, his eyes hot with emotion. He glanced at her just before he passed through the door. Anger, frustration, hurt glittered from those dark depths. Then he was gone.

Her heart turned over. He had barged into the house with no invitation, ruined the engagement party with his dramatic claim to Annabelle, then attempted to usurp Lord Raventhorpe's position as her fiancé with a wild story that rivaled Mr. Defoe's novel *Robinson Crusoe*. Yet despite all that, she couldn't help but feel a certain sympathy for him.

He had braved all for his lady, only to lose.

She slipped from the room, hurrying down the hall on an impulse that, by the time she had reached the foyer, once again had her questioning her own judgment. The matter was closed. What did she hope to accomplish by speaking to him?

The footman was just closing the door behind him when she got there. She yanked the door open herself and hurried outside to where his coach sat in front of the house. He had just raised his foot to climb inside. "Captain!"

Samuel stopped, a shadowy figure in the dimness of the lamplit drive as he turned to face her. "Mrs. Burke? Did they send you to find me?"

His voice sounded rough, and the hint of hope that came through with the last question made her heart soften all the more.

"No," she said, studying his face as she searched for the right words. "Captain, I just wanted to say . . . Well, I am sorry."

He stiffened. "I have no need of your pity, Mrs. Burke. Better your efforts should be turned toward preventing this disastrous marriage."

"It is not pity, Captain. And it is a good match for Annabelle. I just felt badly—"

He leaned closer. "Raventhorpe tried to kill me, Mrs. Burke, and I'm not the first, just the one who survived. Annabelle is marrying a murderer."

Before she could respond, he climbed into the coach and slammed the door, then rapped on the roof. The coach pulled away with a jerk, leaving Cilla standing in the drive with her thoughts awhirl.

Slowly she turned back toward the house.

Annabelle is marrying a murderer.

The words staggered her. Had Captain Breedlove only said that to muddy the waters, to throw doubt that the earl was the best match for Annabelle? Her late husband had certainly been able to tell a convincing tale of woe if it furthered his own ends. Was Samuel Breedlove the same type of man? Had he said that only to gain her sympathy?

What if he told the truth?

She needed this wedding to happen. She was counting on the sterling reputation she would get from the affair to be the driving force behind her fledgling business; otherwise she was just one more ruined debutante trying desperately to survive. She doubted that unforgiving society would give her a second chance. But if Lord Raventhorpe truly was a villain, would she be able to stand by and watch Annabelle marry him, knowing the girl might be putting herself in danger? How could she in good conscience put her own dreams ahead of Annabelle's safety?

She couldn't.

Either Captain Breedlove was lying or Lord Raventhorpe was. Somehow she needed to find out which one. The American's words would haunt her until she did.

Chapter 3

John had turned the coach back toward the inn where they were staying, leaving Nevarton Chase behind them. Alone in the vehicle, Samuel found no peace in what should have been a comforting darkness. Emotions roiled through him like a stew pot on full boil. Pain. Betrayal. Regret. Disbelief. When a man's dreams got ripped away, it hurt.

Annabelle had ended their engagement. His heart should have broken at the news, but the defection of Virgil and Dolly had struck harder and deeper than losing their daughter.

How could they possibly think so little of him? How could they believe Raventhorpe's lies? Annabelle had changed from the sweet farm girl he had once known into just another haughty society heiress. And Virgil and Dolly had judged him before he'd even begun to tell his side of the story. Perhaps before he'd even walked through the door.

He acknowledged that he had shocked them. Perhaps their reactions had simply been a response to his sudden reappearance in their lives, especially since Raventhorpe had apparently blackened his name while he'd been gone. Maybe he needed to give them more time.

But would more time really make any difference? He could try again in a day or so, but he couldn't ignore the growing evidence that the bond he thought he had with Annabelle wasn't as strong as he'd believed. Certainly not as strong as should exist between a husband and wife. He'd been gone nearly two years, most of that time spent alone on an island. An experience like that changed a man. He'd had way too much time to think, to judge his own worth. To ponder who he was and what he wanted. To face both his strengths and his flaws and learn from them.

He wasn't the same man who had proposed to Annabelle, and apparently she wasn't the same woman. Not if she could so easily believe the worst of him on another man's say-so. He could allow for the fact that she was young, only twenty, and perhaps given to impulsive decisions. But what excuse could he create for Virgil and Dolly? Yes, he understood that Raventhorpe had lied to all of them. The deceitful snake had even fooled Samuel at one time, not normally an easy task. But how could the Baileys believe the worst without giving Samuel the benefit of the doubt, especially after all the years they'd known each other?

And what about their claim that he had returned now simply because they had become wealthy? If they only knew how little their money meant to him.

The confrontation in the study had been like shouting into the wind, the Baileys' trust and affection slipping further away with each word exchanged. None of his accusers had paused to consider his feelings, only charged ahead with their allegations, Raventhorpe leading the way.

The only person in that house who had even given a single thought to his reaction about what had happened tonight had been Dolly's assistant, Mrs. Burke.

She'd run after him. Offered him sincere compassion at a moment when everything he had ever valued in his life had just fallen apart. When she'd darted out of the house and called for him, his heart had leaped at the thought that they'd changed their minds, that they had sent her to stop him from leaving.

That they had decided to believe him.

He'd known his hope had reflected in his voice. But he'd realized the truth the instant the words had left his lips. He would never forget that regretful, sympathetic look in her big brown eyes as she'd stood in the drive and smashed his hopes with her simple "I am sorry."

His temper had flared, and he'd snapped at her. Shocked her even. He wasn't proud of his loss of control. Nineteen months without any human contact had weakened his skill with people, and tonight's disaster had pushed him too far. She hadn't deserved his brusque words. But his anger at himself, at revealing how pitifully eager he was for acceptance back into the family, had made him lash out at her.

Not his proudest moment.

But he needed to look forward now, not dwell on the past. He could accept the broken engagement.

In fact, he suspected his heart had never truly been involved. Marrying Annabelle had simply seemed the next logical step in his relationship with the Baileys, and he could let that go with more regret than pain. It might even be possible that he was not the marrying type. Some men weren't. His father hadn't been.

But he could not accept the people he considered surrogate parents thinking the worst of him; all he had left now was his honor, and now that was being challenged. Nor could he accept Annabelle marrying Raventhorpe. The man was a killer, and despite their history he still cared enough that he could not let Annabelle put herself in danger.

The answer was clear then. He had to stop this wedding, whatever the cost.

Cilla came back inside the house just as Annabelle and Dolly came out of the study.

"Cilla, where did you go?" Dolly asked as the two ladies quickly traversed the hallway. "You ran out so quickly!"

"She went after Samuel." Annabelle frowned at her. "Why did you do that, Mrs. Burke? Can't you see how he has torn this family apart?"

"I was making certain he left the house," Cilla improvised.

"Good. I never want to see that man again." Annabelle's words rang with the bitter peal of a woman scorned.

"Now, Annabelle—"

"Mama, don't tell me you're still fond of him, even after what he's done?"

"He seemed genuinely sorry, darling."

Annabelle stared at her mother in horror. "He promised to marry me, then just disappeared when he changed his mind. If Pa hadn't asked Richard what happened, I might still be sitting there waiting like a fool." Her voice broke. "I'm very tired. I think I will go to bed."

"Don't you want to wait and say good night to Lord Raventhorpe?"

"Frankly I don't want to see another man for the rest of the night." Annabelle glared at a passing footman, who tried to sidle down the hallway unnoticed.

"All right, dear. Your father will say your goodbyes for you. Perhaps I should bring you one of my toddies when I come up?"

"That sounds wonderful. Make sure you put extra whiskey in it. I'm going to need it to deal with the gossip that's sure to come of all this." Gathering her skirts, Annabelle began to climb the stairs, her stomping footfalls evidence of her ill humor.

Dolly watched her go, and when her daughter was out of earshot, she turned back to Cilla. "She's right, you know."

"About the gossip? I fear there is no way to avoid it after that very public display."

"Not about that. About me being fond of Samuel." Dolly's expression softened. "I practically raised the boy. I just can't fathom his behavior. He used to have such lovely manners."

Cilla frowned. "So you believe his wild story?"

"Of course not. But I also can't believe he simply

left Annabelle waiting at the altar. There's probably some explanation that falls in the middle." She sighed. "I wonder if Virgil was too hard on him."

"From all accounts, your husband has every right to be angry with the man who abandoned your daughter."

"It's not just that." Dolly glanced around before lowering her voice. "Samuel spent quite a bit of time at our house as a young man. I believe Virgil saw him as the son I was unable to give him, and once Lord Raventhorpe told us what happened, my husband felt betrayed. Even though none of us wanted to believe the tale at first."

"But you seem to believe it now."

Dolly shrugged. "What else could we think? The boy never contacted any of us. We could only draw our own conclusions based on the facts we knew. Virgil was adamant that Samuel had callously broken our girl's heart. There was no persuading him otherwise."

Cilla frowned, thinking back to the pain she had seen in the captain's eyes when he'd stormed from the study—not at all the expression one expected from a cad. "Tell me, is Captain Breedlove the type of man to tell tales if it suits his needs?"

Dolly pursed her lips as she considered the question. "He never was before."

"And when was the last time you saw him before tonight?"

"Nearly two years ago when he came to say goodbye to Annabelle. He had taken the captain's position on Lord Raventhorpe's ship when the previous captain left his post rather abruptly. It was a wonderful opportunity for him."

"So he planned to marry Annabelle after he came back from this voyage."

"Oh, yes. Lord Raventhorpe had offered a generous salary since he needed a captain so desperately. Annabelle and Samuel would have been able to marry as soon as he returned." Dolly frowned, her expression troubled. "The earl told us that he and Samuel had quarreled and that Samuel had left his post mid-voyage. Just disembarked somewhere in the Caribbean, leaving the ship with no captain! If Virgil hadn't asked what had happened to him, we would never have known what to think."

"Did Lord Raventhorpe say why they had quarreled?"

"No, he never told us."

"Mama!" Annabelle's petulant summons echoed from above them.

"I'm coming, darling!" Dolly let out a long sigh and gave Cilla a tired smile. "This has been an exhausting evening."

"Indeed it has. You do realize that what happened tonight is going to fuel the gossips all over the area."

"I'm trying not to think about that. At least not until tomorrow." Dolly patted her on the arm. "I'm certain that by breakfast time, you'll have thought up a wonderful plan to take care of that little problem. Your knowledge of English society is one of the reasons I hired you."

"Of course." Cilla managed a smile that conveyed a reassurance she did not feel.

"Mama!" came Annabelle's call again.

"I'd better go up to her before she gets herself in a state. Good night, Cilla."

"Good night." Cilla watched Dolly ascend the stairs for a moment, then turned toward the great hall. She would check on the progress of the servants cleaning up the great hall, and then she would retire to her tiny bedchamber in the corner of the house. Dolly was depending on her to come up with a plan to stave off the gossip by tomorrow, and she would need her rest.

But later when she lay in bed, sleep eluded her. She found her thoughts constantly coming back to Samuel Breedlove. Strangely it was not his dire words about Raventhorpe that claimed her attention, though she intended to investigate that matter more thoroughly. No, it was the pain and confusion in his eyes that had touched something inside her. She had seen what remained unspoken, something raw and compelling and terribly familiar.

His heart had been broken.

Hadn't she felt the same way when she'd discovered that her husband had only married her for money—money that never materialized because her father had disowned her? Edward's bitterness had exposed the sham of his proclaimed love, and only anger had gotten her through the nightmare of her marriage. Anger and a desire to never be dependent on anyone ever again.

So yes, she understood. She and the captain—they were the same. If he was lying about abandoning Annabelle, then why the torment in his eyes? She would expect a scoundrel to show a lack of emotion, or perhaps cold calculation. Not the utter pain and loss she had witnessed.

But men could be deceptive, and she had been duped before. She knew she could not trust her own instincts when it came to the male of the species. Still, her heart ached for him.

Even if that made her a fool.

"I admit I don't know what to think," Dolly said, slicing her ham at breakfast the next day. "I would never have expected such behavior from Samuel."

"That's for sure," Virgil answered, scooping some eggs into his mouth.

"Cilla, have you come up with a plan to deter the gossips?"

"I have some ideas." Cilla sipped at the tea she had reluctantly accepted when Dolly insisted she breakfast with the family this morning. As a mere employee, she did not merit dining at the same table as her employers. However, at heart Dolly Bailey was still a farmer's wife from Virginia, and she saw nothing wrong with her paid assistant sharing a meal with her.

Unfortunately the other servants disagreed, as indicated by their furtive, disapproving glances at Cilla.

"Excellent. We can talk about it after breakfast." Dolly let out a sigh of relief. "Thank heavens Lord

Raventhorpe did not seem to hold Annabelle responsible for last night."

"And why should he?" Virgil demanded. "She did nothing wrong. Samuel's at fault here."

"But what about the consequences? The gossip? The earl is a very proud man. I'm just worried all this fuss is going to make him change his mind about marrying our baby." Dolly's lip quivered, and Virgil reached out a hand across the table to cover hers.

"Don't you worry about that, sugarplum," he said. "I won't let him hurt our little girl."

Dolly gave him a tremulous smile in return. The moment held such love, such intimacy, that Cilla had to glance away. The cool courtesy of English marriage paled in comparison to what she witnessed now.

"If it helps at all," Cilla finally said after a long moment, "it would be considered the utmost of scandals for His Lordship to cry off. A lady might change her mind about an engagement, but never a gentleman."

"Well, thank goodness for that!" Breaking eye contact with her husband, Dolly placed her hand over her heart and let out a relieved sigh.

Annabelle chose that moment to enter to breakfast room. "Good morning."

"Sweetheart!" Dolly sprang to her feet and went to hug her daughter. "How are you this morning? Should you be out of bed so early?"

"I'm fine, Mama." Annabelle smiled at her mother, then pulled away and went to kiss her father on the cheek. "Good morning, Pa."

"Morning, sweet pea."

"Are you well enough to eat?" Dolly asked.

"Of course, Mama."

Even as Dolly looked around, the maid, Liza, set a place across from Dolly at the table. "Will you have tea, miss?" she asked Annabelle. "Or would you prefer chocolate?"

"Chocolate, please," Annabelle said, taking her seat. "Good morning, Mrs. Burke."

"Good morning, Annabelle." Cilla studied the girl's face. "You look well."

"Better than you expected?" Annabelle laughed as she reached for her napkin.

"You seemed upset last night, but I am glad you are in good spirits this morning."

"Truly." Dolly sat down again. "Darling, if you had decided to take to your bed for a week, no one would have thought a thing of it!"

"That wouldn't help matters at all, now would it?" Annabelle said. "Yes, it was a shock to find that Samuel had come back and expected me to still be waiting. However, I'm engaged to Richard, and there is nothing he can do about it." Liza set a cup of steaming chocolate in front of her, and Annabelle lifted the cup to take a sip. "Besides," she said sharply, "he surely wasted no time in taking his leave, wouldn't you say?"

"Forgive me," Cilla said, reacting to the girl's bitter tone, "but I recall that last night you wanted nothing to do with men, even Lord Raventhorpe."

"Yes, darling," Dolly said. "You told Samuel to leave."

Annabelle waved a dismissive hand. "I was upset. I feel better now."

"That boy had best stay far away from you," Virgil said.

"Now, Pa."

"Don't you try and sweet-talk me, young lady. You know what I mean." He sent her a look, hard with meaning.

Some of the light dimmed from Annabelle's face. "All right, Pa."

"What's the matter?" Dolly asked. She sent a quick, searching glance at Virgil, who merely sipped his coffee.

"Nothing," Annabelle mumbled, sipping her chocolate.

Just then the butler entered the breakfast room. "I beg your pardon, sir. Lord Raventhorpe has come to call on Miss Annabelle."

"Lord Raventhorpe? Tell him to come in, Evers," Virgil said.

"Yes, Mr. Bailey." Evers disappeared.

"Annabelle!" Dolly hissed.

Annabelle nodded at her mother, then patted her hair and pinched her cheeks for color before smoothing her hands over her dress.

Evers reappeared. "Lord Raventhorpe."

The earl entered the room. Virgil stood and shook his hand. "Good morning, my lord. Are you hungry? We have plenty."

"No, thank you." The earl smiled, but Cilla saw no matching emotion in his eyes. "I apologize for disturbing you at so early an hour, but I was concerned about Annabelle."

"How nice of you," Dolly said, a relieved smile spreading across her pretty face. "Do sit down, my lord. There's a seat right there next to Annabelle."

"My thanks, Mrs. Bailey." With an elegant bow, the earl made his way to the other side of the table. "Good morning, my dear." Taking Annabelle's hand, he pressed a soft kiss to it.

"Good morning, Richard." Annabelle pinkened as Raventhorpe sat down beside her.

"I hope I am not interrupting."

"On the contrary," Virgil said. "We were just talking about you."

"Were you?" He arched his brows.

"We were talking about last night," Dolly said. "Such a shock, Samuel showing up from nowhere. My heavens!"

"Indeed. I had no idea there was competition for your hand, my dove." Raventhorpe gave Annabelle an intimate grin.

"Oh, Richard!" Annabelle said, laughing.

"My lord, I have been wondering about something since last night. Where exactly was the ship when the captain quit his post?" Cilla asked.

Raventhorpe glanced at her in surprise, as if astonished by her audacity in addressing him. After a long moment of silence—which conveyed his disapproval in the most unmistakable way—he gave her a barely polite smile. One that did not take the chill from his eyes. "Why do you ask?"

"Curiosity." Though she kept her voice respectful, she did not cower. The earl's haughty, deliberate demeanor had always struck her as rather cold, but she had always dismissed it as a result of being full of his own consequence.

Now she wondered if it hid something deeper.

"Yes, I would like to know that, too," Virgil said. He signaled the maid to bring more coffee. "How did all this happen?"

"Since *you* ask, Virgil, we were in the Caribbean. The captain had gone ashore for . . . private reasons." The earl met Virgil's eyes for a significant moment.

Virgil's mouth tightened. "Go on."

Annabelle glanced down at her hands.

"He came back late for his watch. We argued about his dereliction of duty. He resigned his post and left the ship immediately."

Cilla glanced at Dolly and could see the same puzzlement she was feeling at the unspoken secrets between the others. "And where did you say that was, my lord?" Cilla asked.

"The Caribbean. Near Cuba perhaps. I don't recall precisely." Raventhorpe picked up Annabelle's hand and kissed it. "I was quite upset at the time."

"Of course you were," she breathed, a delicate flush creeping into her cheeks.

Lord Raventhorpe turned away from Annabelle and focused on Virgil and Dolly. "When we got back to America, I tried to find Breedlove to settle matters."

"Of course," Virgil said with a nod. "Any man would do the same."

"You can imagine my shock when you told me the blackguard had not returned home. That he had deserted his fiancée."

"Shameful," Dolly murmured.

Virgil shook his head and drank his coffee.

"And then when he did come back, after nearly *two years*, he tried to excuse himself with that ridiculous story." Annabelle set down her chocolate with a click. "I am hardly a fool. Even if he had changed his mind about the marriage, he still should have told me."

"Clearly he is a disrespectful rogue, my dear," the earl said. "You are better off without him."

"I agree." Annabelle curved her lips in a flirtatious smile.

Had Cilla not been watching the earl, she might have missed the momentary glint of triumph in his eyes. Perhaps he was simply pleased to have won the lady, but she could not ignore the dislike that swept her when she witnessed that look. Did he seem overly pleased at such a small thing, or was she jumping at shadows?

"You do not feel you dismissed the captain somewhat hastily, Mr. Bailey?" Cilla asked. "From what I understand, he was a longtime friend of the family."

"No," Virgil answered in a tone that brooked no argument.

Raventhorpe whipped his head around to pin her with a sharp look. "Why would you ask such a thing, Mrs. Burke?"

Due to the angle, no one but she could see the threat in his eyes. She exhaled slowly and lifted her teacup as if nothing were amiss. "Only because he seemed so determined to be heard. One would think that a friendship that had endured for so many years would at least merit a longer discussion." Calling on years of deportment lessons to keep her hand steady and her expression serene, she sipped the hot beverage.

"He hurt my daughter," Virgil said. "And maybe you don't know all the facts. Either way, this is none of your business."

"I apologize." Cilla dropped her eyes to her lap. "It is just that he did not seem like a man who would give up easily." When Raventhorpe's eyes narrowed, she wished she could call the words back.

"Perhaps Captain Breedlove simply recognizes the importance of a strategic retreat, Mrs. Burke," the earl said. "Which calls to mind a question that has been plaguing me since first I made your acquaintance."

Cilla raised her brows in polite inquiry. "My lord?"

"I have felt since our first meeting that I have seen you before, but the connection has eluded me until this moment. Are you not the daughter of Admiral Robert Wallington-Willis?"

Startled, Cilla set down the teacup. "Yes, but—"

"Ah, I thought so." The earl turned to the Baileys. "Admiral Wallington-Willis is one of Her Majesty's most respected and decorated naval admirals. He is accepted at the highest level of society."

"Why, Cilla, we had no idea!" Dolly exclaimed. "I mean, you had said that you knew all about society, but I figured that was all book learning."

Cilla managed a smile even as she silently wished the earl to the devil. Her departure from society had been less than decorous, and she couldn't help but wonder if the earl knew it. Or was he simply probing for a weak spot in response to her persistent questions? "I have been gone from England for several years. Certainly the connection is of little import now."

"Why, Mrs. Burke, you are too modest," the earl said. His tone conveyed affability while the threat of something darker lingered in his eyes. "Surely it has not been so long that all London society will have forgotten the daughter of one of our most treasured heroes."

"You flatter me, my lord."

"Nonsense." The earl waved away her objections.

"Your family lives in London?" Annabelle asked.

Cilla nodded. "Ever since Papa retired from commanding his own vessel."

"Cilla, for goodness' sake, why didn't you tell us?" Dolly exclaimed. "Why, we were all invited to London to attend Lady Canthrope's ball Monday next. You simply must come with us."

"No, no." Cilla held up her hand in protest. "One simply does not attend a ball when one has not been invited. I am perfectly content to remain here as we planned." *Especially since my presence in London might be a detriment to Annabelle.*

"An easy remedy," Raventhorpe said, a smirk curving his lips. "I shall procure an invitation for Mrs. Burke."

Annabelle clapped her hands together. "How generous of you, Richard! It would simply be wonderful if Mrs. Burke could accompany us."

"I agree," Dolly said. "I am certain Cilla still has lots of friends in London. After all, it hasn't been that long, has it, dear?"

"Four years." Dread surged through her at the direction of the conversation. "But I really do not think my presence is appropriate."

"I will be arriving at the affair much later due to a previous engagement," Raventhorpe said. "It would be a great favor to me if you would take my betrothed and her mama under your wing until I arrive."

"But—"

"Please, Mrs. Burke?" Annabelle wrung her hands, her lovely blue eyes wide and pleading.

"You simply must come with us, Cilla," Dolly said. "It's the perfect opportunity to introduce Annabelle to London folks. After all, she's going to be a countess soon."

She longed to refuse. She glanced at Lord Raventhorpe, and there it was again, that slyness flashing across his face. She knew pushing him about Captain Breedlove had made an enemy of him, but she could not do otherwise. The captain's emotional response to the confrontation still resonated with her, and Raventhorpe's subtle attack was enough to make her question the earl's version of events. But for now—how to get out of this situation?

The last thing she wanted was to go back to London at this juncture, before the wedding had occurred. She had left society in disgrace. She intended to return in triumph.

"We'll have to get you a ball gown," Dolly said.

"Oh, but I could not—"

"But you must, Mrs. Burke." The earl glanced around at everyone seated at the table, then back at Cilla. "You do want to make a memorable impression on society, do you not?"

Gleeful satisfaction emanated from him even as knots twisted in Cilla's stomach. Had he deliberately exposed her secret to the Baileys as a way to discomfit her? Edward had often done the same thing, flinging her missteps in her face and then punishing her for her transgressions. Perhaps Raventhorpe expected her to embarrass herself in front of her employers by refusing to go.

She refused to be manipulated by spite.

Folding her hands in her lap, she said, "Naturally I will go where my employer bids me."

"Glad to hear that," Virgil said. "Since His Lordship is going to all the trouble of getting you an invitation and all."

"Yes, thank you, my lord." Cilla smiled at Raventhorpe, more at the frustration simmering in his eyes than gratitude for the invitation. "I appreciate your assistance."

Raventhorpe gave a curt nod and turned to engage Annabelle in conversation.

Cilla smothered a smile. She would wait until the pompous earl had taken his leave and then she would explain the situation to Dolly in private. Surely she would understand why Cilla simply preferred not to show herself in society—at least not until after the success of Annabelle's wedding.

Perhaps leaving for London early was the answer to the gossip problem caused by the events of the night before. And if the family departed for the city and left her behind, it would give her an opportunity to try and discover more information about Samuel Breedlove.

"Are you certain you want to do this?" John asked. "You could go back again this morning. Perhaps the Baileys would be more willing to listen without Raventhorpe there."

Samuel tucked the last of his clothing into his satchel, trying to function beyond the grief of having lost the respect of his adopted family. "No, they were all quite adamant in their views. They think I am a fortune hunter."

"More like a fortune *finder*. Did you tell them that? Sometimes gold speaks louder than words."

Samuel shoved the last item into the bag and closed it, then turned around. His friend and sometime coachman watched him from the doorway of his room at the inn, a smile playing about his lips. Simple clothing marked John a man of modest means, yet he had about him an air of regality that had always struck Samuel as being directly at odds with his humble appearance.

And sometimes, John's odd sense of humor irked him no end.

"They seem to worship gold entirely too much already. And I cannot buy back what I have lost."

"I did not come back and rescue you from that island only to have a Virginia farmer get the better of you. If they did not listen last night, you must simply try again."

"That's why we're headed to London. We're restrategizing and moving our battle to a different field."

John grew serious. "Samuel, as an earl, Raventhorpe will have the advantage in London. You might have more luck here in the country."

"No, I think this is the right move. It was you who gave me the idea when you passed on that little tidbit you learned from the servants last evening."

"Bless them. I told you the servants' network is the fastest and most accurate way to transmit knowledge."

"It's served us well to this point. First alerting us to where we could find Annabelle, and now with the knowledge that the Baileys travel to London in a few days."

"And that Raventhorpe is scheduled to leave for Cornwall to visit the orphanages he sponsors. He will join his fiancée in time for the Canthrope affair on Monday."

"Ah, yes. Raventhorpe the philanthropist." Samuel gave a disbelieving laugh. "When we get to London, I want you to start collecting information on those orphanages, John. There might be secrets there we can use to prove his character to the Baileys."

"It would be just like Raventhorpe to turn a charitable establishment into something sordid."

"We both know what he is capable of, and sincere donations of the heart are not in his repertoire."

"While I am doing that, what do you intend to accomplish in London?"

Samuel smiled and picked up his bag. "I intend to make a spectacle of myself. Rent a house. Buy a carriage, horses. How else will I make an impression on the wealth-obsessed members of London society except by an extravagant spending of gold?"

"Which will get all of London talking about the mysterious rich American." John laughed. "Well done!"

"The Baileys don't yet know about my change in fortunes. I like to imagine their faces when they find out."

John chuckled. "Even though you are a lowly American, the color of your gold will open the doors of society for you."

"The color of *our* gold, John. I told you I would divide the treasure I found on the island with you as reward for returning for me."

"I have no need of treasure," John said, waving a hand in dismissal.

"Nevertheless, I have a need to give it to you. I could open an account for you—"

"No." John shook his head. "If you insist on bestowing your riches on me, I trust you to hold it until such a time as I may require it. For now I am content to be your coachman."

Samuel gave a quick laugh. "John, you are much more than a coachman."

"Very well. Your companion, then."

Samuel gave his friend a sharp look. "You are more than that as well. But if this is how you want it to be . . ."

"It is. Trust me, Samuel. It is much better if I stay invisible to the authorities of England. And how better to do that than to be in plain sight as a servant?"

"John, I know you are no mere servant. Anyone who exchanges more than a few words with you would know it."

"Then I shall endeavor to remain silent whenever possible." When Samuel opened his mouth to comment further, John held up a hand to silence him. "Please, Samuel."

His plea convinced Samuel to let the matter drop. "Very well. Let's leave for London directly after breakfast." He headed for the door, then grinned and tossed his bag to John, who caught it. "If you insist on being a servant, you'll have to act like one."

John adjusted his grip on the bag and moved out of the doorway. "I see your humor has improved."

Samuel followed John into the hallway and turned to lock the door to the room. "I intend to stop this wedding, John, and I *will* win back the Baileys' trust in me."

"You'll need a plan for that."

Samuel thought of Mrs. Burke and the sympathy in her eyes when she'd come after him. "I may have already found one. The next time the Baileys see me, it will be a different Samuel Breedlove who greets them."

Chapter 4

London, a week later

I should have stayed behind," Cilla said as she regarded the crush in Lady Canthrope's London ballroom. "My presence may do more harm than good."

"Nonsense." Dolly waved her hand in dismissal. "You have done nothing wrong, my dear, except to follow your heart."

"You have a different view on marriage than the English," Cilla said. "I caused quite a stir when I eloped with Edward. And the memories of society matrons are long and detailed."

Annabelle sent her a worried glance. "I certainly hope no one is rude enough to mention such a thing."

"I am not concerned for myself. It is you. I do not want to see your reputation harmed by my foolish decisions. It is bad enough that everyone around Nevarton Chase is buzzing about what happened at the engagement party."

"Enough," Dolly murmured as a group of people

passed by the niche where the three of them had gathered. "Cilla, we talked about this. It was a brilliant notion to leave for London early to escape the wagging tongues. By the time we return, the whole scandal should have blown over."

"That is my hope. But here in London . . . I tried to tell you that my marriage was not well received. Some people might slight you because of me."

"Nonsense. You should hold your head high and don't let any of those busybodies rile you. It's not like you ran off with the man to live in sin, after all!"

Annabelle giggled. "Mama!"

"Well, it's the truth." Dolly gave Cilla a righteous nod. "You married the wrong man, dear. A mistake many women make, let me tell you. I'm just lucky I met my Virgil."

"Where *is* Pa?" Annabelle asked, glancing around.

"Off in the card room as usual. You know he detests dancing." Dolly snapped open her fan. "Goodness, it's warm in here. How in the world do they fit so many bodies in one room?"

"'Tis a matter of consequence," Cilla said. "No London hostess can consider her event a success unless the guests complain about the terrible crush."

"Seems silly to me." Dolly waved her fan with more vigor. "Makes more sense to just invite the people you like and have room to breathe than to stuff your house full of a bunch of strangers. How we'll find Lord Raventhorpe in all this I do not know."

"I'm certain Richard will find us without any

problem," Annabelle said. "He probably attends these sorts of affairs all the time."

"No doubt," Dolly agreed. "And that means you'll be attending them too, sweetheart. How exciting!"

"I can hardly wait." Annabelle gave the smug smile of a woman who knew her worth. "Mrs. Burke, how were you ever able to leave such a thrilling life behind? Don't you miss it?"

Before Cilla could respond, Dolly said, "Of course she did, dear, but she was in love. And when one is in love, everything else seems trivial."

Annabelle glanced at Cilla as if for confirmation. Reluctantly she nodded. What else could she do? She dared not voice the disappointment of her marriage to the young girl. The private shame was her own to bear.

Dolly, in the meantime, was watching the crowd like a hawk over a flock of pigeons. "Aha! There they are." Closing her fan with a snap, Dolly beamed at Cilla, an unnerving twinkle in her eyes. "I asked Lady Canthrope to invite someone for you, dear. She is a close acquaintance of the earl's family and was only too pleased to grant my request."

Dread shot straight into her throat. Not another eligible gentleman! She had already deflected the well-meaning American's not so subtle attempts at matchmaking from the moment they had left the shores of New York until just a week ago, when Dolly had determined a local squire might be perfect husband material. "Dolly, we discussed this—"

"No, no." Dolly waved a dismissive hand. "It's not

a man, though I haven't given up looking for a new prospective husband for you, dear. I still think that you're far too young for widow's weeds."

Cilla let out the breath she had not realized she had been holding. "I appreciate your concern, but as I have told you before, I am not looking for marriage."

"No, this is a much more wonderful surprise." Dolly clasped her hands together with a clap, fan dangling from the tie on her wrist. "I've invited your family."

"What?" Cilla snapped her head around, following the path of Dolly's gaze. Her mother and sister were approaching—and much too quickly for Cilla to hide.

Genny had grown, was her first thought. Then she met her mother's gaze—the hope lurking there, the uncertainty. *Oh, Mama.*

Dear God, she was not ready to face them. Not yet. But it was too late now.

"I told Lady Canthrope we would be waiting in this lovely alcove and to send them over once they had gone through the receiving line." Dolly took up her fan again and tapped Cilla on the arm with it, her face beaming. "I imagine it's been years since you've seen your family."

"Yes." Nearly four years, and her father's pronouncement of disinheritance still echoed in her heart.

"When I discovered they lived right in London, naturally I had to arrange for you to see them. After all, the wedding takes so much of your time and we'll only be in the city for a few more days." Dolly's face creased in concern. "I certainly hope it was all right of me to do that. You don't seem very excited."

"The shock." Cilla forced a smile as her family reached them. "It was kind of you to think of me, Dolly."

"You're very welcome, dear." Turning to Cilla's mother, Dolly held out her hands and trilled, "Mrs. Wallington-Willis, I sure am glad to meet you. I'm Mrs. Bailey, but you can call me Dolly. And this is my daughter, Annabelle."

"A pleasure to meet you both. It was kind of you to ask Lady Canthrope to invite us." Helen Wallington-Willis accepted Dolly's greeting, then sent a hesitant smile to her daughter. "Cilla. You're looking well."

"Thank you, Mama." How many times had she imagined this meeting? But always in her mind she had swept into the midst of society on a wave of success, not in the position of a mere employee. Swallowing past the tightness in her throat, she glanced at her sister. "Goodness, Genny, you're all grown up."

"I *am* eighteen," Genny said. No kindness lurked in her green eyes, only the banked fires of resentment. "It's been nearly four years after all."

"Genny has already been presented to Her Majesty," Helen said.

"How wonderful." Cilla looked at her mother. "Where's Papa?"

Helen's smile never wavered. "The card room. You know how your father is."

"Yes, I do." So, he still had not forgiven her. That,

more than her mother's reserve or her sister's hostility, burned straight to her heart.

"Men and their cards." Dolly sighed, rolling her eyes. "Heavens, do they think we can dance with ourselves?"

"I agree," Helen said. "It seems that once a man has acquired a wife, he feels his days of dancing are over."

"Richard is an excellent dancer," Annabelle said. "I bet we'll dance together all the time, even after the wedding."

"My daughter is engaged to Lord Raventhorpe," Dolly explained to Helen, pride shining in her eyes.

"I saw the announcement in the *Times*. Best wishes, Miss Bailey."

"Yes, best wishes." Genny shot a sideways glance at Cilla. "Is it true that my sister is arranging the wedding festivities?"

"Why yes," Dolly replied. "She's a godsend. I couldn't have navigated English society without her."

"But you are standing in a corner," Genny said, and with jerk of her dark curly head toward Cilla, added, "with the hired help. I fail to see how this counts as navigating society."

Cilla's face burned, and Helen gave a little gasp. "Genevieve!"

"My apologies," Genny said to Dolly and Annabelle. "I meant no offense to you."

No, Cilla thought, not to them. But Genny had made it more than clear what she thought of her older sister's life choices. What had happened to the cheerful young sprite who had followed her around everywhere before her marriage?

"Young woman, that was about the rudest thing I have ever heard," Dolly said. Steely anger tinged her voice, a direct contrast to her normal cheerful demeanor. "She is your sister."

The glee faded from Genny's eyes. "I apologized."

"We shall talk about this later," Helen said. "I would like to apologize as well for my daughter's behavior. To *all* of you."

Annabelle eyed Genny with dislike. "It's clear to me that you don't know your sister at all."

Genny stiffened. "Not anymore." She looked at her mother. "Mama, I see Marguerite Jaxton. May I go speak to her? I want to see if she has heard more about that dashing American captain. It is rumored he is to make an appearance here this evening."

Helen closed her eyes as if praying for patience and sighed. "Fine. Go. But I will come and find you in a few minutes. See that you stay close to Mrs. Jaxton."

"I will. Nice to meet you," she said to the Baileys, then turned and made her way toward her friend a short distance away.

"I apologize again for my daughter," Helen said. "Especially to you, Cilla."

"Already forgotten," Cilla said, though Genny's attitude had indeed stung. But another matter had claimed her attention. "If I might ask—what dashing American captain was she talking about?"

"Oh!" Clearly grateful for the safer topic, Helen smiled. "About a week ago, a mysterious fellow they are calling the captain took London by storm. He's rumored to be phenomenally rich. People have been whispering about him for days. He rented a town house in Mayfair and paid in gold!"

"My heavens!" Dolly looked at Annabelle. "Do you suppose . . . ?"

"He paid in gold?" Annabelle shook her head. "Then it can't be Samuel."

"Oh." The spark faded from Dolly's eyes. "You're right."

"Who is Samuel?" Helen asked.

"A long story," Dolly said, patting Annabelle's arm. "Annabelle was once engaged to a sea captain named Samuel, and he recently came to call on us at Nevarton Chase. But she ended that engagement, and now she is to marry the Earl of Raventhorpe."

"An earl is certainly a better catch than a mere sea captain," Helen said.

Dolly nodded. "My thoughts exactly. My Annabelle is as thrilled as bees at a honey festival to be marrying a real English lord."

Helen blinked at the phrase. "Of course she is. What girl would not be?"

"Samuel didn't have a lot of money, certainly not enough to pay for a house in gold," Annabelle said with a shrug.

"So this captain cannot be your Samuel," Helen said.

"Oh, no," Annabelle said. "It's impossible."

Helen turned to Cilla. "All this talk of marriage

reminds me, Cilla. I saw Prescott Allerton as I came in."

Cilla stifled a groan. "Indeed?"

"Quite. He is still unwed."

"Who's this Prescott Allerton?" Dolly asked. "An old beau, perhaps?"

"I believe he held a *tendre* for Cilla at one time. He has advanced in rank to lieutenant in Her Majesty's Navy." Helen gave Cilla a conspiratorial smile. "He is a man even your father would approve as a suitor."

"Why that sounds just perfect!" Dolly beamed at Cilla.

Cilla shook her head. "I am certain Lieutenant Allerton has forgotten me after all these years, Mama."

"Do not dismiss him out of hand," Helen said. "I warn you, I intend to engage him in conversation and test his memory."

"Mama!"

Ignoring Cilla's protests, Helen said, "If you will all excuse me, I had best find my daughter. I hate to leave her alone in this crush for long." She reached for Cilla's hand and squeezed it. "I am so pleased to see you, my dear."

Longing for the warmth of her family clogged her throat. Still she managed, "It was good to see you, too, Mama."

Helen's serene expression faltered for a moment, and she released Cilla's hand. "I must find Genny. Please excuse me." With a nod to all of them, she turned and disappeared into the crowd.

Cilla watched her go, her heart swelling with more emotion than she cared to entertain while standing in the middle of a crowded London ballroom. She had missed her mother desperately, the ache inside her made even more wrenching by their all-too-brief conversation. For one sharp moment, she dearly missed her old life in London society.

"Your mother is a darling lady," Dolly said.

"She is." Cilla blinked her stinging eyes. She would not weep for all London to witness. Such a loss of control would be the crowning glory for the gossips who watched her with avid attention, circling like carrion birds as they waited for her to make a mistake that would give the rumor mill more fodder. Only the presence of the incredibly wealthy Baileys had kept them at bay this long.

"Can't say the same about your sister," Annabelle said. "Really, why was she so rude? If I had a sister like you, I'd be pleased as all get out to show her off to everybody."

"Annabelle, hush," Dolly murmured. "Your sister is young, Cilla. She must have missed you when you left."

"Maybe so. But—" She broke off as the murmur of conversation in the ballroom dipped noticeably, though the orchestra continued playing and the dancers continued dancing. "What is happening?"

"I can't see much of anything through this crowd," Dolly said.

The people around them began to shift.

"Maybe it's the queen!" Annabelle breathed.

"Her Majesty does not usually make an appearance

at functions like this," Cilla said. "But apparently someone of note has arrived."

The crowd began to part in front of them, heads turning toward the three of them, curiosity evident.

"I believe that's Lady Canthrope," Dolly said. "She has someone with her."

"Maybe it's Richard," Annabelle said.

"I don't think so. It looks like a dark-haired man, and His Lordship is blond. Perhaps—" Dolly sucked in a quick breath. "Heavens!"

"Mama, what is it?"

The people nearest them moved aside, revealing Lady Canthrope leading Samuel Breedlove straight to their alcove.

Annabelle gasped. Dolly gaped. And Cilla maintained her hard-learned discipline with effort as the couple reached them. *What was he doing here?*

Elegant black evening clothes accented by a neck cloth, shirt, and waistcoat of snowy white fit his powerful build as if tailored specifically for him. His long dark hair had been clipped to a shorter, more fashionable style, curling slightly at the ends in a way destined to make a lady's heart quicken. Rather than bringing to mind the working classes, his sun-bronzed complexion served to accent his dark eyes and wicked grin in a rakish way that could not be matched by any of the pale Englishmen in the room.

Cilla's heart gave a hard thud in her chest before her pulse quickened. The man simply embodied virility, and her body responded to his presence like a flower opening for the rising warmth of the sun.

Her visceral reaction alarmed her, and she reached for her well-learned discipline. He was too handsome for his own good. And American. And determined to stop the wedding she was trying to arrange. And he was most probably a liar.

But that secret softness inside her didn't care. He affected her as no other man ever had, and that made him dangerous.

"Mrs. Bailey, look who has arrived! Captain Breedlove tells me he is a close family friend, so of course I felt I should escort him to your side myself!" Lady Canthrope's plump face creased in a huge smile, her small eyes glittering with anticipation.

"Mrs. Bailey. Annabelle." Samuel executed a perfect bow. "Mrs. Burke."

"Samuel! My goodness, we had assumed you had gone back to America," Dolly said.

"I'm afraid you aren't rid of me that easily."

Annabelle lifted her chin and looked away over his shoulder. "Oh, Samuel, really."

"I couldn't leave England without saying goodbye, Annabelle. We've known each other too long to part in anger."

Annabelle jerked her gaze back to his, clearly moved despite herself.

Even Cilla's heart melted a bit at the romantic phrasing, but she steeled herself against further softness toward this man. What was he about? How had he infiltrated the closely guarded doors of London society?

"The captain has been the talk of London these past few days," Lady Canthrope gushed.

So, the mysterious captain *was* Samuel.

"We have been hearing the most incredible stories about you, Captain Breedlove," Cilla said. "Exaggerations, surely."

"Gossip is a frivolous waste of time," Lady Canthrope declared with a sharp look at Cilla. "However, I must admit that I, too, have been subjected to such innuendo. Perhaps the captain might dispel such rumors for us, his close friends?" She beamed up at him.

Samuel looked perplexed for a moment, and Cilla felt a twinge of sympathy for the man. Even before Cilla had left England, Lady Canthrope had been the biggest gossip in London. It would be quite a coup if she learned his secrets from the man himself.

"I can understand you must have questions," Samuel said, quickly recovering his aplomb. "But I will only reveal my secrets to Annabelle—if she grants me the pleasure of the next dance."

Annabelle jerked her gaze to his. "Isn't that against protocol? I *am* an engaged woman."

"Not at all, my dear," Lady Canthrope gushed. "After all, your betrothed has not yet arrived, and your mama and I are here to chaperone. I see nothing wrong with an innocent dance, especially with an old family friend."

"I don't know if that's such a good idea," Dolly said. "I wouldn't want Annabelle to do anything that would upset Lord Raventhorpe. And after what happened at the engagement party—"

"Oh?" Lady Canthrope's gaze glittered like that of a raven sighting a shiny object. "What happened at the engagement party?"

"Water under the bridge," Dolly said. "Though I must admit to curiosity, Samuel."

"It's up to Annabelle," Samuel said.

"Oh, Mama, Richard isn't even here yet." Annabelle pouted and cast her big blue eyes at her mother. "And apparently there is more to Samuel's story than we know. I'm certain one dance won't hurt anything."

Dolly visibly melted. "Cilla, what do you think?"

"I don't—" Cilla began. Samuel slanted a sharp glance at her. Their gazes held for a brief, potent moment.

"This is my ball, Mrs. Burke, and I give permission." Lady Canthrope glared at Cilla. Had consequence been a physical thing, hers would have been flaring like a peacock's plumes. "I see no harm in it, and if His Lordship objects, I will tell him I sanctioned it."

"My dear Lady Canthrope, your support is greatly appreciated." Samuel took the lady's chubby hand in his and pressed a kiss to it.

"You rascal." Blushing like a schoolgirl, Lady Canthrope giggled. "Go on, now. Dance with Miss Bailey before I set my cap for you myself."

"'Tis my loss that Lord Canthrope won you first." Turning to Annabelle, Samuel held out a hand. "Annabelle, may I have this dance?"

Annabelle took his hand, her face smug with triumph.

As the two of them moved to the dance floor, Lady Canthrope clasped her hands at her bosom. "Such a man. If I were only twenty years younger." With a dreamy sigh, she moved off.

Cilla watched Samuel and Annabelle take their places. The orchestra struck up a waltz, and they whirled into motion. They made a striking couple, he so dark and she so fair. They waltzed together as if they had done so many times in the past—which, given their history together, was entirely possible. If not for a tragic twist of fate, they might have been married long ago.

If Samuel was to be believed, he had braved the challenges of Ulysses to return to Annabelle. But if Raventhorpe was to be believed, Samuel was a desperate liar trying to win back the woman he had abandoned. Both stories were fantastic. Which man was telling the truth?

And was she a fool for wanting to believe it was Samuel?

Certainly he was handsome. Tall, good-looking, strong, and able-bodied. He fit every woman's fantasy about the dashing hero coming to rescue the fair maiden. And his genuine pain about losing Annabelle was enough to soften any female's romantic heart, especially hers. Was this why she wanted to believe him? Had the attraction she felt for him colored her opinion of him?

She had been wrong about Edward. What if she was wrong this time, too? It was more than her future on the line.

The crux of the matter came down to whether

Annabelle was truly in danger if she married Raventhorpe. And how had a poor sea captain come into enough funds that he could pay for his rented town house in gold? There were too many unanswered questions. The captain had eluded her at the engagement party and then again later, when she had quietly inquired about him at the local inn, only to discover he had indeed been staying there but had already departed. However, she would not allow him to escape her again.

Tonight she would get her answers.

"I've missed you, Annabelle." Samuel relished the victory of luring Annabelle to the dance floor. He had counted on her curiosity when he'd issued the invitation, and now she would have to listen to him.

"You always were an excellent dancer." She moved in perfect harmony with him, a nostalgic smile playing about her lips.

"A man achieves a strong sense of balance walking the deck of a moving vessel."

"I imagine so." She looked up at him, caution in her eyes. "Why did you do it, Samuel? If you changed your mind about getting married, you should have told me."

"It wasn't my choice to stay away."

"So you said." Her expression darkened. "Richard told me how the two of you argued and you resigned your post in the middle of the voyage. Your temper betrayed you, not him."

Samuel swirled her around as they swept the room.

"Did Richard also tell you that he pushed me off a cliff and left me for dead?"

Her mouth formed an O of horror. "What a terrible thing to say!"

"It was a terrible thing to do."

"Jealousy does not become you, Samuel."

He nearly stopped in the middle of the dance floor, but kept going before he caused a collision. "Jealousy! Is that what you think?"

She gave a little shrug. "What am I supposed to think?"

"You're supposed to trust me, damn it. I'm no liar."

She ignored his profanity. "But he is? Richard is an earl, Samuel. A member of the House of Lords. Surely a man as important as he is wouldn't bother to try and kill a mere sea captain."

"Now I'm a *mere* sea captain?" He curled his lip. "A mere sea captain was good enough for you before your father discovered that coal mine under his farm."

She flinched. "We've all changed."

"Some more than most, apparently." They fell into a strained silence, whirling around the room in perfect physical harmony.

But never had he felt so far away from her. For the first time, he was grateful she had broken their engagement.

"Don't they make a wonderful couple?" Dolly sighed and clasped her hands to her bosom. "Such a shame. I was always fond of Samuel. Still am, I suppose."

Cilla sent her a startled glance. "Even after all that has happened?"

"Well, I still don't understand why he never came back until now, and then when he did he made all those accusations about Lord Raventhorpe. He broke my Annabelle's heart."

"But when he tried to explain, you didn't believe him."

Dolly gave her a look of incredulity. "I had to take my daughter's side. Surely you know that."

"What if the captain's story is true?" Cilla asked.

"I can't believe that Lord Raventhorpe would deliberately strand Samuel on an island." Dolly waved a hand in dismissal of the idea. "It's more likely Samuel was too embarrassed to come home."

"But you all thought the captain was a fortune hunter. Clearly he is not."

"You don't know him like we do, Cilla. Between the way he was raised and his temper, Samuel has been known to do one or two unwise things."

Before Cilla could reply, a gentleman in naval dress appeared before her and bowed. His crisp uniform emphasized his light brown hair, startling green eyes, and handsome features. "Miss . . . I mean, Mrs. Burke, Lieutenant Preston Allerton at your service."

"Lieutenant Allerton." Startled—and not a little unnerved by the gleam of interest in Dolly's eyes—Cilla automatically extended her hand for his greeting.

He took it, brushed a kiss against the back of

it. "Pray forgive my impertinence, but your dear mother encouraged me to approach you to renew our acquaintance."

I bet she did exactly that.

Dolly coughed, and remembering her manners, Cilla said, "Mrs. Bailey, allow me to present Lieutenant Preston Allerton of Her Majesty's Navy."

"Charmed to meet you." Dolly held out a hand, and the lieutenant obligingly bowed over it.

"A pleasure, Mrs. Bailey." He looked back at Cilla. "Mrs. Burke, I am hoping that our lengthy acquaintance over these past years will compel you to accept me as your partner for the next dance."

Cilla opened her mouth to refuse, but then Samuel and Annabelle swept by. Samuel's tall form moved easily through the steps, one hand firmly on Annabelle's waist, the other hand joined with hers. However, Annabelle did not look to be enjoying the dance as much as one would expect; in fact, Cilla recognized the flush in her cheeks and the stubborn set to her mouth as clear indications of ill humor in her young friend.

What were they saying?

Leaping to a decision, she smiled at the officer in front of her. "What about this one?"

She could tell she had startled him, but he recovered quickly. A pleased smile curved his lips at what he no doubt assumed was eagerness on her part. "The waltz?"

"*This* waltz. If you are amenable, Lieutenant."

"Most amenable. Shall we?" He extended his arm, and Cilla took it, barely aware of Dolly beaming at her. The lieutenant led her to the dance floor, placed his hand on her waist, then whirled her into the rhythm of the waltz.

"Speaking of changes," Annabelle said, "what's this rumor about you paying for a London town house in gold?"

Ah. He had wondered when she would ask.

"I've come into good fortune and find myself richer than any man could dream. Certainly richer than your precious Raventhorpe, for all his title and pretty manners."

She stiffened. "Richard has explained to me that his estates are terribly expensive to maintain. I know he's not a wealthy man, but I have money enough for the both of us."

"So you know he's a fortune hunter then. And now I've told you how he tried to kill me, yet you still defend him."

She tightened her lips, glancing about them as if to make certain no one was listening to their conversation. "What I *know* is that you abandoned me after swearing to marry me. Richard comforted me. He was *there*."

"It wasn't my choice, Annabelle."

"It was a terrible time for me, Samuel. Horrible memories. I expected more from you, especially with the way you claimed to value honor."

"I would have been at your side if Raventhorpe had not betrayed me. A reef around the island shattered every raft I made."

"Will you please stop saying such things?"

"For pity's sake, Annabelle, why don't you listen to me? Why would you wed him knowing he only wants your fortune?"

"The fact that Richard needs my money doesn't bother me. In fact, it means he won't abandon me. Even if he runs through my dowry in a blink, the only way he'll be able to get more money from Pa is if he keeps me happy."

"And alive?" He stared down into her pretty face. He could see the hurt he had caused her—hell, that Raventhorpe had caused both of them—but he also saw a glimpse of the same sweetness and naïveté that had once made him choose her as the mother of his children. "Tell me this, Annabelle. Who inherits the money if something happens to your parents?"

"Me, of course, though that's a terrible thing to say!"

"Is it?" He leaned down to bring his lips closer to her ear. "And if something were to happen to you after that, Raventhorpe would inherit everything."

Shock rippled across her face just as a hand landed on his shoulder, forcing them to halt mid-turn. Mrs. Burke, in the arms of a naval officer, dodged around them to avoid a collision as Samuel turned to face Raventhorpe.

"Still sniffing after my bride, Captain?" the earl sneered.

"You were late." Samuel shrugged. "If you're that worried, you shouldn't keep your lady waiting so long."

"She knew I was detained." He tugged Annabelle's hand from Samuel's. "Didn't you, my dear?"

"Richard, please don't cause a scene," Annabelle whispered, glancing around them.

"I am simply defending you from unwanted attentions." The earl glared, his social mask slipping to reveal the murderous rage beneath. Samuel braced himself for battle.

Annabelle made a mewl of distress and laid her hand on Raventhorpe's arm. "Richard, please."

"Nothing to say, Breedlove?"

Annabelle's anxiety kept Samuel's anger in check. A public altercation would not advance his cause with the Baileys. His months of solitude had taught him to control his temper, but Raventhorpe would not know that. He would be expecting Samuel to react as he had in the past.

"She came willingly," he said. "Just ask your dear friend Lady Canthrope. But unlike you, Raventhorpe, I have no desire to instigate a brawl in the middle of a dance floor." Samuel sketched a bow. "Thank you for the dance, Annabelle. Think about what I said." He gave the barest hint of a nod. "Raventhorpe."

Without another word, he turned away. Barely sparing a glance for Mrs. Burke and her escort, who lingered close enough to have certainly overheard the conversation, he left them all standing there as the rumbles of speculation began.

Chapter 5

Samuel found solace in the garden. He stood on the path, staring up at the night sky. The stars looked smaller here in the city than they had on the island, but focusing on them allowing him to get a firm rein on his temper. This should have been easier. Annabelle should have believed him.

But what had he expected? Women had a different sense of loyalty than men. They always allied themselves with males who were wealthy or powerful, men who would give them things. And when the generosity dried up, the woman would move on to another man. His mother had taught him that lesson.

He had known the nature of women going into his engagement with Annabelle. At the time, she was the most beautiful girl in the county, even though her father was only a poor farmer. Her beauty was the only asset she possessed to attract a decent husband, and he could not fault her for using it. After all, hadn't he selected her for her looks and sweet nature? Her life as a farmer's daughter meant that she understood the rewards of hard work and would make a good mother for his children. Not to mention there was a strong possibility those children would inherit their mother's handsomeness.

He remembered the day he had asked her to marry him, how she had tearfully accepted. She had gone on about love and happiness, and he allowed her that. Love was how women justified their manipulation of men. For him, marriage was a contract. He wanted a wife and family; she wanted a man who would provide for her. It was an excellent arrangement all around. Logical. Sound business.

But now things were different. Samuel blew out a long breath. He could handle losing Annabelle. He could even understand her wanting to marry another man. After all, it was painfully clear to him that they weren't suited anymore. But not this man, who would as soon slit her throat as bed her. He cared too much for Annabelle and her parents to allow that to happen.

"Captain Breedlove?"

He glanced over at the woman standing on the steps leading down into the garden, silhouetted by the lights of the ballroom behind her. He would recognize that straight spine and lushly curved figure anywhere. "Mrs. Burke, to what do I owe the pleasure?"

She descended the remaining steps, then paused. "I hope I am not disturbing you."

"Not at all." He turned to face her. "What happened to your escort?"

"I asked him to fetch me some punch." She approached him with the caution of a virgin to a dragon.

For some reason her hesitance only heightened his simmering temper. "I thought you would have been comforting Annabelle after what just happened."

"She is with His Lordship."

"Raventhorpe?" He gave a bark of laughter. "Hardly a comfort."

"Even if he is the villain you claim, he will hardly do her harm in front of half of London society." As Mrs. Burke approached him, the flickering light from the torches along the path emphasized the dark pools of her eyes and the inviting cleft between her breasts. He allowed himself to enjoy the pleasant hum of lust for a moment. The lovely widow might very well possess the most magnificent breasts he had ever seen.

It had been a long time since he had enjoyed such a sight.

"At Annabelle's engagement party, you asked me to listen to you," said the owner of the distracting bosom. "And I tried, but you left rather abruptly. I even inquired at the inn the next day, but you had already departed."

"I thought it best to exact a strategic retreat." An excellent idea for this moment as well. Up close, the lady's skin looked even more delectable.

"It left many questions." She paused. "The Baileys think the worst."

His laugh sounded more like a snarl. "And you, Mrs. Burke? What do you think?"

"There was some speculation that you had abandoned Annabelle and only returned when you discovered she was an heiress."

"Is that what you believe?"

"I do not know what to believe. Your explanation for your absence is something out of a novel. Yet at the same time . . ."

"At the same time . . ." he urged when she did not continue.

"I do think you honestly cared for her," she said. "At least a little."

"At last! Someone who doesn't think me the villain of the piece."

"I admit that I have not yet made that determination."

He frowned. "You just said that you believed me."

"I *want* to believe you. But truly, Captain, you might simply be a very gifted liar."

He stiffened. "If you were a man, I would knock you cold for that."

She gasped. "Captain, really!"

He shrugged. " 'Tis the truth. But have no fear, madam." He couldn't stop himself from taking a long, appreciative look at her form. "I can see clearly enough that you are most definitely not a man."

In the relative silence of the garden, he heard her breath catch, and she splayed her hand over her bosom. Was her heart pounding at such a simple remark? How long had it been since she had felt a lover's touch?

Did she even seek a lover? An image flashed in his mind of the comely widow in the arms of the buttoned-and-pressed lieutenant. No, he doubted the naval man had the fire necessary for the job.

Mrs. Burke struck him as a passionate woman who needed a man of equal passion to satisfy her. The lieutenant would leave her wanting. She needed a man of strength, someone comfortable in his own skin, unafraid to take her where she needed to go.

Someone like . . . him.

Once his mind latched on to that notion, it was impossible to let go. The altercation with Raventhorpe had left him edgy, and Annabelle's disbelief had only increased his frustration. Now here was Mrs. Burke, a widow with a body designed to be a man's playground, alone in the garden with him.

Her every word and gesture spoke to him of needs denied. Hunger unsatisfied. He knew without a doubt he could satisfy her. A lesser man might take advantage of the situation.

But he needed her to help him, and he did not consider seduction the best way to convince her. When sex became involved with business, emotions ran high. Too much could go wrong. As tempted as he was, he had to stand strong and keep his eye on the goal. To save Annabelle.

"I thought you were determined to clear your name, Captain," the widow said, her tone ringing with well-deserved rebuke. "To prove your honor. Flirting with me will gain you no ground to that end. Remember, it is my job to arrange this wedding. I have nothing to gain by helping you ruin it."

"Except to save Annabelle from marrying that scum."

"Scum? An unpleasant personality and puffed-up consequence is no reason to think the man a murderer. And I should warn you, sir, I am impervious to the charm of attractive gentlemen, so if you think to beguile me into helping you, it will not happen."

"Beguile? Do I have that power? Interesting." He smiled slowly.

Impossible male!

Cilla took slow, even breaths to calm her racing heart. What kind of man disrupted so many lives for the sake of one woman, then flirted with another? And that clever, engaging grin of his invited a woman to forget herself and follow him anywhere. Edward had been nearly as charming. She would not succumb to such blatant manipulation again. Ever.

"But you do bring up an interesting suggestion," he continued. "You are close to Annabelle. If I can convince you that Raventhorpe is a danger to her, will you help me stop this wedding?"

"If you speak seriously and tell me what is truly happening," Cilla said. "If you cannot do that, I trust you will not waste my time any further."

"Down to business, are we?"

"I am a practical woman, Captain. You must have a reason for trying to stop the wedding when the odds are so clearly against you."

"I told you my reason. Raventhorpe."

"I can understand that—*if* Lord Raventhorpe did what you claim."

His jaw tightened. "He did."

"And Annabelle?"

"Our engagement is at an end."

"You seem to have accepted that rather well."

"We are different people than we once were, but that doesn't mean that I want to see her hurt. I will do whatever I can to stop that wedding."

"I am all admiration at your determination to protect your former fiancée. Which brings us to another question." She folded her arms. "Explain the rumor I heard today where the mysterious American captain paid for his town house in gold."

He chuckled. "For a lady, you sure have no problem cutting right to the heart of the matter."

She shrugged, annoyed he had read her so easily. "Nonetheless, I do not follow anyone down a path blindly. Please answer me."

"You're all assuming I was after Annabelle's fortune, is that it?"

She gave a stiff nod.

He laughed. "My dear Mrs. Burke, in a rather bizarre twist of fate, I find myself part owner in a pirate's treasure."

She couldn't help it—she gaped. "A what?"

"A pirate's treasure. 'Twas hidden on that blasted rock where I spent the better part of the past two years. I split it with the man who rescued me from the island." He leaned forward, crowding close to her in a manner that made her extremely aware of his presence. "I can buy and sell Virgil Bailey several times over. So put your fears to rest. I don't want her money. I just want to save her from Raventhorpe."

"I see." Pirate's treasure? Did she dare believe such a fantastical tale? "Captain, I do not see—"

"Cilla?" Her mother stepped out onto the terrace above them. "Are you out here?"

Cilla clamped her mouth shut, grabbed Samuel's sleeve, and dragged him off the lit path and into the shadows below the terrace.

"Are you certain you saw her come out here?" a man asked.

"Perhaps she is down in the gardens," Helen said.

"We can check. I will escort you."

"Thank you, Lieutenant."

Cilla closed her eyes. Lieutenant Allerton. Was her mother so desperate to see her married to a man her father would find acceptable that she would lead the poor lieutenant to the altar by the hand? The timing could not be worse. Should the lieutenant discover her lurking alone in the gardens with the notorious American captain . . .

The gossips would destroy her.

Samuel appeared to understand the situation without her uttering a word. He lowered his head until his mouth nearly touched her ear. "Come with me."

His breath tickled the flesh of her neck. A swift, powerful surge of delight swept through her, awakening parts of her body she thought long dormant. Praying he had not noticed her involuntary quiver, she nodded in response to his command.

His large hand closed around hers. Willingly she

allowed him to lead her along the edge of the terrace and away from the lit walkway. She could hear her mother and Lieutenant Allerton walking down the stairs, chatting. Suddenly Samuel jerked her away from the terrace and led her through a barely visible opening between two large flowering bushes. The shrubs allowed them to remain concealed from Allerton and her mother, whose conversation echoed back as they strolled the garden path.

As her mother's voice faded into the distance, Cilla looked around. Samuel had led her into some kind of grotto with a stone bench standing between two Grecian columns—clearly meant to be a romantic corner for a rendezvous. Beside the faux ruins stood a quiet fountain with a Greco-Roman maiden pouring water from a jar into a stone pool. Trees and hedges shielded them from the sight of anyone on the pathway or the terrace.

"How did you know this was here?" she whispered, looking around her with wonder.

"I heard the water," he murmured back.

"Clever of you, Captain." She turned back to him and found him watching her. In the dimness of the starry night, his eyes looked darker than ever. The intensity she found there brought forth that quick tingle again. She moistened her dry lips.

His gaze zoomed to her mouth, then downward. "Your skin glows like porcelain in the moonlight."

She glanced down and saw that her sensible dark blue satin evening dress, which had appeared quite proper in the ballroom, now blended into the darkness, emphasizing the bared skin of her modest décolletage in a way that looked quite erotic. She jerked her gaze back to his. "You are flirting again, Captain. And rather boldly."

The flash of his grin only made him look more sinful. "Calm yourself, Mrs. Burke. I'm no ravenous beast to devour you on a garden path, but neither am I blind to your charms. 'Twas merely a harmless compliment."

"I will thank you to keep your conversation to the topic at hand." Even she hated the primness of her tone. But he just chuckled.

"As you wish. But apparently this venue is rife with interruptions. I'm willing to meet you elsewhere to discuss the matter in private."

She raised her brows. "Given your remarks, is that a wise idea?"

"Shall we write letters then? Come now. I'm certain we can meet in some sort of privacy without ravishing each other."

Her face heated, and she was glad of the darkness. "Captain, you are doing nothing to allay my concerns."

He chuckled. "I can't resist. Your prickly demeanor only makes me want to poke at you even more."

"Captain!" Did he . . . Could he mean . . . ?

He burst out laughing. "Oh, you have a wicked mind, don't you?"

"No! I did not . . . I thought you meant . . . Oh, botheration!"

He was still chuckling when they heard the voices again.

"I am certain I heard someone laughing." The

voice of Cilla's mother sounded closer, accompanied by the scuff of footsteps on the garden path beyond the shrubbery.

With a squeak of alarm, Cilla instinctively covered Samuel's mouth with her hand to silence his laughter. The inappropriateness of the action struck her even as the sensuous feel of his surprisingly soft lips against her hand re-ignited the attraction simmering between them all evening. She glanced up at him. Beneath her palm, his mouth curved into a smile, and needs she had long forgotten surged up within her like a steaming geyser.

"It could have come from the ballroom, Mrs. Wallington-Willis." The lieutenant's voice came from just on the other side of the hedges.

Slowly Cilla lowered her hand.

"It sounded as if it were right here," Cilla's mother said.

Samuel captured Cilla's hand before she could retreat completely. He held it for a long moment, then stroked his thumb over her palm. Fire streaked to her loins. Her eyes slid closed; her breath caught.

"It could be anyone, anywhere," the lieutenant said. "Perhaps you were mistaken when you thought you saw her come out here."

Cilla tugged at her hand, and he let it go. Disappointment swept over her like a wail of grief. She suppressed it. A man was not in her future. Especially not this man. She wanted to believe in his innocence, but she had been wrong before. Cilla curled her fingers into her palm as if to hold the memory of his touch.

"I suppose I could have been mistaken," her mother said. "I had hoped the two of you could renew your acquaintance."

"We will have that opportunity on Friday," the lieutenant said. "I am most grateful for the invitation to dinner. You said she will be there?"

"Have no fear of that, Lieutenant. I will make certain of it."

Dinner? She hissed in a sharp breath.

"What's wrong?" Samuel murmured.

She shook her head, not trusting herself to answer.

"Clearly she is agreeable to your attentions," her mother said. "After all, you are the only man she danced with tonight."

"It was my honor. Allow me to escort you back into the ballroom," the lieutenant said.

Cilla listened to their footsteps as they faded into the distance.

"What's wrong?" Samuel asked again.

"My mother appears to be matchmaking." She straightened to her full height—slight though it was—and looked him straight in the eye as she said, "I think your idea to meet privately is a good one."

"I agree," he said. "When and where?"

"Friday," she replied. "I will leave it to you to name the place." Then she turned away.

"Mrs. Burke."

She paused and glanced back at him.

"Why are you willing to believe me when others do not?"

She hesitated, then said softly, "The look in your eyes when you thought you had lost. There were no lies that night."

He did not answer, and she hurried away, leaving him standing alone in the garden.

Before she begged him to touch her again.

Chapter 6

The next morning Cilla joined Dolly and Annabelle in the drawing room of their rented town house.

"Good morning, Cilla," Dolly all but sang. Dressed in a simple morning dress of dark blue, Dolly waved a hand at an empty chair at the large round table where she and Annabelle were sorting through the day's post. Invitations teetered in a large stack in front of them. "Come on now, you just have to help us figure out which invitations we should accept."

"We return to Nevarton Chase in a few days," Cilla said, taking the offered chair. "Plus, Annabelle has her appointment with Madame Legere for the first fitting of her wedding dress this afternoon. I do not imagine you will be able to accept many invitations."

"Nonsense! Everyone wants to see my darling," Dolly said. "We'll accept as many as possible so everyone in London gets to know her."

"What time is my appointment with Madame

Legere?" Annabelle asked, trying to peer over the pile of invitations at Cilla's notebook.

Cilla consulted her schedule. "One o'clock."

Annabelle squealed and clapped. "This is all so exciting! I can't believe that in a month I will be a married lady."

"I can't believe it, either." Dolly sniffed and searched for her handkerchief as her eyes welled with tears. "My baby is all grown up!"

"Oh, Mama," Annabelle rolled her eyes and then grinned at Cilla. "Get used to Mama's spells, Mrs. Burke. It'll only get worse the closer we get to the wedding."

"I just love you so much," Dolly said. She sniffled again, then dabbed her handkerchief on her moist eyes. "Let's change the subject or else I'm going to get these letters all wet. Cilla, we got two for you this morning." She dug around in the pile, then withdrew two notes and handed them across the table.

Cilla took them, her brow furrowing in confusion. "Who would write to me here?"

"Well . . ." Annabelle flashed a conspiratorial look at her mother. "One of them looks like it's from a gentleman."

"Perhaps that dashing lieutenant you danced with last night?" Dolly suggested with a sly grin at her daughter. "Very flattering, wouldn't you say?"

"Very," Annabelle agreed.

Cilla frowned down at the two missives. One bore her mother's distinctive script, but the other had clearly been penned by a man. The bold, slashing letters were unfamiliar. She opened her mother's first.

"Never mind that one. Open the other one," Annabelle urged.

"My mother has invited me to dinner on Friday evening," Cilla said, scanning the note.

"That's your free day, so I don't see any problem with that," Dolly said.

"I shall have to write back to her." Cilla set down the letter and picked up the other.

Annabelle leaned over the pile of invitations and tilted her head to try and read the note Cilla had set down. "Oh! She's invited Lieutenant Allerton for you!"

"Annabelle!" Dolly exclaimed. "Where are your manners?"

"I'm sorry." She sat back in her seat. "Please tell me you're not angry, Mrs. Burke. I'm just so excited that you have a beau!"

"You could have simply asked me to see it," Cilla said. "And the lieutenant is hardly a beau." Then she opened the second communication.

"May I see it?" Annabelle asked.

Without looking up from the second note, Cilla handed the first across the table. She barely heard Annabelle's comments to Dolly about the dinner invitation. It was the words on the other note that captured her complete attention.

Please join me for a picnic lunch on Friday to continue our conversation in a more private set-

*ting as we discussed. I will send a carriage for
you at noon.*

*To continue our conversation in a more private setting
as we discussed.* The note had to be from Samuel. She
had not promised a private meeting on Friday to
anyone else.

A picnic? Such an odd venue for a business
conversation—though it would certainly be
private. Remembering his flirtatious mien during
their time in the garden, her heartbeat sped up.
Certainly he did not intend anything improper at
their meeting.

Did he?

Did she want him to?

"Mama, she's blushing!" Annabelle's voice shook
her free of her increasingly heated reverie.

"She certainly is." Grinning from ear to ear, Dolly
said, "I'm betting that one is from a certain gentleman, isn't it, Cilla?"

Cilla fumbled with the note, trying to refold it.
"Yes, it is from a gentleman."

"I knew it! It's the lieutenant, isn't it?" Annabelle
crowed. "Can I read it?"

"Not this one." Cilla tucked the note away in her
pocket.

"Oh." Annabelle's face fell.

Cilla held out her hand. "May I have the note
from my mother, please? I need to respond to her
invitation."

"Sure thing." Annabelle handed over the other
note and watched Cilla tuck it away. "But you can't

fool me. Your hand is shaking, and you're blushing fit to bust."

"Nonsense." Yet her face heated from chin to hairline.

"Ah, sweet love," Dolly said, and began sorting invitations again with a knowing smile curling her lips. "What else do we have on the schedule today, Cilla?"

Grateful for the change in subject, Cilla eagerly glanced at her notes. "After the dressmaker, we are scheduled for tea with Lady Iften at five o'clock."

"Lady Iften." Dolly sighed. "And her five giggling daughters."

"They are the earl's cousins," Cilla reminded her. "And Annabelle's bridesmaids."

"I need bridesmaids, Mama," Annabelle said. "We didn't bring anyone from home so we have to use Richard's family."

"I know," Dolly said. "I just wish they weren't so . . . cheerful. It sounds like a gaggle of geese have invaded the house!"

Annabelle stifled a laugh. "They're not that bad, Mama. Most of them are very sweet. Except that Edith. I don't like her much, but I didn't know how to leave her out without offending someone."

"Edith, Eliza, Elinor, Emily, and—who was the other one?" Dolly asked.

"Esther," Annabelle said.

"Yes, Esther. Why would a woman name all her daughters with the same letter at the beginning of their names? Makes no sense to me at all. Here, Cilla." She pushed a stack of unopened missives toward her.

"You start on this pile. I hope to have our responses written out before we leave for Madame Legere's."

"Maybe you can answer your own letters as well," Annabelle teased.

Cilla accepted the stack of invitations and began tearing them open, hoping her duty would help her ignore the note in her pocket.

And the man who had sent it.

"A picnic? Do you think that is wise?" Stripped down to his shirtsleeves, John circled in a defensive position, hands spread in preparation to fend off an attack.

"It's perfect," Samuel replied. Also in shirtsleeves, he kept pace with his friend, watching for an opening. A good spar was just what he needed. "We'll be out in the middle of nowhere. No one will see us. No one will ever suspect she's helping me stop the wedding."

"But it is my job to find the nowhere," John grumbled.

Samuel jabbed, and John dodged. "What's wrong with here?" Samuel asked, circling again.

"Here? We're in the middle of a bloody meadow."

"Seems like the perfect picnic place to me." He swung again, and again John eluded. "Besides, you picked this meadow."

"You said you wanted to spar outdoors, in a place where the servants would not gossip about it. This is outdoors, and no one is around for miles."

"Can you suggest a better place for a secret picnic?"

They paced each other. "It just seems rather . . . open," John said.

Samuel stopped and straightened. "I can't meet her at the house or a public restaurant or hotel where someone might see us together. Aside from the fact that it would reveal our relationship, her reputation could be damaged."

"And you care about that?" John straightened as well, though he kept a wary eye on his opponent.

"Of course I care! I need the woman's help; I don't want to harm her."

"And an intimate picnic is the way to convince her to help you."

"Intimate? I'm trying to create a relaxing setting." His mind flashed to last night in the garden, those searing moments of madness when she had touched his mouth—and he had for one moment entertained the fantasy of where he *really* wanted her to put her hand. He pushed the memory away, settling back into fighting stance and forcing himself to think about the present. "Come now. Are we doing this or not?"

"You are the one who keeps going on about the widow." John flashed a grin and took his position again. "Comely thing, isn't she? Just be sure she does not get too *relaxed*."

Damn John's perception. "Don't be ridiculous."

"You have been on an island for nearly two years, Captain. No one would fault you for a pleasant tumble with a fetching woman like Mrs. Burke."

"I would." *At least afterward.* He lunged at John.

John twisted out of the way at the last second, then blocked Samuel's punch with his arm. "Why? Your betrothal has ended. You are not committed to any other woman. Do not try and tell me you do not want to taste her charms."

"Of course I want her. I'm not dead." Spurred by his own frustrations, Samuel landed a punch on John's ribs a little harder than he'd intended.

The slender man sidestepped out of range, pressing a hand to his rib cage. "Then why not enjoy her company?" John came back swinging. His blow glanced off Samuel's jawbone as Samuel tried to dodge.

Samuel moved his jaw from side to side to ease the sting—and to be certain it still worked. "Damn it, you are relentless."

"Just making sure you know your own mind."

"Of course I do." Samuel rubbed the sore spot on his face.

"You know, Annabelle was a sweet farm girl. She had no idea how the world worked. Now the widow Burke—" John gave an appreciative chuckle. "There's a woman who knows how things are."

Samuel scowled and settled back into position. "What do you mean by that?"

"Just what I said." John's mouth curved in a wicked grin. "No doubt she would be glad of a bit of passion to liven up her life. And she is a widow, so as long as you are discreet, there's no harm to anyone."

The same thoughts had occurred to him—more than once. But he had chosen his path, and he would keep to it. "I told you, ours is a business relationship."

"In that case, perhaps you wouldn't mind if I had a go at her." The words had barely left his mouth before Samuel struck. John reeled backward and clapped a hand to his bloodied lip. "Then again, maybe you would."

"She's a paid employee. She hardly chose this situation," Samuel said. "I suggest you keep a civil tongue in your head about her. She can't help the position I'm putting her in."

"Ha, and which position would that be?" When Samuel glared and took a step toward him, John held up one hand in surrender, the other pressed against his lip. "All I'm saying is this: You are no longer engaged to Annabelle, so it would hardly be out of line to seek some comfort from the lovely Mrs. Burke, for purely physical reasons if nothing else."

"How the devil did we get onto this subject?' Samuel snapped.

"You started it, mooning on about the picnic you are planning."

"I'm not mooning," Samuel grumbled. "I need Mrs. Burke's help to stop the wedding. However attractive she is—"

"And a widow," John reminded him again.

"—*despite* being a widow, I have no intention of taking advantage of her."

"Now that is a shame. But then again, perhaps it is best not to mix business and pleasure."

"Exactly. Now let's change the subject. Have you looked into those orphanages of Raventhorpe's?"

"I have. On paper they look legitimate. I would

have to go there to tell if anything is not what it seems."

"Plan on doing that. Soon."

"And leave you all alone to fend for yourself? You would be lost without me."

"I can take care of myself."

Grinning with an amusement that grated against Samuel's battle-scarred will, John fell back into defense posture. "In that case—prove it, my friend. It seems to me in the absence of a dalliance with the widow Burke, a bout of sparring is just what you need."

Samuel smiled slowly. "First man down buys the ale."

"Done."

They took their positions again, circled.

John's grin had a gleeful mischief to it, a taunt ready on his lips. Suddenly his expression changed. "Get down!" he shouted, then leaped for Samuel just as a gunshot cracked across the meadow.

Their horses, tied to a nearby tree, shrieked in alarm. John rolled off Samuel. "Are you hit?"

"No." Samuel rolled onto his stomach, then started inching forward on his elbows toward his discarded coat—and the pistol that lay with it. "Where is he?"

"Just in those trees I think." John gestured toward a small wood, then reached down and slid his weapon of choice—a slender but well-made dagger—from the strap inside his boot. "I'll go around these rocks over here and get behind him. Watch my back."

"John, no," Samuel hissed, but his friend ignored him and headed out, using the nearby rocks as cover. "Damn it." Samuel braced himself, then shot to his feet, racing for his coat while trying to stay as low as possible. He dove for the garment, finding the familiar shape of the pistol even as another shot rang out.

Brandishing the weapon, he looked up and studied the trees John had indicated. A glimmer of sunlight reflecting off something metallic alerted him to the shooter's location. He got to his feet and ran alongside the rocks toward the shooter.

As he neared the trees, a soft whistle reached his ears. Then John emerged from the wood, the rifle in his hands pointed at the back of a fellow dressed in the simple coat of a working man.

Relief unwound some of the tension in Samuel's shoulders. "Well, what have you there?"

"I thought it wise to relieve this gentleman of his rifle," John answered, as calmly as if they spoke of tobacco brands. "He seemed uncertain of his aim."

"Wise indeed," Samuel agreed. "You there. Why are you shooting at me?"

The gunman sent him a sullen glare and remained silent.

"Talkative fellow, isn't he?" Samuel said.

"Quite." John poked the fellow in the back with the rifle. "Answer him."

"I was paid to do it." The shooter spat at Samuel's feet. "Filthy American swine."

"Who paid you?" Samuel demanded.

Their attacker remained silent, though if looks

could kill, Samuel would have shriveled into a corpse.

"As if we couldn't guess," John said. "I suppose we should take him to the magistrate."

"I agree. Let me go fetch my coat." Samuel headed back toward his coat and hat, still piled in the middle of the meadow.

He was halfway there when he heard John shout. The rifle fired. Samuel pivoted and ran back the way he had come, where John and the shooter wrestled for the rifle. He stopped and aimed his pistol. "John!"

The stranger glanced back over his shoulder and saw Samuel poised to fire. He felled John with a hard shove and took off, the rifle sailing through the air and landing on the nearby grass just beyond John's reach.

Samuel fired, but just missed the fellow as he disappeared into the wood. Cursing beneath his breath, he raced forward and crouched beside his friend. "John, are you all right?"

"Yes." It was the tone of disgust in his voice that convinced Samuel he was unhurt. "Bloody hell, he's getting away!"

The distant sound of hoofbeats reached their ears. "I'd say he's already gone," Samuel said. "Come on, let's get you up."

"I'm hardly an invalid." Brushing away his captain's hand, John slowly climbed to his feet. "Bastard took me by surprise." He swiped his hands over his clothing, clearing crushed grass and leaves from the material. "You know Raventhorpe had to have sent him."

"Of course. His Lordship is nothing if not tenacious." Samuel stared off in the direction where the man had fled. "But there's no way to prove anything. We had best watch our backs from now on."

"Agreed." John raised a brow. "So, does this make me the first one down?"

Samuel's mouth twitched. "Considering you knocked me down earlier, I'd say I was the first one down."

"Good, then you buy the ale."

"Done." Samuel turned away. "I'll fetch our coats, and we can be gone from this place."

"Good idea." John picked up the rifle and hefted it in his hands, testing the balance.

Samuel started across the field, then stopped. "Oh, and John . . . I believe you're right."

"About what?"

"This is a very bad place for a picnic."

John grinned. "Maybe next time you will heed my advice before all hell rains down upon us."

Grinning, Samuel continued across the field, pistol in hand. "Where's the fun in that?"

Lady Iften's brood of daughters resembled one another to a shocking degree, Cilla thought, all of them blond and blue-eyed and so pale as to look positively ghostlike. Each one was tall and skinny with the distinctive beak of a nose that characterized the Raventhorpe family—like a flock of storks that had descended upon the blue drawing room.

Except for Edith. While as blond and pale as her sisters, she had been blessed with a sweet feminine bump of a nose and a mouth curved like cupid's bow, lending her a delicate loveliness that branded her the clear beauty of the group.

And she knew it.

"Now, Annabelle, you must allow that I know more about these things than you do," Edith was saying. "Why, you are new to fashionable society. I am certain you will agree that the peach silk will wash out my fair complexion. Certainly you can select another color for my dress."

"I thought the peach was lovely," Annabelle said. "I liked it so much I ordered an evening dress made from it for after the wedding."

"The color looked very well on you," Cilla said.

Edith glared at Cilla. "Kindly do not interrupt, Mrs. Burke." She turned her attention back to Annabelle. "My dear cousin-to-be, you must allow that your coloring is vastly different than mine."

"But you're both blond," Dolly said, a wrinkle of confusion appearing between her brows. "Seems like what would look good on one should look good on the other, don't you think?"

Edith let out a trilling laugh that she had no doubt practiced in front of her mirror. "Oh, Mrs. Bailey! Why, my hair is closer to *moonbeam*, while Annabelle's is . . . yes, wild honey, that's it. A very *dark* blond, nearly brown."

Cilla rolled her eyes and glanced down at her hands before anyone could notice. She had run across her own selection of selfish debutantes in her day, but Edith might top them all.

"I never thought of it that way," Annabelle said.

Cilla heard the hitch in her voice and looked up, trying to catch the girl's eye. *Don't let her do this to you.*

"And your complexion is much more robust than mine," Edith continued. "After all, you were raised on a farm in the country, so you have a certain pinkness to your skin that someone raised in the drawing rooms of London would not." She smiled sweetly, as if to distract from the acid in her tone.

"Perhaps Edith is right," one of the sisters said. Esther? Eliza?

"Of course, I am right," Edith said. "What do you think, Mama?"

Lady Iften looked up from the ladies' magazine she was perusing. "Your taste is impeccable, my dear, as well you know."

"What color would you prefer?" Annabelle asked quietly.

"Perhaps a shade of bronze or dark purple," Edith mused.

"Such as royalty might wear?" Cilla said. When Edith whipped her head around to glare, Cilla met and held her gaze. She wasn't the same scared debutante she had once been.

Edith looked away first with a little titter. "Oh, you are so amusing, Mrs. Burke. The Baileys must be simply delighted to have you in their employ."

Cilla felt the sting but would not allow it to show on her face. Sharper tongues than that of Edith Falwell had attempted to fell her in the past—and failed.

"Indeed we are," Dolly spoke up. "Why, Cilla is

more like one of the family than a plain old employee. I'd be lost without her."

"How nice," Edith said, her perfect mouth pursing as if tasting something sour.

"We think so," Annabelle said. This time when Edith attempted to glare her into submission, she held her ground.

The butler came to the door of the drawing room. "Mrs. Bailey, Miss Bailey, you have a caller. Captain Samuel Breedlove."

Cilla sat straight up in her chair, certain she had not heard aright. She could not take her eyes away as the butler stepped aside and Samuel filled the doorway. The Iften daughters gasped, and Cilla struggled to maintain a calm demeanor despite the flutter in her belly. Samuel's tall, broad-shouldered presence made the drawing room with all its feminine decor seem very, very small.

"Samuel!" Annabelle straightened, then glanced worriedly at the Iftens. All five of them plus their mother wore expressions of stony disapproval.

"Mrs. Bailey." Samuel first bent over Dolly's hand, then turned to acknowledge each of them. "Annabelle. Mrs. Burke."

"Samuel, my stars! We didn't expect you." Dolly fluttered a hand to her throat, clearly uncertain what to do in the face of his boldness. "Do you know Lady Iften and her daughters? Lady Iften, this is Captain Samuel Breedlove."

"I have heard of Captain Breedlove." Lady Iften gave a barely perceptible nod. "My daughters: Miss

Falwell, Miss Esther, Miss Eliza, Miss Emily, and Miss Edith."

"Ladies." Samuel flashed a charming smile, then turned immediately back to Annabelle. "I came to see if you would join me for a carriage ride."

"Miss Bailey, you cannot!" squeaked Eliza.

"You are an engaged young woman," Lady Iften said. "I am certain my cousin would take offense if you were to accept such an invitation from a gentleman not of your family."

"Now, Lady Iften, calm yourself," Dolly said. "Annabelle has known Samuel since she was a child."

"It is not done," Lady Iften pronounced.

Samuel raised his brows. "Who is this cousin you're talking about, Lady Iften?"

"Lord Raventhorpe, Annabelle's betrothed," the lady proclaimed with pride.

"Oh, would me taking Annabelle for a ride in my carriage upset him? How unfortunate." He turned away from the Iften ladies and focused on Annabelle. "What do you say, Annabelle?"

Annabelle scowled at him. "Of course I can't go with you. You know I'm engaged to Richard!"

"Don't you remember our rides together?" His voice lowered to an intimate tone that carried to every straining ear in the room. Cilla tightened her fingers around her needlework. Dear Lord, the man knew how to turn a woman's insides to mush with just a whisper!

"Of course I do, but that was a long time ago. When

I was a child." Annabelle sniffed and cast a glance at the Iften ladies. "My apologies, ladies. Samuel and I were engaged once, *long* ago."

"Why, it seems like just last week to me." Samuel sent a charming smile at Raventhorpe's disapproving relatives.

"But you are not engaged any longer," Lady Iften said. "Therefore, such familiarity is ill-bred."

"Samuel, please don't cause any trouble," Dolly said.

"Trouble? Of course not. I simply wanted Annabelle to join me on a drive. For old times' sake."

"No." Annabelle narrowed her eyes at him. "It would be best if you left now."

He didn't appear fazed in the least. "You know, Annabelle, I thought you had more gumption than to let anybody order you around."

Annabelle stiffened.

Lady Iften shot to her feet. "Enough. Miss Bailey is betrothed to Lord Raventhorpe, sir. I thank you to cease this impertinent behavior and take yourself off."

Dolly rose as well, sending a concerned glance at Lady Iften. "I do not think this is appropriate, Samuel."

He looked from Dolly to Annabelle to the Iften ladies. Finally his gaze landed on Cilla for one long, hot moment, but even as her breath hitched, he looked away again. "Perhaps another time, Annabelle."

"Mrs. Bailey, do you intend to allow this sort of behavior?" Lady Iften demanded.

"Of course not." Dolly gazed at Samuel with true regret. "Please go, Samuel."

"As you wish." He bowed to all of them and headed for the doors of the sitting room. "We shall have our drive another day, Annabelle."

"Insolent cur!" Lady Iften spat. "My cousin shall hear of this!"

Samuel paused in the doorway and gave her a cheeky grin. "Give him my regards, won't you?" Then he departed, leaving Lady Iften spluttering.

Chapter 7

Lady Iften wasted no time in carrying tales to Lord Raventhorpe. The earl came to call later that same day and spoke at length with Annabelle's father—sometimes in quite ringing tones—about his disapproval of Samuel's visit. After an hour or so of such discussion, Virgil emerged from his study and announced they were removing to Nevarton Chase immediately.

By late morning on Friday, Cilla found herself staring out the window of her room at the familiar fields and forests of the Baileys' country estate.

She had managed to post a note to Samuel before they departed London, advising him of their sudden exodus. And the cancellation of their picnic.

She was surprised at her own disappointment. The picnic was simply a business meeting where Samuel had promised he would tell her the whole of what he knew of Lord Raventhorpe and why he felt Annabelle was in danger. Then she would decide if he was telling the truth. And if he was . . . well, could she in good conscience allow Annabelle to marry the earl?

She knew Lord Raventhorpe to be quite full of his own consequence and intolerant of those who would thwart his wishes. She had experienced a taste of that herself in the way he had reacted to her questioning him about the past. The fact that he had deliberately exposed her social connections to the Baileys—no doubt well aware of her ignominious exit from society some years ago—only made her believe he had indeed intended to teach her a lesson of some kind by throwing her back into the turbulent waters of her old life.

Unkind? Yes. A killer? Undecided.

A knock sounded at the door. "Mrs. Burke, the driver is here to take you to the village."

"Thank you, Mary." Cilla picked up her bonnet and tied the ribbons, then took up her shawl and her purse. Since it was her free day, she was going to go to the village and see about getting some lace to trim a dress she was going to redo. Maybe she'd pick up some ribbons for a bonnet as well. Her straw one could use some reworking.

Cilla made her way down the stairs to the ground floor, her mind full of lists and plans. A footman opened the door for her, and she nodded her thanks as she walked outside, adjusting her gloves as she walked. A plain coach sat waiting, a hired hack from the village.

She paused beside the coach and looked up at the bearded coachman. "Please take me to the village green. I will decide where I want to go from there."

"Yes, miss," the coachman grunted.

She nodded to herself, then opened the door and climbed into the coach. As she closed the door behind her, she realized she was not alone.

"Don't be afraid," Samuel said. "We had an appointment for a picnic, remember?"

The coach lurched into motion, and he rested a hand on top of the picnic basket on the seat beside him to keep it from falling.

Cilla recovered her tongue. "What are you doing here? You must have left London as soon as you got my note to get here so quickly."

"You sent a note?" He grinned at that. "So you hadn't forgotten about me. Excellent."

"As if I could forget about you!"

His smile faded, his gaze heating as he studied her from top to toes. "I'm gratified to know I made some sort of impression on you."

Oh, he had made an impression, all right—one that had her heart skipping beats and her cheeks heating. And it was wrong. Perhaps there was some spark of attraction between them, but there was still doubt about his character. She had put her trust in a scoundrel once, and she did not intend to repeat the experience.

But it would certainly be easier to convince herself of that if he wasn't staring at her like he was going to make her part of that picnic lunch he had promised her.

She settled back in her seat, unusually aware of her plain attire, designed for a day of walking through the village. While not ill-fitting or terribly threadbare, she knew her garments were old and out of style.

Had they met years ago when she lived in London with her parents, she would have been dressed by a fashionable modiste in colors that flattered her and clothing cut in a way to draw the male eye to her figure and keep it there.

She had not yearned for such things in a very long time.

"If you did not receive my note," she said, "how did you know we had left London?"

He chuckled. "The servants' network is an amazing thing. I swear it could predict the weather, never mind alert me to the sudden departure of one household."

"Ah." A small smile curved her lips. "I have seen such miracles myself, now that I have joined the ranks of the employed."

"My coachman, John, is very much abreast of the local happenings via the servants. Apparently my call on Annabelle Tuesday had dramatic repercussions."

"His Lordship was most put out," Cilla confirmed. "He and Mr. Bailey closeted themselves away to discuss the matter, but we could hear their voices throughout the house."

A smile of satisfaction curved Samuel's mouth. "Good."

"I am certain he believed that our returning to Nevarton Chase would discourage you from seeing Annabelle."

Samuel laughed. "Has he not heard of the railway? As soon as I received the news of your departure, I made arrangements to follow you. And here I am."

"And somehow you discovered I had ordered a hack to bring me to the village this morning."

"It's a small village. People talk," Samuel confirmed. "I apologize if I disrupted your plans."

"No, no." She shook her head, glancing down at her twisting fingers. "We had an appointment today anyway."

"Was there something you intended to do in the village?" His voice changed, acquired a slight edge. "Did I interrupt some sort of romantic rendezvous?"

"Romantic? Heavens, no." She laughed, but even she heard the harshness of it. "I have no desire for a man in my life, thank you, Captain. I was just running errands."

"What kinds of errands?"

"Normal things. Picking out lace for a dress I am going to rework, perhaps some ribbons for an old bonnet I have. But such frivolities pale in comparison to the importance of our meeting today."

"You like pretty things."

"Really, Captain, what woman doesn't?" She smiled at him. "It is just trimming for a few old, outdated dresses. Annabelle's safety is much more important. I will visit the village store another day."

"If you're certain."

"Of course I am. Where are we going?"

"As I told you, on a picnic. Away from servants and gossip, where we can talk freely."

"Then I am glad I wore my outdoor clothing."

"Very efficient of you," he agreed, and they fell into silence.

He wondered what she was thinking.

Any other woman might have reacted differently to being basically kidnapped—especially if that woman had intended to embark on a shopping trip. But Mrs. Burke had simply smiled and adjusted her plans. Didn't she realize she was going to be alone with him with only John standing nearby? Didn't she realize how a man could take advantage of such a situation?

He certainly did.

The simple dress she wore was plain brown and serviceable, a garment easily maintained for someone who had little in the way of funds to replace clothing. The fitted bodice only emphasized her shapely figure and perfect bosom, with long sleeves that ended at her gloved hands. Her dark hair had been swept up in a simple twist, with a little brown hat perched just above her brow. The hat was just as sparsely decorated as her dress, with only a few flowers and a faded ribbon to relieve its blandness. Yet despite her clearly out-of-date, much-used clothing, Cilla Burke carried herself like a lady dressed in the height of fashion.

He knew she had begun life in the upper reaches of society, but even though she had fallen on more difficult times and had been forced to seek employment, she knew her own value. And for some reason, he found that quiet confidence impossibly attractive. Very strange indeed for a man who had traditionally sought women who needed the strong arm of a male to guide them. Perhaps his time on the island had changed him more than he thought.

Finally the coach stopped, and Samuel opened the

door, stepping out first and then turning to assist Cilla from the vehicle. Once her feet touched the ground, he reached back into the coach and grabbed the picnic basket.

John climbed down from the coachman's perch, a blanket slung over his shoulder. He handed it to Samuel, who put it over his own shoulder.

"Mrs. Burke, this is John Ready, the man I trust most in the world. John, Mrs. Burke."

John tugged at his hat brim. "Madam."

"Mr. Ready."

"I will stay with the horses," John said, "and keep an eye out for trouble."

"Much appreciated." Samuel crooked his arm at Cilla. "Mrs. Burke, may I?"

She laid her tiny hand on his forearm. "Thank you, Captain."

They walked a few yards away—still far enough that they could have a private conversation but close enough that John could watch over them from his coachman's perch. Guiding her beneath a shady tree, Samuel set down the basket, then spread the blanket on the ground and held out a hand to assist Cilla in seating herself. It took a few moments for her to arrange her skirts in a way that she would be comfortable. In those few minutes, he found himself staring at the back of her neck as she bent her head, the tiny curls edging her hairline a nearly irresistible temptation. For an instant he imagined placing a kiss on that delicate nape. Then she reached down to adjust her skirts again and gave him a quick flash of a stockinged calf.

Damn John for being right. He turned away to grab the picnic basket before he forgot the reason he was here.

Cilla glanced over as Samuel sat down on the other side of the blanket and set the picnic basket down between them. "Why don't you tell me what you know of Lord Raventhorpe?"

"I should hate to spoil your appetite." He opened the picnic basket. "The innkeeper has packed sandwiches, a bit of cheese, some lemonade, and, I believe, fresh berry tarts baked just this morning. What would you like?"

"Lemonade sounds lovely."

"Lemonade it is." He went about pouring the lemonade into the wooden goblets the innkeeper had sent along.

"While I appreciate your consideration, Captain, I do need to know about Lord Raventhorpe." She watched his hands as he served. "Because if I help you, the ensuing scandal will put an end to any chance I have of building a future."

"What do you mean?" He handed her the first cup of lemonade.

"I have an idea to start a business where ladies can employ me to assist with planning their weddings. Annabelle's was to be my first, and possibly the most well-known since she is marrying an earl. A big society wedding like that would give me a reputation as the person all young ladies of quality should employ to create the most talked-about event of the Season." She lifted her cup to her lips, then paused, her lip curling. "Failure would force me to marry again to survive."

"So Annabelle's wedding means a lot to you." He stretched onto his side and leaned on one elbow while sipping his lemonade with the other hand.

She tried to ignore how much of the blanket was taken up by his long, muscled body. "Yes, that's right. But if you succeed in stopping her wedding to Lord Raventhorpe, I will have failed in my position and will have trouble obtaining another."

"Another? Why don't you just stay with the Baileys?"

"Because they intend to return to America. My home is here."

"I thought I heard that your husband was American."

"That is true." She pressed her lips together, unwilling to discuss bad memories. "I lived in New York until he died, and for a bit afterwards. The Baileys hired me some months ago to help them navigate through English society and to help plan an elaborate wedding for Annabelle. Part of our agreement was that they would pay my passage here since the wedding is scheduled to take place in the family chapel at Raventhorpe Manor, but that I would remain when they departed for America."

"And if your plans fell into place, you would have pulled off the biggest wedding this year and gotten a heck of a reputation for it."

"Exactly." She tightened her fingers around the cup. "My livelihood depends on this wedding, Captain.

I need to know everything if you expect me to help you ruin it."

"Didn't your husband leave you anything when he died?"

She stiffened. "No. Edward was not very clever with finances."

"So if you help me stop the wedding, you might be left unemployed and penniless."

"It is a distinct possibility." She sighed. "I suppose I could return to America to stay in the employ of the Baileys, but part of my goal was to remain here in England. I miss it."

"You could marry again."

She shook her head. "Not if I can avoid it. I intend to control my own life from now on, not depend on a man to do it for me. Yet another reason why this wedding holds such value for me."

He sipped his lemonade, his dark eyes steady on hers. "I could pay you to help me."

"Absolutely not!" She set down the cup with enough force that it nearly overturned, but she grabbed it before it tipped over. "That strikes me as . . . as . . . unethical, Captain. If I decide to do this, I will do it because it is the right thing to do. Keep your money."

"I'm just trying to help."

"I understand. I do appreciate the sentiment, but being paid by a man to do anything strikes me as too much like . . . well, not good." She cleared her throat and looked at the picnic basket. "Did you say there were sandwiches? I did not have much for breakfast, so I am quite hungry."

"Sure." He sat up and reached into the basket to pull out a cloth-wrapped bundle and set it down before her, then grabbed another one for himself.

Cilla opened the cloth and found a ham sandwich on thick slices of bread. Balancing the creation between her two hands, she attempted to bite into it, but her mouth was not quite big enough. She tore off an edge with her fingers instead. "Tell me about Lord Raventhorpe." She popped the torn bit of sandwich into her mouth and chewed.

"Well, to begin with, Nevarton Chase used to belong to him. He sold the estate to Virgil Bailey when he became engaged to Annabelle. I'm sure the servants are still loyal to him. In fact, the land we are sitting on is very close to what remains of Raventhorpe's lands."

"He is not the first nobleman to sell one of his properties. I do not see how that makes him a villain."

"He had to sell," Samuel said, "because he needed to pay his enormous gambling debts. It seems His Lordship cannot stay away from the tables."

She shrugged. "Unfortunately that, too, is not a new tale when it comes to the nobility."

"You don't seem to understand that this man would do *anything* for money."

"Which is no doubt why he is marrying an heiress." She tore off another piece of her sandwich and nibbled at it. "Mrs. Bailey says you worked as a captain on one of his ships?"

"Yes." Samuel tore off a bite of his sandwich with more force than seemed necessary and washed it down with the lemonade. Then he reached to refill his cup. "Raventhorpe hired me to replace a captain who had left abruptly. He offered an excellent salary, and despite the fact that he would tell me nothing about the cargo, I agreed. I was trying earn enough money so I could marry Annabelle. John tried to warn me about Raventhorpe, but I did not listen."

"What do you mean, he warned you about Lord Raventhorpe?"

"John has a history with him, too. And before you ask: No, I don't know anything about it except that John had to leave England as a result."

Cilla had just opened her mouth to pose the question, but closed it again.

"We had already reached the Caribbean when I discovered His Lordship the Earl of Raventhorpe was not interested in the sugar and coffee I had assumed we were transporting. He was using the vessel for the slave trade."

Cilla set down her sandwich and stared at him, her stomach churning. "Are you certain?"

"Quite certain. We had a rather loud argument about it. He intended to meet a contact in the Indies who had a live cargo."

"I thought slavery was illegal now!"

"Laws don't stop some men when money can be made."

"Didn't your Mr. Lincoln free the slaves in America?"

"He did, but this outside the United States. And it's another kind of slavery. A specialized kind." He paused, as if uncertain if he should continue.

Apprehension swept through her like a gust of icy breeze. "Tell me, Samuel."

"It's not really a tale for a lady's ears."

How long had it been since a man had treated her with such gallantry? "We have come this far, and I should have all the facts if you expect me to help you. Besides, I am a grown woman."

"Grown or not, it's not a pretty story."

"Samuel." She leaned forward and laid her hand on his sleeve. "Look at me. I am hardly a naïve girl."

He did look, his gaze sweeping over her form in a swift assessment that seemed to miss nothing. "No, not a girl, but I think perhaps there is still some innocence about you. And I would not want to be the man who takes a piece of that away."

"Innocence!" She gave a laugh, quick and harsh. "I have not been an innocent in some years."

"I think some part of you is, and I don't want to be the man to rip away your illusions."

She let out a huff and began to rapidly wrap up her sandwich. "Then you might as well take me home, Captain. I will not help you blindly."

"Blast it, woman." He took the sandwich from her hands, slapping it back on the blanket in front of her. "I'm trying to spare you some unpleasantness."

"And I am telling you that you need not spare me anything. I am hardly a fragile flower. I can take the truth, else I would not have asked for it."

Still he hesitated. She started to get up, and he burst out, "It was women. There, are you satisfied? Raventhorpe was interested in selling women as slaves."

"Women?" Stunned, she sat back down. "As in . . . not for . . ."

"A kind term would be 'pleasure slaves.'"

"Heavens." Shocked despite herself, Cilla splayed a hand over her bosom. "Who would engage in such wickedness?"

"Men with no scruples, like Raventhorpe. He and his associates obtain women through kidnapping, blackmail, and sometimes buying them outright from their families. They take them far from home and sell them to rich men abroad."

"As pleasure slaves." Just the words left a bad taste in her mouth. "Would he . . . What about Annabelle?"

"Mrs. Burke, when I refused to go along with his evil purposes, he pushed me over a cliff on that island and left me for dead. The whole crew went along with it; they were loyal to Raventhorpe. This man will do anything he needs to in order to further his own ends and fill his coffers—even kill the Baileys and Annabelle to inherit their fortunes."

"This is . . . . I am having trouble believing all this."

"You are welcome to ask John Ready." He swept a hand toward his servant, who sat on the coachman's bench with a book open on his lap. *A servant who reads?* She barely had a chance to process that bit of information before he was speaking again. "As I said, John also has a history with Raventhorpe. When I did not come back from the voyage, he got one of Raventhorpe's crew drunk and convinced him to tell him where they'd been. Then he came back for me, though it took more than a year."

" 'Tis a fantastic tale." Even as she said the words, she wanted to believe him. She could not forget his face the night Annabelle had jilted him. Could a man feign such intense emotion? "Why do you not bring charges against the earl, if he is as villainous as you say he is?"

"Because I have no witnesses other than John, and he has his own reasons for not wanting to come to the notice of the law. Without ironclad proof of his perfidy, I can't bring charges against Raventhorpe. What chance would an American seaman have in an English court against the influence of an earl?"

"Probably none in the House of Lords, which is where he would be tried. But without proof or witnesses, there is no way to bring him to justice."

"All I can do," he said, "is save Annabelle from him. I intend to take great pleasure in depriving Raventhorpe of what he wants so badly."

She recoiled. "You intend to use Annabelle for revenge?"

"No, I intend to make certain she is safe, and in the process punish the man who tried to steal my life from me." He stared into her eyes, as if obtaining her agreement to his plan was simply a matter of his will. "I know it sounds mad, but I am doing this to save her life—and to prove to Dolly and Virgil that I did not lie to them. That I did not cruelly abandon their daughter."

His passionate whisper sent the blood sweeping into her cheeks. "I believe you."

"Then you will help me?"

"What exactly are you proposing?"

"Talk to Annabelle and build doubts about Raventhorpe. Buy me some time so I can find real evidence to show the Baileys."

"I—"

A soft crunch came from the trees behind them. They turned to see a man dressed in black step out of the wood. When he grinned at them, she noticed he was wearing a mask.

"Stand and deliver," he said in a strangely cheerful tone, pointing a pistol at them.

Samuel sat up straighter. "What do you want?"

"Your valuables of course, my good man." He gestured with the pistol. "Let's start with the lady. What have you got in your reticule, my dear?"

She paled and grabbed the tiny bag. "Please, it's all I have."

"Leave her be." Samuel leaped to his feet but froze when the highwayman cocked the pistol with an audible click.

"I prefer to leave you alive, friend," the highwayman said. "Let's not be rash, eh?"

"Leave her alone," Samuel repeated. "I have gold enough for both of us."

"Such chivalry." The thief smiled as if they were two acquaintances having a pleasant conversation. "I never thought to hear such gallantry from one such as you."

"Such as me? You don't even know me. What have I done to you that you would threaten us this way?"

"Well, 'tis a sad thing indeed. You see, you are on

Raventhorpe land. And I make it my business to take anything that might be Raventhorpe's."

"I had no idea we were on Raventhorpe's land. We simply stopped for a picnic."

"You should choose your friends more carefully, my friend. Raventhorpe is not the type of man to engage in something as unfashionable as loyalty."

"Raventhorpe is a snake of the lowest order," Samuel agreed. "I shall be certain to spit on his land before we leave it."

The highwayman laughed, a booming sound that echoed across the clearing. "Excellent, sir! How gratifying to find someone who shares my view of the pig earl. Very well, I shall take only *your* gold, and I shall leave the lady be."

A shout echoed through the air. John had spotted the highwayman and was racing toward them, a rifle clutched in his hand.

"Your guard approaches. Quickly now. Your purse."

"No."

"Samuel!" Cilla hissed. Was he mad?

"I should hate to shoot you, but I will." The high-wayman held out his hand and snapped his fingers. "Your purse."

"No."

The thief swung his pistol around to point at Cilla but kept his gaze on Samuel and snapped his open fingers again.

"Samuel, don't," Cilla whispered. "I think it's Black Bill."

"Of course I'm Black Bill," the highwayman answered. Samuel pulled out his purse and threw it at the thief, who caught it easily. "Thanks much, my friend."

"Go to hell," Samuel snapped.

"I don't think so." He turned away and ran for the trees.

"Stop thief!" John raced up to them, stopped and lifted the rifle to his shoulder. Fired.

A chunk of tree exploded in front of the thief. Black Bill stopped. He whirled, aimed, and returned fire. John jerked, then fell.

"John!" Samuel raced toward his fallen friend.

Black Bill paused for a moment. "It did not have to be this way," he called with what sounded like real regret, then sprinted toward the woods and disappeared into the trees. Moments later the sound of hoofbeats echoed through the meadow, retreating into the distance.

Chapter 8

"**J**ohn!" Samuel dropped to his knees beside his fallen friend.

Cilla raced over and shoved the cloths from their sandwiches at him. "Use this to staunch the bleeding. How badly is he hit?"

Samuel shoved the cloths underneath John's shirt, then buttoned his waistcoat tightly around the temporary bandage. "Shoulder shot, but still bad from the bleeding. Might have nicked an artery. We've got to get him to a doctor."

John groaned. "No doctor."

"Nevarton Chase—" Cilla began.

"I'll not take him there. The inn is closer." He raised his voice. "John, we have to get you to the carriage."

"What do you want me to do?" Cilla asked. Her voice shook.

"Collect the picnic basket and the blanket. Especially the blanket. We need to keep him warm." Samuel slung John's arm around his shoulders and stood up, dragging the half-conscious man with him. "Damn it, John, I won't let you die. And damned well not before we get Raventhorpe."

John turned his head toward him and locked his pain-dazed gaze on Samuel's. "Raventhorpe."

"Walk with me, John. Help me get Raventhorpe." Samuel started for the coach as quickly as he could, half dragging the stumbling, wounded man.

Cilla raced back to the picnic site and threw everything into the basket willy-nilly, snapping it shut and hefting it in one hand and the blanket in the other. Then she raced as fast as she was able, burdened by her load and hampered by her skirts, to meet Samuel at the coach. She set the picnic basket on the ground and flung the blanket into the vehicle, then shoved her shoulder under John's arm to help steady him.

"Can you hold him?" Samuel asked. "I'll climb into the carriage and grab him under the arms, and we'll drag him in. You can get his feet."

She nodded, winded from wrestling with the nearly unconscious man. Then she let out a soft *oof* as Samuel eased out from under John's arm and jumped into the carriage. Cilla staggered beneath the increased weight. Slowly John started to sink to the ground, dragging the much shorter Cilla with him. "Samuel!"

"I've got him." Crouched on the floor of the coach, Samuel grabbed one of John's arms, relieving her of a good part of his weight. "I need you to help me turn him around so when we drag him in here, he'll be on his back."

She blew a loose curl out of her face and nodded, her bonnet askew and dangling from its ribbons. Between the two of them, they managed to get John turned around. Then Samuel hooked his arms under John's armpits and hauled him backward into the coach. As soon as John's feet left the ground, Cilla cradled his legs in her arms and swung them around to help get him all the way in.

Samuel squeezed out from under John and propped him against the seat. "You need to ride in here and apply pressure to his wound. I'll drive us back to the inn." He stood in the doorway and held out a hand to her, assisting her into the coach. He paused before climbing out, looking into her eyes without relinquishing her hand. "Keep him alive for me."

"I will." She squeezed his hand. "Just get us there with all possible speed."

He nodded and hopped out of the coach. He picked up the picnic basket and tossed it on the seat before closing the door behind him. Then he climbed up into the coachman's seat and set the team racing for the inn.

By the time they reached the inn, Cilla was very worried about John. The cloths she had been pressing against the wound had become soaked with blood, and he had fallen unconscious. She was despairing of what to do next when the coach thundered into the yard of the Caruthers Inn.

Moments after the vehicle stopped, Samuel flung open the door, shouting for help. Grooms ran over in response, and three of them helped Samuel ease John from the coach and carried him into the inn. Cilla sat on the floor of the carriage, her hands shaking with emotion. Slowly she climbed out into the yard.

A groom held the horses and tipped his hat to her as her feet hit the ground. She nodded to him, then stiffly made her way to the door of the inn.

Inside, bedlam reigned. Samuel and the grooms carried John up the stairs under the direction of an older man who had to be the innkeeper. Cilla stood uncertainly in the middle of the madness until a young woman spotted her.

"May I help you, miss?" she asked.

"Missus," Cilla corrected out of habit. She pointed after the people on the stairs. "I am with the wounded man who was just brought in."

"Oh, of course! You're with Mr. Breedlove. Come upstairs, Mrs. Breedlove, and we'll get you settled right away."

"I am not—" She took a breath. "I would like to see the wounded coachman, please."

The girl gave her an uncertain look. "Are you sure about that? They've sent a lad for the surgeon, but it might be a while if he's not at home."

"Please take me to him."

The girl shrugged. "Come with me." She started for the stairs.

Samuel appeared on the landing. "Cilla! There you are. Come up."

The girl smiled at Cilla. "See there? All's well, Mrs. Breedlove. Just you go on up with your husband."

Cilla gave the girl a nod. "Thank you."

She climbed the stairs, and Samuel met her halfway.

"Mrs. Breedlove?" he murmured, offering his arm.

"She assumed and I did not feel like explaining," she said as they climbed the stairs together. "I am told they sent a boy for the surgeon."

"Yes. We've got his boots off and stripped off his shirt. I've arranged for a private dining room, so perhaps you would rather—"

"Captain, I am a widow. I have seen a man without his shirt before." She swept a hand before her. "Do lead the way. I want to check that bandage we cobbled together."

"The innkeeper's wife is sending up some clean cloths and hot water."

"Good." Cilla straightened her bonnet. "Lead on."

The woman was not what he thought she was.

Samuel led Cilla to the room where John lay with sweat misting his forehead. They had laid clean handkerchiefs over his wound, but already drops of blood had begun to seep through. Cilla stepped into the room without a qualm, her eyes on John as she removed her dangling bonnet. Smoothing her hair, she turned to Samuel.

"When was the hot water requested? The sooner we clean that wound, the better."

"The innkeeper's wife should be bringing it at any moment." He stroked a flyaway tendril of hair behind her ear. "Are you certain you would not rather retire to another room and recover from this shock?"

"I have not swooned yet, Captain." Easing away from his touch, she set down her bonnet on the bureau and went to John's bedside. She bent over

him, pressing her hand to his forehead. "I believe
he is already becoming fevered."

The innkeeper's wife came up behind Samuel where
he stood in the doorway. He moved aside, letting the
lady enter the room with her basin of water. "The
surgeon should be here at any moment," she said,
bustling to the small table beside the bed. "He lives
just down the road." Cilla stepped out of her way as
the woman carefully lowered the bowl, then set down
the cloths that had been hanging over her shoulder.

"He seems very warm," Cilla said.

The innkeeper's wife frowned in concern and
rested her hand briefly against his cheek. "Indeed
he is. Best get that wound cleaned." She glanced at
Cilla. "Nothing you can do for now, Mrs. Breedlove.
I'll see to your coachman. We've got the private dining
room set up for you."

"We'll wait until the surgeon gets here," Samuel
said. "Mrs. . . ."

"Caruthers," she replied, dunking one of the cloths
into the water and wringing it out. She moved to
John and lifted the handkerchiefs they had used as
the last bandage, then pressed the damp cloth gently
against the ugly hole just below his left shoulder.
John groaned and shifted. His eyelids lifted for just
a moment, then fell again.

Footsteps pounding up the stairs drew Samuel's
attention away from his friend. An older man
thundered up the staircase at a pace he would not
have believed possible. But the surgeon—a short,
square-shouldered, balding man with spectacles sliding down his nose—reached the doorway in record

time, and Samuel found himself moving out of the lively man's way.

"Mrs. Caruthers," the surgeon said. "What has happened here?"

"Their coachman was shot, Mr. Emerson," Mrs. Caruthers said.

"Who shot him?"

"A highwayman," Cilla said.

"Indeed?" The surgeon bent over John, lifting his lids to peer into his eyes.

"Black Bill," Samuel clarified.

Emerson sighed. "That young man certainly keeps me busy."

"He seems to be well-known around here," Samuel said.

"Indeed he is. Notorious even." The surgeon waved away Mrs. Caruthers and lifted the damp cloth to study the wound. "Well, your friend was lucky. I think Black Bill missed the artery."

"He seems warm—" Cilla began.

Emerson sent her an impatient glance. "Of course he does— he's been shot! What did you expect would happen?"

Samuel came forward and took Cilla's arm. "Will he live, Mr. Emerson?"

"We'll know in a few hours. As long as this fever doesn't worsen, I expect he will make a full recovery."

"What can we do?" Cilla asked.

Emerson barely spared her a glance. "Stay out of the way. We'll call you once we've got him comfortable."

"Cilla." Samuel tried to tug her away. "Come, let's go downstairs. I've ordered dinner."

"We have a fine lamb today," Mrs. Caruthers said. "Go on now. Your coachman will be here when you get back."

"John," Cilla corrected, her eyes on the wounded man's face. "His name is John."

Emerson looked up at that. "We'll care for John. Off with you."

Slowly she turned away. Samuel slid a guiding hand around her waist as they left the room and made their way downstairs. She did not protest. The farther away from the sickroom they got, the slower her movements became. He signaled to Caruthers, the innkeeper, then followed the man to the private dining room, feeling by the time they reached it that Cilla had somehow left a part of herself upstairs with John. It was as if he guided a life-sized doll to the table where a steaming feast awaited.

"Would you like some wine?" Caruthers asked.

"No—" Samuel began.

"Yes," Cilla replied, sitting down at the foot of the table. She stripped off her bloodied gloves.

Caruthers glanced at Samuel.

"Bring some water with the wine," Samuel said, and then the innkeeper slipped from the room. Samuel ignored the place setting at the far side of the table and pulled out the chair right next to Cilla. "Are you all right?"

"I thought I was." She stared at her stained gloves, an affront to the neatly set dining table, then glanced up as Samuel took the discolored pair away and stuffed them into his coat pockets. "It all happened so quickly."

"You were magnificent." Samuel placed his hand over her restless one. Her skin was soft, her bones delicate. "If you hadn't kept your head, John would be dead."

"I would be better if I could be up there with him. Sitting here doing nothing—it's frustrating."

"From what Mrs. Caruthers said, this Emerson is supposedly an excellent surgeon. Best we give him the room he needs to do what needs to be done."

"I know, but—" She raised her gaze to his, her dark eyes wide and troubled. "I suppose I function better when I am the one handling the problem."

"Dolly Bailey has been known to say she could not manage without you."

"That is kind of her."

"Kindness has nothing to do with it. You forget, I have seen you in your capacity as a lady's assistant. You are frighteningly efficient. Scared the devil out of me the first night we met."

She let out a reluctant laugh. "If that were true, Captain, you would never have disrupted the party."

"Nonetheless, I knew you were the one who might actually succeed in stopping me. You were the one I watched."

"Well." She licked her lips and dropped her gaze to their touching hands. "I suppose I should be flattered."

"It was meant as a compliment."

Caruthers entered the room, bearing a tray with a bottle of wine, a pitcher of water, and two glasses.

Samuel took his hand from Cilla's. Her brisk efficiency of the previous hour was slowly giving way to some sort of panic. He knew what to expect from the strong, efficient Cilla who managed details as easily as he commanded a ship. But this other woman—pale, sober Cilla with the trembling fingers—this woman was a stranger. One who was quietly losing her composure.

"I'll pour the wine, Caruthers," Samuel said as the innkeeper started to uncork the bottle. "Please leave us. The lady needs a few moments in private. And please ask the staff not to disturb us."

"Of course, of course." Caruthers placed the contents of the tray on the table, then gave a bob of his head and left the room, closing the door firmly behind him.

"I apologize." Her whisper came out on a quivering breath. "I do not want to be any trouble."

"Nonsense. This has been a harrowing ordeal, especially to someone who is not accustomed to that sort of thing."

"Are you? Accustomed to it, I mean?"

He shrugged and reached for the wine bottle. "I've spent many years at sea and seen my share of unpleasantness."

"I feel like a ninny. Like a pale, simple *woman*." She sucked in a breath and straightened her spine. "Again, I apologize."

"You're a human being, Cilla. No reason to apologize for that." He worked loose the cork on the wine bottle. "I believe some wine might help." He poured her a glass. "And for the record, my dear, you *are* a woman."

"Perhaps, but I do hate to be missish."

He gave a bark of laughter. "The last word I would ever use to describe you, Mrs. Burke, is 'missish.'"

She picked up her wineglass and slanted him a look from beneath her lashes. "Mrs. Burke? I was Cilla a few moments ago." She sipped her wine, never looking away from him.

He turned his attention to pouring his own wine. "I hadn't noticed. I do apologize for using your Christian name without permission."

She laughed, such a startling sound that he bobbled the wine bottle with a loud clink against his glass.

"After all of this, Captain—and given that we are essentially conspiring together—I believe it is appropriate for you to call me Cilla."

He recovered control of the wine bottle and topped off his portion. "Then perhaps you should call me Samuel." Setting down the bottle he raised his glass. "To John."

Her expression sobered. "To John," she echoed, and touched her glass to his. "I do hope he is all right. It was very brave of him to chase off that highwayman."

Samuel took a swallow of wine—a surprisingly decent bottle of red, given the inn's humble ambience—and set down his glass. "I am in his debt again. The man seems to make a habit out of saving my life."

"He saved you from the island." She sipped more of her wine. "Given John's actions this afternoon, I feel inclined to believe your story. I mean, that he would come back for you—if that was indeed the situation."

"He did come back for me. Rescued me from that blasted rock. And he saved my life again on Tuesday, no doubt why he reacted so quickly today." Samuel swirled the wine in his glass, then took a healthy swallow. "I don't want him killed because of me."

"What happened Tuesday?"

"Someone tried to shoot me. John went after the fellow and captured him, but then the shooter got away from us."

"My heavens." Cilla splayed a hand over her bosom, then finished off her glass of wine in one gulp. "More, please."

Samuel raised his brows. "Perhaps you had best eat something. Too much wine with no food in your belly will knock you flat."

"I am not hungry."

"You should still eat something. You barely got any of that sandwich before our picnic was so rudely interrupted." Samuel grabbed the platter of hot sliced lamb. "Allow me to serve you, milady."

"Do you listen to nothing I say?" She watched him fork several slices of lamb onto her plate. "I told you I am not hungry."

"Cilla, be reasonable. You don't want to get all muddled from the wine, do you? After all, Emerson will not stay forever and I will have to take you home. I doubt you want to return to the Baileys inebriated."

The mutinous light left her eyes. "I suppose you are correct. Very well, I will eat. Perhaps some of those potatoes?"

"Certainly. And here, try the French beans." He served her each dish, passing her the loaf of bread once her plate was full.

"I will not be able to eat all of this."

"Just eat some of it and I will be content. And then you can have some more wine."

She shot a narrowed-eyed glare at him. "I am not a child, Captain."

"Samuel. And I am well aware you are no child."

"Then stop treating me like one."

"You were overset. I was only trying to help."

"I was not overset! I was simply—at a loss."

He toyed with his wineglass, amused by the myriad of expressions flickering across her face. Did she have any idea how easy she was to read? "You were at such a loss that you forgot the basics. What would you advise a young woman who had just been through such an ordeal? Been threatened at gunpoint by a highwayman? If she were overset, I mean."

"If she were overset, then I would advise her to have some hot tea and take to her bed until her nerves had recovered." She lifted her brows and held up her empty glass. "This is not tea, Captain; therefore, I am not overset."

He chuckled and filled her glass halfway. "You *are* overset. We agreed you would call me Samuel, but now you are back to Captain. Therefore, you are overset."

She pressed her lips together, no doubt to restrain some unladylike epithet. "Thank you for the wine."

"No more for you until you have eaten some of that." He pointed at her plate.

"I should inform you that I drink wine regularly, Cap— er . . . Samuel, and that I have yet to become inebriated. I do know my limitations."

"That's good to know. A person should always know his limitations."

She sliced off a sliver of lamb and popped it into her mouth. "And what are yours?" she asked when she had swallowed.

He sliced his own lamb. "My limitations? Given that I have been on my own since I was fifteen, I imagine my limitations are somewhat less than yours. I have had to test myself many times over the years."

"Fifteen? Heavens! Where was your family?"

"The truth is I never knew who my father was. My parents were never married. And my mother died when I was fifteen, so I went to sea to make my living." He focused unduly on cutting his meat into bite-sized pieces so he wouldn't have to see the shock on her face.

"How terrible for you, Samuel." She touched his hand, and he looked up. Her soft brown eyes melted with sympathy rather than the rejection he had expected. It reminded him of the night she had run after him. "Fifteen is too young to lose your only family."

He shrugged, pulling away from her touch on the pretext of reaching for another piece of bread. "I survived. It did me good to learn I can stand on my own. Besides, I had the Baileys. When things got unpleasant at home, I went there."

"No wonder you were so upset the night we met."

"Yes." He ripped apart his bread with deliberate care. "The Baileys were closer to me than my own mother had been. That they would not believe my tale . . ." He fell silent, his throat working to dislodge the knot forming there.

"And you were fifteen when you went to sea?" She sliced another piece of lamb as if she hadn't noticed his momentary lapse, though he knew she had. "You were hardly more than a child."

He cleared his throat, regained control. "I became a man quickly because I did the work of a man. Eventually I earned my way into the captain's position. I had my own ship, my own business. I would never be dependent on anyone else ever again. But then my ship was lost to fire, and I had to take on work as a captain on other men's vessels."

"That's how I felt after Edward died, that I would finally be independent." She clamped her mouth shut as if the words had escaped against her will, then popped a piece of potato into her mouth as if to prevent more such outbursts.

Her distress intrigued him. If she was going to help him save Annabelle, he needed to know everything about her . . . especially if she would betray him.

Since she was finally eating, he picked up the wine bottle and topped off her glass. "Tell me about Edward."

"You do not want to hear such an old story, surely." She dug into the food as if suddenly ravenous.

"Cilla." He laid his hand over hers before she could

lift the fork to her mouth. "Tell me about Edward. I want to understand."

She laid down her silverware with a clatter, slipped her hand from beneath his, and took up her refilled glass. "Edward is dead. He is in the past. Surely we can leave him there."

"Now, Cilla." He gave her a charming smile. "You know everything about me. About my parents, about Raventhorpe. Is it unreasonable I should ask questions about you? After all, you are going to be my partner in all this."

"I *may* be your partner. I have not yet decided if I believe your wild stories."

He sighed. "What must I do to convince you I tell the truth? Do you have so much love for Raventhorpe?"

She wrinkled her nose. "I cannot say that I do. The man truly does seem rather self-serving most of the time. And what you told me at the picnic was positively chilling."

"All right then." He leaned closer to her. "Knowing that, which one of us do you trust more? Me or Raventhorpe?"

"I—" She stopped.

"Has anything I have ever told you been proven a lie?"

She shook her head.

"Have you ever seen me harm anyone or heard about me harming anyone?"

"Just Thomas."

"Who the devil is Thomas?"

"The footman you struck when you pushed your way into Nevarton Chase."

A satisfied smile curved his lips. "Ah, yes. Thomas. I do apologize. I tend to be rather single-minded when I want something, and he was trying to block my way."

"Single-minded? Yes, I have observed that about your character."

"My honor is at stake, Cilla. My word is being doubted by the people who were closest to me. Please understand that I truly believe Annabelle will be in danger if she marries Raventhorpe, and I will do anything to stop this marriage."

She set down her fork. "You are asking me to sacrifice everything to help you."

"I know I am, and I am sorry. But isn't saving an innocent girl's life more important than anything else?"

"More important than your honor?"

"Yes." He held her gaze, willing her to believe him. "I have only my word to support my argument. John might even tell you his story in hopes of convincing you. I am not trying to marry Annabelle myself or steal her fortune. I just want to make sure a woman I once cared for does not end up married to a man I know to be a killer. I will even dance at her wedding to another man, as long as that man is not Raventhorpe."

"Oh, Samuel." Her lovely face softened with sympathy. A sheen of dampness brightened her eyes. "I will consider it, but I need time to reflect on everything you have told me." She dabbed at her eyes with the edge of her sleeve. "Please forgive my manners, but I used my handkerchief for John's bandage."

"I would lend you mine, but I used that one for John, too." He gallantly offered his napkin. She took it and dabbed at the corners of her eyes.

"Thank you." She took a sip of wine, clearly struggling to regain her composure. Finally she looked at him again. "Clearly you loved Annabelle very much, to go to such lengths to protect her."

"Not exactly." He looked away, toyed with his fork.

"Not exactly? Are you telling me your affections for Annabelle have changed?"

He looked at her sweet face, her dark eyes misty with romantic tears, and he almost didn't tell her. But he was an honest man. "I was never in love with Annabelle, Cilla. I've come to the conclusion I'm not capable of it."

Chapter 9

Cilla stared, certain she had not heard aright. "Of course you are capable of love."

"I don't think so. I was very fond of Annabelle, but the people I came from were not very loving. I don't consider myself a romantic man, and I've never 'fallen in love' as they say. I don't think it's in me."

She listened to him say this, his voice completely steady and his expression serious. He truly did not believe himself capable of love.

"For myself, I'm beginning to believe love does not exist," she said, and drained her wineglass.

He frowned at her. "Come now, Cilla. Of course you believe it exists. You married for love, didn't you?"

"I did." She reached for the bottle, but he grabbed it before she could. She almost protested—until he tipped some wine into her glass. "I married for love. Embarrassed my family, left my friends and the only life I ever knew behind, all because I fell in love." She leaned forward and fixed him with a fierce stare. "I was stupid."

"Don't say that, Cilla. All women know how to

love—at least what they think love is. There are many women who do the same thing you did, every day."

"Then we're all stupid to believe a man's lies. All Edward wanted was the money he thought I had. But he didn't expect my father to disown me, did he? All I had when we ran off together were the jewels I had inherited from my grandmother. And he took them, every one, and sold them for cash that he lost at the gaming tables." She leaned back in her chair, suddenly exhausted. "That was my love, Samuel."

"Is that why you don't want to marry again? Certainly a romantic woman like you longs for a lover."

"Ha! A lover? Who would fill the position, Samuel? You?"

"I believe you have had enough wine." He took her glass away and placed it on his other side, beyond her reach, then moved a goblet of water in front of her. "Drink this. It will steady you."

She took up the glass and drank, then set it down and looked at him with her mouth set in defiance.

"As for me being your lover—" he began.

"I was not suggesting that!"

"Weren't you?" He fixed her with a knowing stare that made her heart skip beats. "I admit, the thought has crossed my mind. You are a very attractive woman. I've been tempted since the first moment I saw you."

The breath left her lungs. "What—"

"And I do know how to make love to a woman. To take her breath away with a kiss. Melt her knees with a touch." He raised her fingers to his lips. "To bring her pleasure that will make her scream my name."

"Then why—"

"I think you want a lover, Cilla, but it can't be me. Not if we're going to work together."

Stung, she snatched her tingling hand away. "Nonsense. I do *not* want a lover. Why would I? Women were created to endure men's lusts, not enjoy them."

"Surely you don't believe that."

"Surely I do."

"That's a pity, Cilla. Not to speak ill of the dead, but I'm sorry your husband did not properly see to your needs."

"My needs? I do not know what you are talking about."

"My, my. Do realize the challenge you pose with those words? I'm almost tempted to show you myself."

"I doubt you could show me anything new, Captain."

He chuckled. "Well then, how about a wager?"

The gleam in his eye made him appear a little too pleased with himself. She regarded him with suspicion. "What type of woman do you take me for?"

"The type to engage in a harmless wager between friends."

"And are we friends?"

"We're certainly not enemies."

"True." She nibbled her lower lip. "What type of wager?"

"I will wager that I can make you cry out my name in pleasure—without me removing a single piece of your clothing."

Her common sense urged her to deny his claim, to slap his face in outrage, but she hesitated. Part of her was intrigued by his boast. Certainly it was impossible. How could a man do such a thing if she remained fully clothed? But his seductive words of moments before had sent her blood thundering to unmentionable places, and she found herself ensnared by the idea that he just might be able to do what he claimed. "Are you mad?"

"Not mad," he said. "Confident."

Oh, she wanted to wipe the smirk right off his face. "What would we wager?"

"A guinea," he said.

"How can you have a guinea when the highwayman stole your purse?"

"I have John's purse. How else did you think I was paying for the inn?" He produced the purse and took out a guinea, laying it on the table. "If you win, you get the guinea."

"And if you win? What do you get, Captain?"

"A kiss," he decided. "And not one of those little pecks on the cheek. A real woman's kiss."

The thought of kissing him left her breathless. "This is probably not a good idea."

"What are you afraid of?"

She eyed him for a long moment. She did not truly believe he could do as he claimed, however exciting the fantasy, but she did have to admit to a certain curiosity. Her attraction to him had bubbled steadily from the moment she had first seen him.

Dear God, how long had it been since anyone had touched her?

"I accept your wager," she said. "And I will be pleased to accept your guinea when you lose."

He gave her a slow smile that sent a streak of heat straight to her woman's parts. "I have no intention of losing."

"So what happens now? Do you mesmerize me with your wicked stare? Recite poetry designed to incite me to such a state that I disrobe of my own volition? Tell me, Captain, how to you intend to accomplish this miracle?"

"Hardly a miracle, my dear. And I told you to call me Samuel."

"Samuel," she said, wrapping her tongue around his name as if it were hot taffy.

He sent her a sizzling look that made her toes curl. "Do you taunt me, Priscilla?"

She wrinkled her nose. "I dislike my proper name, Samuel. It always seemed so prim and uninteresting."

"I don't know about that. It rolls off the tongue with a rhythm that pleases me. Priscilla." He pushed his chair back from the table. "Perhaps we should do something about the way you feel about your name."

Anticipation shot straight to her loins. "What are you doing?"

"You certainly don't expect me to pleasure you from a distance, do you?" He rose and removed his coat, which he draped over the back of his chair. Then he stepped behind her chair. Her skin rippled with goose bumps at his nearness. What was he doing? *Why* had she accepted the wager?

"Perhaps this was not such a good idea," she said. She glanced over her shoulder. She could see the lean line of his waist and part of his hip from the corner of her eye. "I am a bit worse for the wine."

"You're far from intoxicated, my dear. I would never approach a lady who was not in control of her faculties. And you've already accepted the wager. You cannot refuse now." He pulled her chair away from the table and turned it so she faced him. When he crouched down in front of her, their faces were level with each other. "It's a matter of honor, Priscilla. Are you afraid your resolve will not withstand my persuasion?"

Yes, she thought. "No," she said.

"Don't fear me, sweet one. I only want to make you feel good." He traced a finger down her cheek. "Soft as satin. You're a very beautiful woman, Priscilla."

"I am plain. Brown eyes, brown hair, a tad plump—"

He placed his finger on her lips. "Hush. You are far from plain. And you are certainly not plump. You are shaped like a woman, an enticement to any male. Your brown eyes are so soft a man could drown in them. And your hair is beautiful. See the way it curls at the nape of your neck?" He touched one of the curls, tugged at it. Or was he wrapping it around his finger? She couldn't see. Didn't dare ask. Her heart pounded.

"It is a terrible bother," she murmured. "It is

so curly that I have a hard time making it behave properly."

"So you tame it into this sober knot every day? How terrible." He touched her coiled hair.

Was he going to remove the pins? Her breath nearly stopped at the thought. One part of her wanted him to do it, to pull the pins from her hair and release her . . . it . . . from its fetters. Would he think her beautiful then?

He found one pin, started to tug it loose.

"No." She covered his hand with hers to halt him. Dear heaven, his skin was warm. "I consider my hairpins part of my clothing."

"Come now, Priscilla—"

She lifted her chin. "Will you lose the wager so easily, Samuel?"

He studied her face for a long moment, then gave her a slow smile that sent warmth flooding through her body. "I won't let you win so easily, Priscilla."

She licked her suddenly dry lips. "I know."

His gaze narrowed on her mouth, and he slid his hand from the back of her head to the back of her neck, urging her forward. Dear God, he was going to kiss her!

"Hold." She halted him with a hand on his chest when he would have tugged her closer. "I thought the kiss was to be your reward, Captain."

"Samuel."

"Samuel. How can it be your reward if it is part of your seduction?"

He sat back on his heels. "You are intent on making this a challenge, aren't you? Are you so afraid of feeling again that you would deny yourself pleasure?"

His comment struck home, but she had come this far. "Are you so lacking in confidence that you would take the prize before you have won it?"

"I am not lacking, my dear—not in any way that would matter to a woman."

Heat seared her cheeks. Wicked man! Was he referring to . . . "No hairpins. No kisses. Are we agreed?"

"No hairpins. And no kisses on the mouth."

She gave a little laugh. "Of course. Where else would one kiss?"

A gleam lit his eyes that made butterflies explode in her stomach. "Ask me that again afterwards."

He rose to his knees and curled his hand around the nape of her neck again.

"Samuel—"

"Hush." He bent his head and pressed his mouth to the side of her neck above the collar of her dress.

A quick burst of heat shot through her, and her eyes nearly rolled back in her head. When his teeth scraped her sensitive flesh, she nearly jumped out of her chair.

"Easy," he murmured against her throat. He nibbled his way up from the high collar of her dress to her ear, tiny nips that didn't hurt but sent tremors along her nerve endings. Without stopping what he was doing, he took her hand and began toying with her fingers.

What was he doing to her? She stopped the moan before it left her lips, but she didn't fight the need to let her head fall to the side to give him better access. She kept her eyes closed, enjoying his touch way too much. Craving it.

He reached her ear and breathed gently across the sensitive lobe. She shivered and tried to move away, but his hand at the back of her head was relentless. He tangled the fingers of his other hand with hers. "Relax, Priscilla. Enjoy what's happening to you."

"I do not know what is happening to me." She clamped her lips shut. Goodness, had she actually said that?

"Don't be afraid of your feelings." His tongue touched the rim of her ear, and she jerked away. He pulled back to look into her eyes. "If you don't want this, simply say so. We can forget the wager." He raised her hand to his lips and pressed a kiss to the palm. "Or you can trust me to show you a true taste of a woman's pleasure."

She nearly told him to stop. The part of her who had been raised as a London debutante wanted to default on the wager and run away, no matter how cowardly it seemed. But the part of her who had married the wrong man and been forced to rebuild her life hesitated. She really wanted to know—finally—what every other woman her age seemed to know.

"I have never felt anything like this," she murmured.

"You were married. Did your husband never touch you like this?" He brushed the tip of his tongue against the palm of her hand.

She gasped and fought the impulse to close her

fingers around the now highly sensitized area. "No," she managed. "Never like this."

"He was a fool. You are so responsive. How could any man resist?" He slowly took her pinky into his mouth.

She whimpered. There was no other word for it. His mouth was hot and moist, and he tickled the pad of her finger with his tongue before releasing it. Then he took her hand and placed it against his cheek. "Touch me, Priscilla. I know you are as curious about me as I am about you."

His skin was hot, the slight roughness of a late day beard brushing the heel of her palm. His hand remained at the base of her neck, his thumb gliding gently up and down the sensitive flesh.

She raised her other hand, cupping his face between her hands. Good Lord, she was curious. Edward hadn't liked being touched—except in one particular place. Never had he offered to let her explore him. He had usually groped her breasts and buttocks, thrust his tongue in her mouth in a semblance of a kiss, and then thrust his manhood into her body with little or no warning. Occasionally he had come home too intoxicated to even do that much and made her fondle him until his rod stiffened before he took her. She had learned to lie still and wait for him to finish. Never had she felt the urge to discover his body.

But she felt the urge to discover Samuel's.

"Let me help you." He sat back on his heels again, out of her reach, and dropped his hands from her flesh to the fastenings of his waistcoat. She wanted to cry out at the loss, but then her curiosity was caught as he opened the waistcoat and then the panel of buttons on the shirt beneath to reveal part of his bare chest, sun-kissed and lightly sprinkled with dark hair. He shrugged off the waistcoat and tugged the shirt out of his trousers, then leaned up again, taking her hand and pressing it against the expanse of male muscle exposed by the open buttons. "Indulge your curiosity," he murmured.

She should have pulled away. But the heat of his skin surprised her—that and the way the curling hair tickled her palm. She trailed her fingers along his flesh, lured by his warmth, the solidity of his form. She leaned forward, pushing farther beneath his shirt, brushing his male nipple in her exploration. He hissed, and she pulled away.

"No." He grabbed her hand and flattened it against his chest again. "It feels good. Don't stop."

"It sounded like I hurt you."

He gave her a tender smile. "No. Let me show you." He cupped her breast right through her dress and rubbed his thumb across her nipple.

Pleasure sliced through her body, centered on her womb, and squeezed. Her eyes closed as she gasped for breath.

"It works both ways," he said. "You touch me. I touch you. We set each other on fire."

"Please." She opened her eyes and fixed her gaze on his face. "Please show me."

"Ah, my sweet Priscilla. That's exactly what I intend to do." He leaned in and licked her throat, never removing his hand from her breast.

She slid her hands up around his shoulders, pulling him closer as he licked and nibbled his way from her throat to her other ear. When he took the lobe between his teeth, she let out a soft cry.

"Yes, that's it," he murmured. "Let it happen. Let go." He slid down her body, rubbing his cheek against one breast as he fondled the other with his hand. "I liked your evening gown better. It seems a crime to hide such beauty beneath so much cloth. If only I could taste this sweet flesh." He closed his mouth around one nipple and teased it with his tongue. Her body reacted even through layers of clothing, and she, too, wished she were wearing anything but her high-necked traveling dress.

She let her head fall back, surrendered to the heaviness sweeping into her limbs, and opened herself up to his touch. She clung to his shirt as the only safe harbor to be found in this wild storm of sensation. He continued to savor her nipples as if the layers of cloth were not even there, sending streaks of pure fire straight to her loins. When he reached for the hem of her skirt, she had given up pretending that she wanted him to stop.

"Shall I kiss you?" he whispered, lifting her skirts until her stockinged calf was bared to him.

"Yes, kiss me." Anything to ease this growing ache.

He brushed his fingers along the underside of her knee, teasing the sensitive flesh. She trembled, her breath coming in short pants as he slid his both hands beneath her skirts, easing his fingers beneath the edges of her drawers to toy with the ties to her garters.

"What are you doing?" she asked, though it came out as more a plaintive wail.

"Touching you. Learning you. Making you feel good." He leaned forward, gently squeezing her cotton-clad thighs. "Trust me."

His fingers trailed up and down her thighs, each time coming closer and closer to the heat between her legs. Dear God, was he going to touch her there? He wouldn't—would he? Did she want him to?

God, yes.

"Please," she whispered.

"What, sweet Priscilla? What is it you want?"

"Please touch me."

"I am touching you." He drew circles on the very tops of her thighs with his fingers. So close.

"More. Please, Samuel. Please."

"What do you want, Priscilla? This?" He traced her inner thighs right up to her center . . .

. . . then stopped. A whimper escaped her lips. So close. Right there. Right there. "Right *there*."

She hadn't realized she had spoken until he said, "Right here?" And pressed his palm against the ache between her legs.

"Yes. Dear God, yes." She bent her knees, digging her heels into the seat of the chair as she raised up to better feel his touch. "More. Please, Samuel. More."

"All right, beautiful Priscilla. I know what you need." He took her ankles and hooked her bent knees over his shoulders.

"What . . . what are you doing?" She gripped the arms of the chair, fearing she would fall off the seat.

"Giving you what you need." He nipped the inside of her thigh through her drawers. "God, you're so ready for this, aren't you? The scent of you is intoxicating. Let's give you what you need, sweet Priscilla. Let's show you what you've been missing."

Then he leaned in and kissed her, right between her legs.

She nearly screamed. He was really . . . How could this . . . Dear God, it felt so good. *So good.*

She could feel his tongue slipping past the slit in her drawers. Teasing her. Licking her. Rubbing against that one spot that burned, that one spot that sent tremors through her entire body. The pressure built. She should make him stop. Surely this wasn't right . . .

The hell it wasn't. She clenched her fingers around the arms of the chair, arching toward him, pulling him toward her with her legs hooked over his shoulders. He chuckled, and the vibration against her sensitized flesh sent her over the edge. Her world exploded. Her mind went blank. Her body burst into flames hotter than the sun.

She didn't realize she was crying until she came back to herself to find him murmuring soft words of comfort and dabbing at the tears on her cheeks with the edge of his shirtsleeve.

Her loins still throbbed, though the sensation had started to ebb. Her arms and legs tingled. At some point he had set her skirts to rights and now knelt beside her chair, his brows furrowed with concern. She looked into his eyes and let out a long sigh.

"Oh," she said.

"'Oh' indeed," Samuel said. He helped her sit up. "There you are. Not so much as a hairpin removed."

"You cannot say the same." She slid her gaze over his bared chest, and the hunger in her eyes nearly made him burst his trousers.

"True, but the wager said nothing about removing *my* clothing." Quickly he did up the buttons of his shirt. He dared not look at her as long as she had that just-pleasured flush to her cheeks, else he would be unable to resist finishing what he'd started.

"Why, Samuel?"

He glanced up at her soft query, tucking his shirt back into his trousers. "Why what?"

"Why did you make the wager?"

He shrugged on his waistcoat and began to button it by touch. "Because I wanted to show you how wrong you were about a woman's pleasure. What you would be missing by not marrying again. A beautiful woman like you should not allow your passions to die simply because you have never been loved properly before."

"So I should marry again simply to satisfy my physical passions?"

"Why not? It's as good a reason as any if you don't believe in love." He picked up his glass of wine and swallowed the last of it. "I had best check on John. If he is doing well, I will be able to take you home."

She started to rise. "I shall come with you."

"No." He held up his hand. "Stay here and finish your meal. I shall be back directly." He reached for the door handle.

"Samuel."

He paused and looked back at her.

"I happen to think you are very capable of love."

"Sex isn't love, Cilla. But thank you anyway."

Chapter 10

Samuel drove Cilla back to Nevarton Chase himself, playing coachman in John's absence. Alone inside the coach, Cilla watched the scenery pass by, her mind a whirl of confusion.

Samuel had returned to the dining room with news that John was resting comfortably and that he would see her home. He made no mention of the intimacies they had shared, nor had he attempted to collect on his wager. Instead he had efficiently escorted her out to the waiting coach and handed her in before climbing up to the coachman's box.

His calm dismissal of their passionate interlude puzzled her. He had instigated the wager, as she recalled. He had indicated that he found her attractive, but immediately afterward he had regained his aplomb as if nothing had happened. She had heard from other women how men could indulge their sexual curiosity and then walk away without guilt. Was it that curiosity had led Samuel to touch her so intimately?

She should never have let it happen. She knew very well that as sincere as he appeared, this man might still be a trickster. She liked to think that she had learned something from being married to Edward, but deep down inside, she didn't really believe that. She still worried about being fooled by a man. About having her heart broken.

Yet here she was, her body still humming with the pleasure he'd brought her, having allowed him liberties she'd never imagined she would.

He threatened everything she was trying to build, yet somehow he had convinced her that Lord Raventhorpe meant Annabelle harm. She was actually considering helping him stop the wedding based merely on the facts he had given her and her own evaluations of the two men involved. He made Raventhorpe sound like a heartless villain, and Cilla was starting to believe him. Certainly the earl had not impressed her with his generosity to humankind. But did that make him dangerous?

She didn't want to believe the worst of Samuel. He appeared to be honorable and loyal, and she was impressed with his determination to protect the people he considered family. As she had seen herself, he cared—deeply. On top of all that, he was handsome and made her head swim whenever he was near. But was that physical attraction getting in the way of her common sense? She must have gone a little mad to agree to his wager, but the combination of the wine with the shock of John getting shot had lowered her defenses. Was she such a slave to her emotions?

Heaven help her, but had he given her pleasure

as a way to soften her toward his cause? She didn't like to think he was so devious, especially after all that talk about keeping things businesslike between them, but she could not ignore the possibility. Was he using her as much as Edward ever had?

The thought chilled her. He had admitted he did not think himself capable of real love, and she had to confess that he seemed to have more control over his impulses than she did. If she was going to make a sound decision regarding Annabelle, she would have to keep a level head. The girl's future was at stake, and if Cilla felt Samuel was telling the truth, she would help him. If she decided he was a liar, she would block his attempts to stop the wedding.

Even though her body still cried out for his touch.

What the hell had he been thinking?

Why had he given in to the temptation to touch Cilla? He knew it was a bad idea to get involved with her on a sexual level, especially since he needed her help. What was it about this woman that drew him so strongly? Was it her stubborn determination to stand on her own that sparked his reluctant admiration? Her willingness to learn the truth about Raventhorpe, though it threatened her own future? Or the fact that he could tell that she was a sensual woman who had never been correctly initiated into the world of passion?

Watching the startled pleasure spark in her eyes had excited him so much he had nearly climaxed himself. He could barely resist the innocent lure of her unawakened sexuality, especially with the taste of her still on his lips. The wine had not washed the sweetness away. He had wanted to bury himself inside her, to watch her face as he took her.

Stopping the wedding should be his focus. Annabelle's life depended on it. He could not allow himself to be distracted by his powerful attraction to Cilla.

Maybe John had been right. Perhaps he had been too long without female companionship. How else to explain his outrageous behavior with the lovely widow? Her declaration that had betrayed her lack of experience with lovemaking had proven a nearly irresistible lure.

He knew she had probably drunk too much wine, and coupled with the trauma of the robbery and John being shot, he was certain she had been in a vulnerable state. But watching those sensual lips say the words that made him realize she had never truly experienced sexual pleasure, had made him reckless.

John Ready was his close friend, the one man he could trust implicitly. John's brush with death had left Samuel shaken himself. Bantering with the widow Burke had seemed a good way to blow off some steam—until it had ignited the sexual attraction already simmering between them.

Not that he hadn't enjoyed being the first man to introduce Priscilla Burke to the world of sensual pleasure. What man wouldn't relish the taste of her as she had climaxed for the first time? And the look on her face . . .

Damn, just the memory was making him hard again.

He shifted in the driver's seat and adjusted himself. He needed to focus on the business at hand. Annabelle. Raventhorpe. The wedding.

Cilla had seemed quiet when he'd fetched her from the dining room. She'd been happy to hear about John, of course, but other than that she had said little to him. He'd been too intent on getting her to the coach to think much of it—and somewhat relieved she hadn't attempted to talk about what they had shared. But the farther they got from the inn and the closer they got to Nevarton Chase, the more his concern grew.

Had his actions tonight alienated his best ally?

Blast it. Sex ruined everything. He knew that, knew better than to let his loins overtake his brain. But that logic had flown out the window tonight.

He stopped the coach in the drive of Nevarton Chase and hopped down from the coachman's box, then opened the door and extended a hand to help Cilla down.

"Thank you," she said. But she did not look at him.

He frowned as she walked past him toward the door. "Priscilla."

She stopped but did not turn. "My name is Mrs. Burke. Or Cilla. Good night, Samuel."

He started to go after her. Then a footman opened

the front door. She hurried up the path, and he turned away, not wanting the footman to recognize him. He hated the way she darted into the house as if eager to get away from him. Damn it all. Had he ruined everything with one passionate impulse?

He climbed back into the driver's seat and, once the front door had closed behind her, snapped the reins over the horses' backs and set them to a lively trot.

The sooner he got back to John, the better.

Cilla awoke the next morning still wrestling with her decision. The notion that she might be manipulated by her own desires shamed her nearly as much as being married to Edward had. Her husband had gotten into one scrape after another, but he had always had a charming smile ready and an explanation at his disposal. And she had always believed him—had always *wanted* to believe him—because she simply could not face that she had been foolish enough to wed an untrustworthy man.

But once he had died and left her scarred by scandal and burdened with his debts, she had made herself face the facts. Edward had been handsome and persuasive enough to convince an angel to buy a house in hell, but he had always cared more for himself than anything or anyone else in his life.

She had chosen him. She had gone against her family's wishes and wed him, so certain that love would make everything all right. She had turned a blind eye to his flaws, made excuses for his lack of consideration. Everything that had gone wrong in her marriage could be laid straight at her door. Clearly she did not know how to discern a decent man from a scoundrel.

Yet now she was being asked to make that same decision about Annabelle's fiancé, based solely on her own instincts and observations. Raventhorpe intended to move forward with the wedding, and Samuel intended to try and stop it. Either way, Cilla had to choose a side. A neutral position was not an option.

If she chose to align with the Baileys and Lord Raventhorpe, Annabelle would marry well and become a countess. Cilla would earn a reputation that would help her start her business and launch her to success. However, if Samuel was right, Annabelle might well come to physical harm at the earl's hands.

If she chose to be Samuel's ally, Annabelle would be safe, though she would have lost a titled fiancé. Still, the girl was young, beautiful, and rich, so finding another husband would not prove difficult. But Cilla would be destroying everything she was trying to achieve for herself. Certainly the Baileys would not trust her to work for them any longer, and once rumors got out as to why she had been discharged, she would never be able to have her own business. Heavens, she would be lucky to even find a new position, especially with the scandal of her marriage still lingering in the memories of the London matrons.

The question came down to how much she was willing to risk to potentially save a girl's life. The answer: Whatever it took.

The decision was clear. She would help Samuel. She had trusted him enough that she had allowed him liberties with her body. She knew the potential consequences of her choice. As long as she went into the situation with her eyes open, it would have to be enough.

Samuel had said he wanted her to talk to Annabelle and build doubts about Raventhorpe to give him some time to find real evidence. No better time to start than now.

She found Annabelle seated on a stone bench in the gardens, reading a book. As she neared the girl, she could make out that it was one of those romantic novels that so enchanted the young girls these days. "Annabelle?"

Annabelle jerked her head up and stared for a long moment, her cheeks flushed with color. "Mrs. Burke!" She snapped the book closed.

"May I join you? I had wanted to discuss the guest list for the wedding."

"Of course." Annabelle shoved the book aside—cover facedown, Cilla noticed—and made room on the bench. "Would you prefer to go inside?"

"Not if you do not want to."

"I love being outside." Annabelle raised her face to the sun and closed her eyes for a moment, as if worshipping. "I miss the outdoors now that we are always off to some ball or another."

Cilla sat down on the bench next to her. "But I thought you enjoyed being out in society."

"Oh, it's quite fun." She flashed a smile. "I enjoy meeting all the people and seeing all the beautiful dresses. But I grew up on a farm, Mrs. Burke, so I'm used to spending a lot of time outside."

"Once the season is over, you will probably spend more time in the country. There are many events—house parties, horse races—"

"Picnics," Annabelle finished for her. "I do adore picnics."

Cilla pushed aside the distracting memory of a certain memorable picnic. "There will be many opportunities for all sorts of outdoor activities once you are a married lady."

"I can hardly believe it is less than a month away. I often dreamed about who my future husband might be." She laughed. "I certainly never imagined myself marrying a real lord!"

"What did you imagine your husband to be like?" Cilla busied herself by pulling out the pages of her guest list.

"Well . . ." Annabelle's eyes sparkled. "Handsome, of course. Kind. And someone with a solid trade so he could provide for a family."

"Well, an earldom is hardly a trade."

"You're right about that. But now that Pa is so rich, I don't have to worry so much about money."

Cilla laid the list flat on her lap and smoothed her hands over it. "You're very lucky."

"That Pa found that coal mine? Don't I know it!"

"I wanted to ask you something. You seemed angry at Captain Breedlove while you were dancing with him at Lady Canthrope's ball a few days ago. I imagine you are still upset about his defection."

Annabelle sighed. "Yes, I was angry. I didn't realize how angry until I saw him again, big as life." Her normally animated features dulled with remembered pain. "He humiliated me."

"He seems genuinely apologetic."

"Can you believe that? He was gone for almost two years, Mrs. Burke. *Two years.*"

"He claims he did not abandon you."

"I know, but he insists on trying to make me believe that ridiculous story that Richard left him on some island. I don't know where he was for those two years, but I know where he *wasn't*—and that was with me."

"What if he is telling the truth?" Cilla asked.

Annabelle gaped at her. "Have you heard the story? Painting Richard as some kind of monster out to kill him?" She shook her head. "Richard has never been anything but a gentleman to me. I have a hard time believing he is some sort of villain." She traced the binding of her book, her expression pensive. "I don't know why Samuel could not simply tell me the truth, even if it meant he found . . . someone else."

Cilla frowned at the girl's odd hesitation. "If he had found someone else, he would hardly have come here to claim your hand. And you cannot say it is for the money because apparently he has his own."

Annabelle shrugged. "Money hardly matters anymore. If I marry Richard, I can become a countess, and no one will ever tell me I'm not good enough. If I had married Samuel, I'd just be rich—well, richer than I am now."

"Who would ever tell you that you are not good enough?" Cilla shook her head. "You are bright and beautiful and kind. That is more than I can say for many of the so-called quality of English society."

Annabelle chewed on her lower lip. "I'm going to tell you something, but please don't tell Mama that you know."

"All right." She braced herself for a story of some sort of scandal, but Annabelle surprised her.

"When Pa first got rich, we went to New York. Mama had heard all about the rich people who lived there, how they all wore beautiful clothes and traveled to wonderful places and led exciting lives, and she wanted that, Mrs. Burke. I mean, she wanted it bad."

"Wanted to go to New York?"

"No, wanted to be part of New York society. So we went there. Pa got us a house and Mama tried to be friends with everyone, but no one would talk to her. They thought we weren't good enough. Too countrified to fit in." Her pretty face hardened. "I bet a countess would fit in, though."

"I bet a countess would."

Annabelle looked down and twisted her fingers together. "When Richard asked me to marry him, I knew he was having money troubles. But I thought, Pa is rich, and I could be a countess. My son would be an earl. And Samuel was gone, so . . ." She shrugged. "I figured I'd marry Richard and then maybe Mama could get her New York society."

"Annabelle . . ." Cilla paused, considering her

words carefully. "You should marry for your own reasons, not for someone else's."

"I love my mama, Mrs. Burke. When we were poor as church mice, she would sneak some of her food onto my plate. She thought I didn't see. And when we got a little money, it was always me who got the new dress, not her." Annabelle's mouth curved in a small, satisfied smile. "Samuel was gone, and Richard had been kind to me. So when he asked me to marry him, I said yes."

"But now Captain Breedlove is back."

"Yes." Annabelle sighed and picked up her book. "It seems so easy in the novels, Mrs. Burke. If a lady is torn between two gentlemen, one of them is always a villain. But is that true in this case?"

"The captain says Lord Raventhorpe is the villain."

"And Richard says Samuel is so jealous that he is making up this whole story to make me fall in love with him again. As if that would happen after what he did!"

"Were you in love with him before?"

"I thought so. He's handsome, isn't he? And commanding, and rich now, too. If only he hadn't done what he did—and had a title—he would be perfect."

"Perfect?"

"The perfect husband." Annabelle picked up her book and flipped through the pages, her mind clearly on other things. "I just wish he had had the decency to write to me if he wanted to break the engagement. He didn't have to lie."

Cilla looked down at the list of wedding guests on her lap, knowing as she hesitated that Annabelle's next words would settle her decision on the matter. "What if he did not lie?" she asked softly.

"Of course he did," Annabelle said with a laugh.

"Has he ever lied to you before?"

The girl's brow creased in confusion. "Not until all this happened."

"Then why would he start now? Why would he leave you for two long years and let you think he had abandoned you, then show up out of nowhere with fantastical stories?" Cilla shook her head. "Annabelle, what do you really know about Lord Raventhorpe?"

"He's an *earl*, Mrs. Burke. He has no secrets."

Cilla gave a sharp laugh. "Annabelle, everyone has secrets, especially the peerage."

"I don't have any secrets."

"You just told me one about your mother. Have you forgotten?"

"Well, that . . . that's more in the way of being a confidence rather than a secret. And you swore you would not tell Mama that you know."

"And so I shall not. But you must admit you do have a secret."

"Fine. Yes, that is a secret."

"So do not believe you know everything about the earl. He may have hidden depths that you do not suspect."

"So could Samuel."

Cilla nodded. "You are right. However, I believe

you know more about Samuel Breedlove than you do about Lord Raventhorpe. Perhaps you could get the earl to talk more about himself. Or I could make discreet inquiries through the servants. The earl used to own Nevarton Chase, and the staff did not change when your father bought the estate."

"What could the servants know about a lord?" Annabelle scoffed.

Cilla raised her brows. "You can tell a lot about a man from his servants. They see everything and hear everything and yet are often not seen or heard themselves. You can also learn much about a man from how he treats his employees."

"I don't know. It seems rather rude, don't you think?"

Cilla touched the girl's arm. "Annabelle, it is no secret that my own marriage was not the best. I married the wrong man. Do not make the same mistake. Be certain."

Annabelle bit her lower lip. "I don't know . . ."

"If the earl has nothing to hide, then you can marry him without the shadow of uncertainty marring your wedding day. If, however, it turns out that he is not the man you think him, better to know now than to find out when you are bound in the eyes of God."

"Perhaps you are right. I suppose it would not hurt to ask Richard to tell me more about himself."

"Do not forget about the servants."

Annabelle shook her head. "I couldn't go behind his back like that. It doesn't seem right."

Cilla knew when not to push the issue. "As you wish. I just want you to be certain, because marriage is forever." When Annabelle remained quiet, Cilla patted her hand and rose from the bench. "We can talk about the guest list later."

Annabelle nodded, paging aimlessly through her book. Cilla turned and left her in the garden, certain she had planted the seeds that might make her look more closely at Raventhorpe.

She was doing the right thing, she assured herself. If Raventhorpe turned out to be less than a gentleman, she could not let Annabelle wed him—even though it meant she might lose her position as a result of it. As much as she longed for financial independence for herself, she had to follow her instincts. Had all worked out as planned, she could have held her head high and perhaps won back some of the acceptance of her family—especially her father—with the accomplishment of launching a successful business.

But by doing this she probably ruined her chances of success. She could probably find work in one of the factories, but she knew the hours to be long and the pay very little. How could she face her family with such prospects? In such dire straits, her only alternative would be to return home to live with her parents, who would do their best to marry her off—which meant she needed to be equipped to choose a good husband.

One thing her interlude with Samuel had clearly illustrated was that she was way more passionate than she dreamed, and that she did have needs even she hadn't realized. And that there was much for her to learn about the world of sexuality in order to choose correctly this time.

Her hours of thought had concluded in a single truth that might resolve her struggle between survival and her attraction to Samuel. If she was going to put her entire future on the line to save Annabelle from marrying a monster, then she would have to learn how to tell the good men from the bad ones.

And Samuel was going to help her.

Chapter 11

He had sent her three notes over the past three days, and still no response. It seemed as if he had indeed frightened off the only person who was willing to help him save Annabelle.

Samuel climbed the stairs of the inn and made his way to John's room. He opened the door and found his friend out of bed with his trousers on. "Where the devil do you think you're going?"

"Is there a law against knocking?" John replied, shrugging into his shirt. "I am sick of being abed and thought to go down to the stables."

"You were shot, or don't you recall?" Samuel shut the door and went over to grab the edges of John's shirt as his friend tried to fasten the buttons.

"Samuel, you had best let go of my shirt or we are going to have something of a problem."

"Damn it, John, you were at death's door only days ago." Samuel eyed the bandage on John's shoulder. No signs of blood. "It looks well enough. I suppose you can get up today."

"Thank you, Mother." John jerked his shirt out

of Samuel's hands and walked across the room to the looking glass.

"Someone has to look out for you. You would have died if Cilla and I hadn't rushed you back here and nursed your wounds."

John met his gaze in the reflection of the looking glass. "Cilla, is it?"

"Mrs. Burke."

"Aye, I know who she is." John arched his brow. "A lot must have happened while I was abed."

"Not so much." Beneath John's steady stare, Samuel relented. "Well, maybe. We had an . . . encounter . . . the day you were injured."

John grinned. "An encounter?"

"Never you mind," Samuel grumbled. "It's not quite what you're thinking, though I might well have ruined everything."

"Why is that?" John tucked his shirt into his waistband and went to fetch his coat.

"I drove her home that evening and she wouldn't even look at me. I've sent her three notes. No response."

John sighed and shook his head. "You are lost without me, Samuel, I can tell."

"I'm sorry, John. Of course I'm glad you're feeling better."

John chuckled. "I know you are. This widow of yours—she has got you tied up right and tight, hasn't she?"

"I need her, John. She's the only person who is willing to convince Annabelle to jilt Raventhorpe."

"Is that all?"

"What else would there be?"

John smothered a grin. "What else indeed?" He shrugged into his coat, wincing as he maneuvered his arm into the sleeve. "I am starved. What say you we go downstairs and get some food, and we can figure out a way to get you back into the widow Burke's good graces, eh?"

"I would be glad of your advice." Samuel headed to the door. "Especially since you were the one who encouraged me to pursue her."

John followed him out of the room and down the hall. "Me? As I recall I was courting death in the bed there while you were making advances to the lady."

"Have you forgotten our conversation just last week? The one where you suggested I should begin an affair with her?"

"Samuel, when a man has snatched his soul away from the greedy hand of death, not much else lingers in his mind. I am afraid I do not recall much before I was shot."

Samuel stopped at the top of the stairs and slanted him a look. "That nonsense won't work for long, you know."

"I know, but I was hoping it would last until at least after breakfast."

Samuel ignored the levity. "I'm truly concerned, John. What if I have botched things and she won't help us?"

"Then, my friend, I suggest you formulate some

sort of alternative plan. But not on an empty stomach."
With a reassuring grin, John preceded him down
the stairs.

Cilla arrived at the Tuesday night local assembly
ball with the Baileys. It was the first assembly ball
of the year, and the Baileys had decided they had
best get to know their neighbors. With Annabelle
marrying Lord Raventhorpe, they expected to be
visiting their home in the area quite frequently, even
after they had returned to America.

"So many people!" Annabelle said.

"Anyone can attend a public ball," Cilla told her,
"as long as they can afford the price."

"Lord Raventhorpe doesn't know what he's missing," Dolly said.

"Richard believes affairs of this sort are for the
lower classes," Annabelle said, with a sniff.

"Lord Raventhorpe can be a little too full of himself," Virgil said. "This just looks like a bunch of
regular folks having a good time."

"That is what it is, for the most part," Cilla said.

"Mrs. Burke, isn't that your mama?" Annabelle
asked, pointing.

Cilla gently pushed the girl's hand down. "I believe
it is, Annabelle. My goodness, what are they doing
here?"

"Let's go see." Dolly charged ahead, leaving the rest
of them to follow her. "Hello there! Mrs. Wallington-
Willis!"

Cilla hurried after her with Annabelle and Virgil

right behind her, well aware of the whispers Dolly's behavior generated.

Helen glanced up, then disengaged from the group she was talking to and turned a gracious smile upon them. "Mrs. Bailey! How are you?"

"I am wonderful as always." Dolly paused, catching her breath.

"Hello, Mama." Cilla came up beside Dolly. "What are you doing here?"

"We are staying nearby with the Fitzwarrens." Helen smiled, a twinkling of mischief in her dark eyes so like her daughter's. "Your father just went to fetch us some lemonade."

"Mama, may I introduce Mr. Bailey? And you remember his daughter, Annabelle."

"Pleasure," Virgil said with a little bow.

"How lovely to meet you, Mr. Bailey. And of course I do remember the lovely Annabelle. My own daughter Genny is taking a turn with Mercy Fitzwarren and should be back directly." She looked at Cilla. "Perhaps now we can have that family dinner."

"I am sorry I had to cancel—" Cilla began.

"Entirely my fault," Virgil interrupted. "I whisked my ladies back to the country so fast they had no time to change their plans."

"Oh, Pa, it wasn't your fault," Annabelle said. "Richard was the one who insisted we come back so early."

"Annabelle, hush!" Dolly said. She turned a commiserating look upon Cilla's mother. "These young girls just burst out with the darnedest things."

"I understand completely, having two daughters of my own." Helen smiled suddenly, looking beyond them. "Ah, here comes the lemonade."

As they all turned to follow her gaze, Cilla's attention was captured not by her bearded, distinguished father, but by his tall, familiar companion.

"Heavens, that's Samuel!" Annabelle gasped.

"Ah yes, as I recall you are acquainted with Captain Breedlove," Helen said. "He and my husband have struck up quite the friendship this evening. Men of the sea and all that."

"I had heard he was still in England," Virgil said grimly, "but I have not spoken to him myself."

The two men reached them, and Cilla's father handed his wife a cup of lemonade. "Here you are, my dear." He looked at his daughter and immediately away again. "Priscilla."

Priscilla.

Even as her father's dismissal stung, Cilla couldn't help but glance at Samuel. His mouth curved in a secret smile. An answering heat sprang to life inside her. For a moment, it was just the two of them again alone in the dining room at the Caruthers Inn.

She made herself look back at her father. "Hello, Papa. I hope you are well."

"And who is this charming lady?" her father asked, looking at Dolly.

Dolly flushed and extended her hand. "Mrs. Dolly Bailey."

"Mrs. Bailey, I am Admiral Wallington-Willis." He bent over her hand.

"Pleasure to meet you, Admiral." Dolly withdrew her hand and indicated Virgil. "This is my husband, Virgil, and our daughter, Annabelle."

"Mr. Bailey." The admiral gave a respectful nod before turning to Annabelle and giving her a brief bow. "Miss Bailey, you are nearly as lovely as your mother."

Annabelle dimpled at him. "Thank you, Admiral."

The admiral indicated Samuel. "And this is—"

"The Baileys are acquainted with Captain Breedlove," Cilla said.

For the first time, her father looked directly at her. "They are?"

"Yes, we are." Virgil did not extend his hand to Samuel. His gaze remained steady on the younger man.

Samuel gave him a brief nod. "Sir."

The admiral looked from one man to the other, his expression curious. But he did not ask.

"We thought you were still in London," Dolly said.

"The delights of the city pale without your company," Samuel said. "Perhaps you will allow me to call on you while I am in the country."

An awkward silence fell.

"I don't know—" Dolly began.

"Perhaps—" Annabelle started.

"I would like to talk to you, Samuel," Virgil said. "Now, if you don't mind."

Samuel's expression grew guarded. "Very well."

"This way." Virgil stalked off. With a murmured apology and a quick bow, Samuel went after him.

Helen and the admiral looked at Cilla. She gave a slight shake of her head.

"Let's all get some lemonade," Dolly said.

Virgil stormed out the doors of the assembly hall and walked around the corner of the building. Samuel followed and found Virgil waiting for him in the shadows, arms crossed and legs braced.

"What in God's name are you up to, boy?" he demanded. "You better not still be sniffing after Annabelle. She's marrying Raventhorpe and that's that."

"You can't let her marry him," Samuel said. "He's not the man you think he is."

"Bollocks. You just want her for yourself. Well, you should have thought of that about two years ago."

"I didn't leave her on purpose. Why don't you believe me?"

"Raventhorpe told me all of it, Samuel. *All* of it."

"All of what, Virgil? If I told you what I have learned—"

Virgil threw up his hands. "I don't want to hear it unless you've got proof to show."

"I don't. But I know what kind of man he is."

"I used to know what kind of man *you* are, but you've disappointed me."

"I'm sor—"

"How could you do it?" Virgil burst out. "How could you take up with other gals when you knew Annabelle was home waiting for you?"

"What?" Samuel gaped at the man he considered his surrogate father. "You think I chased other women while I was engaged to Annabelle?"

"The earl told us what went on whenever you were in port."

"The same way he told you that I lost my temper and abandoned my post?" Rage coiled inside him like a striking snake. "I have never before given you any reason to question my honor."

"Until—"

"Never," Samuel repeated, ice in his tone. "I don't know why you are taking the word of a complete stranger over someone you've known for over ten years."

"He's an earl . . ."

"He's a man first, and a poor example of one to boot. His social status does not guarantee good character."

Virgil blinked, startled. "But . . ."

"I have done nothing to shame you," Samuel said. "But when I needed you to believe in me—when I *counted* on you to believe in me, you let me down."

"*I* let *you* down . . . ?"

"You listened to the lies of another instead of the word of the man who—" He stopped, took a deep breath. "I wish there was some way to prove all this to you, but I can't. Did you ever think to ask Raventhorpe for proof of his accusations? Because right now, it's my word against his—his and the crew who work for him. Not exactly an unbiased group. And it's a shame that all our years together aren't enough for you to give me the benefit of the doubt."

Virgil said nothing, but Samuel could tell by the

look in his eyes that he appeared to be considering Samuel's words.

"Annabelle is what matters now," Samuel said. "And if I can leave you with any impression at all, it's to reconsider the kind of man you're giving your daughter to."

He turned and walked back inside, leaving Virgil alone in the dark.

Cilla was watching for Samuel. He came back into the hall alone, his jaw tense and his eyes hot. He looked around, saw her where she stood with her parents and the Bailey women, and started toward her with a resolve that sent a thrill through her.

"There's Samuel," Dolly said. "I wonder where Virgil is?"

Samuel reached them. "Mrs. Burke? Would you like to dance?"

"Well, I . . ." She glanced at Dolly.

"Oh, go on, girl," Dolly urged.

Cilla inhaled a deep breath. "Yes, Captain, I would love to dance."

Annabelle frowned, looking from one to the other.

Samuel held out his hand and Cilla took it. "I believe the next dance is a polka. Let's go get our places."

Cilla slid a look at her parents and was surprised to see approval there, even from her father. "Lead on, Captain."

Cilla allowed Samuel to lead her away from the group, more than conscious of Annabelle's puzzled expression. Once they were out of earshot, she murmured, "I do not think Annabelle likes this."

"She made her choice." Samuel led her to a place on the dance floor. "We're no longer engaged, so it shouldn't matter to her who I choose to partner."

"Does that bother you?" she asked as the music started.

"The broken engagement? Not anymore." He slid one hand around her waist and took her other hand in his, pulling her against his warm, lean body. "My real motivation was to hold you in my arms."

His words sent a thrill through her even as he led her into the spirited polka.

Joy bubbled up inside her. How long had it been since she had felt the excitement of a man's arms around her as they stepped to the music? She had danced once with Lieutenant Allerton only days ago, but that experience could not compare to the whirlwind of being in Samuel's arms.

He never looked away from her as he guided her expertly around the room. His dark eyes held an intensity that made her pulse trip over itself. "You have not answered my letters," he murmured.

"I know." She bit her lower lip in guilt, and his gaze dropped to her mouth. Passion bloomed low in her body, loosening her muscles. She relaxed in his arms, letting herself lean against him a little more. "I have been thinking about the situation, and I believe I have come to a conclusion."

"If your conclusion is that you regret what happened at the inn—"

"No." She met his gaze squarely. "No regrets."

He seemed to relax. "Good. I did not want to offend you."

"You appear to have been honest with me, Captain." Her lips curved in self-deprecating humor. " 'Twas not your fault that I did not want to hear that honesty at the time."

He raised his brows. "And now?"

"Now I have come to believe that perhaps you were right. About a lot of things."

"Excellent."

"I need to talk to you alone," she murmured.

"Not here. Too many busybodies. Do you suppose you could develop a headache?"

"Of course, but then the Baileys will just take me home."

"Not necessarily." He gave her a grin that held a hint of the wickedness she had seen when he had so eagerly won their wager. "Just become ill as soon as I take you back, and leave the rest to me."

"Perhaps I should become ill during the dance rather than after?"

His look of approval warmed her. "Even better."

"Then let us begin." She sagged in his arms.

He kept moving so as not to cause a calamity on the dance floor, then expertly slipped out of the formation. Slowly they made their way back to her parents and the Baileys. Virgil and the admiral were nowhere in sight, but Genny had joined the group of ladies by this time, along with Mrs. Fitzwarren and her daughter Mercy.

Helen noticed them first. "Cilla, are you feeling all right? The set has not yet completed."

"She felt dizzy," Samuel said.

"Perhaps I grew too zealous." Cilla clung to Samuel's arm and sent them all a wan smile. Annabelle looked dismayed and Genny just watched her with narrowed eyes. "A headache has been plaguing me since before we left this evening, and I think the exertion of the dance has made it worse."

"Oh, you poor dear!" Dolly exclaimed.

"Captain Breedlove must be an energetic dancer," Genny remarked.

It took effort for Cilla not to respond to her sister's goading tone. "Perhaps if I find a place to sit down . . ."

"Now, Cilla, you know how your headaches are." Her mother glanced at Dolly. "Ever since she was first presented at court, she would get terrible headaches. Only a darkened room and hours of sleep would get rid of them."

"Oh, no!" Dolly said. "We should leave at once then and get Cilla home to bed."

"Yes, we should," Annabelle said. "I am sorry you are not feeling well, Mrs. Burke." Disappointment echoed in her tone.

"No, I do not want you all to leave on my account. You have been looking forward to this all week. I will find a chair along the wall."

"If you will allow me," Samuel said. "I will be happy to escort Mrs. Burke home so you ladies do not have to disrupt your evening."

"Oh, but I couldn't—" Dolly began.

"Please, Mrs. Bailey. It is no trouble at all, and this way Annabelle can continue to enjoy the dancing."

He gave them all a charming smile. "I will escort Mrs. Burke home in my carriage and return forthwith."

"If you do not mind . . ." Dolly glanced at the other ladies.

"That sounds like an excellent idea," Cilla's mother said. "The sooner she gets to her bed, the better."

"I see no issue with it, young man," Mrs. Fitzwarren said. "Provided you return as soon as you have completed your mission so there is no gossip."

Samuel gave a half bow, since he was still supporting Cilla. "I will not even descend from the carriage, merely escort her home safely and return promptly."

"Thank you, Captain," Cilla whispered.

"I will help you get her to the carriage, Captain," Cilla's mother said. "Genny, do stay with Mrs. Fitzwarren until I return."

"Very well, Mama."

"Come, Captain Breedlove." Helen led the way through the throng.

Cilla hated to deceive her mother. The genuine concern on Helen's face made her feel as guilty as a little girl stealing sweets. But there was no other way to speak to Samuel alone without generating suspicion from the Baileys. And she needed to tell him her terms for helping him stop the wedding— before she lost her nerve.

It seemed like forever before the carriage arrived— with John in the coachman's seat, she noticed—and she and Samuel were finally alone in the confines of the dark carriage.

"Nicely done," he said when the coach lurched into

motion. "You are quite the actress, Mrs. Burke."

"I hated to deceive my mother that way, but I wanted to speak to you face-to-face."

"I was worried when you did not respond to any of my notes," he said. "But you have already said you were not offended by what happened between us."

"No." She glanced down at her hands, grateful for the dark that hid her blush from him. "But it did inspire me to think about what you said."

"About?"

"About me knowing nothing about passion. I'm afraid you were right. Edward was not a very good teacher."

"Then Edward was a fool. You, my dear Priscilla, are a marvelously passionate woman who deserves the satisfaction of a skilled lover."

"You are kind to say so."

"Kindness has nothing to do with it. As I said, if I had not proposed our business liaison, I would be tempted to pursue you myself."

Her breath caught. The growl beneath his tone underscored his words in a way mere persuasion never could. "And are you a skilled lover, Captain?"

He was silent for a long moment. "I thought we had established that."

"I get the feeling that what you showed me is only the beginning."

His harsh intake of breath sliced through the darkness of the carriage. "What are you about, woman?"

"If I help you by convincing Annabelle to jilt Lord

Raventhorpe, I could be destroying any chance I have of making my dreams of independence come true."

"I know. I wish there were some other way."

"Perhaps there is. With no business to sustain me, the only respectable recourse for a woman of my background is to wed again. And you know how I feel about that."

"I have offered to compensate you for your loss."

"And I have refused your offer. I will not trade any of my assistance for gold. Are we clear on that? I am not for sale."

"I never said you were."

He was angry; she could tell from the steel in his voice. "But I will help you in exchange for you helping me."

He was silent again. Perhaps she had surprised him. Finally he said, "What are your terms?"

"First, let us discuss exactly what you need me to do."

"Talk to Annabelle. Leave doubts in her mind so that she might reconsider marrying him. John is going to be searching for evidence of illegal activities down in Cornwall while I will remain here to keep an eye on Raventhorpe."

Cilla said, "He cannot jilt Annabelle without causing a huge scandal. It simply is not done. He will not risk it."

"It can't hurt."

"No, it certainly cannot," she agreed. "So your best chance is still to find some evidence against him while I try to convince Annabelle to call off the marriage. It is more acceptable for the lady to jilt the gentleman, and Annabelle will escape with less scandal attached to her."

"Thank you for being willing to do this."

"Which puts us right back where we began. You are asking me to sacrifice my one chance to make a reputation for myself that will help me launch my business. If word gets out that I betrayed my employer's trust, no one will ever hire me. I must either go to one of the mills or marry again. Since I have no desire to acquaint myself with the mills except as a last resort, that leaves marriage."

"Which you don't want."

"That's true. I am not eager to put my future in the hands of yet another man who might mishandle it. However, you have shown me that there is much I do not know about men or the sexual side of marriage. I chose badly with my first husband. I do not want to make the same mistake a second time."

"You want me to find you a husband?"

She laughed. "No. I want you to teach me about men and lovemaking so I am equipped to choose my own."

Her proposal shocked him. There was no other word. He was willing to do whatever it took to keep Annabelle from marrying Raventhorpe, but this . . . ?

"Let me see if I understand correctly," he said finally. "You are asking me to teach you about men and sex so you can pick a good husband?"

"Exactly. I need to learn the difference between desire and love."

"And how did you determine I would accomplish this?"

She hesitated only a moment, but long enough for him to realize that this wasn't as easy for her as it appeared. "By becoming my lover."

Her quiet words shot straight to his groin. Immediately his mind flew back to that interlude at the inn—her stocking-clad legs, the sweet scent of her arousal, her innocent astonishment when she had climaxed for the very first time beneath his touch. He was hard in mere minutes, ready to start the lessons right here in the carriage.

"Samuel?" Her tentative tone brought him out of his memories.

"Forgive me, Priscilla," he said, hearing the hoarseness in his voice as he struggled to get his body under control. "You took me by surprise."

"I know it is bold of me to ask this of you, Samuel, but you are asking much of me as well. It will be a fair trade I think."

He gave a rough laugh. "You are innocent indeed if you do not comprehend what such a proposal can do to a man."

"Then you are willing?"

"Aye, I'm willing. What man wouldn't be? But are you sure this is what you want?"

"This would be a business arrangement, Samuel. I have no intention of throwing my cap after you. As long as we both remain honest with each other, we should both be able to each get what we need. It's not as if we will fall in love with one another."

Naïve, he thought. She was very much the type t•
fall in love. "How long would we be lovers?"

"How long will it take you to teach me what I
need to know? One day? Two?"

He laughed. "More than that, dear lady."

"Oh. Really? Well, then let us not set a time limit
on it. We shall say that our affair will end when you
decide I have learned everything I need to know or
if either of us should determine it is best to end the
relationship."

"An intriguing notion. I suppose I could find a
cottage close by where we can meet in secret for
your education."

"That would be ideal. I have free days all day
Friday and a half day on Sunday. Though I do not
imagine people make love on Sundays, do they?"

He laughed out loud. "They make love whenever
the mood strikes, and sometimes *wherever* the mood
strikes. There has been many an assignation in a
moving carriage, for instance."

"That seems somewhat unlikely given the lack of
room. Why, two people cannot even lie down."

"Ah, dear Priscilla, how much you have to
learn."

"But you will teach me?"

"I will. On one condition."

"What is that?"

"You must pay your wager to me first."

"My wager?"

"From the inn. You lost, or do you not recall?"

"I recall."

The husky tremor in her voice shot straight to his cock. "Then, Priscilla, I believe you owe me a kiss."

"I do."

He waited. "Aren't you going to kiss me?"

"Now? In the coach?"

"What better time? We're alone where no one can see us. And what better way to seal our bargain?"

"Very well." He heard her suck in a breath. "You will have to tell me how to go about this."

"First come over here to my side of the coach. Take my hand."

Cilla reached out and caught his hand, butterflies exploding in her belly as she considered what she had just agreed to. He gave her hand a little tug, and she let out a squeak of surprise as he pulled her out of her seat and sent her stumbling toward his. She landed sprawled atop him, his knee between her legs, his face pressed against her bosom.

"You smell delicious." He nuzzled her breasts, which were half bared due to her evening dress. His hot breath on her bare skin made her flesh prickle with excitement. "How I wish you had been wearing something like this that day at the inn."

She swallowed. The soft cotton of her chemise rubbed against her breasts in a way that made her loins ache. "I owe you a kiss," she reminded him.

"That you do." He gripped her waist with both hands and edged her backward, then guided her to the seat beside him. She landed on her bottom, more or less correctly seated. "Women's fashions are a darned nuisance when it comes to lovemaking."

"I imagine so," was all she could think to say.

"Look at me, Priscilla." He laid his hand along her cheek, turning her face toward his. "I am going to teach you to kiss me. When we meet again to begin your lessons, I want you to remember this."

He had barely finished speaking before he was kissing her. His mouth was hot, moist, and softer than she'd imagined. At first she kept her lips closed, her mind spinning away with the amazing feelings that coursed through her body. After a moment, the gentle pressure of his fingers on her jaw and the teasing of his tongue against her lips made her open for him. He seized the opportunity, taking her mouth with a fervor that sparked an answering inferno inside her. Her breasts swelled, her nipples tight and aching. The place between her legs flared with burning need. She wanted to rub against him, quench the fire that seemed to blaze higher with every second that the kiss lingered on.

He finally pulled away, running his thumb along her lower lip before sitting back in his seat. "Honor is satisfied," he said, his voice rough.

She sought a moment of peace, struggling to calm the raging storm within her. Outside the window, the lights of Nevarton Chase shone in the distance.

She had high hopes for her instruction at his hands. Already in the space of time it took to travel from the assembly hall to the manor, he had taught her how to kiss.

And she would remember the lesson.

Chapter 12

The note came late Wednesday, delivered by a young lad at the kitchen door.

Friday at noon. I'll send the carriage.

Cilla's heartbeat sped up as she read the note a third time. It was set then. Samuel was sending the coach for her Friday so he could teach her the ways of the opposite sex.

A scullery maid came into the kitchen, and Cilla quickly folded the note and slipped it into her pocket, then hurried up the back stairs to the first floor, where Annabelle awaited her in the music room. The knowledge that she would soon have a secret lover bubbled inside her like a stew simmering on the stove. Dear Lord, Friday was two days away. Samuel had certainly moved quickly in finding a place for their liaison. He was a man who knew what he wanted and acted appropriately to obtain it.

And apparently *she* was what he wanted. She had noticed the hardness of him when she'd stumbled against him in the carriage. He was primed to bed her, that much was certain, and part of her thrilled to the idea that she could affect a man so. Edward had always seemed to covet her grandmother's jewels more than her body. What would it be like to be intimate with a man who wanted only what her flesh could offer him?

Warmth flooded through her as she imagined Samuel kissing her again. Touching her as he had at the inn. Making her feel that incredible pleasure that had exploded through her like fireworks. Was it the same for him? She knew he would put his rod inside her. Men seemed to like it, though it was not all that enjoyable for the woman. But if Samuel brought her pleasure first, she would willingly let him thrust himself inside her, no matter the discomfort.

She paused before exiting the stairwell, hand pressed to her pounding heart as she struggled to regain her composure. She did not want to appear in any way agitated for fear Annabelle would ask her what was wrong. Once she had calmed herself, she exited the servants' stairs and made her way to the music room.

The sound of quiet sobbing shook her out of her daydream. Alarm streaked through her, and she opened the door to the music room to see Annabelle seated at the pianoforte, head on her folded arms atop the instrument as she wept.

"Annabelle, what has happened?" She hurried to the girl's side, sliding onto the bench beside her and slipping an arm around her shoulders. "Tell me, please, what has upset you so?"

Annabelle looked up, her blue eyes brilliant with

tears in her blotchy face. "I've ruined everything, Mrs. Burke! Everything!"

"Now, now." Cilla took out her handkerchief and pressed it into Annabelle's hand. "Tell me what happened, and we shall set it aright."

"I don't know if it can be set right!" Annabelle swiped at her damp eyes.

"I will do my best to help you, no matter what it is." She rubbed the girl's shoulder, hoping to soothe her.

"It's Richard," Annabelle said with a sniffle.

Cilla froze, every warning Samuel ever uttered bursting through her mind. "Did he hurt you, Annabelle? Tell me, please."

"He was horrible." She sucked in a shaky breath. "I couldn't believe it was the same man."

"What did he do to you?" She turned on the seat and grasped Annabelle by the shoulders. "You can tell me, Annabelle."

"He was so nasty." She took another shuddering breath. "All I did was ask some questions as you suggested, and he . . . he . . ."

"Did he strike you?"

"No!" The girl sounded so shocked that the tension automatically left Cilla's shoulders. "But he said the most horrible things. I don't know what I did wrong. And now . . . now . . ." She started to cry again.

"Now . . . what? What did he say?"

"He . . . he called me a crude American." She covered her mouth as if she could not bear to have said it. "He said I should mind my place if I had any chance of making a decent countess."

"Oh, no." Cilla took the handkerchief from Annabelle's hand and wiped away a stray tear. "That is indeed horrible. What brought on such talk?"

"I was just asking questions like you suggested. His favorite food, his favorite book. About his family and his childhood. His favorite pastimes. Who his friends were."

"That does not seem like anything that would incite such a violent reaction."

"I didn't think so, either, but he went a little mad. Accused me of being too meddlesome." She let out a big sigh. "When I was engaged to Samuel, we used to sit outside on the porch at night and talk about all kinds of things like that while Mama and Pa sat just inside the house. Sometimes Mama would read to Pa, and Samuel and I would sit quietly listening through the window. I always thought that's what my married life would be like."

Cilla resisted the urge to cheer that Raventhorpe had begun to show his true colors. "It seems natural to me that a woman would want to know such things about her future husband."

"That's what I thought, too. But I guess English lords see asking questions as being nosy."

"I never heard of such a thing," Cilla said, "and I have known some English lords in my day."

"We were just walking through the garden, talking. He asks me questions all the time. About America, about when I was engaged to Samuel. I always answer them."

"He asks you about Samuel?"

"Well, yes." Annabelle shrugged. "I think he's

a little jealous, actually, because I was engaged to Samuel first."

"Men can be that way," Cilla murmured. Her mind raced with the implications.

"I just hope I didn't ruin everything by asking too many questions," Annabelle said. "My wedding dress is nearly ready, and I've so got my heart set on being a countess. If Richard changes his mind, I would just die."

"He won't change his mind," Cilla said automatically.

"Perhaps you're right. I know he's marrying me for my money." She dropped her gaze to her hands and twisted her fingers together. "I just thought maybe he was starting to love me . . . maybe a little."

"Oh, Annabelle." Cilla sighed and stroked the girl's arm.

"Things weren't like this when I was going to marry Samuel," Annabelle said with a sniff. "Sometimes I wish Pa had never found that coal mine."

"We cannot undo the past." Cilla paused, trying to find just the right words. "The earl will probably not call off the wedding. It would be a terrible scandal and would blacken his reputation. In order for the engagement to be over, you would have to be the one to jilt him."

"Oh, I don't know if I could do that!"

"I have faith that you can do anything as long as you know it's the right thing to do. Just follow your heart, Annabelle."

"I don't know what my heart wants!"

Cilla smiled at the frustration in her voice, recognizing a kindred spirit. "You will. In the meantime, let us go up to your bedchamber so you can splash some water on your face. You do not want to worry your mother."

As expected, the mention of Dolly spurred Annabelle into action. The girl leaped to her feet and headed for the door. Cilla followed behind. It seemed Lord Raventhorpe's temper had begun to sow the seeds of his own destruction. Perhaps it would only take a little nudge to encourage Annabelle to call off the wedding.

Would Samuel leave England once he had accomplished his mission?

They had not discussed the possibility that Cilla might succeed in her part of the plan right away. What if Annabelle was so upset at Raventhorpe that she called off the wedding this very day? How long would Samuel stay in England once that happened?

Cilla was keeping her side of the bargain, and she was determined that he would keep his. They needed to set a minimum time frame on their affair so that if Annabelle did call off the wedding sooner than expected, Cilla would be guaranteed a certain number of lessons before Samuel returned to America. There was much she needed to learn in order to pick the right husband this time.

She was gambling on Samuel's sense of honor to see the bargain through. God save her if she was wrong about him.

Raventhorpe reflected on the disappointment of his assassin's failure with a hatred that ate at him like acid. How he longed to do the deed himself, to take Breedlove's life and watch him die as he thought he had done on that island.

But the damned American had the devil's own luck—marooned on a deserted island and instead of finding death, he found gold. And somehow got himself rescued as well.

Aye, the captain had more lives than a cat. But Raventhorpe could count higher than nine. He would just keep trying to get rid of the irritating American until he was successful. Here in England, he was nearly untouchable. And he was a patient man.

Had he not courted Annabelle for nearly two years in order to get her to marry him? She had been grieving for her lost betrothed, so it had been over a year before she had even begun to see him as a suitor. Her father had only just struck it rich from the huge coal deposit under one of his fields, and Raventhorpe had made it his business first to comfort Annabelle, then to court her. The Baileys were impressed with his title, and he used it to dazzle Annabelle into accepting his offer of marriage.

He hadn't counted on Breedlove returning from the dead just as he was about to wed one of the richest heiresses in the world.

And now that he was thinking about it, he realized it was more important than ever that he apologize to Annabelle for losing his temper earlier today. But the chit had started prying into his past, asking a hundred questions that were none of her business, and he had finally snapped. She'd dissolved into hysterics and babbled something about Mrs. Burke telling her to ask him these things.

Mrs. Burke. Now there was a troublesome one. Between her and Breedlove, the two of them threatened to ruin everything he had carefully built. Breedlove would be dealt with soon enough—permanently this time. And as for Priscilla Burke . . .

She was a fetching thing with her generous bosom and her fine, rounded arse that begged for a man's attention. That tongue of hers could be put to better use than filling Annabelle's head with nonsense. Like around a hard cock. Aye, with her fair skin and lush figure she would certainly command a good price in the slave markets overseas, even though she wasn't a virgin.

Perhaps, he thought as his own loins stirred, he would try her out himself before he sold her into someone else's keeping. Always best to test the merchandise.

He rose from his desk to ring the bell. He would have one of the chambermaids come in and take care of his swelling sex—perhaps the new, young one with the pert breasts. He might even close his eyes and pretend she was the widow Burke as she serviced him.

Tomorrow he would go to Nevarton Chase to set things right with Annabelle. Abject apologies and pretty words should do it. Perhaps he would even speak of love. Whatever it took to make the little bitch forgive him.

The door opened in response to his call, and he

nearly grinned as he saw it was the delectable young maid he had intended to summon.

"It's about time," he growled, returning to his chair. He sat down, pushed the chair far back from the desk, and sprawled his legs wide. The girl hesitated on the threshold. "Get in here and close the door behind you. I have a task for you, and you had best do it well or else you will be turned out immediately."

She shut the door and hurried toward him, round little breasts jiggling in her haste, as he reached down and unfastened his trousers.

Thursday morning began with a call from Lord Raventhorpe.

Dolly and Annabelle had gone out to pay calls on their neighbors, leaving Cilla home alone to work on Dolly's correspondence. Every time she tried to focus on one of the letters, her imagination had turned toward her rendezvous on Friday, and so very little got done. When the butler showed Lord Raventhorpe into the parlor where she was working, she jumped to her feet and smoothed down her skirts before sketching a curtsy.

"Good morning, my lord. I am afraid you have missed Annabelle."

"So I have been told." He sent a look at the butler, who bobbed his head and scurried out of the room, closing the door behind him.

So Samuel was right. The servants at Nevarton Chase *were* still loyal to Raventhorpe. Cilla refused to be intimidated by his show of power. "May I help you with something?"

"I wished to have a private word with you, Mrs. Burke. About your place here." He drew himself taller, a reed-thin man with blond hair and narrow blue eyes that focused on her so intently she fought not to fidget. "You have overstepped your boundaries one time too many. I believe you have forgotten that you are no longer of the quality."

The threat in his voice shook her as he no doubt intended, but she would walk barefoot in hell before she let him see it. "How so, my lord?"

"It has come to my attention that you are putting treasonous ideas into the head of my betrothed."

"I do not understand."

"Do you not?" He strolled across the room until he stood over her, glaring from his lofty height as if he regarded some offal on the street. "You have been encouraging Annabelle to ask questions."

Fear shivered through her, and she assumed an obedient stance, folding her hands before her. "She was curious about the man who will be her husband."

"She has never been so curious before. I wonder what encouraged her to do so now? Or should I say *who*?" He actually stepped closer, crowding her backward nearly to the desk. "My sweet betrothed should be preoccupied with wedding preparations and instead she quizzes me on my associations."

Cilla looked down, hoping he would not see her nervousness. "Obviously she finds you very interesting, my lord. I believe it is only natural for a woman to want to know about her future husband."

"And do you know what I believe?" He whipped

out his hand and jerked her chin up so she was forced to look at him. "I believe you are putting ideas in her head that have no business being there. And be warned, Mrs. Burke, that if I discover you are saying anything to Annabelle that would turn her from me, it would go very badly for you."

She tried to jerk her face free, but he pinched her jaw harder between his powerful fingers, forcing her to stay where she was.

"The world is a terrible place at times. I would hate for anything . . . unfortunate . . . to happen to you."

"You flatter me with your concern, my lord." She pried his hand loose and shoved it away. "Kindly do not touch me again."

His lips curled in a snarl, and he leaned in, crowding her, surrounding her with the menace that emanated from him. "You should have a care for that insolent tongue," he whispered. "You forget your place." He jerked away from her. "I will call again later to speak to my fiancée."

She swallowed hard and nodded, too stunned to speak.

He reached the door and paused with his hand on the knob. "No impudent response? I see you are a quick learner. That bodes well for the future. Good day, Mrs. Burke."

As the earl exited the room, Cilla rubbed her hands together, suddenly chilled. Now that she had seen the malevolence Samuel had described, she wanted to find Annabelle and hide her from Raventhorpe.

She did not want him in the same room with the girl, much less wedded to her.

For the first time, she no longer felt any uncertainty at all about helping Samuel. Raventhorpe was evil, and Samuel was doing the right thing in trying to stop the wedding. And she was going to assist him.

It was worth the price.

John returned from Raventhorpe's orphanages in Cornwall late Thursday evening.

"What have you learned?" Samuel asked, waving John into his room.

"The blasted orphanages look perfectly normal," John said, weariness dragging his steps as he entered the room. "The employees all sing the praises of the generous and caring Lord Raventhorpe."

"I think I might be sick."

John grinned as he sat down in a chair. "I almost was. I was able to visit two of orphanages, since they weren't far from each other. At both the places I went, the matrons acted as if Raventhorpe deserved sainthood for his generous sponsorship. The facilities are clean and well maintained. The children are healthy. Well nourished. Educated in a school built on the grounds."

"Strange. I have heard that Raventhorpe Manor is falling to ruin around his ears, yet the orphanages are in excellent condition?"

"Exactly."

"What else were you able to find out?"

"I indicated that I was on a mission for a wealthy

man who was interested in adopting a daughter. One of the women was quite enthusiastic to tell me everything about how they operate. Healthy boys are often released into apprenticeships or the military. Healthy girls are taught art, music, and dancing, as well as basic reading and ciphering. When the girls turn sixteen, they are entered into a program started by Lord Raventhorpe himself. A program where they are matched up with potential husbands."

Samuel frowned. "Husbands?"

"Yes, these husbands apparently live abroad, sometimes in America. Raventhorpe personally makes the matches."

"I bet he does."

"There is also a program for boys where they might be shipped out of the country to take advantage of employment opportunities overseas."

"I'll be damned."

"Mrs. Waltham at the Beedleville facility says His Lordship is quite the humanitarian and frequently sends them orphaned children he comes across in his travels."

"You can see what he is doing."

"Indeed I can. And so can you. But to everyone else?" John shook his head. "They think these children are really being sent out to start new lives. As far as I can see, there is nothing to prove anything illegal is going on."

"Curse that slippery snake!" Samuel paced the length of the room. "I was hoping to find something concrete to show the Baileys. Even if what he is doing isn't technically illegal, it's bloody immoral."

"I can tell you from personal experience that Raven-thorpe has been operating for at least seven years, if not longer. Rumors among the servants in the area indicate that his father was cut from the same cloth. If no one has caught him at something before now, he must be very, very good at what he does."

"Too good." Samuel swiped a hand over his face. "I was so hoping to knock the bastard off his pedestal this time."

"Looks like you will have to rely on your other plan if you are to stop that wedding."

"I know."

"What will you do if Mrs. Burke fails to convince Annabelle to jilt Raventhorpe?"

Samuel fisted his hands. "Whatever it takes."

Chapter 13

Finally Friday came.

Lord Raventhorpe had been successful in tendering his apologies to Annabelle Thursday afternoon, but Cilla thought she now saw a caution in the way the girl dealt with Raventhorpe that had not been there before. The earl had actually helped Cilla's cause by revealing a glimpse of his odious nature.

And his visit yesterday morning had not contained a bit of subtlety. If he decided for certain that Cilla was trying to turn Annabelle against him, there was no telling how he would retaliate—but retaliate he would, and probably in a most painful manner. Better to allow him to think she feared him too much to meddle further, which might have actually been true had Samuel not been her ally.

She lingered in the foyer at noontime awaiting the carriage Samuel was going to send, grateful that the Baileys had left earlier with Lord Raventhorpe to attend a boat race some distance away. The last thing she wanted was questions about her plans for the day. She had never been the type of woman for secret assignations; even her late husband's courtship had been common knowledge, if not accepted by her family. But this . . . this was something out of one of the romantic novels that Annabelle was always reading, the young widow preparing to meet her lover on a lazy afternoon.

Her lover. Heat crept into her cheeks despite her efforts to remain calm. Samuel Breedlove would become her lover this afternoon. He would teach her about men and intimacy, the sorts of things most widows already knew. The sorts of things that would help her to choose a well-suited husband. It was business.

Though business rarely included removing one's clothing.

Once the thought had entered her mind, there was no stopping the images that flowed in its wake. Memories of the inn burst to life, and she could clearly see Samuel's bare, hair-roughened chest in her mind. Edward had not been a particularly hairy man, and she found herself wondering if that hair was all over Samuel and how it would feel against her naked flesh. And another question—how large would his rod become when he was aroused? She had heard enough talk from other women that the size differed based on the man. What if he was too big to fit? Edward had not been particularly large, and he had hurt her more than once.

The carriage came down the drive, and she realized she was twisting her fingers together like a green girl. She had been married. She had seen a naked man. Samuel had touched her intimately and not hurt her. Quite the contrary, in fact. She had never felt such pleasure in her life.

He had indicated there would be more, so she should cease fretting about the unknown like an empty-headed fool. She trusted Samuel. He would teach her what she needed to know, show her the secrets of sexual pleasure, and remain discreet. No would know of their bargain, but they both would benefit from it.

The carriage stopped in front of the house. She opened the door and stepped out just as the coachman climbed down from the box.

"John!" She smiled, pleased to see him up and about. "You look well. I had not realized you had recovered so completely."

"It takes more than a bullet to fell John Ready." He opened the carriage door for her and held out a hand.

She took his hand and allowed him to assist her into the vehicle. "I am pleased you are doing so well."

"Thank you, Mrs. Burke." With a warm smile, he shut the door.

Cilla sat back in the seat, trying to control her skittering nerves. The coach rocked as John climbed back to the coachman's seat. With a shouted command and a crack of the whip, he set the team in motion.

The adventure had begun.

The simple, unassuming cottage stood on a grassy knoll on the edge of the woods. A crumbling stone wall encircled the house with a gap where a gate must have hung at one time. A well-worn path led to the front door, and a curl of smoke drifted from the chimney. Samuel was already here.

He opened the door as the coach stopped in front of the gateway.

Her heart leaped into her throat as she saw him standing there, the afternoon breeze ruffling his dark hair. He wore no coat or waistcoat, only his shirt and trousers, as if he were just a man relaxing at home while waiting for the return of his wife. He smiled when he saw her, and her pulse went wild. What was she doing? Did she really intend to become intimate with this man who was essentially a stranger?

John hopped down from the box and opened the door. "Mrs. Burke," he invited, extending a hand.

She hesitated. "What will you do while we . . . while we are visiting?"

His dark eyes softened with compassion. "I have to go back to town and see about getting the horses reshod. I believe it will take all afternoon."

"Oh. I see." She reached out her hand.

"I've got it, John." Samuel appeared behind the coachman, his gaze steady on her. John moved aside, and Samuel took her hand. Even through her gloves she noticed the heat of his skin. Good Lord, what was she *doing*?

"It's all right, Priscilla," Samuel murmured. "Come out of the coach. I have a nice luncheon waiting for us."

Food. So he would not leap on her and ravage her like a beast? As soon as the thought went through her mind, she dismissed it. Of course he would not.

He had had every opportunity to do such a thing with her at the inn, and he had not acted on it.

"It sounds lovely," she said, and allowed him to help her descend.

He closed the door and, still holding her hand, glanced up at John in the coachman's seat.

"I expect to be back at about six o'clock," John said.

"Understood." Samuel gave a nod and turned toward the house.

"Good-bye, John," Cilla called. The coachman tipped his hat and then cracked his whip. The team took off at a brisk trot.

She and Samuel were completely alone.

The notion sank in with a hint of panic to it. At the inn they had been alone in the dining room, but she had always known there were other people about. That if she called for help someone would probably hear her. Here at this isolated cabin, the only ones who would hear her would be the woodland creatures.

"Have you changed your mind?" he murmured as he led her up the path to the open door. "We can simply have a nice lunch, and you can go back with John later. I do not want you to feel forced into anything."

"This was my idea." The words were as much a reminder for her as for him. "I keep my promises, Captain."

"I have asked that you call me Samuel. Captain seems so formal."

"I am sorry. I was taught to be formal as a child."

"Sweet Priscilla." He paused just before the threshold, still holding her hand. "I intend to give you nothing but pleasure today. If I say or do something that makes you uncomfortable, you must tell me immediately."

"I am certain you will not—"

He laid the forefinger of his other hand on her lips, then let it drop away. "Honesty between us, Cilla. That is the only way this can work. You tell me if you are uncomfortable. Everyone has different tastes, and this afternoon is about discovering what yours are."

"I thought it was so I could learn about men."

"That, too. But first you must learn about yourself. And I intend to help you." He held up their joined hands. "Are you ready?"

She glanced at the open doorway, then back to him. "I am."

"Then come with me, Priscilla Burke, and allow me to introduce you to the world of pleasure."

He stepped across the threshold, and she followed without hesitation. As he closed the door behind them, she got a sudden feeling of finality, as if she had indeed bid good-bye to one world and entered another.

A low fire burned in the grate, a steel cooking pot hanging over it with steam drifting from it. The savory scent of stew reached her even as she noticed the fresh bread on the table and the bottle of wine.

"I do not expect I will need the wine this time," she said with a laugh.

"Perhaps not." He looked down at her hand in his. "Will you remove your gloves?"

The rough timbre of his voice sent ripples along her flesh. Keeping her gaze on his, she began to remove her gloves, one finger at a time.

"And your hat," he added. "We might as well be comfortable while we eat."

He held out his hand for her gloves, and she gave them to him, then removed her hat. He took that, too, and went to hang it on a peg near the door, then placed her gloves on a small table near it, which stood beneath a mirror. As he came back, a ripple of excitement curled low in her stomach. Already she had willingly discarded her hat and gloves. How much longer before the rest of her garments followed?

"The first thing you should learn about a man," he said, taking her bare hand in his, "is whether or not he treats you like the treasure you are. If he does not, you should reject his suit and look elsewhere."

"How will I know?"

He led her to the table, then pulled out her chair. "He should treat you like royalty. Put your needs before his own."

"That is how all gentlemen are raised," she said, sitting down.

He leaned down and murmured, "They are all taught, but many do not practice. If a man does not treat you like a princess before you are wed, how can you expect him to do so afterwards?"

His breath tickled her ear. Her body responded with a quiver that surprised her, and even as she turned toward him, he drew away and sat down in his own seat to her right. "If you do not care for wine today," he said, "there is water for tea, though I will have to heat it."

"A little wine would not be amiss." She could not help but watch his hands as he uncorked the bottle and poured some into her glass, then poured his own.

"Is something wrong?"

She jerked her gaze up, realizing she had been staring. "I was looking at your hands."

"They are rough, I know. I will apologize now. The life of a seaman tends to leave nicks and calluses behind." He set down the bottle.

"No, that is not what I meant." She reached for his hand before she thought to stop herself and turned it over so she could run her fingers along his strong, smooth palm. "Your hands are so much bigger than mine, see?" She laid her palm against his, noting how much longer his fingers were than hers. "For some reason I find the differences between us fascinating."

"Your hands are little and soft." He closed his fingers around hers. "I remember how they felt against my skin."

Her mouth fell open even as heat flooded her face. "I . . . I remember, too."

"Before this afternoon is through, I want to feel them on me again." He brought her hand to his lips and kissed it. "Are you hungry?"

The truth slipped out before she could stop it. "Not really."

"I had hoped to seduce you gently, to ease you into

bed with wine and food and civilized conversation."
He licked between her knuckles. The shimmer of
sensation nearly sent her jerking out of her chair. "Now
I wonder if perhaps you are as curious as I am."

"You are curious?" Was that husky whisper really
her voice?

"I've been curious about you ever since I first saw
you." He turned her hand over and nipped the pad
of her finger. "You are so sensual—I don't think you
even realize it. It's completely unconscious, which
makes it all the more tantalizing."

"I do not know what you mean."

He nipped another finger and soothed this one
with a quick lick of his tongue. "The way you move.
Your figure—so lush and inviting. Your big brown
eyes and those gorgeous, soft-looking lips. A man
gets ideas from a mouth like that."

"I do not intend . . . I . . ." He touched the tip of his
tongue to her palm, challenging her comprehension
of the English language. "Surely men do not see me
like that," she managed.

"We do. There's something you should understand
about the male of the species, Mrs. Burke." He leaned
forward. "A man is always stimulated to bed women.
Even if he has no intention of actually doing so, he
is always distracted by the urge. Tempted. And you,
Priscilla, are quite tempting indeed."

"I never—" She cleared her throat, though her
voice still came out huskier than normal. "I never
thought of myself that way."

"That's part of what is so fascinating about you.
Here you are with the body of a goddess, yet the

innocence of a virgin. An irresistible lure to any man with blood in his veins."

"Is that how you feel?" She squeezed her eyes shut as she realized what she had blurted out.

"Haven't I just told you so? Or perhaps you don't believe me." He stood up, his chair scraping backward across the wooden floor. "Here. Undeniable proof." He pressed her hand against his groin.

She nearly snatched it away again. His rod was big all right, bigger than Edward's, it seemed. How could this possibly work? Yet even as she contemplated snatching back her hand, her fingers seemed to move on their own, stroking with curiosity over the turgid flesh straining against the cloth of his trousers.

He let out a breath on a hiss and closed his eyes. "Priscilla, you are going to make me embarrass myself if you keep doing that." He took her hand by the wrist and took a step backward.

"I am sorry. I do not know what came over me!" She snatched her hand back.

"You did nothing wrong, love. When a man goes a long time without bedding a woman, his control falters."

"Do not call me your love, Samuel." When he met her gaze with surprise in his, she held it fast, needing to emphasize the seriousness of what she was saying. "Never call me your love unless you mean it."

"Very well. May I call you sweetheart?"

"You may."

"What about darling?" She nodded. "Sweetness?" Again she nodded. "So anything but love."

"Not unless you truly mean it."

"All right." He rubbed a hand over the back of his neck, his brows furrowed as if he were puzzled.

"So you have been too long without bedding a woman?" she asked.

He gave a short laugh. "Sweetheart, I was nearly two years alone on an island."

"I would have thought that after you were rescued—"

"No. I've never had a taste for whores, and I considered myself betrothed. I thought I would wait."

"That is unusual for a man, is it not?"

"Not for me. I like to feel something for my partner, even if it's just respect. Frankly no woman has really tempted me since I came back, until you."

The breath left her lungs. "Oh."

"Have I offended you? That wasn't my intention."

"No, no. It's just that . . . well, to be the first woman you have . . . well, two years . . ." She bit her lip. "I have never been very good at intimacy. What if I disappoint you?"

He chuckled. "You won't."

"You do not know that."

"Actually I do." He paused. "After our encounter at the inn, I was incredibly aroused. Hard as a rock."

Her mouth fell open at his candor. "What . . . How does a man . . . Oh, I do not even know what I am asking."

"A man can take care of these things. But it's not the same thing as having a woman."

"I see." She didn't, but she figured he would explain at some point.

"You get my blood hot, Priscilla, with that combination of siren's body and angel's face. If you're really not hungry, I'd like to take you to the bedchamber and start teaching you what you came here to learn."

"Now?"

"Right now,"

"But John will not be back for hours. What will we do afterwards?"

A slow grin spread across his face that hinted at a secret she did not share. "It's going to take more than one lesson."

"More than one time?"

"More than one time, more than one afternoon."

"Heavens!"

"I'm leaving it in your hands, Priscilla. We can eat first if you want to wait, or you can come with me now to the bedchamber."

She eyed her wineglass, the loaf of bread, the savory stew simmering on the hearth. "You had best take the stew off the fire."

"Done." He swung the arm that held the stew pot so the food no longer hung over the flames.

Cilla stood and smoothed her skirts. She could hardly believe she was doing this, but she wanted to know. She wanted to see and hear and taste and feel everything she had missed over the years of her marriage. She held out her hand to him. "You will need to show me what to do."

He took her hand and led her away from the table toward the tiny hallway at the rear of the cottage. "I will. Have no fear."

"I do not want to disappoint you." She stopped so he would look at her. "If I am not pleasing you, you must tell me at once."

"Stop worrying." He cupped her face in his palm and pressed a kiss to her mouth.

Her body remembered him. Heat flooded her limbs as he nibbled at her, tangling his tongue with hers. Her knees softened into pudding, and she tightened her grip around their entwined fingers. He gave a low groan, dropped her hand, and deepened the kiss, dragging her full against him as he devoured her mouth.

Sweet God in heaven! Her body exploded with sensation, and she could only cling to him as he worked his magic on her. One of his hands clenched in her skirts and the other gripped her back, fingers clenching and unclenching. He fell backward against the wall of the hallway, taking her with him, and ripped his mouth from hers, leaning his head back as he sucked in great gulps of air.

"We need to slow down," he said in between harsh breaths. "I'm too hungry and you're too innocent. We need to take this more slowly."

Her entire body vibrated like a plucked harp string. She stared up at him, distracted by the sun-darkened flesh of his throat. When had she ever seen a man's throat so exposed before? It was because he wasn't wearing a neck cloth, that was it. He was half naked. That expanse of male flesh beckoned her, and she leaned up to touch her tongue to it.

"Christ in heaven." He grabbed her by the shoulders and moved her away, though he did not let her go. "I thought you said you were inexperienced."

"I'm sorry. I don't know what came over me."

"So you didn't mean to . . . God help us both." He closed his eyes. "We may just burn each other up once I finally get you naked."

"Get *me* naked?" She had no idea where this strange playfulness came from, but it seemed right. Felt right. "What about you?"

He opened his eyes. There was a gleam there that made her nervous and excited all at once. "Saucy, aren't you?"

She should back down, not play with a fire she didn't know how to handle. But . . . "Perhaps."

He laughed, full and hearty. "Oh, sweetheart, this is going to be fun. Hurry." He grabbed her hand and sprinted the last few feet of the hallway, dragging her behind him into the bedchamber.

A large bed dominated the room. A looking glass stood in the corner to her left, and a simple bureau with a washbasin and pitcher caught her eye on the right side of the bed. She halted in the doorway, a glimmer of uncertainty piercing her arousal. But as usual, he seemed to know what was wrong even if she didn't.

"Honesty, right, Priscilla?"

She tore her gaze from the bed to look at him. "Yes."

"You are certain you want to do this?"

She hesitated only a beat. "Yes."

"Do you trust me to guide you?"

"Yes." No hesitation there.

"All right. The first thing we need to do is to start getting you out of those clothes."

"Just me?" She laid a hand over her bosom as if to prevent him from ripping the garments from her.

He grinned. "Your clothes take a lot longer, sweetheart. I promise, I won't rush you or do anything you don't like."

"All right."

"Turn around. I'll play lady's maid."

She slowly turned around and immediately felt him plucking at the long line of buttons down her back. She kept her arms crossed in front of her, uncertain what she should be doing. Then his lips brushed the back of her neck. Her eyes slid closed and a low moan escaped her lips as he continued to trail kisses down her spine with each button he unfastened. Her arms uncrossed to hang limply at her sides.

"Your skin looks like fresh cream." The top of her dress loosened, and she allowed him to tug it down her arms and off, leaving the top hanging at her waist. "Look at how beautiful you are."

She opened her eyes and realized she was facing the mirror in the corner. Her dress bunched at her hips, held suspended by her petticoat. Her shoulders, her arms, and a good part of her bosom were revealed by the simple white chemise and corset that she wore beneath her clothing. He loomed behind her—so much taller, so much bigger. He reached around and cupped her breast as she watched, his large, sun-browned hand nearly encompassing the soft globe.

"Do you see what I see? Tempting, like a delicious cake in the bakery window." He bent and kissed the side of her neck, gently fondling her breast through the incredibly thin cotton. "I see you like this, and I want to kiss you everywhere. I want to see more, touch all of you."

"Yes." Was that her reflection, that sultry-looking woman with her eyes half closed and a blush on her cheeks?

He used one finger to tug one edge of her chemise down her arm. His expression fascinated her, like a man intent on a very important mission. He stopped just before baring her completely and traced his finger along the tops of her breasts. "So soft. I want to take my time. Or at least as much time as I can stand."

"If it is painful for you, we can—"

"No, not painful," he interrupted. "Not yet." He met her gaze in the mirror. "I want you ready for me, Priscilla. So ready that when I slide inside you, it will be maddening for both of us."

She clasped her hand over his. "I want to please you. Please tell me what to do."

"Bare yourself for me." He removed his hand from her breast. "I want to watch you uncover your beauty for me."

She tried to hold his gaze in the mirror, but when she reached for the top of her chemise, she couldn't help but drop her eyes in modesty. Without unfastening her corset, she tugged the front of the chemise down as much as she could so her breasts were completely exposed to him.

"That is true beauty." He cupped both of her breasts in his hands, rubbing the nipples with his thumbs. "Look at yourself, Priscilla. You are so beautiful."

She glanced at the mirror. The intensity in the way he looked at her made her entire body come to attention. Her skin felt that much more sensitive. The scent of him—somewhere between soap and outdoors—made her heady. The sight of his dark hand on her pale flesh excited her more than she had ever dreamed. Wet heat bloomed between her legs.

"This is what it should be like, always," he murmured, nibbling along her shoulder as he continued to gently fondle her breasts. "This hunger growing inside you. Do you feel it? Does your mouth water for the taste of my kiss?"

"Yes." His words seduced as much as his hands.

"Do you want my mouth here?" He pinched her nipples. The unique pleasure-pain had her gasping.

"Yes. Please."

"And what about here?" He slid one hand down her waist, under the dangling top of her dress, to press between her legs. She leaned back against him, her knees losing all strength.

"Yes."

"I want you naked, Priscilla."

"Yes."

"I want you to welcome me into your body."

"Yes."

"I want you to forget about everything you thought

you knew about men and women." He nibbled a trail along her neck, then met her gaze in the mirror. "Trust me to take care of you."

She nodded, nearly incapable of words.

"Unfasten your corset. I will get this dress off you. I want to feel *you* against me, not twenty petticoats."

"I have only one." Obediently she began to unclip the fastenings on the front of her corset.

"Even one is too many." The dress loosened around her hips, and he tugged it down. Her petticoat followed. "Step forward."

She obeyed, stepping out of her dress and petticoat as she managed to unclasp the last fastening of her corset. The stiff undergarment came off in her hands, leaving her clad only in chemise, drawers, and stockings.

"I'll take that." He flung it away, then turned her around and brought her close for a hot, openmouthed kiss that sent her mind spinning. Her naked breasts rubbed against his cotton shirt, and even the soft material stimulated her sensitized flesh to a near unbearable peak. Now that the layers of clothing were all but gone, she could feel his hardness stiff against her stomach. Instead of being frightened, she pressed closer.

He made a growling noise in his throat and clasped both hands on her bottom, grinding against her. She clung to his shoulders, uncertain yet willing to be led where he would take her.

He ripped his mouth away. "I need you, Priscilla."

"Yes," she replied, then gasped as he reached

down and dragged her chemise over her head. The garment caught on her hair, but he tugged it loose. A pin went flying.

The plink of it hitting the floor caught his attention. "Let down your hair. You refused me at the inn. Let me see it now." He rested his forehead against hers, pulling her close against him. "Please, Priscilla."

She could not resist his plea. She reached up to pull the pins from her hair. The movement thrust her breasts forward, and he bent to take one nipple into his mouth. The damp scrape of his tongue against her tight nipple incited a little moan from her throat. Blindly she jerked at the hairpins, dropping them to the floor as quickly as she yanked them free. Her dark hair tumbled in long, curling hanks around her shoulders.

He let her nipple slide slowly from his mouth, licking it one last time before straightening and thrusting his hands into her loosened hair to hold her head while he kissed her.

Her body vibrated with strange, compelling sensations; dark, sensual emotions that she did not understand but instinctively craved. His blatantly sexual kiss, the touch of his tongue and teeth, his greedy hands that seemed to explore all of her at once—it all drove this demanding, irresistible need to a higher pitch.

He broke the kiss. "I cannot wait any longer. Forgive me, Priscilla, for not taking more time." He yanked at the fastenings of his shirt, then leaned forward and gave her another quick kiss. "I promise that next time I will have more control."

She tried to help him remove his shirt, but he stopped.

"No, don't. I don't have much control left at all. Ah, hell." He stripped the shirt off and threw it on the floor, then curled his arm around her waist and pulled her against him. Bare flesh met bare flesh. He rubbed her against him, the hair on his chest grazing her sensitive breasts with delicious friction. He kissed her again and slid his hand between her legs, through the slit in her drawers, and slipped one finger inside her.

She jerked, breaking the kiss, and grabbed his shoulders as her breath shuddered from between her lips.

"God, you're so ready for me." He closed his eyes, resting his forehead against hers again, teasing her damp, swelling loins with his fingers. "One more minute of this and it will be too late for me." With evident reluctance, he pulled his hand free. "Take off your drawers, Priscilla, and lie on the bed."

Arousal vibrated through her at the rough command. She slid the drawers off and dropped them on the floor, leaving her still clad in her stockings, garters, and shoes. She bent over to unfasten her shoes.

He stroked a hand over her head. "You have no idea how arousing that position is, sweetheart. But that is for another time. Leave the bloody shoes on and go lie on the bed."

She straightened and sent him a puzzled look.

He took her chin in his hand and stroked his thumb over her lip. "Please."

She went to the bed and lay down on it, a quick dart of guilt shooting through her at the thought of placing her shoes on the clean coverlet.

He began to unfasten his trousers. "Spread your legs. Don't be shy, sweetheart. I think you're beautiful."

Hesitantly she opened her legs, blushing at the lewd display she must be providing him. But he never took his eyes from her as he discarded the rest of his garments and then approached the bed. His rod rose proudly from the nest of hair between his thighs, stiff and much, much bigger than she had expected.

He knelt on the bed between her legs, pausing a moment to nudge her knees into a bent position that seemed to open her up even more, then shifted and settled with his hardness pressing against the core of her. "Easy, sweetheart," he murmured, then pushed inside her.

She had expected pain, not this hot, wild stretching. His eyes closed, and he groaned, then he grabbed her by the hips and held her fast as he plunged inside her to the hilt.

She arched her hips instinctively, allowing him to set the pace as he began to move. She could barely think, could only feel. This was different, she thought briefly. This was good. Then thought spun away on a tidal wave of emotion.

His muscled body surrounded her, pressing her into the mattress as he drove them higher with strong, urgent thrusts. She clutched his shoulders, torn from within her small, safe world to ride on the wind with him. His eyes were closed, his face a rictus of concentration. She watched him, the only stable force in her world at that moment.

Suddenly he stiffened and cried out. He slipped from inside her and grabbed himself, shuddering as he spilled his seed on her belly.

Protecting her, she realized.

He opened his eyes, his rod still in his hand. "I'm sorry, sweetheart. I couldn't wait for you."

She smiled. "It was lovely, Samuel."

He barked a laugh. "Lovely? We're nowhere near finished, darling. Don't move, and I will show you."

Chapter 14

She lay where he left her as he got off the bed and went in search of a cloth. Between her naïve ignorance about sex and her sinful-looking body, he was amazed he had lasted as long as he had. His climax had come harder and faster than he had anticipated. Hell of a teacher he was.

He found the towel beside the washbasin and wiped his cock, then turned back to her. She lay where he'd left her, his semen gleaming on her belly. A primal surge of satisfaction surged through him. She looked incredible, naked in his bed with his claim upon her.

But they weren't finished, not by a long shot.

He joined her on the bed and wiped up the fluid on her belly. She watched him with those huge dark eyes, patience and curiosity evident on her face. He set the towel aside and bent to kiss her lips. "Your turn now, love."

The word slipped out before he realized it. Even as she frowned, he slipped his hand between her legs and began stroking her. He could tell she was close. Her juices flowed over his fingers, her flesh swollen and warm. He teased her clitoris, watching the awareness and surprise flicker across her face. It didn't take long; if he'd been able to resist her for just a few more minutes, he would have seen to it she finished before he did. But there was time for that. They'd barely begun. And there was something to be said for having taken the edge off his appetite so he could enjoy the pure shock that rippled across her face as she climaxed.

She arched her hips and let out a long, low moan, her eyes drifting closed as her loins exploded in his hand.

"Good girl," he whispered, and kissed her slack lips.

When Cilla came back to herself, Samuel was stretched out beside her, his head propped on one elbow as he idly stroked his hand along her torso.

"Oh," was all she could think to say, and he burst out laughing before leaning down to kiss her.

"I hope that means you liked it." He kissed her again, nibbling on her lower lip for a moment before releasing her.

"Yes." She took a deep breath. "Is it always supposed to be like that?"

"It depends on the people involved. I try to make sure my partner enjoys herself as much as I do. It's no fun otherwise."

"I do not think all men feel the same way."

"Your husband?"

She nodded. "He was always very quick and rough."

He frowned. "A man needs to prepare a woman

for sex or else it will be uncomfortable for her."

"I believe you are correct. This was not uncomfortable for me." She reached up to stroke his face. "This was beyond wonderful. Thank you."

"Oh, sweet Priscilla." He dropped a kiss on her lips. "There's a whole world you cannot even imagine."

She gaped at him. "More than this?"

He chuckled. "Much more."

"My heavens. How does anyone do anything else once they have discovered this?"

He roared with laughter, rolling backward onto his back. "Good Lord, Cilla, you amaze me."

"Why?" She shifted up onto her elbow, amazed that she felt not the slightest bit embarrassed about lying next to him, both of them stark naked. "I am curious is all. Had I been more careful in my choice of husband, I might have discovered all this earlier."

"Well, now you know what to look for."

His voice sounded strange, and she belatedly wondered if it was *de trop* to speak of one's late husband while naked in bed with another man. Inconsiderate at the least, she decided. "You are an extraordinary lover," she murmured, and leaned down to kiss his mouth.

He caught the back of her head when she would have retreated and held her in place, deepening the kiss as her hair fell down around them. Even when he broke off the kiss, he held her where she was. "Can you take me again? I don't want to hurt you."

Excitement exploded in her belly. "I will tell you if you do."

"Agreed. Come here." He dragged her on top

of him, but her shoes banged his shins and suddenly seemed to her like a terrible hindrance in her lessons.

"Wait." Rolling back, she sat up and quickly unfastened her shoes, then threw them both over the side of the bed before lying back down again. "Now I'm ready."

The fond smile on his face made her heart melt as he pulled her on top of him once more and took her mouth in a long, slow kiss that left her dizzy. "You're going to ride me, sweetheart."

"Ride?"

"Yes. Slide yourself down on me and make yourself feel good."

"I'm not sure how." She bit her lower lip. "Though I do like the way your rod feels inside me."

He chuckled. "My rod? Hell of a term. I call it a cock, sweetheart. And I like the way it feels inside you as well."

"You will have to help me."

"Just sit up and brace yourself on my chest until you can get my—"

"Cock."

"—cock inside you. Do you know how arousing it is to hear you say that word? Not a lot of women will utter it."

"Cock. I like it. Short and to the point."

"Not too short, I hope."

"No." Following his instructions, she succeeded in lowering herself down on the rigid length of him. "Not short at all."

"Glad to hear it." He guided her with his hands

on her hips, showing her the rhythm he wanted.

She picked it up quickly, bracing her hands on his chest so she could retain more control over her movements. Being on the top was an unusual experience. She experimented a little bit: slowly versus quickly, easing backward so he went a bit deeper, grinding forward so he rubbed against that spot between her legs that had brought the explosion of pleasure. Each time she altered her movements, his expression changed or he would utter a sound that she took to be approval. She rapidly learned which pace pleased him the most.

He reached up to play with her breasts, and his thumbs rubbing against her nipples started a fire burning in her loins that nearly distracted her from what she was doing. She began to work her hips in a way that made his rod . . . cock . . . rub against her center of pleasure. His whispers of praise encouraged her. She forgot about everything but feeding the growing hunger, building it into a demand that could not be resisted. It exploded inside her, making her arch her back, her cry nearly a scream, before she collapsed on top of him.

She came back to herself moments later. He was whispering to her, kissing her forehead, running his hands in soothing strokes down her back.

"Oh," she murmured, and he laughed, the sound echoing in his chest pressed against her ear.

"Is that what you will always say when you reach your climax?" he asked, amusement still heavy in his voice.

She glanced up at him but couldn't see much past

his chin, and the lethargy of utter satisfaction kept her from lifting her head. "I suppose so."

Moments passed while he stroked her hair. His heart beat in steady rhythm beneath her ear. Warm in his embrace, she nearly dozed. Then he gently disengaged their bodies and eased her to the side.

She startled back to full consciousness. "What . . . ?"

"Hush, it's all right." He kissed the top of her head. "You can sleep if you want."

She lifted her head to look first at his groin, then at his face. "You did not . . . what's the word? Climax?"

"No. I nearly did because watching you explode like that was too captivating for words. But I don't want to get you with child, and the best way to avoid that for now is to not spill my seed in you."

"I certainly appreciate that. Though it seems unfair that I took my pleasure but you did not get yours."

He chuckled. "That is easily remedied, sweetheart. I'm very close, so if you will help me, the score will be even once more."

She eyed his erection. "How?"

"Just take your hand like this . . ." He guided her fingers around his shaft. "And stroke it like this."

She ran her fingers up and down as he had shown her. "Like this?"

He let out a hiss of pleasure and closed his eyes. "Just like that."

"You must tell me if I do it wrong." Curious now, she stroked him, watching his flesh respond, listening to his whispers of encouragement that quickly gave way to mutters of barely intelligible words. Beneath her fascinated gaze, his cock hardened even more, responding to her slightest touch. Then he closed his hand over hers, jerking once, twice. A long, low moan escaped him as he arched his hips and his seed exploded out of him, splattering over her hand, his chest, and his belly. His hand stilled, and she went to stroke him again, but his grip tightened, halting her.

"No," he muttered.

She would have to ask him to explain that later, she thought as she looked at his now peaceful features. But she had to admit that it had been an education watching him reach his climax. Was that how she looked?

She took her hand away, and he opened his eyes. "There should be a towel on the bed somewhere."

She glanced around and found it amid the sheets, then wiped off her hand and turned her attention to him, gently cleaning off his belly and chest. When she was finished, she got up from the bed and set the towel on the bureau, then opened the top drawer and found more towels. She poured some water from the pitcher into the basin and washed her hands, drying them with the clean towel.

She turned back toward the bed. A flash of movement caught her eye, and she glanced over, then stood stock-still, arrested by the sight of herself in the mirror across the room.

She looked like the veriest wanton. She was stark naked except for her stockings and garters. Her hair was tangled about her shoulders and her lips were slightly swollen from his kisses. A gentle flush lingered in her face.

She looked soft and relaxed and extremely satisfied.

"You look incredibly wicked, Priscilla," Samuel said. When she glanced at him, his lazy smile of approval warmed her from top to toes.

"I cannot believe I made love with my shoes on the first time."

"Can you not?" he teased.

The smile spread across her lips before she could help it. "I suppose I forgot about them quickly enough."

"I suppose you did." He gave a great sigh and stretched, his lithe body rippling with muscle like some kind of jungle cat. "If you are finished with me for now, my lusty wench, I find that I am starving. Do you suppose we might salvage the stew?"

She propped her hand on her hip, that strange playfulness sweeping over her once again. When had she become such a flirt? "So now that I have eased your lusts, sir, you are demanding I cook for you as well?"

"You haven't eased my lusts completely." The flash of desire in his eyes made her breath catch in her throat. "That was only the beginning. And I'm a passable cook myself, so don't assume that just because you are the woman that you will be forced to prepare the meals."

"That's a woman's usual role, isn't it?"

"Perhaps." His wicked grin spurred heat back into her cheeks. "But there's another 'usual woman's role'

I have in mind for you, and I prefer you save your energies for that."

"Samuel!" She picked up her chemise from the floor.

"Oh, no." He jumped off the bed and took the garment from her hand. "No clothing for you, my lovely."

"But I thought we were going to eat?"

"You don't need clothes for that." He took her by the hand and turned toward the door.

She dug in her heels. "I cannot sit at the dinner table naked!"

"You're not naked. You're wearing your stockings."

"You know what I mean."

"Why the shyness? Who's going to see you besides me?"

Well—" She stopped herself, realizing he was right. "There are no servants here, are there?"

"No." He lifted his hand to her lips and brushed a kiss against her fingers.

"And John will not return in the middle of dinner?"

"No." He tugged her close and dropped a kiss on her mouth. "He knows better."

"Thank heavens for that." Her blush burned her face from forehead to throat.

"Now, don't be embarrassed."

"I cannot help it."

"That's something we can work on." He squeezed her fingers. "You must not be ashamed of your body, Priscilla. You're beautiful."

"No one has seen me without at least my shift since I was a babe."

"Not even your husband?"

"Especially not him." She shook her head. "I always wore my nightdress."

"Oh, sweetheart, no wonder you came to me." Samuel pulled her into his arms. "Don't you like it?" he murmured. "How our bodies fit together?"

"Yes." Her whisper came so softly she barely heard it herself. "Does that make me a whore?"

"Good God, no!" He pulled back enough to look into her eyes. "There is a vast difference between a passionate woman who simply enjoys sex and a woman who sells it for money. There's no shame in liking what we do together, sweetheart."

She bit her lip, doubt and guilt nipping at the memory of the pleasure he had brought her. "I will try to remember that."

He let out a sigh. "You, my dear Priscilla, are thinking too much. I can see it is time for another lesson." He went back to the bed and sat on the edge of the mattress. "I would like you to take off your stockings."

"But—"

"And do it slowly. A man likes to watch a woman disrobe for him." His steady gaze brooked no argument.

"All right." She bent over to unfasten one garter.

"No, not like that. Turn sideways so I can see more of you than the top of your head. In fact, prop your foot on the bed just here and slowly roll off your stocking."

She propped her hands on her hips. "I am not a performing animal, Captain!"

"No, you're a beautiful woman who can seduce me with the simple act of removing your stockings."

She blinked at him. "I can?"

"Of course. Men like to look at naked women. And you peeling off any of your clothing for me . . . well, it's damned arousing."

His passionate words stoked the fire still simmering within her, and she realized she was curious. Was that true? Did a woman have some kind of power over a man where the mere baring of flesh could affect him so strongly?

He chuckled. "I see that sly gleam in your eyes, sweetheart. Go ahead. Indulge yourself. Drive me mad with desire."

She came over to the bed and propped her foot up on the edge of the mattress just inches from his hip. His gaze skimmed along her stocking-clad limb, then dropped lower between her legs before he looked away. But that brief glance had seared like a touch. Her blood warmed and embarrassment faded. She unfastened the garter and slowly slid it down her leg.

He followed it with his eyes. She tugged it off and dangled it from her finger like a prize she had won before boldly dropping it on the floor. He grinned, but the expression faded to something much more intent as she began to peel off the stocking.

His cock stirred, fascinating her as it grew harder of its own volition. She had never witnessed the process before and could not tear her eyes away.

Her absorption both aroused and embarrassed her. When she had completely removed the stocking, she teasingly draped it across his lap, covering the proof of his interest. Then she switched legs, resting the other foot on the bed.

In this position she was much more open to him. He reached out and fondled one of her breasts as she removed the garter and worked the stocking down her leg. Then he dipped his hand lower to stroke between her thighs. She let out a squeak of surprise and almost fell over. He grabbed her by the waist and steadied her. They remained that way for a long moment, staring into each other's eyes.

"I think we'd better eat," he said finally, tugging off her stocking the rest of the way. "I have a feeling I will need my strength later." He tossed both discarded stockings on the bed, then ran his hand down her calf.

"I think I might need my strength, too," she murmured. "Heaven help me."

He laughed at that, then stood. "I suppose we had best see if we can salvage the stew."

Slowly she lowered her leg, a bit dazed by his utter lack of embarrassment about walking about naked, especially with his arousal so exposed. And a bit astonished at herself and the ease with which she had accepted this introduction to the world of sensuality.

She didn't dare think too much about the things that had happened in this bedchamber, or about the fact that she so docilely allowed him to lead her bare as the day she was born into the main room of the cottage, where dinner still awaited them.

He went to the hearth and swung the stew pot back over the fire. "Just a few moments to heat this, I think."

She winced. "Be careful, Samuel." She waved a hand at his groin. "You do not want to get burned."

"I think we both already did." Grinning, he came over and kissed her mouth, then reached for the wine bottle. "I think it's safe to have a bit of this now, don't you think?"

"My head is already spinning. I think I might prefer tea."

"You just want me to go back to the fire," he teased.

"No! That is . . . oh, bother." She clasped her hands over her warming cheeks. "Will I never have the upper hand with you, Samuel Breedlove?"

"Is that what you want?" He moved to his own seat and poured himself a glass of wine. "To be in control?"

"I do not know. I am confused and embarrassed and oh, so many things."

"Did you like being with me, Cilla?"

She looked up in surprise. "Of course."

"Did you enjoy what we did together?"

"Yes, heaven help me."

"There's nothing to be embarrassed about. You're a young, passionate woman and I am a healthy man. What happened in there was perfectly natural. We did not harm anyone."

"I suppose you are right."

He went to stir the stew, then looked back over his shoulder toward her. "Are you pleased with our bargain so far?"

"I was not certain what to expect, but I have no complaints."

"Good." He seemed as if he would say something else, but then he turned his attention back to their meal.

She indulged herself with a leisurely study of his muscled back and buttocks, even as she wondered what he had intended to say, but hadn't. She thought about bringing up the subject of when their relationship would end, but decided she did not want to spoil the moment. "Are *you* pleased with the bargain?"

He tasted the stew, then took the pot off the fire. "More than pleased. I have wanted you almost from the very first moment I saw you."

A thrill shot through her, and she tried to maintain a calm demeanor. "A very romantic statement from a man who claims he is not capable of love."

"Because I have never felt the way the poems and songs say I should. If the state of love exists, I remain unconvinced." He scooped stew into her bowl.

"Why, Samuel? You seem to like women well enough. That is, you do not strike me as a man who hates females and thinks they are beneath him."

He flashed her a wicked grin. "Not that I have any objection to females beneath me, you understand . . ."

"Samuel!"

". . . but no, I do not think women are inferior.

Weaker than men, physically that is, and more emotional, which in itself can be considered weakness by some."

"By you?"

He shrugged and ladled some of the steaming fare into his own bowl, then turned and set the pot near the hearth. "I certainly understand the drive of passion. The bond of loyalty. The warmth of friendship. I simply don't see the need to romanticize every relationship the way women do."

"So then where does marriage fit into your world?" She reached for the wine bottle, but he grabbed it first and poured her a glass.

"Marriage is a partnership. A man and woman decide to spend their lives together as partners. They take risks together, raise children together, grow old together. I can like and respect a wife and even lust after her without being in love with her."

"You have never known real love, have you?" She traced the stem of her wineglass as she contemplated his face. "How very sad."

"I had the Baileys. I thought that was real." He sat down and reached for his napkin to spread on his naked lap. "As I recall, Mrs. Burke, you cannot claim a grand romance yourself."

"No, but I believed I had." She dipped her spoon into the stew, rather astonished at how easily she had accepted dining naked. "Edward said all the right things and made me think he loved me. He could not have done that if I had not believed in a love that lasts forever."

"You still believe that, don't you? In an everlasting

love? Despite that nonsense you tried to tell me at the inn?"

"Yes," she admitted, and kept her eyes on her meal, not wanting to see the derision or, God help her, pity in his eyes.

"Then why do you need me? If all you want is romance?"

She risked a glance at him. No pity. No derision. Just curiosity. "Because clearly I cannot trust my own judgment when it comes to understanding the male of the species. I was young and naïve when I met Edward, and I knew nothing of men and women other than what I had learned from my parents."

"Which was?"

"That a man and woman can be happy in a marriage. It is not easy being married to a naval man. My mother had to become strong to manage everything while he was away at sea. When he came home, she knew he did not want to hear about any troubles that had occurred while he was gone. He wanted to bask in the love of his family. We wanted that, too." She smiled, bittersweet memories coming to the fore. "Mama always played the stalwart seaman's wife, able to tackle any problem, able to keep her emotions under control when it came time for him to leave again. He knew that under that serene expression she was already mourning him, but it served both of them to pretend."

"How did he know she was pretending?"

She glanced up at the strange note in his voice. A stillness had come over him that brought a hint of concern, but the glint of warning she saw in his eyes told her he did not want her to pry. Like her mother, she carried on as if nothing were amiss. "Papa always whispered in my ear to take care of Mama because she was not as strong as she thought she was. He always knew."

"So you have used your parents' marriage as a model for what you hope to achieve."

"I think most people look to their parents as a model for what they should be as adults. Even you, I would expect."

"No, not me." He began to eat his stew.

She waited, but he did not elaborate. "Why not?"

"I told you, my mother never married. But there were men in her life."

The edge in his voice told her this was a sore subject, but her curiosity about the man with whom she had just shared her body made her probe deeper. "Men? Like . . ."

"Men. Lovers. She had a child to provide for, and this was all she knew."

"Oh, Samuel."

"Some of them were all right. They tolerated me, brought me sweets. One of them taught me how to whittle."

"Thank heavens for that."

"But not all of them were like that. Some saw me as an inconvenience. Those didn't usually last long. For all that she needed the money they gave her, she didn't want to see me mistreated. But she always cried so much after they left." He curled his lip. "Because she was *in love*."

"I see now why you do not seek love for yourself." Cilla reached for a slice of bread and tore it in half.

"Is that right?"

"Of course. For the same reason I did not seek another husband. Edward had ruined the fairy tale for me."

"So you're saying my mother ruined my fairy tale?" He gave a harsh laugh. "My dear lady, clearly you have no concept of the misery of growing up a bastard."

"Of course I do."

"Bollocks to that. You know who your parents are. I bet you could name your ancestors all the way back to the Conqueror."

"Good Lord, yes." She rolled her eyes. "My father keeps the family Bible on a table in his study. When we were small, he used to lecture Genny and me about the great deeds of our forefathers. I believe he was terribly disappointed neither of us had been born a son."

"Then how can you think you know what it is like to be born a bastard?"

"Because you and I are the same, I think."

"Oh, really." He leaned back in his chair and folded his arms. "How so?"

"I know what it feels like to be looked down upon by others. After Edward died, I had to make my own way. He left me penniless, nearly starving. I even had to beg for food once or twice. All I could think about was coming back here. Back home." She let out a derisive laugh. "Here in England, my choice of husband is looked upon as a liability. 'Poor Cilla, married to a scoundrel without a sou to his name. Whatever will become of her?' "

"His misdeeds were not yours. You simply married the wrong man."

"I *chose* the wrong man. You did not choose to be born out of wedlock. I admit I am partly to blame for my misery of a marriage. But you had no choice at all."

"Tell that to the fellows who thought it would be fun to dunk the little bastard's head in the horse trough."

She winced. "I would have assumed your mother would have told you something about your father. His name at least."

"Well, she didn't. Maybe he was such a sorry piece of scum that she thought it would make matters worse." He finished off his glass of wine and reached for the bottle again.

Cilla touched his arm. "I apologize if I overstepped. Shall we change the subject?"

He remained with his fingers on the bottle for a long moment while he studied her face. Then he dropped his hand. "What shall we change it to? The weather? The latest gossip?"

"Anything more cheerful than our mutual unhappy pasts." She raised her glass, then sipped her wine.

He grinned at her, and this time she could tell it was genuine. "I have an idea. After dinner, let's play a game."

Her heart fluttered in her chest at the devilish gleam in his eyes. "What kind of game?"

"Chess."

"Chess!" She laughed. "I thought you meant something much more scandalous."

"Can you play chess?"

"I can, actually. My father taught both me and Genny. Mama never liked it so Gen and I were his best opponents."

"Excellent. I look forward to our match."

Still smiling, she lifted her wineglass again. "You are certainly full of surprises, Samuel. Are you not concerned about being bested by a woman?"

"Not at all. I happen to be an excellent chess player. Many's the time I've whiled away the hours on board ship with a good game of chess."

"Then we should be well matched."

"I agree. Though I have never played naked chess before, so this should prove interesting."

She choked on a sip of wine, clasping her hand to her chest. "What?"

"Naked chess." He waggled his eyebrows. "I look forward to thinking up unusual methods to distract the opposition."

That newly discovered playful part of her came to the fore and pushed aside the proper lady. Stretching her arms above her head, she noticed with satisfaction the way his gaze dropped to her bare breasts. She gave him a smile that she hoped was inviting. "I might have a few distractions of my own."

His slow, sensual smile made her stomach flip. "I've always loved a challenge."

Chapter 15

Annabelle ducked her head down behind the bushes, shutting her journal as the footsteps drew closer. She did not want to see anyone. Sometimes she liked to be alone, to scribble her thoughts in the book her mother had given her when they'd first learned of Samuel's disappearance. Her mama had hoped that writing down her feelings would help with the pain. And it had, at least at first. But then her thoughts had taken on a life of their own, and now she craved isolation whenever she wrote down the fancies her imagination created.

This corner of the garden had proven to be the perfect place. The small grotto was hidden from the walkway by the tall hedges, and all it contained was the stone bench on which she sat. Sometimes the servants passed by on their way to fetch flowers for the dinner table. When that happened, she stayed very still and quiet, hoping whoever was out there would pass by, ignorant of her presence.

This evening, footsteps along the path and the

hushed murmur of female voices alerted her to the fact that she was not alone.

"Are you certain?" a woman hissed. Annabelle recognized the voice as belonging to Melly, the upstairs maid. She peered between the hedges and confirmed her suspicions.

"My Tom heard it at the tavern last night. 'Tis the honest truth." The other girl—a scullery maid named Gladys—marched alongside Melly. "The girl had been working at Raventhorpe Manor only two months before she bolted."

"Are you certain she bolted?" Melly stopped to examine a scraggly pink rose on a nearby bush.

"What other explanation is there? I've worked for His Lordship's family for nearly a decade. All his servants are fiercely loyal to him."

"A decade, is it? I've worked here in this village for nearly twenty years, Gladys, and I can tell you that there have been times the people around here have doubted His Lordship."

Gladys gasped. "Doubted him! How could you say such a thing?"

"Well, what do you think?" Melly snapped. "A fetching young maid has disappeared from Raventhorpe Manor. Why would any girl willingly leave a position where she lives in a fine house and makes a good wage? It's not the first time I've heard of pretty women disappearing from this area."

"I bet the tart shared his bed," Gladys said. "Got with child and tried to blackmail His Lordship into wedding her. Well, he showed her, didn't he? Probably turned her out on the street without notice."

"Then why has she not returned home? No, I don't think that's what happened at all." Melly glanced around her, then lowered her voice. "When I was a girl, we heard tales around the village. Tales about the old lord and how young women disappeared from his properties. Young pretty women, never to be seen again."

"Oh, certainly that's an old wives' tale."

"Perhaps. But strange how it's happening again now that the new earl is in residence."

"Melly, what are you saying? That His Lordship is making these girls disappear?"

"I don't know. But over the years there have been stories. Young Nell is not the first girl to vanish from the area without anyone knowing what happened to her. And I can't help but remember the stories I heard about old Lord Raventhorpe. The liking he had for young, comely girls—some of them barely old enough to be considered grown."

"Even if his father was the worst sort of lech, that doesn't mean the son has followed in his footsteps."

"No," Melly said. "I fear the son may be far worse." She let out a long sigh. "Let's check the other side of the garden. I don't think these roses have been getting enough sun."

As the servants headed off down the pathway, Annabelle turned back around on the bench. Her heart pounded. They spoke of Lord Raventhorpe—her fiancé—as if he were guilty of some terrible crime. And was he? One thing she had learned, thanks to

Mrs. Burke, was that the servants often knew more about what went on in people's houses than the home owners themselves. So what did they know about Richard?

A shiver rippled through her, and she clasped her arms around herself, fighting the growing disquiet that welled within her. She had noticed Richard's distraction of late. His short temper, his reluctance to discuss their future married life. And now all this talk of young women disappearing from the village. The notion that Richard might be responsible for the rumored disappearances was simply ridiculous. He thought way too much of his title and his position in society to endanger them with anything underhanded or illegal. She was certain he had nothing to do with the young women vanishing. Most probably they had run off for their own reasons, and the speculation among the servants was simply that—unfounded theories based on gossip and hearsay. Everyone loved a good story.

Nonetheless, the chatter had done nothing to quell her own growing unease. Lately she had gotten the distinct feeling that Richard's regard for her was dwindling, even though he kept talking of moving up the wedding date. Her mother would not allow any such thing, of course, fearing speculation about the *necessity* of a speedy wedding, but still Richard continued to suggest that they might want to change their wedding date, which was two weeks from now, and get married earlier. His impatience would have thrilled her had she believed its cause to be his great passion for her, but she knew it was not. Therefore she could only determine that his eagerness came from his urgent need for funds.

She knew he was marrying her for her fortune. Country girl she might be, but that didn't mean she was completely oblivious to the way the world worked. But was it so terrible to expect your future husband to at least *like* you before you joined your lives together?

Darn it, why couldn't he just ask her for the money and do away with all this tension?

She bit her lip as she considered the question. Arrogance came to mind. Or did he think her so conceited that she would not wed him if she knew how badly he needed her dowry? Didn't he realize that she would stand by her husband, no matter what? Or maybe he just thought she was one of those fluff-brained women who didn't think of anything else but fashion and hairstyles?

The idea that he might think her a fool stung her pride. Back in America, plenty of men had assumed that a pretty face and kind heart meant an empty head. Samuel had never made that assumption, which was one of the reasons she had accepted his marriage proposal. She was not a china doll who would smile adoringly when her husband deigned to pay attention to her. She intended to be a partner to the man she married, just as her mama had always been to her pa. She was a hardy American girl, the daughter of people who wrested their living from the bare soil of the earth. If Richard thought she would easily turn her back on her own nature, he had another think coming.

She jerked to her feet, sending her journal tumbling to the ground. She scooped it up, then began to march back toward the house. Perhaps she had been too hasty in rejecting Samuel when he'd returned. While she still wanted the social prestige that came with marrying an earl, she could not deny that she wanted to be happy, too. And how could she be happy with a man who had so many shadows in his past? A man who refused to confide in her, yet expected her to vow herself into his keeping for all time?

Samuel had always been honest with her, even when the truth had not been pleasant to hear. Yes, he had disappeared for two years, then returned with a crazy story about Richard trying to kill him. She had been angry at Samuel for being gone—irrational, to be sure, and that anger and hurt had only made her more determined to marry Richard when Samuel had reappeared.

She realized now the childishness of her reasoning. She still wanted to achieve social prestige so her mama could have the fancy New York social life she craved, but did she want that at the cost of marrying a man who could not share his secrets with her? What if Richard really had tried to kill Samuel? Then again, what if Samuel had raised all these questions out of simple competition? She didn't think it was out of jealousy. Samuel had never professed his love for her. Not once. Then again, neither had Richard.

Did either man love her, even a little?

She shook her head, dizzy from all the questions flying around her mind. Samuel's claims about Richard. Richard's claims about Samuel. The maids speculating about the disappearing women. Her doubts about Samuel's motives. Her own instincts that were telling her something was wrong in her relationship with her betrothed.

She stopped just outside the door to the house and covered her face with her hand. She needed to regain control of herself before she went inside. Her mother had a nearly supernatural instinct to realize when her daughter was distressed, and Annabelle did not want to answer any probing questions until she had recovered her equilibrium. She needed advice, but she wanted to avoid her mother's emotional reactions to bad news.

Perhaps Mrs. Burke could help her.

Relief washed over her. Mrs. Burke was a widow, and she knew all the parties involved. Surely she would have some words of wisdom as to what the next step should be. She was the only one, other than Mama, who would be able to help Annabelle decide if she had chosen the right husband.

Some of the worry receded, and she opened the door.

All these years, she had been living only half a life.

Alone in her room back at Nevarton Chase, Cilla stripped off her gloves and then slowly untied her bonnet. Every movement seemed more vivid now that she had become so much more aware of her body. Every nerve ending tingled. A delicious languor lingered in her muscles, and she found herself smiling about nothing at all.

She walked to the bureau and poured some water into the basin, then looked up to meet her own gaze in the mirror hanging there. She looked mostly the same as when she had left the house that morning, except for the new awareness lingering in her eyes. Anyone could attribute the flush on her cheeks to a harmless cause, but that knowing gleam spoke of carnal knowledge learned and enjoyed.

Perhaps if she and Samuel had not engaged in the chess game, if there had been some time between their last coupling and John's arrival, the change in her might not be so obvious. But with both of them making exaggerated attempts to distract the other, they had soon ended up on the floor beside the hearth making love again. Afterward while they had lingered in each others' arms, they had heard the coach on the road outside and had been forced to flee to the bedchamber to regain some semblance of decency before John knocked on the door.

John knew what had happened between them, of course. She had seen the flicker of it in his face before he masked it, and her cheeks burned with chagrin even now. He had acted the gentleman—so much more than a mere servant, that one—and said nothing as she and Samuel had climbed into the coach to begin the journey back to Nevarton Chase.

Samuel had held her in his arms most of the way, brushing kisses upon her temple, but as the lights of the manor appeared on the horizon, he had moved to the seat across from her.

"We will meet again on your next free afternoon,"

he had said. "Unless my plan against Raventhorpe works and the wedding is called off."

The reminder of the wedding had jolted her from the sensual daydream she had been weaving in her mind. "What do you mean?"

"I've bought all Raventhorpe's gaming markers, and he knows it. I've told him I'll demand payment if he proceeds with the wedding and forgive them if he walks away from Annabelle. Any sane man would accept the deal."

"Or he might move up the date of the wedding in the hopes that Annabelle's portion would satisfy the debt."

His sigh had echoed through the carriage even over the crunching of the wheels over the graveled drive of Nevarton Chase. "There is that. We will have to hope that he wants to rid himself of debt more than he wants an heiress as his bride."

"Which do you think he will choose?"

"My dear lady, that is anyone's guess."

A knock at her bedroom door jerked her out of her memory and back to the present. She stared wide-eyed at herself in the mirror for a moment as she collected herself, then called, "Come in."

The door eased open, and Annabelle peeked around the edge of it. "Mrs. Burke, I'm so glad you're back."

"Come in, Annabelle. I am simply freshening up before dinner." Seizing a moment for herself, Cilla splashed water on her face, then with her eyes closed she grabbed the towel by feel and dried her skin. She heard the door close, and the soft shuffle of skirts told her that Annabelle had entered the room.

"I know I shouldn't be bothering you on your free day," Annabelle said, plopping down on the edge of the bed, "but you're the only one I can talk to about this."

Cilla set the towel aside and turned to face Annabelle. "You know you can tell me anything, but I am surprised you have not gone to your mother with whatever is bothering you."

"I don't want to upset her. She's so weepy these days over the wedding and all." Annabelle traced one of the narrow black stripes on the skirt of her pretty pea green dress.

Cilla sat down in the chair by her writing desk. "Tell me what is troubling you."

"It's Richard."

"What about him?"

"I don't know if he really likes me."

The girl's plaintive whisper brought instant sympathy to the fore. Words of reassurance bubbled to her lips, but Cilla stopped them just as she remembered that she was supposed to encourage the girl to second guess her engagement to the earl, not advocate the match.

Apparently her own newly found contentment was urging her to make sure everyone else was happy as well.

"Perhaps you are misinterpreting his demeanor," she said. "Lord Raventhorpe is a member of the peerage and can be quite high in the instep."

"It's not just that. I mean, sometimes he does tend to treat me like I'm not as good as he is because I'm

American, but that's not the real problem. I know he's marrying me for my money. I just don't know if he knows that I know."

"I imagine the subject is not one you have discussed."

"No, I've been too afraid to bring it up. He thinks I'm pretty, I suppose, but I get the feeling he would marry me even if I looked like one of the plow horses in the fields as long as Pa's fortune goes with me. But is that all he thinks of me? That I am pretty and rich? Doesn't he want to know if I am smart or funny or kind or anything else a man might want in a wife?"

"You already said you believe he is wedding you for your fortune."

"I *know* he is." She lowered her voice and looked down at her hands. "I guess I just thought he would eventually fall in love with me . . . even just a little."

Sympathy washed over Cilla as she studied at the girl's bent head. She wanted to comfort her, but she also did not want Annabelle wed to a man who might harm her. "I am certain you realize that love is not something that is taken into consideration by the upper classes where marriage is concerned. Very often two people marry for other reasons that have more to do with fortunes than with hearts."

Annabelle looked up. "Your sister said much the same thing to me two nights ago at the Collingwood affair. But I thought she was simply being mean."

Curse your sharp tongue, Genny. "Perhaps she was

simply trying to help you avoid a broken heart."

"So it's true then? Richard might really feel nothing for me? Nothing at all?"

The despair edging her voice tested Cilla's determination, and her heart turned over in her chest at her young friend's fallen expression. "I am going to tell you something, Annabelle, which might disturb you."

"Oh, my heavens! What is it?" The girl clenched her hands together, blue eyes wide with anxiety.

"I have heard tell that His Lordship is deeply in debt."

Annabelle remained frozen for a long moment. "Is that it?"

"Yes. He has amassed quite a number of gaming debts, which forced him to sell this estate to your father. Marrying you will also get him enough funds to pay the men he owes."

Annabelle gave a sigh of relief. "Heavens, Mrs. Burke, I thought you were going to tell me that the earl was already married or something horrible like that."

"Debts are no laughing matter. A man who cannot stay away from the tables can bankrupt his entire family. *Your* entire family."

"Oh." Annabelle frowned. "I suppose that is a problem."

"Marrying you may be his only solution, and unfortunately it does not require that he fall in love with you."

"Like I said, I already knew he needs my money. And now that I know that he has these gambling debts, everything makes sense." She gave Cilla a smile. "At least you didn't mention that silly rumor about Richard making young girls disappear from the area."

Cilla froze. "What rumor?"

"I overheard the servants talking. Something about a girl who worked at Raventhorpe Manor disappearing. They thought that Richard might have something to do with it. Naturally it is nonsense."

Cilla wrestled with her instincts for a moment. Should she tell Annabelle what Samuel had divulged to her, or should she follow her intuition and shelter an innocent girl from a sordid truth? Protection won the battle. Rather than revealing information that might possibly shatter Annabelle's innocence forever, she would instead build on the doubts the servants had raised and convince Annabelle to jilt the earl. "Naturally such talk about one's betrothed would generate second thoughts."

"Oh, but I don't believe that crazy story," Annabelle insisted. "It's just talk. Still . . ." Her voice trailed off, and uncertainty flickered across her face.

"Doubts."

"I shouldn't feel this way," Annabelle burst out.

"Better to address your concerns now rather than after you are wed."

"Fine. Let's talk about doubts. What about Samuel's ridiculous story? Claiming that Richard tried to kill him." She shrugged as if to dismiss the charge, but Cilla heard the lack of conviction in her voice.

"Has Captain Breedlove ever lied to you?"

"No, but that was before he disappeared for two years."

"All right, allow me to play devil's advocate for a moment. Is the captain the type of man to make up wild stories to further his own ends?"

"Of course not."

"And what are your reasons for believing Lord Raventhorpe over Captain Breedlove?"

"Well, Richard's an earl."

Cilla waited, but the girl said nothing more. "That is your only reason?"

"Of course. An earl would have no reason to lie."

"Annabelle, I know America has no gentry as we do here in England, so you must take my word when I tell you that an earl can lie just as easily as any other man. Sometimes more so because their position in society will often shelter them from punishment for their misdeeds."

Annabelle frowned. "You mean Richard could commit a crime and never go to jail for it?"

"That is exactly what I am saying. If his crime is severe enough, he can be brought up on charges and be tried in the House of Lords. The other peers will decide his fate, though sometimes the accused still goes free."

"That doesn't seem very fair."

"But that is the law of England, the law that will govern the earl. Now, knowing that, is there any reason why you should believe Lord Raventhorpe over the captain?"

"Richard never abandoned me."

"And the captain has already stated he never intended to abandon you. You have admitted that Lord Raventhorpe needs money. He and the captain were in business together, yet only His Lordship returned from their voyage. What happened to the captain's share?"

"Once Samuel resigned his position, his share was divided amongst all the investors."

"Including the earl."

"Of course." Annabelle furrowed her brow. "I do not like your implications, Mrs. Burke."

"All I am saying is that *if* Lord Raventhorpe were in desperate need of funds and *if* he were the type of man who would resort to desperate action when cornered, he might indeed be tempted to do away with his enemies. What if Captain Breedlove was somehow getting in the way of Lord Raventhorpe making more money?"

"So you are saying that Samuel was trying to keep Richard from making money from the voyage, so Richard tried to kill him, then returned to America and claimed part of Samuel's share since everyone thought Samuel had deserted the ship."

"Correct. But the captain was marooned, which is why he was gone for two years with no communication. His first act upon being rescued was to come and find you."

"Oh, my." Annabelle bit her lower lip. "It sounds crazy."

"Not if you combine it with the rumor you heard from the servants."

Annabelle was silent for a long time, and Cilla began to hope she might have successfully sowed the seeds of doubt. But then the girl said, "Now allow me to be devil's advocate."

Cilla nodded.

"What if Samuel was lying to me the entire time we were courting? He never said he loved me, you know."

"Neither did Lord Raventhorpe."

"Nonetheless, Samuel courted me before I was an heiress and never told me he loved me, even when I said the words to him. Then he disappeared. Maybe not coming home was just easier than breaking our betrothal."

Cilla chuckled. "Do you really think Captain Breedlove is that dishonorable?"

"Well, there's more." She twisted her fingers together. "Richard told me that there were other women."

"What?"

"He said that whenever they would put into port, Samuel would take up with . . . well, you know. Prostitutes."

"Good God! Lord Raventhorpe talked to you about *prostitutes*? That is most ungentlemanly behavior, Annabelle, I must tell you."

"But is it true?" Annabelle picked at her skirt again. "Samuel did not love me, and I knew that. What was to stop him? When I told Pa—"

"You told your father? No wonder he was not willing to listen when the captain tried to plead his case." Cilla rubbed her suddenly throbbing forehead. "Annabelle, you have known Captain Breedlove for many years, correct?"

"Since I was five."

"And has he ever in all that time acted the slightest bit dishonorable?"

"Well, not that I ever saw. But I was just a child."

"Yet you and your family are willing to listen to Lord Raventhorpe over a man who has essentially been a member of your family for some fifteen years."

"Well, when you put it like that . . . But Lord Raventhorpe is an earl. We didn't think he'd have reason to lie. And his crew told the same story when Pa asked them."

"As I said, everyone has secrets. Let me ask you this. Had the captain not gone missing, would you have chosen to marry the earl instead if you had been given the choice?"

"Of course not," Annabelle scoffed. "Once I give my word, I keep it. That's what's so difficult about this whole situation. I gave my word to both men."

"But you gave your word to Lord Raventhorpe only when you thought the captain had abandoned you. And if that's not true, some could argue that Captain Breedlove has prior claim."

"Not if he stayed away on purpose and only came back after Pa got rich. I would never marry a man like that."

"If you distrust the captain so much, why did you agree to marry him to begin with?"

"I didn't distrust him at the time. He was so handsome and strong and made a good living at sea." A nostalgic smile crossed her lips. "Samuel used to sing to me some nights as we sat on the porch together. I don't know if he loved me, but I could tell he liked me a whole lot."

"So you would have wed him and been happy?"

"I thought so. We wanted the same things. A home, family."

"Do you want something different now?"

"Well, I told you about the ladies in New York. If I were a countess, Mama could have the society life she wants."

"Do you think she wants that more than she wants your happiness?"

Annabelle sighed. "Probably not."

"And is Samuel Breedlove the type of man to marry a woman for money?"

"I didn't think so. But . . ." Her voice trailed off.

"But we know now that the captain has a sizable fortune of his own, which means he is not a fortune hunter. If you believe that, then you must look more closely at the earl, a man you have already determined is *only* wedding you because you are an heiress. Besides, you have already said you used to trust Captain Breedlove."

"I don't know what to think anymore!" Annabelle buried her face in her hands.

Cilla went to sit beside Annabelle on the bed. Sliding a comforting arm around the girl's shoulders, she said, "You realize it is within your rights to cry off."

Annabelle turned to Cilla with uncertainty in her eyes. "Won't that cause a scandal?"

Cilla shrugged. "There will be some gossip, but it would be short-lived. The important thing is that you do what feels right to you. Marriage is forever, and you do not want to spend forever with the wrong man."

"You expected to be with your husband forever, right?"

"Of course. No bride expects otherwise." She could not control the terseness in her tone.

"I'm sorry to have brought up such sad memories. I'm sure you miss him."

Cilla hesitated, then decided that the situation deserved the truth. "Actually he was quite the bounder. Gambled, drank, and could not maintain a position of employment for any length of time. The best thing he ever did for me was make me a widow."

Annabelle's jaw dropped, and Cilla glanced away. Why had she confessed such a thing to this young girl? They were talking about Annabelle's future, not Cilla's mistakes.

"I had no idea you were unhappy," Annabelle said.

"It is the truth." Cilla gave her a small, embarrassed smile. "My marriage was not a happy one, but I plan to choose better the next time I take a husband."

"So you want to marry again?"

Cilla thought of the delights she had discovered in Samuel's bed and could not stop the small smile that crept across her lips. "I would certainly consider it."

"I always wanted to get married. To have a passel of children for Mama to spoil."

"Lord Raventhorpe would require an heir."

"For his title, right?" She shrugged one shoulder. "I just want babies and lots of 'em. Samuel wanted a bunch of children. Neither of us had any brothers or sisters."

"If you are not absolutely certain about your engagement to the earl, I would advise you to talk to your mother."

"I just don't know what to think. Richard has been acting oddly these past couple of weeks."

"Since Captain Breedlove returned."

"Yes!" Annabelle leaned forward, her face animated. "Do you think he might be jealous?"

"It is possible."

"I would never allow one man to call on me while I was engaged to another. Though Samuel did call on me, do you remember? Richard was furious, even though I didn't do anything."

"Some men are not rational about their jealousy. Even if the lady has done nothing wrong, a man might yet think the worst."

"That doesn't seem very fair."

Cilla laughed. "When a man is impassioned about something, fairness does not come into play."

"If he was jealous, at least it would mean that he felt *something* for me."

"But that, too, could be a problem. A jealous man could be a dangerous man."

She had expected Annabelle to brush aside the warning. Instead, the girl fixed her with a serious look. "I'm beginning to wonder how much I truly know about Richard."

"Then perhaps you should wait. Postpone the wedding until you make a decision."

"Postpone it! I wish I could."

"Of course you can. No one would find fault with you taking the time to consider such an important step in your life."

Annabelle chewed the inside of her lip. "Do you think so? I don't know what Richard might do if I tell him I want to wait."

"All the more reason to go to your mother. She wants you to be happy, so I imagine she would support your decision. And she could convince your papa to put off the wedding until you are more certain of your choice of husband."

"That's a wonderful idea!" Annabelle slid off the bed. "Will you come with me, Mrs. Burke? I don't want Mama to think I am just being fickle."

"Of course I will."

"If we go right now, we can talk to her before dinner. Then she can talk to Papa afterwards. He's always more cheerful after he's eaten."

"Just give me a moment to change my clothing."

"Mama's in her sewing room, so let's meet there."

"I will be along momentarily."

"Thank you, Mrs. Burke!" Annabelle gave her a quick hug, then jumped off the bed and raced from the room, closing the door behind her.

Cilla stared after her, wondering if she had done the right thing. Certainly Raventhorpe was a villain, and it was in Annabelle's best interest to postpone the wedding and reconsider marrying the earl. Why, then, did Cilla feel as if she had done something underhanded in keeping her knowledge of Raventhorpe's more nefarious deeds from Annabelle?

Confirming the girl's worst fears would have driven Annabelle away from Raventhorpe in a trice. Annabelle would have been safe, the only cost being her naïve outlook on the world. But Cilla had wanted to protect that virtue awhile longer. She knew how it felt to have one's innocence ripped away like a blindfold in bright sunlight.

A postponement of the wedding was a far cry from calling off an engagement, but it was a step in the right direction to save Annabelle. But would it be enough?

Chapter 16

Saturday morning found Samuel on the doorstep of Nevarton Chase. When the door opened, Samuel found himself face to face with Thomas the footman. The servant's eyes widened for a moment before narrowing. Samuel did not bother to stop the grin that curved his mouth. "Good morning, Thomas. I'm expected."

For a moment he thought the footman was not going to allow him entrance, but then the servant stepped backward, jerking the door open. Samuel stepped inside as the servant closed the door behind him.

"Come to see Miss Annabelle, have you?" the servant asked, bristling with nearly visible hostility.

"Actually it was Mr. Bailey who summoned me."

Surprise flashed across the footman's face before he masked it. "Wait here," he muttered, then stalked toward the hallway.

"Thomas."

The footman stopped and turned, his hands fisting at his sides. He waited.

"Glad to see the lip healed well," Samuel said.

The footman glared, then spun on his heel and marched down the hallway.

Long minutes passed as Samuel was left to cool his heels in the foyer. Two other footmen passed by, each at different times. Both stiffened and scowled as they caught sight of him, but neither of them spoke, nor did they stop in their duties. Samuel was just beginning to think the summons from Bailey was some sort of trick when he heard his name.

"Samuel." Cilla looked over the rail at him from the floor above. "Good heavens, what are you doing here?"

"I've been invited."

"Wait, I will come down." She disappeared from sight but then reappeared moments later, holding her skirts out of the way as she hurried down the stairs. Her breasts bobbed in time with her rapid descent, reminding him of how they had looked, rosy and bare, while he had made love to her in the cottage just yesterday. She reached the ground floor, her cheeks pink. Was that from exertion or from seeing him again?

Her hair was back in its familiar coil, and she brushed at the wisps that danced along her temples as she reached him. But though she was once again dressed in her conservative dark colors, he could imagine beneath the layers of buttons and petticoats the sensual creature who had eagerly embraced all the sexual arts he had taught her that afternoon in the cottage. And as she met his gaze, he could tell that she was remembering, too.

"Samuel," she murmured.

That quickly they were back in the cottage, bodies naked and straining against each other as they raced toward the pinnacle of pleasure.

"Priscilla." A spark lit her eyes as he murmured her name, and a primal urge to claim this female rose within him. What was it about this woman that made him want to carry her off and have her, consequences be damned?

"Why are you here?" she whispered. A maid passed through the foyer, reminding them they were not alone.

"Bailey sent for me."

She nodded. "Of course. I should have expected as much."

"Why is that?" He glanced around, more than aware that another servant could walk by at any moment. "Where can we talk alone?"

Her eyes widened. "That is not wise."

"The hell it's not. I need to know what's going on. Five minutes alone with me will hardly destroy your reputation." He grinned at her. "Though I take it as a compliment that you think I could do enough in five minutes to cause such scandal."

Her face flamed, but her eyes lit with a carnal interest that had never failed to arouse him in all the hours they had spent together. She turned and strode to a nearby doorway. "The dining room is through here. Mr. Bailey will be summoning you at any moment, so we must be quick about it."

"Perhaps that should be our next lesson," he murmured as he passed by her to go through the doorway. Her sharp intake of breath told him she had heard him, and he found his mind wandering down the road of dangerous possibilities as she shut the door behind them.

"Are you mad to say such things here?" She stormed past him, hugging her midriff. "Our arrangement was to remain a secret."

"And so it is. But I can't help how I respond to you . . . or how you respond to me." He moved closer to her, then trailed his fingertip along the shell of her ear. As expected, the caress made her visibly quiver. "Perhaps we should indeed use our five minutes for another lesson."

"Have you no shame?" Her voice lacked the rebuke it should have had, and he could swear he could see her nipples straining against the dark gray dress she wore. "Anyone could come in here at any moment."

"Then I suppose you had better tell me what's going on. Why did Bailey summon me here?"

"I have convinced Annabelle to postpone the wedding."

"Postpone? Not call off?"

"No." Cilla shook her head. "For now, she is uncertain enough about Raventhorpe that she spoke with Dolly last evening about her concerns. Dolly talked to Annabelle's father this morning. Now you are here, so I can only assume that Mr. Bailey has made a decision about the matter."

"Perhaps he intends to have me keelhauled."

"Do not be ridiculous. Virgil Bailey is a fair,

levelheaded man. More likely Annabelle may have convinced him that they misjudged you."

"That would be a miracle indeed."

"At least postponing the wedding buys you more time to find evidence against the earl." She bit her lower lip, her lovely brown eyes reflecting her apprehension. "I decided not to tell Annabelle the whole truth about Raventhorpe. Let her have her illusions about life for a little while longer."

He tipped her chin up with one finger so her gaze met his. "You're a softhearted little thing, aren't you?"

"Nonsense." She pulled away from him, but not before he noticed the pulse pounding in her throat. "I simply do not see any purpose in telling Annabelle such sordid tales unless it is absolutely necessary."

"You know that by telling her the whole truth, she might very well drop Raventhorpe like a hot rock."

"The thought did occur to me, but I truly believe she should be spared if possible. Besides, if I did carry such accounts to her and she did not believe me, she might tell her mother and then I would be dismissed. I am not willing to take that chance."

"Is that the real reason?" He trailed his finger down the side of her neck, smiling as his suspicions were confirmed. Her pulse was racing like a rabbit's.

"Of course. You know Annabelle's safety is of the utmost importance to me."

"Or were you worried that I would end our bargain as soon as we attained our goal?"

She glanced away. "I thought of it."

He bent down until his mouth hovered near her ear. "Whatever happens with the wedding, our bargain stands."

"Until when?" she murmured. "You do not intend to stay in England indefinitely."

"No, but neither do I have pressing business in America. There is no shame in wanting more, Priscilla."

She didn't answer.

"Is that why you've convinced Annabelle to postpone the wedding instead of jilting Raventhorpe outright?"

"No, that is not why I made the suggestion." She turned her head and locked eyes with him, her mouth only inches from his. "My own naïveté was destroyed by my husband, and I do not have the life I wanted. I do not want that for Annabelle. She still has a chance at happiness."

Damn, but he wanted to taste that mouth again. But this was not the place or the time. There was business to attend to. "I'm not objecting. We can try it your way for a while, but if it does not work, we'll have no choice but to tell her the whole of it."

"I know. I just think we should lead her to jilt Raventhorpe and believe it is her own idea. She will be better off in the end."

"In the meantime, you have delayed the wedding, which is in our favor." He looked down at her lips, so full and soft. The temptation was killing him. "Your mouth is a man's fantasy, do you know that?"

Her lips parted and a sound came out—some kind

of squeaky, half-shocked gasp. Even that stirred his desire.

"I have some ideas involving that mouth." He raised his brows. "You still have a free afternoon on Sundays, don't you?"

"Yes, but . . ." She glanced around as if expecting the vicar to jump out from behind one of the curtains. "It still feels scandalous to indulge such appetites on a Sunday."

"If you intended to make love in the church, I would agree with you. Otherwise, Sunday is just another day."

"I attend services with the family on Sunday mornings."

"What time are you released from your duties?"

"I begin my half day at two o'clock."

"I will send John around at two o'clock then." Distracted again by the lure of her lips, he took her chin in his hand and pressed a quick, hard kiss to her mouth. "You have no idea how much you tempt me to forget this meeting with Bailey," he muttered. "But he summoned me, and I have to admit I am very curious as to what he has to say."

She slanted him a look that told him she shared his regret. "Be sure to tell me what happens."

"I will." He started for the door, then paused. "Are you coming?"

"I will be along in a moment." She took a deep, shuddering breath. "It is better if we are not seen together."

"Until tomorrow then." He gave her a nod, then left the room.

* * *

Samuel entered Virgil's study at the behest of the surly Thomas. Virgil sat behind his desk, spectacles perched on his nose. He glanced over as Samuel closed the door behind him.

"Come and sit down, Samuel. Thank you for coming."

"Your summons took me by surprise." Samuel seated himself in a chair before the desk. "I had not expected to hear from you after our conversation the last time I was in this room."

"I know, I know." Virgil took off his spectacles and laid them on the open book in front of him. "You've got every right to be angry."

"Why did you call me here?"

"Not going to give an old man a shot, eh? That's all right. I'd be steamed if I were you, too. Anyhow, I wanted to tell you that I thought about what you said."

Samuel simply nodded.

"And you're right, I should have believed in you." Virgil pinched the bridge of his nose. "The thing is, Annabelle was devastated when you didn't come home. After a while, I was so burned up at seeing her cry all the time that I was ripe for the picking when Raventhorpe came around with his story about how you were no good."

"Do you believe that he lied?"

"I don't know what to think except this: Something extraordinary must have happened to you because nothing short of that would have prevented you from keeping your word to my baby."

"That's right."

"So I'm not choosing between the two of you, saying who's right and who's not. I can't do that. Your word against his, you understand?"

"I would hope you would give weight to my word since you have known me longer."

"Like I said, without evidence, I can't make a true decision. But what I can do is follow my gut. And my gut says you belong back home."

Emotion welled up, tightening in his chest. "What made you change your mind?"

"You did, son. You and those principles of yours. Once the dust settled, Dolly told me that she didn't believe you'd run off like a coward. She thought something else must have happened, something that prevented you from coming back to Annabelle."

"Raventhorpe happened," Samuel said. "When he came to you to tell you his tale—probably to cover his own tracks—and he saw how pretty Annabelle was, and how rich, he must have seen a golden opportunity. The man gambles too much and always needs money."

"Well, Dolly believed in you, and then Annabelle told us about how Lord Raventhorpe started treating her after you came back. Looking down on her because she was American and trying to push up the wedding. Sort of made me think."

"You place too much importance on having a title."

"I'm starting to see that. After Annabelle told us what sort of things went on and why she was thinking maybe she'd misjudged you, it occurred to me that earls and those types are born into their positions. They don't earn them. You, son, you earned your way to the captain's spot. That says something about a man."

Samuel gave a short nod, struggling to remain collected in spite of the emotion welling up inside him.

"Tell me, were you taking up with other gals while you were away?"

Samuel stiffened. "No."

Virgil nodded. "And did you stay away of your own free will?"

"No."

"All right then. That's all I'm going to ask you. The rest is water under the bridge. Forgotten."

Surprise made him blink. Could *he* forget the pain of his surrogate family not believing in him? Could he forgive that easily?

He looked into Virgil's eyes and saw reflected back the same man who had been like a father to him. Stubborn, resourceful, proud, and honest as the day was long. If Virgil wanted to move forward on the understanding that Samuel had not acted like a cad, it might be the best he was going to get. He would take it.

"If you're willing to forgive an old fool, I'd like to shake your hand on it."

Samuel nodded and extended his hand. The older man took it and shook firmly.

"What now?" Samuel asked. "Are you willing to hear what I've learned about Raventhorpe?"

"You got evidence?"

"No."

"Then no, I don't want to hear any rumors or gossip or what have you. Let's just leave it at the fact that you two fellows don't like each other very much. And that Lord Raventhorpe can act like a jackass sometimes."

"You'd be right."

"Then let's not talk about that. Let's talk about Annabelle."

"What about Annabelle?"

Virgil sat back in his chair and folded his hands across his stomach, a grin stretching across his face. "I'd like to offer you the chance to court her."

"Court her? But she broke our engagement."

"Well, she was mad at you. Thought you'd abandoned her for some senorita down Mexico way or some nonsense."

"That *is* nonsense."

"Well, she's postponed the wedding to Lord Raventhorpe. She can't make up her mind about which one of you she wants for a husband, so she wants you to both court her so she can make up her mind."

"But she's still engaged to Raventhorpe."

"We haven't torn up the agreement, if that's what you're asking. I talked to him about the situation this morning."

"And he went along with this?"

"Oh, he's madder than a long-tailed cat in a room full of rockers, but the truth is, he had no choice." Virgil's mouth thinned. "If he wants to win Annabelle, he's going to play by my rules, and I say we're postponing the wedding. What my baby wants, she gets, and right now she wants to be courted by both of you."

"I'm flattered, Virgil, but I'm not interested in courting Annabelle."

"Not interested?" Virgil sat up in his chair. "A few weeks ago you busted into my house and raised a ruckus about marrying Annabelle."

"And afterwards I realized that she and I have both changed. We're not the same people we were, and getting married now might be a mistake."

"Well, hell. What am I going to tell her now? She wanted the two of you to fight for her hand or some female foolishness. If you're not interested, then she's probably going to end up with Raventhorpe just to soothe her ruffled feathers."

"There are a dozen equally eligible bachelors she could choose from. Why him?"

"He helped her through a tough time, so I reckon she has a soft spot for him."

"He *caused* the tough time." Virgil held up a finger in warning, and Samuel let out an impatient sigh. "But you have no proof of that. I understand."

Virgil sat back in his chair again and eyed Samuel. "I was hoping you'd end up being my son-in-law, boy. Maybe you could humor an old man. Get to know Annabelle again. *Not* court her, just be her escort to a couple of social get-togethers. Maybe spend some time talking."

"I don't want to lead Annabelle to think I'm angling to marry her," Samuel said.

"That's fine," Virgil said. "I'm just thinking that maybe with you hanging around her some, she might not be so quick to jump back into Raventhorpe's arms."

He could tell from the gleam in the older man's eyes that Virgil was hoping Samuel would decide to rekindle his relationship with Annabelle. Samuel knew that would never happen, but it might be wise to go along with Virgil's plan as a way to keep Annabelle and Raventhorpe apart. Anything he could do to buy more time to dig up evidence on Raventhorpe.

"All right. I will make an effort to get to know Annabelle again, as long as it is clearly understood by both you and her that I am *not* attempting to woo her into marriage. My role will be that of a family friend, someone who occasionally escorts her to social events."

"Sure, sure. I'll explain all that to her."

"This is important to me, Virgil." He caught and held the man's gaze. "I have already been falsely accused of being a cad once. I have no desire for history to repeat itself."

"Absolutely, my boy. I'll make sure Annabelle understands completely. She and Dolly are out visiting right now, but I'll sit down with her as soon as she gets back."

"As long as we understand each other." Samuel stood and held out his hand to Virgil. "Thank you for the apology. I hated to think there was bad blood between us."

Virgil stood and shook his hand. "Me too, son. Me too."

* * *

She was not eavesdropping, Cilla thought as the study door opened. She simply happened to be passing by on her way to the gardens. If she chanced to overhear anything, it was completely by happenstance.

"There's the Archer thing on Wednesday. You could escort Annabelle to that," Virgil said, clapping Samuel on the back.

"I will be pleased to do so."

"Ah, Mrs. Burke." Virgil beamed at her. "Do show Samuel out, won't you?"

"Of course, Mr. Bailey." Cilla met Samuel's gaze. He was escorting Annabelle to a ball? What had happened in that room?

Was Samuel going to start pressing his suit with Annabelle again?

"I'm glad we had this chat, son," Virgil said.

"I am, too. I will see you Wednesday." Samuel stepped out into the hall.

"Yes, you will." With a gleeful grin, Virgil slipped back into his study and closed the door, leaving Samuel and Cilla alone in the hall together.

"Is there somewhere we can talk?" Samuel asked, glancing at a maid passing by at the end of the hall.

"I can show you out through the garden gate." Her blood seemed frozen in her veins. If he was going to be pursuing Annabelle again, he would no doubt be ending their arrangement. She should have expected it. He had never made any secret about the fact that he would do anything to break up Annabelle's marriage to Raventhorpe.

But he had also given her reason to believe that he and Annabelle were not suited. Had he lied to her? Had he simply used her to accomplish his own ends?

Had she once more allowed a man to make a fool of her?

Numb, she led him toward the door in the rear of the house, where they could slip out into the garden unnoticed. Cilla was very aware of Samuel's close proximity as they started down the path leading to the side gate.

They walked for a couple of minutes in silence. Each second that ticked by, she waited for his announcement that the Baileys had accepted him back into the fold again and that he would once more be pursuing Annabelle.

Finally he stopped her with a hand on her arm. "Wait a moment."

She squeezed her eyes closed for a quick second, bracing herself for disappointment. "What's the matter?"

"I can tell you are upset."

"Nonsense." But she couldn't meet his eyes.

"Come here." He took her hand and led her beneath an arbor and behind some tall shrubbery. A marble bench sat in the hidden alcove. "Sit with me for a moment."

"How did you know this was here?"

"John and I studied the garden's layout extensively. Just in case."

"We should not linger. Someone will be missing me shortly."

"Don't fret about that." He tugged on her hand until she sat on the bench, and then he settled beside her. "Dolly is out with Annabelle, so you can stay with me for a few minutes."

"Very well. But only for a few minutes." She tugged at her hand, but he continued to hold it.

"I like touching you," he said. "Now tell me why you're so unhappy. Our plan is working."

"Working so well that you are now escorting Annabelle to the Archer ball."

"Is *that* what this is about?"

"What am I expected to think? You have made no bones about the fact that you are determined to see Annabelle parted from Raventhorpe, no matter what the cost."

"True, but—"

"I had thought that postponing the wedding would serve as a solution until I could convince Annabelle to break off the engagement. But apparently you have found a different way." Her voice broke on the last word. She sucked in a deep breath. She would *not* act like a ninny and fall in love with Samuel Breedlove. What they had was not love. It was sex.

"Cilla, you are overreacting. Yes, I have agreed to escort Annabelle to a ball or two, but I made it clear to Virgil that it is just as a family friend."

"It is not so great a leap from family friend to suitor."

He tilted his head, trying to see into her face as she continued to look down. "Do you regret your decision to help me, Priscilla?"

"I really had no choice, Samuel. If I did not act,

then Annabelle would be marrying a man capable of murder and any number of other terrible acts." Now she met his gaze, the heat of her emotions behind her words. "I chose to save Annabelle. And I made that choice again when I decided not to tell her about Raventhorpe's horrible crimes. Yes, she would have jilted him immediately, but it would have been at the cost of that sweetness and faith in people that is what makes Annabelle the person she is."

"I'm not disputing that."

"You asked me if I did it so we could have more time together."

He looked stunned at her outburst. "Good God, Cilla, I was just teasing you when I said that. Never have I met a more generous person than you. It never occurred to me that you would ever do anything so unethical. It's not in your nature."

She let out a breath. "Oh. All right, then."

"No, it's not all right." He took both her hands now, holding her fast when she would have gotten up from the bench. "Everything since we met has happened with more drama than Shakespeare's plays. It bothers me that you would believe that I think so little of you. That you think I would so quickly turn back to Annabelle after I have already told you that I have decided we do not suit. Did you truly believe you were just a means to an end?"

"You do not have to tell me fairy tales, Captain. I know how the world works."

"Calling me captain again, eh? I know you only do that when you're put out with me. Listen to me, Priscilla Burke. You and I are the same. We're both people whose lives have been displaced by circumstances beyond our control. All we can do is make the best of matters and move forward."

"I understand."

"I don't think you do. You claim to know how the world works, but I believe you have only seen the bad in the world and none of the good." He looked down at her hands in his, caressing the backs of them with his thumbs. "Our bargain came about because I asked you to do something that could ruin your life. It was selfish of me, but it was the only way I could possibly get between Annabelle and Raventhorpe."

"You do not have to explain to me."

"Apparently I do." Real anger rode his words as he leaned closer. "If you and I had met under normal circumstances, I have no doubt we would have ended up together. You are everything a man could want in a woman. Beautiful, smart, passionate. I would have pursued you."

"Ah, but if we had met under normal circumstances, I might not have accepted your suit." She saw the surprise in his expression and hurried to continue. "I still believe in love, Samuel. I still want a husband who loves me above all else, and we both know that you cannot provide that. So perhaps it is better that our relationship is just what it is."

"I have no intention of courting Annabelle."

"What? But Mr. Bailey said—"

"He asked me to, but I refused. I told him I was willing to escort her to a couple of events to mend fences, but I only agreed to that to buy us time. I would never officially court her unless I was serious about marrying her, and I changed my mind about that the night you and I met."

He'd surprised her. "Well, just so you know, if you *were* courting her, then I would not feel comfortable continuing with our arrangement. It would not be right."

"I agree."

"And you are not courting her now."

"No. My relationship with her stands firmly in the category of family friend."

"All right. Then I expect we will be meeting at the cottage as scheduled."

"You're sure you still want to meet?"

"Of course. I am no fool, Samuel. Our time together is teaching me a great deal about men and physical relationships that it would take me years to learn otherwise. I cannot thank you enough."

"I don't want you to thank me, damn it!"

"It has been an emotional day." She stood, jerking her hands from his. "I should show you to the east gate."

"I know where the blasted gate is." Samuel surged to his feet. "Why are you denying what we have, sweetheart?"

"What we have is a physical relationship. Though I am yet curious as to who is the better chess player." She managed to smile, taking refuge in training from years of governesses teaching her to hide her emotions.

"I know you still want me." He edged closer to her, hemming her in between the bench and his body.

"I do still want you." She reveled in his closeness, excited even more by the way her pulse skipped wildly when he came near her. "I never denied it. But neither of us are children, so we should not entertain fantasies. Thank you for reassuring me about your thoughts of my character. I was concerned."

"You want me to think you can control your emotions about us? I've had you naked beneath me, Priscilla, and watched you explode in my arms. In that moment of release, you can't hide anything, sweetheart. I see it all."

She swallowed hard, unnerved that she might indeed reveal more than she intended in moments of sexual ecstasy. "What do you want, Samuel? Do you want me to fall in love with you? How will that benefit either of us? You said you are not capable of love. We would end up miserable in each other's company. Better to enjoy our affair and remember it fondly when it is over."

"Damn it, Cilla."

"Do not try to make this more than it is." She stood on her toes and brushed a kiss to his lips. "I have been gone too long. I will see you tomorrow at the cottage, Samuel, barring any dramatic changes in our circumstances."

She tried to pull free of him, but he snagged her wrist when she would have left him. "If you kiss a man, Priscilla, do it right."

He tugged her into his arms, pressing her against his lean, warm body. The scent of him—plain soap and water with a hint of sea salt—triggered instant arousal. Her body recognized him, and she had no desire to fight the attraction. He lowered his mouth to hers. She had expected hot passion, perhaps the edge of the anger she had heard in his voice. Instead he took her mouth with a leisurely skill that ravaged her meager defenses. He tasted her. Nibbled at the sensitive flesh of her lips. Soothed the sting with his tongue. Mastered and owned her with a devastating thoroughness that had her swaying when he finally released her.

"I'll see you tomorrow." The roughness in his voice told her he was as aroused as she was. Before she could respond, he left the alcove, heading with unerring accuracy toward the east gate.

Leaving her with a new appreciation for a man who knew where he was going and how to get there.

Chapter 17

Saturday passed into Sunday. Cilla was wait-ing when John Ready arrived at two o'clock to fetch her.

The cottage was as she remembered it. She walked in the door and shut it behind her, then turned to find Samuel coming down the hallway. He wore only his trousers and shirt, and the shirt was unfastened. Her mouth watered as she feasted her eyes on his sun-darkened throat and the hint of hair peeking from where the shirt gaped open. He stopped as he saw her.

They looked at each other for long moments across the common room. Finally she unbuttoned her gloves at the wrists. "Good afternoon, Samuel."

"Priscilla." The rough purr of his voice made her fumble as she moved to tug off her gloves one finger at a time. She paused to regain her composure.

"Do you need help with that?"

She jerked her gaze over to him. He leaned in the doorway between the hallway and the common room, arms folded as he watched her remove her gloves.

She had seen a cat once watch a mouse in the same way—right before it pounced.

"No, thank you." She stripped off one glove, noting how his gaze followed the movement as if bewitched. Heat flared through her along with a hint of power. The heady feeling awakened her wicked, playful side, a teasing creature who reveled in his attention. She tossed the glove on the table, then started on the other one with a mischievous smile.

"Playing with fire, are you?" he asked, his lips curving.

"I suppose that depends on how hot you are feeling." She stripped off the other glove and tossed it onto the table before reaching for her bonnet.

"Pretty damned hot." He swept his hungry gaze over her. "I've been thinking about this all day. All yesterday, too. Since the moment you were last here, come to think of it."

She paused in setting her bonnet on the table. "You were?"

"Oh, yeah."

"What exactly were you thinking?"

"About you. About us. About your next lesson."

"And what is today's lesson?"

"I think you're working on one of your own." He shrugged away from the doorway and came toward her. "A man likes to watch a woman undress for him."

"Oh?" Her belly clenched with hunger as he pulled out a chair from the table and sat down.

"Sure. Since you started already, I figure I'll sit and watch the show."

She bit her lower lip, suddenly worried she might have gone too far. "So you want me to continue?"

"Absolutely."

She hesitated. Should she take her pins from her hair? But then it would be that much more difficult to unfasten her dress. Perhaps her shoes. This reminded her of how much he'd seemed to like watching her take off her stockings. She pulled out another chair, but rather than sitting on it, she braced her foot on the seat.

He shifted in his chair, his dark eyes alight with interest.

She tugged up her skirts so her entire stocking-encased lower limb was exposed. Then she bent to work on her shoe. She discarded the first one and glanced up to find him watching her with an intensity that made warmth bloom between her legs. With a little smile, she switched legs and bent to her second shoe.

The scrape of his chair across the floor made her look up just as he reached her.

"I can't wait," he said, then plundered her mouth like a drowning man exposed to air. Her body flared to life, and she clung to him, all rational thought sizzling away like drops of water thrown on a griddle.

Long moments later he ripped his mouth from hers. "I wanted to teach you something new, but right now I just have to have you."

"Yes," she murmured.

"I know I should be more patient—"

She laid her fingers across his lips, silencing him.

"Take me to bed, Samuel. I want you until I feel like I will die from it."

He scooped her up in his arms and carried her down the hallway to the bedroom.

"Why don't you believe you're capable of love?" Cilla lay in bed with Samuel sprawled halfway on top of her. An hour or more had passed since he had carried her off, and her body still sang with passion. Her lips curved as he drew lazy circles on her breast with his fingers.

"I'm just not built that way." His voice sounded muffled because he had buried his face against her neck.

"I have trouble believing you've never loved *anyone*, Samuel."

"The notion that someone can love someone else more than themselves? Nonsense. Survival instinct always takes over."

"You don't really believe that, do you?"

"Yes."

"We're all born believing in love." She caught his head in her hands as he began to drop nibbling kisses along her throat and made him look at her. "What changed you, Samuel? Did a woman break your heart?"

"Why do you females always think that?"

"Because there must be some explanation. Your attitude goes against what most normal men believe."

"Then I am an original thinker." He curved his fingers around her breast, rubbing his thumb across the nipple. "Guess what I'm thinking now?"

"What was her name?"

"Blast it, woman!" He sat up and gave her an exasperated look. "Before Annabelle, the only woman in my life was my mother. No desperate, secret loves in my past. Are you satisfied?"

His mother. His *unwed* mother who had died when he was fifteen. The defensiveness in his tone made her realize she had touched a wound. What had his mother been forced to do to survive on her own with a young son? Her heart broke as she imagined how harsh reality must have destroyed the illusions of a young boy.

His guarded expression warned her to leave well enough alone for now. Instead she stretched her arms above her head, arching her body toward him. "Satisfied? Not quite."

"Demanding wench." He lay back down beside her and palmed her breast again. "Is your plan to exhaust me?"

She flushed. "I am sorry. It's just . . . this is so delicious. I want to take as much as you are willing to give me. I am not ready for our time together to end."

"Is that so?" He tongued her nipple, the wet, raspy flesh sending quivers along her nerve endings. "I'm not exactly finished with you, either. There is too much to explore. Too much to teach you."

He clamped his mouth around her straining nipple and sucked, and she arched her back, her breath sighing from her lips. "There is more?"

A grumbling noise of assent reached her ears but she did not care anymore. Just as her brain melted into simmering porridge, he slowly drew back, her damp flesh sliding from his warm mouth. The cool air made her nipple contract, and he gave it one last lick before resting his forehead against hers. "Ready for another lesson?"

The hungry gleam in his eyes both excited and scared her and nearly made her say no, but she found herself nodding anyway.

"Good. Turn over." He whipped the pillow from beneath her head as she rolled onto her stomach, then tucked it under her belly so her hips arched up. "If I'm doing something you don't like, yell 'bowsprit.'"

"Bowsprit? That is a strange word."

"But it's not something you might yell in the heat of passion. If you yell 'bowsprit,' it means you had to think about it." He got on his knees behind her, taking her hips in his hands. "You ready?"

"What is a bowsprit?"

"It's a spar that sticks out from the stem of a ship."

"What's a spar?"

He leaned down so his mouth was near her ear. "It's a long pole that holds the rigging." He nudged the head of his sex against her female folds as if to illustrate, then slipped inside her.

She let out a cry of surprise at the depth of his thrust.

He stopped. "You all right?"

She nodded, unable to speak from the sensations thundering through her. His hands caressing her hips. Her sensitive nipples rubbing against the bedding.

His cock so deep inside her. The way he surrounded her on all sides, covering her, his warm belly against her bottom.

"You want to say 'bowsprit'?" he asked.

She shook her head no. Vehemently.

He chuckled. "Then hold fast, Priscilla. We're in for a wild ride."

The Mertletons' dinner party was just a small affair—only forty guests—and even Cilla was invited since the Mertletons were good friends of her parents. As she entered the room behind the Baileys and Lord Raventhorpe, she looked forward to seeing her mother but hoped there would be no matchmaking on Mama's part this evening.

She saw him as soon as she stepped into the room.

Samuel stood with her parents and Genny as the guests lingered in the drawing room waiting for dinner to be announced. Raventhorpe and Annabelle strolled across the room ostensibly to greet friends, but veered so close to where Samuel stood that Cilla was certain it had been a deliberate move on Raventhorpe's part. Clearly the earl was gloating. Samuel, to his credit, barely looked at them.

"Why, Cilla, there are your parents," Dolly said, obviously having followed her daughter's path.

"Lady Mertleton and my mother are quite close friends," Cilla said. "I was hoping they had been invited."

"And there is Samuel talking to them."

"He is acquainted with my father."

"I hope he intends to behave himself," Dolly murmured.

"I expect that he will. Your husband has given him a second chance, and he is not a man to take such a thing lightly."

"True." Dolly slanted her a glance. "You have come to know him well."

Cilla concealed the flare of nerves. "When it looked as if he was going to disrupt the wedding, I made it my business to find out everything I could about him."

Dolly's brow cleared. "You are so efficient!"

"I try to be."

"Excuse me. Mrs. Burke?"

Cilla turned to see who had addressed her, and her heart sank as she recognized the earnest young naval lieutenant who had appeared at her elbow. "Oh, good evening, Lieutenant. Mrs. Bailey, you remember Lieutenant Allerton."

"I sure do. Good evening, Lieutenant," Dolly said with a dimpled smile.

"Mrs. Bailey." The lieutenant sketched a bow, then looked at Cilla. "We are partnered for dinner, Mrs. Burke."

"How lovely." Cilla glanced at her mother and found that lady smiling at her. She let her exasperation show for just a moment so her mother would get the message, then turned back to her assigned escort.

"Excuse me while I greet our hostess," Dolly said, then walked away.

"Lieutenant," Cilla said, "I see my mother across the room. Please excuse me while I go to speak her."

"Allow me to escort you." The lieutenant crooked his elbow.

Left with no other recourse, she took his arm and allowed him to lead her over to where her family stood talking. Her father saw her first, but rather than stiffening with rejection as he had done in the past, he greeted her with a welcome smile.

"Good evening, Cilla! And to you, too, Lieutenant."

"Admiral." The two men shook hands.

"You know my wife and daughter," the admiral said to Allerton.

"Indeed, I do. A pleasure to see you, Mrs. Wallington-Willis. And you, Miss Wallington-Willis."

"And this is Captain Samuel Breedlove."

"Captain?" Allerton extended a hand. "Military?"

"No," Samuel said. He shook the man's hand in one short movement, then withdrew. "I was the captain of a ship, though not any longer." He glanced at Cilla. "Good evening, Mrs. Burke."

She nodded. "Captain."

Allerton cast her a quick questioning look. "You are acquainted with Captain Breedlove?"

"Through the Baileys."

"The captain is here as our guest this evening," Cilla's mother said. "He was gallant enough to offer to escort Genny."

Cilla shot a frown at her sister and was greeted with a smug smile.

"Papa and the captain have struck up a marvelous friendship," Genny said.

"I think a sea captain is a perfect match for my daughter." The admiral chuckled.

"Robert, you are going to embarrass the captain!" Cilla's mother said.

"Nonsense."

Cilla couldn't help but glance at Samuel. He was listening to something Genny was telling him. He glanced up and caught her eye just as they were summoned to dinner, and the brief, intense stare seared her in places she dared not mention. Lieutenant Allerton offered his arm. She went with her escort, her emotions a hard, tight knot in her chest.

He didn't like that Allerton fellow putting his hands on Cilla. Not in the slightest.

All through dinner he was aware of young Genny Wallington-Willis chattering on about social acquaintances he did not know, but while he managed to make the appropriate responses, he focused his attention farther down the table to where Cilla conversed with the naval man.

He had never considered himself a jealous man. Even his actions regarding Annabelle and Raventhorpe, who sat close to their hostess, had not been generated by jealousy so much as a need to set things right. But when it came to Cilla Burke, everything he had come to know about himself in the past no longer applied. He wanted to shove the lieutenant away from her and then drag her off somewhere where they could be alone.

Sex. That's what it was. That's what it *had* to be. There was some kind of unique sexual attraction between himself and Cilla that he had never felt before. Perhaps it was a male sense of possession. He had never been a man to share his women, which was one of the reasons he never patronized whores. When he took a lover, it was an exclusive relationship until one of them walked away.

Seeing Annabelle on Raventhorpe's arm bothered him, but in a less intimate, more something-in-the-world-is-awry kind of way. Like a loose knot in the ropes that needed tightening or a meal of soup that did not include a spoon. Seeing Cilla being fawned over by the uniformed lieutenant struck him in a completely different way. More intense. More urgent. More a ship-is-on-fire-and-the-gunpowder-is-going-to-blow kind of way.

He certainly felt as if he was going to blow if the lieutenant gave her one more flirtatious grin.

"Captain, did you hear what I said?"

Samuel pulled his attention back to Genny. She had brown hair like her sister, but her eyes were green, her figure was more slender, and her mouth wasn't as full. At the moment her lips were pursed in a pout that told him he had missed something. "I apologize, Miss Wallington-Willis. My mind wandered."

She gave a big sigh, no doubt designed to draw his attention to her low-cut décolletage. "Shall we change the subject?"

"Good idea. Tell me more about your family."

"My family? You already know Mama and Papa."

"Tell me about your sister."

"Cilla?" She sent an incredulous look down the table to her sibling. "She ran off and got married and has been living in America ever since. Then her husband died."

"Did you ever meet him?"

"Oh, yes. I could see he was a complete bounder from the very beginning, but there was no talking her out of wedding him. Even Papa couldn't convince her."

"Because she was in love."

"Yes." Genny rolled her eyes. "Anyone could see he was after her money. Even me, and I was only fourteen at the time."

"She made a mistake. It happens."

"She was a fool."

"Everyone is, at one time or another."

"Cilla abandoned her entire family for him. I do not ever intend to be a fool over a man." Her eyes widened as if she hadn't mean to verbalize the thought. Then the empty-headed flirt was back, asking him about America and his stay in England, but it was too late. He had seen the truth in her eyes. For all that Miss Genny Wallington-Willis publicly disdained her sister, in private she mourned her absence.

She could not hide it from him, because he felt the same way.

Lieutenant Allerton finally left her side to fetch her some punch, and Cilla sought out her mother. Her parents stood together watching Genny dance with Samuel.

Cilla managed not to look at the couple on the

dance floor as she stopped in front of her parents. "Mama, please do not attempt to match me with Lieutenant Allerton anymore."

"But why not?" Helen asked. "He's handsome and from a good family."

"Good sailing man," her father added. "Steady income. Could do worse."

"No," Cilla said, holding her mother's gaze. "He is not the type of man that interests me."

Her father stiffened. "What is wrong with a navy man, might I know?"

"Nothing, Papa. He is just not the type of husband that I want."

"Then you do want one?" her mother asked.

"Perhaps," Cilla replied, "when I find a man who will make a good partner. Like you have been to Papa."

Her father looked startled. "What are you talking about, Priscilla?"

"I want what you have. Nothing less will do." She looked from one parent to the other. "But you must let me decide."

"We let you decide before," Robert grumbled.

"I was young and did not realize there was more to marriage than a wedding ceremony. I have been married now. I know better. Now please do not include me in your matchmaking attempts going forward."

"I just want us to be a happy family again," her mother said, her eyes moistening.

"That is up to Papa." Cilla looked her father in the eye. "Edward was not the right choice for me.

I should have listened to you, and I am sorry I did not."

Her father remained silent for a long moment. "I tried to spare you heartache."

"I know you did."

"You were stubborn and would not listen to reason."

"I was."

"I just want you to be happy and safe, Cilla." Her father cleared his throat. "If you want to come back home, you are welcome."

"Thank you, but I am not yet certain where I will be living after Annabelle's wedding."

"Here comes your sister," Helen said.

The orchestra had stopped. Cilla glanced over her shoulder and found Genny and Samuel only paces away. And Samuel was staring at her. A quiver rippled through her at the look in his eyes. She had seen that look before, but never when she had been fully clothed.

The couple reached them.

"You are a wonderful dancer, Captain," Helen said.

"Thank you." He gave Genny a little bow as she moved to stand beside her mother. Then Samuel looked at Cilla. "Might I have the next dance, Mrs. Burke?"

The heat in his eyes touched something inside her and made the world fade away. She extended her hand, and he took it, leading her out to the floor as the orchestra struck up a country dance. She had hoped for a waltz so she could be held in his arms again, but this was better than nothing. They took their positions.

She performed the steps by rote. Promenading with their arms linked together. Facing each other, hands touching. Turning toward Samuel, then away from him, as if flirting with him. Good heavens, how was it she had never noticed how sensual dancing was?

Their set ended with them facing each other, breathing with exertion. Sweat glistened on Samuel's forehead, and she, too, felt overheated. Was that because of the exercise or the sizzling attraction between them?

Samuel offered his arm. She took it. He bent his head close to her ear.

"I need to be alone with you. Meet me in the garden in ten minutes."

I need to be alone with you. Meet me in the garden in ten minutes.

The passionate whisper played itself over and over in her mind. Had she imagined that Samuel had said such a thing in the middle of a crowded ballroom? She had thought he would spend the evening obsessed with Annabelle and Raventhorpe, but he had barely spared them a glance. He had been watching her, Cilla, since their arrival.

Had it been ten minutes yet? Samuel had left the ballroom after escorting her back to her parents and the lieutenant. After what she determined to be the correct amount of time, she made an excuse and left the ballroom.

She found the door to the garden and slipped outside, then wondered how she was supposed to find Samuel. Was she mad to be doing this? What if someone saw her or came looking for her? She should go back inside right now and forget this foolishness.

She didn't.

She followed the path. She'd gone only a few paces when someone grabbed her by the wrist and yanked her into the shadows. She was pushed against the wall of the house, and a mouth came down on hers, demanding and hungry. She knew the feel of that muscled body pressing her into the warm stone, the scent of him, the taste of his kiss.

"Samuel," she whispered when he pulled back.

He rested his forehead against hers. "I had to touch you." He traced a hand down her breast and along her waist.

Tingling followed in the wake of his caress, but one of them had to remain coolheaded. "We cannot stay here. Someone will come looking for me."

"I know. I'm being selfish." He bent his head and nuzzled her throat. "Be selfish with me, just for a few minutes."

She should say no. She should push him away. Instead she leaned her head back against the wall and moaned as he kissed a path from her neck to the edge of her low-cut bodice.

"Thank God you are wearing a ball gown." He drew his fingers along the expanse of bosom revealed by the daring décolletage. "I told you once your skin looks like cream. But it tastes even sweeter."

"Samuel, I have to go back inside."

"Just a few more minutes." He let out a slow breath. "I haven't been able to take my eyes from you all night. I'm feeling quite murderous toward that shiny young lieutenant who is so smitten with you."

Words caught in her throat. "What about Genny?" she managed.

"Genny is a child. You are..." His voice trailed off.

"Convenient?"

"No! Passionate. Caring. Intelligent. The list goes on." He searched her eyes in the dim light from the nearby path. "Wednesday I must escort Annabelle to the Archer ball. Are you going?"

"You will be Annabelle's escort, so what does it matter?"

"I want you there." He brushed a kiss across her lips. "Tell me you will come."

She sighed. "As it happens, the Baileys requested I attend with them so I probably will be there."

"Not probably. Say yes."

She relented. "If the Baileys want me there, I will go. I cannot go just to see you."

"Or the lieutenant?"

"I have no interest in Lieutenant Allerton. That is my mother's doing."

"Good." He cupped her breast through her dress. "I have no claim on you, yet I feel the urge to cosh that young man over the head and dump him in the Thames."

She laughed, almost a sob. She did not have the strength to ask him to stop touching her. She did not want him to stop; she wanted him to touch her *everywhere*. "I wish it were Friday."

"Let's not wait until Friday."

Her breath caught. "Are you mad? I cannot get away on days I am working for the Baileys."

"Perhaps I am. You've become irresistible for me." He kissed her again, openmouthed, his tongue exploring with rough possession. "If you didn't have all these petticoats on, I could take you right here."

Sweet longing swept through her, and she curled her fingers around his shoulders. "You make me want things no lady should think about."

"And you make me want things I never wanted before."

"I have to go back inside. Someone will miss me for certain."

"Yes." He kissed her again. "I will."

"Samuel . . ."

"I will see you Friday. Noon."

"Noon," she agreed and fled the garden before she decided to throw caution to the wind and beg him to take her.

Chapter 18

The Archer affair on Wednesday night was an exercise in torment.

Samuel escorted Annabelle, and Cilla accompanied the Baileys as per their request. Her parents and Lieutenant Allerton were not on the guest list, and the wedding to the earl had been postponed, so Cilla's only duty this week had been to watch over Annabelle. And watch her she did.

Watched her waltz in Samuel's arms.

Once again she was struck by the sheer handsomeness of the couple. He so dark, she so fair. They moved together like swans gliding across a lake. If they had married, their children would have been beautiful.

The thought clenched around her heart like a fist and would not let go.

She barely noticed when their host walked up to them. Sir Harry Archer was a local squire, a baronet with a jovial disposition and an injured leg that required he walk with a cane. He was a handsome enough gentleman with dark hair, hazel eyes, and spectacles, and some found his perpetual cheerfulness grating. He almost never spent any time in Town, preferring his country estate and his horses and hounds to the pleasures of the Season. The most noteworthy thing about Sir Harry was the fact that he was Raventhorpe's old hunting companion, though he could no longer sit a horse, and often followed the earl about much like one of his beloved hunting dogs.

"Good evening, ladies!" he said. "Mrs. Bailey, so lovely to see you again. And I believe this is Mrs. Burke?"

"Indeed it is, Sir Harry," Dolly said.

"So pleased to make your acquaintance, Mrs. Burke," Sir Harry said, bending over Cilla's hand. "I do not believe you were able to attend my picnic some weeks ago."

"Unfortunately my duties required I remain at Nevarton Chase," Cilla replied, "but I am delighted to be present this evening."

"And I am delighted to have you!" He grinned. "If not for this bothersome leg of mine, I would ask you to grant me the pleasure of a dance."

"I am honored," Cilla murmured.

"Since I cannot dance, perhaps you will grant me a turn about the room instead, eh?"

"Oh! Well, I—" Cilla glanced at Dolly, silently hoping for a savior.

"A wonderful idea," Dolly said, acting oblivious to Cilla's pleading look.

"Excellent! Come along, Mrs. Burke. And do not

fear that I will topple over during our perambulation. Despite my cane, I am quite adept on my feet." He extended his arm, and she had no choice but to take it.

"You are too kind," she said, and allowed him to start her along a path past the matrons seated along the side of the dance floor.

"Your father is Admiral Wallington-Willis, is he not?"

"Yes."

"An admirable gentleman. I had the pleasure of meeting him at one of the public balls. Your mother and sister, too."

"I am certain the pleasure was mutual, Sir Harry."

He chuckled. "Very well said, certainly more polite than what you are probably really thinking."

Cilla shot him a quick glance. "What do you mean?"

"I mean that neither of us is the type to exchange inane pleasantries when there are topics that are much more interesting, such as why young Annabelle is suddenly torn between two suitors."

She nearly stumbled, and he caught her by the arm with a strength that surprised her. "It is not in my nature to gossip, Sir Harry."

"I believe you, Mrs. Burke, but as Raventhorpe's closest—if not only—friend, I would like to know the true story of how that upstart American has managed to wedge himself between an earl and his betrothed."

"He is no upstart," she replied, keeping her tone even with effort. "Annabelle was engaged to him first. But he was . . . away . . . for a long time, during which Lord Raventhorpe claimed her hand."

Sir Harry clucked his tongue. "Come now, I am certain there is much more to it than that. How is it a young woman can even consider choosing between an earl and a lowly sea captain?"

Cilla clenched her teeth. "Captain Breedlove is hardly lowly."

"If I may summarize what you have already told me . . . This Breedlove was betrothed to Miss Bailey, then went away for a long time? Is that true?"

"Yes."

"For how long?"

"I hardly see—"

"Now, now, do not insult the intelligence of either of us." He halted, forcing her to stop as well. The look in his hazel eyes froze the excuses on her tongue. "How long was he gone, Mrs. Burke?"

She relented beneath the sharp intelligence in that implacable gaze. "Nearly two years."

"He abandoned that angel for two years? Criminal!"

"It was not his fault," she snapped. "He was marooned."

"Marooned?" Sir Harry laughed out loud, earning them curious glances from those nearby. Jerking his head as a signal to move forward, they began to stroll again. "That is certainly the most original excuse I have heard for such disgraceful behavior. Why, the man's a cad."

"He is not a cad, though I'm certain Lord Raven-thorpe must have given you that impression."

"Really?" A curious note entered his voice. "Why do you believe that?"

"I have said too much already." They neared the other side of the room, and she stopped, her attention caught by the distinctive pink of Annabelle's evening gown as the girl disappeared through the doors of the darkened terrace on Samuel's arm. Cilla's heart twisted into the knot that had become so familiar to her.

"Ah, my dear Mrs. Burke." Sir Harry's voice held a note of compassion that was echoed in his eyes. Eyes that seemed to strip away her façade of calm and see the roiling emotions beneath. "I believe it is what you *don't* say that is the most captivating."

She glanced away from that perceptive gaze. "I do not understand your meaning."

"Yes, I have been told that quite frequently." He indicated the terrace doors. "Do you care for a stroll on the terrace?"

She eyed the doors, bit her lower lip. Samuel was out there with Annabelle. She trusted that he was not yet ready to end their arrangement, but would the nostalgia of being alone with him prove too much temptation for young Annabelle? Curiosity about what might be happening ate at her.

She could go out there, be the chaperone she was supposed to be, and break up whatever intimacies might be occurring. Annabelle would not think anything of it. And Samuel . . . well, Samuel on a dark terrace was too tempting. Even in a crowded ballroom. Even with gossips in every corner. Even with Sir Harry beside her and Raventhorpe lurking about somewhere.

She could pretend that it was duty that motivated her, but she knew the truth. She had turned into a creature that craved a man's touch as much as she craved air to breathe. And not just any man. Samuel.

Curse him. She had wanted him to teach her how to choose a husband, and instead he had only taught her to want *him*. She ached for his kiss, the stroke of his hands on her skin. She burned to feel him inside her again.

"Mrs. Burke?"

She took a deep breath. "I would love some fresh air."

"I've always loved the moonlight," Annabelle said, slanting a sideways glance at Samuel.

He could not mistake the invitation in her voice. She looked like a vision, all blond curls and blue eyes and pink silk. Her skin glowed alabaster in the moonlight, her lips half pursed in welcome. A man would have to be deaf and blind to misinterpret her intention.

She wanted him to kiss her.

How many times had he imagined a scenario just like this one as he lay alone beneath the stars on that blasted island? In his fantasies, he had always accepted the siren's call with eagerness, feasting on Annabelle's pretty mouth and slender body, greedy to possess her. He had indulged himself in imagining how she would look naked in his bed or big with his child. Always before, the tantalizing visualizations had left him hungry, hot, and hard.

Now here they stood, alone for a few precious moments in the dark. And he didn't move. Didn't even want to. Clearly Virgil had not made it clear to Annabelle what Samuel's intentions were.

Or maybe she had just decided she was too irresistible for a mere man to resist.

Confusion flickered across her features, but then she turned to face him, one hand flat on the stone balustrade. A small smile played about her lips. Did she realize how her posture thrust her breasts at him? How her white throat arched just so, begging for his mouth to trace the pulse there?

He observed all this as if from a distance, unmoved by what would once have been a compelling enticement.

"Samuel, why did you want to marry me?"

The question surprised him. "That's a silly question. You're sweet and pretty, and you'll make a great mama some day."

She pouted. "Is that how you see me? As somebody's mama?"

"Now don't get all upset. Most fellows want children."

"I guess." She bit her lower lip, glanced at him from beneath lowered lashes. Hell, every man alive knew what that look meant.

"Now, Annabelle . . ."

"Oh, Samuel!" She threw her arms around his neck and kissed him.

Her lips were soft and her skin smelled sweet, and her young body felt pleasant pressed against his.

Pleasant. Nothing more.

He broke off the kiss and eased her back a step. "Annabelle, we're supposed to be getting to know each other again, not sparking."

"I thought we *were* getting to know each other."

"Not like that."

"Oh, all right." She sighed and rested her cheek against his chest. "You always made me feel safe, Samuel. That's why it hurt so much when you left me alone."

"I didn't intend to leave you that long." He gently eased her back a step.

"I know that now." She looked up at him. "I'm not mad at you anymore, you know."

"That's good." What else could he say? "I think we'd better go back inside before someone comes looking for you."

She giggled. "Yes, like Mrs. Burke. She would scold me for being indiscreet."

Just the mention of Cilla hit him like a splash of cold water. The secluded privacy of the terrace suddenly struck him as wrong. The intimate darkness closed around him like water over his head. What was he doing out here? How could he not have realized what Annabelle intended when she'd suggested they get some air?

"Time to go back," he said, and took Annabelle's arm to steer her toward the ballroom.

Cilla and Sir Harry filled the doorway.

"Good evening," said Sir Harry. "Breedlove, isn't it?"

"Yes. Good evening, Sir Harry." Samuel nodded at the baronet, and then his gaze slid over Cilla. "Mrs. Burke."

"Good evening, Captain." Cilla looked at Annabelle. "I believe your mother was looking for you, Annabelle."

"Oh, dear," Annabelle said.

"I will escort her back straight away," Samuel said.

"Good idea, Captain. Best not to give the gossips any more to chew on," said Sir Harry. He looked out at the night sky and gave a huge sigh of satisfaction. "Beautiful night, do you not agree, Mrs. Burke?"

"It is indeed."

"Allow me to point out the constellations to you." Sir Harry led her toward the balustrade.

Cilla could feel Samuel's gaze on her as she moved past him, but she did not dare meet his eyes. She did not know what she might do if she saw the slightest invitation there.

Sir Harry pointed at the sky, then glanced back at Samuel. "If you would not mind, Breedlove . . ."

"Not at all. My apologies." His voice sounded tight and a bit gruff to Cilla. "Come, Annabelle. Your mother is waiting for you."

The two moved off; she could hear the rustle of Annabelle's skirts. Gripping the balustrade with both hands, she lowered her head and let out a long, slow breath.

"If it is any consolation," Sir Harry said, "he did not like the idea of you being out here with me."

She straightened. "Nonsense. Why would you think such a thing?"

He merely looked at her with those too-perceptive eyes, his face a study of compassion. "Why, indeed."

She raised her chin. "You were about to show me the constellations?"

"Quite so." He pointed. "If you follow my finger, you will see the North Star . . ."

Samuel escorted Annabelle back toward her mother, but his mind was still out on the terrace with Cilla.

Cilla and Sir Harry Archer.

Looking at the stars.

On a dark terrace . . .

He'd "looked at the stars" with a lady a few times in his life, and the heavenly bodies had nothing to do with his motivations for taking the woman outside for a moment of privacy in the dark. Had Cilla begun to look for a new husband already? Was she considering Sir Harry Archer?

He didn't like the idea, and his jealousy threw him off balance. First the navy man, now Archer. Hell, his fiancée had been engaged to another man, and he hadn't even felt a hint of the green-eyed monster, only a determination to set things right. But now? He rubbed a hand over his heart. Now he was surprised his jacket wasn't in shreds from the monster's claws.

"Samuel, are you all right?"

He'd nearly forgotten about Annabelle, though she held his arm as they navigated the crowded ballroom. "Of course," he said, forcing a smile as shame cringed inside him.

"Then let's dance. I do love it when you hold me in your arms." She flashed her coquette's smile at him.

"I thought I was taking you back to your mother?"

"Come now." She quickly stroked her fingers along his sleeve, a movement that would incite a firestorm of gossip if anyone noticed it. "Don't you want to spend more time with me?"

"Of course."

"Besides . . ." She gave a quick jerk of her head. "Richard just came in and he looks like a thunderstorm. I sure hope he hasn't lost again. Maybe we can avoid a scene if we're dancing."

He frowned. "Annabelle, I can handle Raventhorpe."

"I'm sure you can, but he wasn't pleased that Pa's letting you escort me around, so I'd rather just avoid him when we are together."

"I won't hide from him."

"We're not hiding. We're avoiding. Please, Samuel?"

"Very well." He led Annabelle onto the dance floor to set her at ease, but dodging the earl did not sit well with him. "I don't want you to be afraid of him, Annabelle. If he starts trouble, I'll finish it."

"This is no place for a brawl, and I don't want Richard embarrassed. He's a very proud man."

"And I am not?" The orchestra started up, and he swept her into an energetic polka. "I'm civilized enough not to start a brawl in the ballroom, Annabelle. Certainly you know that."

"Now, Samuel, don't fret." She gave a soothing pat to the shoulder she clung to as they danced. "I know you're brave. I just think it's better to avoid a scene. Surely you can do that for me?" Her smile was all coaxing and sugar. She might as well have yanked on a leash.

Was this the life he had once strived for? Was this the woman he had imagined as the mother of his children for all those long months on the island? This uninitiated flirt who thought to control a man's actions with fluttering lashes and a smile? If so, then he'd had a lucky escape the day Annabelle had broken their engagement.

"How old are you, Annabelle?"

She laughed. "Now Samuel, you know it's not polite to ask that."

"Humor me. The years have gotten away from me."

Her merriment faded to be replaced by compassion. "I'm so sorry. Of course they have. I'm twenty years old, though I'll be twenty-one in June."

"Twenty-one." Hell, she was just a baby. Had he really considered her for his life's partner?

He caught sight of Cilla strolling down the edge of the dance floor with Sir Harry. Her womanly curves never ceased to draw his attention. Cilla and the baronet appeared to be in an animated discussion. Her eyes flashed with intelligence as she laughed, the husky sound getting lost in the volume of the music. Her hand rested on Sir Harry's sleeve. Now that was a woman suitable for a long-term partnership.

Friday couldn't come soon enough.

Chapter 19

Friday dawned bright and cheerful. Cilla glanced at the note in her hand, her heart stumbling over itself as the words sank into her consciousness.

I will send the coach at noon.

She folded the paper as if were made of moth's wings, then tucked it into the tiny wooden box that held her simple jewelry and other treasures. Someday when she was much older, she would find these notes and remember with fondness how she had indulged in one wild love affair.

She had thought after watching him with Anna-belle Wednesday night that Samuel would not want to see her again. But when the young boy had arrived at the kitchen door yesterday afternoon with the missive in his hand, it was all she could do not to snatch up the lad and kiss him soundly. One more day with Samuel brought joy to her heart.

She loved him. How could she not? Here was a man who sacrificed anything necessary to do what was right. A man who fearlessly pursued the honorable path, even though it might seem an impossible task. No wonder he had survived the trials of his captivity! He had bound himself to Annabelle two years ago and strived from the moment of his release to keep his promise to her. She could respect him for that.

A knock came at the door. She tied the ribbons of her bonnet, then hurried to open the portal. Annabelle stood outside in the dim hallway. "Oh good," she said, twisting her fingers together. "I was hoping to see you before you left for the day."

"Is something wrong?" Cilla tightened her hand around the doorknob. *Please, God, let nothing go awry that would keep me home today!*

"Not wrong. I just wanted to talk to you for a moment. Might I come in?"

"Certainly." Cilla stepped backward, opening the door wider.

Annabelle darted inside, and stood fidgeting as Cilla shut the door. "Mrs. Burke, I need your advice."

"Of course." A bit alarmed by Annabelle's nervousness, Cilla indicated the chair of her tiny writing table. "Would you like to sit down?"

"No, I can't sit still."

"Are you sick? Is something wrong?"

"No, no." The girl shook her head.

"Is there a problem? Was someone cruel to you?"

"No, nothing like that."

"Did you—"

"I've decided to break my engagement to Richard so that Samuel can court me, too," Annabelle blurted. "That is, let both Samuel and Richard court me so I can decide which one to marry." She sucked in a breath and bit her lower lip, eyes wide as she awaited Cilla's response.

Cilla, on the other hand, had no breath. Surely every whisper of air had left her lungs. Her heart had stopped. The world stood still, then sharply turned over on its axis, tossing Cilla aside like a discarded handkerchief. Annabelle was actually talking about jilting Raventhorpe, but the price would be Samuel stepping to the role of suitor.

He had already told her that he had no intention of taking his relationship with Annabelle any further than close family friend. But if courting her got him the goal he wanted—keeping Annabelle from Raventhorpe—would he then consider it? And once in the position of contender for her hand, would he then be compelled to follow through with marriage? Would his honor demand it?

If he agreed to any of it, their arrangement would end. And she wasn't ready.

"Mrs. Burke, you haven't said anything."

Cilla inhaled slowly. "Does he know?"

"Samuel? No. I still need to break my engagement with Richard first before telling Samuel."

"You made this decision after one evening in his company?" Cilla asked, her lips dry.

"He was going to marry me before, so I know my money doesn't matter to him. And I know him. I'm comfortable with him."

Cilla nodded. Words lodged in her throat, unable to wedge past the emotion welling up there.

"I haven't told anyone yet," Annabelle said. "I wanted you to be the first to know."

"Thank you." Was that raspy croak really her voice? She cleared her throat. "Thank you, truly. I am honored to be the first to know."

"I'm off to tell Mama and Pa." Annabelle grabbed Cilla in a huge hug. "Thank you for being such a wonderful friend, Mrs. Burke. I don't know what I shall do without you when we return to the United States." She opened the door and rushed out, leaving Cilla stricken and alone.

John helped her down from the carriage. Samuel came to the doorway of the cottage, shirt untucked and his hair askew as if he'd run his hands through it. When he saw her, a smile swept across his face, and her chest seized.

Dear God, how could she ever walk away from him?

He stepped forward as she neared the doorway and pulled her into his arms, his mouth coming down on hers in a kiss that fueled her own passion. She clung to him, clenching her hands in his shirt as he gave her what she'd been craving.

Him. Just him.

Tears pricked her eyes, but she forced them back. Later she would cry. Later she would curl into a ball and let pain carry her away. But for now—

Dear God, she needed to tell him. How could she form the words?

He must have sensed something because he pulled back, slowly as if he couldn't bear to stop, and looked into her eyes. His brow furrowed. "Priscilla, sweetheart, what's the matter?"

She opened her mouth to speak and could not, not while she was looking into that face, those eyes. Beloved face, beloved eyes. God help her, but she did not want to let him go.

"We should go inside," she managed.

"Of course." Samuel gave a salute to John, who returned the gesture and snapped the reins over the horses. Samuel curled his arm around her shoulders and led her into the house.

Once inside, she didn't know what to do with herself. She stared around her, at the tiny cottage and the memories that lingered there. She wanted to moan like a grieving widow, to beat her breast. She could not do this. She wasn't strong enough.

"Cilla, my darling." He took her by the shoulders and peered into her face, his own a study of concern and confusion. "What is it? Tell me."

Tell him. Yes, she needed to tell him. She sucked in a deep breath. "I have news, Captain."

"Captain?" He reared back a bit, as if uncertain. "Something has happened. What is it?"

"Good news." She forced a smile to her lips, hating its falsity, trying to project a cheerfulness she would never feel. "Annabelle told me this morning she wants you to court her. She is going to break off the engagement to Lord Raventhorpe completely and allow both of you to compete for her hand."

"Both of us?" he repeated, his voice flat. Shock, perhaps?

"You should be happy. We are closer to our goal."

"Indeed." He frowned and looked down at the floor, hands on his hips. "Certainly this is a time to celebrate." Her insincere smile was going to crack her face if it got any wider. "Maybe some of that wine you are always offering me."

He jerked his head up, his eyes intense in his face. "Are you pleased about this?"

"I am happy for you. I am not pleased about losing my position now that the wedding may not happen."

"Hang your position! Aren't you the least bit upset about us? That our arrangement might have to end, even for a little while?"

"We knew it would at some point." She strolled about the room, touching a table here, a glass there, trying not to shatter as pain crept through her with enough force to splinter her bones. "We are adults. We must do what is necessary. What is right."

"To hell with what is right." He swept her into his arms, and she didn't have the strength to even pretend to resist. "You are all I can think about and I would make love to you for weeks until you begged me to stop."

His passion stirred her own. "I would never beg you to stop," she breathed.

"I want you, Priscilla Burke. If this is our last afternoon together, let's bloody well make it the memory of a lifetime."

"Oh, God, yes." She bit her lip, trying to control the sobs welling up within her, but she lost the battle. Tears trickled down her cheeks. "She is telling Raventhorpe today."

"She hasn't told me anything yet, therefore I don't know anything about it." He cupped her face in his hands. "Come to bed with me, Priscilla, and let me take you to places you never imagined."

"Yes." She jerked at the ribbons to her bonnet. "This is all we have. Our last time together."

"And we'll make it memorable." He helped her with her bonnet, then tossed it across the room. Both of them tore at her clothing, all the buttons and petticoats and layers, leaving a trail down the hall as they made their way to the bedroom. All the time he kissed her, murmuring words of affection, of praise, against her mouth. By the time they reached the bedroom, she was nearly naked.

He sat on the edge of the bed and pulled her, clad only in her undergarments and stockings, between his spread legs. He snagged the strings of her corset and set about unlacing it as she stroked her hands through his hair.

Such a woman. Samuel tossed the corset aside and filled his hands with her breasts. God, he loved touching her. Abundant curves formed a woman's body that begged for his passion and invited him to play. That bee-stung mouth—he had plans for that today. She was a grown woman, not some too slim, immaculate virgin who squealed every time he touched her. No, this was a partner who would arouse him as much as he did her, who would tease him and torment him until they both exploded.

He fell back on the bed, dragging her with him. She laughed, that husky sound that drove him wild, and wiggled against him as she struggled to pull her chemise over her head. Finally her bare breasts crushed against his chest. He cupped her bottom through her drawers and rubbed his hard cock against her through their clothes. Sounds of pleasure erupted from her throat, and she pushed against his chest, forcing him down on his back while she straddled him.

He grinned, and she laughed, throwing back her head like a madwoman. Her hair was starting to droop, and she speared her hands through the sedate bun, sending pins flying as she shook her head, her hair exploding around her like some kind of wild mermaid.

God damn, but he loved her.

The thought took him by surprise, shaking him to the core. Love? How many times had he said he didn't think he was able to love?

She jerked at his shirt, and he allowed her to remove it. Then she tugged at the fastenings of his trousers. The fumbling of her fingers on the fastenings sent his lust soaring like a cannon shot. He tried to help her, and between the two of them they managed to open or remove enough of his clothing that his cock sprang free.

She pounced on it, making a growling noise that reminded him of a cat with a bowl of cream. She toyed with him, stroking her fingers along the length with a maddening slowness that made his brain slow down.

He loved her. Why wouldn't he? This woman who had braved disinheritance for love, who had survived when any other woman would have crumbled. This sensual creature who relished sex as much as any man and seemed to have no inhibitions, no fears. Of course he loved her. Of course.

She dropped a playful kiss on the blunt tip of his cock, and while rockets went off inside his head, she sat up, braced herself on his chest, and sank down on him, taking him inside her through the slit in her drawers.

He grabbed her hips and held on as he thrust upward. Her warm body welcomed him, caressing the length of him with sweet, quivering flesh. He closed his eyes, hungry to spill his seed inside her, to claim her. To make her his.

She made a little cry, and he opened his eyes. She threw her head back, her hair a wild tangle around her slender body as she rode him, her plump breasts bouncing with her rhythm. He reached up, grabbed a hank of her hair, and pulled her forward. She tumbled onto his chest, catching herself, her dark eyes wide and dewy with desire. For a long moment he held her there, the connection between them taut like a vibrating harp string. Then he wrapped her hair around his hand and pulled her mouth to his, greedy to brand her as his, and rolled over so she was beneath him.

"Samuel."

His name on her lips drugged him like wine, and he grabbed her wrists, stretching her arms above her hand. "Say it again."

"Samuel." She made a sound in her throat as he thrust hard. "Samuel."

"Yes. Say it." He worked his flesh inside her, driving both of them higher and higher. All the while he stared into her eyes, willing her to understand, to know, that she was his. Always. His.

"Samuel!" She arched her hips.

"Take me," he demanded, then crushed his mouth to hers. "Take my love, damn it."

Her eyes flew open. She gasped just as he buried himself deep, arching his back as his climax exploded over him. Too late. He started to pull away, tried to save her. But she curled her legs around his waist and would not let him go.

"Mine." She gripped him with surprisingly strong limbs. "Stay."

"God help us." He stayed, settled as the last tremors of his climax shook him. "I shouldn't have—"

"Shhh." She leaned up and kissed his mouth. "No regrets."

"But—"

She kissed him again, softly. "This is all we have now, and I want to take all of it."

He let out a long breath. "Wanton wench."

"Yes."

"All right. We won't speak of it now." He took her lower lip with his teeth and tugged, then let it go. "Are you hungry?"

"Only for you."

He chuckled. "Dear God, what have I done?"

"Brought me to life." She stretched beneath him, her eyes slitted like a cat's, her lips curved in a knowing smile. "And I cannot thank you enough."

"I bet you can."

Her laughter echoed through the cottage as he rolled over and started all over again.

She loved him.

There was no doubt in her mind as, hours later, she lay in the bed with Samuel half on top of her, his face buried in her neck as gentle snores shook his body. She toyed with his hair, staring up at the ceiling and thinking about what came next.

This afternoon was all they had. Today or tomorrow, Virgil Bailey would summon Samuel and offer to let him officially court Annabelle.

Had Samuel wanted this all along? He claimed that the courtship would be simply a delaying tactic until Annabelle was safe. That their lessons would stop only temporarily, until Raventhorpe was permanently out of the picture. What if he could not resist the temptation of marrying the woman he had fought so hard to come home to?

No, she could not believe that of him.

He was exactly the type of man she had always dreamed of, a man who could share with her all the pleasures of the flesh and yet still be counted upon when times were bad. A man who would do anything to win his lady.

A man who kept his word.

But both of them knew the truth. They could not continue their relationship if Samuel had to court Annabelle. It was the right thing to do—even if it broke her heart.

Samuel groaned in his sleep and turned his head. His eyes drifted open, and a sleepy smile curved his lips when he saw her. "Hello."

"Hello." She almost choked on the word as she reached up to stroke his hair.

"Did I fall asleep?"

"For a little while."

He frowned. "I must be heavy."

"No—"

He shifted onto his back, taking the delicious weight from her, but then he dragged her against him, tucking her head on his shoulder. She curved against him as if she'd been made for him. "There. Much better."

"I was fine."

"I'm sure you were." He tipped up her face with a finger beneath her chin and pressed a kiss to her mouth. "You are the finest woman I have ever met."

Her heart fluttered in her chest. "You do not need to flatter me, Samuel. I am already in your bed."

"That's not what I was trying to do." He traced her cheek with his finger. "I was speaking from the heart."

"Oh." Her insides melted. Such lovely words. But she wanted more. And that determination to make sure she did things right the second time gave her the strength to resist his sweet words.

Sweet words that did not include the one she most wanted to hear. Love.

She sat up, her insides churning. What they had was so close to what she had dreamed, and yet . . . "We must be realistic. Things are changing."

"What are you talking about?"

"Annabelle."

"Blast it, I told you I don't want Annabelle."

"I know. But you *are* committed to saving her. We both are, which is why we hatched this mad scheme to begin with—so you could keep her safe from Raventhorpe. And I helped you do it. I helped you drive a wedge between them, but now she wants you to court her . . ." She paused, struggling with a control that was rapidly slipping from her grasp. "I am worried I may end up losing you."

"Come here, Cilla." He sat up and tried to pull her into his arms, but she shrugged him off.

"We were fooling ourselves. Or at least I was fooling myself." She jerked away the covers and stumbled from the bed, tripping over one of the shoes she had discarded earlier. "I thought I could have an affair with you and walk away whole. But I cannot. I will never forget you, and any man who comes after you will pale in comparison." Naked, she began collecting her clothes, which were scattered around the room.

"I don't want to hear about other men, damn it." He got out of bed, shoving the covers to the floor. "There won't be any other men."

"There have to be. I must find a husband, Samuel. And you are not *capable* of giving me what I want. What I need." She found her drawers and pulled them on, tying them swiftly.

"Love." He fisted his hands, the mere word setting him on edge.

"I have told you how important that is to me. The longer you pretend otherwise, the harder it will be to walk away from each other." She bent down to grab her chemise from the floor. "And if you start courting Annabelle, our affair must end. We agreed on that. What if you decide you want to wed her after all?"

He jerked her up with his hands around her upper arms, making her drop the garment. "Blast it, Cilla, that won't happen."

She gave a violent shrug, shaking him loose, then snatched up her chemise again. "You don't know that. We have no choice, Samuel. We must end this affair now if we are to live with ourselves."

"God damn it!" He ripped a hand through his hair. "This is why I didn't let myself believe in love all those years. It hurts too damned much."

"Please accept my apologies for making you feel some sort of emotion!" She jerked the chemise over her head and tugged it down around her hips. "Had you continued the way you were, you would have grown into a bitter old man."

"I might have been better off." He scowled as she retrieved her corset. "Don't go yet. John won't be here for another hour."

She stilled and looked at him. "Perhaps this is better. A clean break."

"I'm not ready."

The words sounded as if they'd been ripped from him against his will, and she couldn't stop the tender smile that curved her mouth. "Neither of us are. But it must be done, whether now or an hour from now. The day will not stop simply because we will it to."

"God damn it!"

She could tell from the frustration on his face that he'd accepted that she meant what she said, though he didn't like it. He stood in the center of the room, stark naked, his hands clenching and unclenching into fists as he watched her collect and put on her garments. With each piece of clothing she donned, her insides steadied, as if the attire represented the walls she was building inside herself. Finally he stalked across the room and found his trousers, jerking them on.

She finished dressing, but then ran into a problem with her hairpins. They'd scattered all over the room, so she began looking for them on the bed first. Just the memory of his hands raking through her hair, strewing the pins all over the place, made her heart twist. By the time she had finished searching the bedclothes, he stood waiting with a handful of pins he had found on the floor. She scooped them out of his hand, her fingers tingling just from touching him, and went to the bureau to look in the mirror.

"I don't suppose you have a hairbrush—"

A crash came from the other room. Samuel jerked to attention, striding to his coat hanging from a hook on the wall and digging a pistol out of the large pocket. He waved her toward the corner of the room as he took a position beside the door, attention focused outward.

"Samuel!" someone shouted.

He lowered the pistol. "It's John." He gave her a quick glance as if to assure himself that she was decent, then opened the door. "In here, John. What's wrong?"

The bearded coachman appeared in the doorway. He glanced at Cilla, gave a nod, then turned his attention back to Samuel. "Raventhorpe has kidnapped Annabelle."

"What!" Cilla cried.

"That bastard!" Samuel's eyes narrowed. "What happened?"

"Bailey invited Raventhorpe to come so Annabelle could end the engagement. The fool left them alone so she could tell him herself."

Samuel shook his head. "Bailey always put too much store in the honor of noblemen. So he took her then?"

"Mrs. Bailey saw Raventhorpe carrying off Annabelle from the parlor window. Of course those bloody servants are all loyal to him, so none of them stopped him. Mrs. Bailey ran after them and tripped on the stairs. She fell, and then it was all bedlam because she hit her head and injured her leg. Probably broke it."

"Oh, my heavens!" Cilla splayed a hand over her bosom. "Is she all right?"

"I don't know. Bailey sent a lad around to the

inn to tell you to come," John said to Samuel. "I think he wants you to go after Annabelle."

"Absolutely. I trust you brought the rifle?"

"And your other pistol. He looks to have headed north. Most probably—"

"Gretna Green. That scum. Does he really think she will wed him after all that?"

John nodded. "Annabelle delights in her new social status, and being trapped overnight with a man not her husband is enough to ruin her."

"Doesn't seem like that would matter to Annabelle. No one ever made her do anything she didn't want to," Samuel said.

"John has a point," Cilla said. "Her reputation *would* matter to Annabelle, but not for herself. For her mother. She wants Dolly to be able to go about in society."

"God damn it. So she might marry him to save her mother some grief."

"Yes."

"We'll just have to make sure they don't stay somewhere overnight." Samuel handed his pistol to John. "Take this while I get dressed. I'll be ready in a minute."

"And what about Mrs. Burke?"

Samuel glanced at Cilla. The regret in his eyes echoed her own. "We can't leave you here. I guess you have to come with us. We'll make up some story."

"All right. Let me finish getting ready." She walked over to the mirror and began coiling her long hair into her familiar style. She watched Samuel in the mirror as he searched out his clothing. So handsome. So strong and sure. Everything a woman could want in a man.

A pang of longing shook her. Their arrangement had come to an end. Never again would she see the inside of this little cottage where she had learned so much. About men. About herself.

The adventure truly had ended.

Chapter 20

Annabelle awoke in a carriage. She could tell from the movement and the scent of leather and horses. Her head ached, and her tongue felt made of cotton. She groaned, opening her eyes.

"Ah, you are awake." Richard smiled from the seat across from her.

She realized she was lying down and pushed herself into a sitting position, the blanket that covered her slipping to the floor. Her head spun for a moment, but then settled. "What are you doing? What happened to me?"

"You do not remember? You tried to refuse my suit, my dear. I could not allow that to happen, so I had to take desperate measures."

She frowned. "I just remember talking to you, and then you took my arm . . ."

A pinprick, she remembered. Then dizziness.

"What did you do?" She studied his face, so familiar, and yet the look in his eyes that of a stranger. "You did something to me, didn't you?"

"Just gave you a little something to keep you quiet so I could get you out of the house. I had the feeling you would not come with me willingly."

"You drugged me? Then kidnapped me?" She jerked aside the curtain to reveal the countryside whipping by, then glanced back at him. "Why?"

"Why? Because you were about to jilt me for that lowborn American! Luckily I still have friends among the servants in your household, and they warned me." He smiled, and the expression chilled her. "So I came prepared."

"To kidnap me and hold me for ransom? Are you crazy?"

He narrowed his eyes. "Ransom has nothing to do with it. We're going to Scotland. I own an estate there, and you're going to marry me."

"You really are crazy if you think that's going to happen!"

"And you should have a care with your words, Annabelle. You do not want to insult me, not when I hold your life in my hands."

Another outburst bubbled up inside her, but she clamped her lips shut.

He laughed. "Very good! Obedience is a desirable quality in a wife, and it is rewarding to see that you already know its value."

"I'm not going to marry you," she said.

"You are." He arched his brows, a nasty gleam in his eye. "Do you know what will happen to your reputation once word gets out that you spent the night alone with me on the road to Gretna Green? Or at my Scottish estate? Your reputation will be ruined."

She shrugged.

"And if your reputation is in tatters, your mother's will soon follow."

She gasped. "Mama didn't do anything!"

"Her good name would be tarnished because of yours, my dear. And then who in New York society would allow her to darken their door? No, she would be an outcast."

She clenched her hands into fists in her lap. "I'm sorry I ever told you about that."

"We all have regrets, my dear."

Samuel walked into Nevarton Chase without knocking, Cilla on his heels and John behind her. A footman stepped forward to stop him. He grabbed the servant by his liveried coat. "Where's Bailey?"

The footman looked as if he would not answer, but Samuel gave him a shake. "Upstairs with Mrs. Bailey," he said.

"How is she, Jeffrey?" Cilla asked. "I was told she was injured."

"Took a tumble down the stairs trying to catch His Lordship. Knocked her head pretty good and broke her leg."

Cilla met Samuel's gaze. "I need to go to her."

"I'll come with you." He shoved the servant aside. "Bailey did send for me, after all."

"Sent for you!" the footman burst out.

John stepped closer and loomed over the shorter man. "Sent for him," he repeated.

Cilla let out a sigh of frustration. "We are wasting time." Gathering her skirts, she spun away from them and hurried up the staircase.

Samuel bounded after her.

John remained, calling up to them, "I will stay here and keep the horses warm."

Samuel reached the landing first, his longer stride carrying him more quickly up the stairs. He reached for her hand as she caught up with him, but she shrugged him off and raced down the hallway. Her rejection stung, but then he remembered where they were. There would be questions as it was about how Cilla came to be with him. They didn't need to expose their true relationship to the entire household.

"Samuel!" She signaled to him from outside a bedchamber at the end of the hall. As he sprinted toward her, she went inside the room.

When he got there, Cilla was seated on a stool beside the bed, holding Dolly's hand. The normally joyful Dolly looked like a pale reflection of herself, her hand limp in Cilla's, a bandage on her forehead. Her blue eyes, normally full of kindness and good cheer, stared straight ahead, dull and lifeless.

Virgil paced by the bedside, throwing concerned looks at his wife. When Samuel entered the room, some of his tension eased. "Samuel, thank God. You need to go after them. You need to go get my Annabelle."

"I will." Samuel stepped up to the bed. "Mrs. Bailey, don't you worry. I'm going to catch him. I'll bring your daughter back to you."

Dolly turned her head and stared at him, a flicker of hope lighting her deadened eyes. "Swear to me."

"I swear. I won't let him get away with this."

"How could we not know?" Her eyes reddened

as moisture gathered in the corners. "I thought an earl would be an honorable man. How could we not know of his evil?"

"Some men are very clever," Cilla said, patting her hand. "Do not blame yourself."

"I would go myself," Virgil said, "but Dolly—"

"Stay with your wife," Samuel said. "Leave Raventhorpe to me."

"Cilla should go," Dolly said.

"No, I will stay here with you," Cilla said, leaning closer.

"No. Do this for me." Dolly met and held Cilla's gaze, her blue eyes glittering with intent. "Take care of my baby. She's going to need a woman with her. Especially if he . . . if he . . ." Her voice broke, and tears overflowed.

"There has not been time," Cilla murmured, patting Dolly's hand. "He is in a rush to get to Scotland so they can wed. He will not risk stopping."

Dolly looked at Samuel. "Tell her."

"She's right." Samuel clenched his jaw. "A man can accomplish a lot of things in a moving carriage, and he might decide it's better to assure that she's ruined."

"Samuel!" Cilla bit her lip, glancing with concern at Dolly.

"If I ever get my hands around that varmint's neck . . ." Virgil muttered.

"He will pay for this," Samuel vowed.

"Go with him, Cilla. Please. Take care of my baby. She might need a woman to comfort her, and I can't be there, not with this stupid leg."

"All right." Cilla looked at Virgil. "Are you certain you do not want me to stay here with her?"

"I can take care of my Dolly. You just go fetch my little girl back."

"Come on. We should leave right now. He's already got a lead on us." Samuel grabbed her hand and tugged her from the chair.

"But . . . should I not . . ."

"Thank you, Cilla," Dolly whispered, her expression full of hope.

"Take anything you need," Virgil said, clapping Samuel on the shoulder.

"I have my carriage, and John knows the way." Samuel glanced from one to the other. "I will bring her back safely. Come, Mrs. Burke."

"We will bring her home," Cilla said. She followed Samuel as he quit the room. Hurrying down the hall to keep up with his long strides, she asked, "Are you certain John knows the way to Gretna Green?"

"Hell yes." Samuel reached stairs and started down them at a pace that was almost too fast for her to keep up. "He got married there once."

"Oh."

Annabelle had come to the conclusion that she would have to do something drastic.

Richard had made one huge mistake in her opinion; he underestimated her. He saw her as a pretty, empty-headed doll like most debutantes. But she wasn't like that at all. She was an American girl, born and raised to think for herself. But if he was foolish enough not to realize that, she wasn't about to tell him. No sirree. If he wanted a feather wit, then that's what she would be.

"I certainly hope you planned for this trip, Richard," she said. "I simply cannot go without a change of clothing."

He looked at her in surprise. "We will buy anything you need."

"Buy! As in factory-made clothing?" She shook her head and clucked her tongue. "I'm an heiress now, and soon to be a countess if you have your way. I simply can't wear factory-made clothing. We must visit a modiste as soon as possible."

"Do not be a fool. You will take what I buy you and wear it with pleasure. Or I can keep you naked. It's your choice."

A shocked blush warmed her cheeks, but it went with the character she was trying to portray. "Richard! I can't believe you said that to me!"

"Believe it." He took in her body with a covetous gaze that made her want to cringe. She fought the urge to wrap the blanket even tighter around her. She had to play his game.

But when this was over, she would scrub her skin raw.

"I can't imagine how you would explain such a sight to people," she said finally.

"We would not see any people. Once we're married, I'm taking you away to one of my other properties so we can be alone." He chuckled. "I am looking forward to claiming my bride."

She wanted to say something but could not think of anything suitably dim-witted that would fool him.

Not when she wanted to tear into him with her nails until she drew blood. She settled for looking out the curtain again at the passing countryside. The sky burned pink with the setting sun. Soon it would be dark. And Raventhorpe in the dark scared her more than anything.

She settled into her seat and prepared to wait for opportunity.

As the coach sped along the road, Cilla held on, trying not to remember another time when she and Samuel had been alone in his coach, the night he had taught her how to kiss him. So many memories, so many feelings. Would the simplest things always remind her so vividly of Samuel?

"We will catch up to them, Cilla."

His voice sounded reassuring, but she could see the banked anger in his eyes. She had learned to read him so well. "I hope we are in time. Raventhorpe is unpredictable."

"I won't let him have her."

She looked outside at the passing countryside. "At least it is reasonable to assume that she will not choose Raventhorpe as a husband after this."

"Thank God for small favors."

"We need a big favor today."

"We'll find them. And if he's hurt her, he'll answer to me."

A gunshot rang out through the night.

Annabelle cried out and squeezed back against the seat. Richard leaned forward, flipping aside the curtain to look out at the road. A large dark object fell past the window, rolling away from the carriage as it sped along.

"That was the bloody coachman!" Raventhorpe leaned out the window, looking up toward the coachman's box. Then he slid back into the vehicle. "Someone else is driving, and I'm going to find out who." He pulled out a pistol and held it ready, then met her gaze. "Do not fear for my safety, my darling."

"I won't."

He narrowed his eyes at her, then opened the door and eased out, gripping the side of the vehicle. Clearly he intended to work his way up to the coachman's seat. Or was he just going to shoot the poor man? Surely that would be suicide for all of them!

She slid across the seat to the other side of the carriage and opened the window there, then stuck out her head. "Watch out! He's got a gun!"

The driver glanced back at her, but she could not see his face in the dimness of twilight. She ducked back into the carriage and turned to see Richard glaring at her from where he clung to the coach on the opposite side. His sneer promised retribution, but at the moment she was willing to take her chance on the strange driver rather than the familiar earl. Good God, what if she'd married this lunatic?

A shot rang out.

Raventhorpe turned toward the coachman, his expression startled, then lost his grip and fell off into the road. The driver slowed the horses. Moments later the coach came to a halt. Annabelle looked around her but no weapon appeared. Clutching the blanket, she shrank back into the seat and waited.

The door to the coach opened. A man stood there in a black hat and coat, black driving gloves on his hands. He smiled at her, and only then did she realize he wore a mask.

"Well, hello there. You must be another one of Raventhorpe's collection, destined for some rich pasha's harem, no doubt."

"What are you talking about?" She took pride that her voice quivered only a little.

"Raventhorpe. He captures innocent women and sells them as slaves overseas. I assume you are here against your will?"

She nodded, too aghast to speak.

"Then 'tis lucky I came along. Excuse me a moment while I go tie up His Lordship before he makes a nuisance of himself."

"But . . . who . . . ?"

"Who am I?" He tipped his hat. "Black Bill. Now stay right there while I take care of business." He closed the door to the coach.

Annabelle stared at the place where he'd been. Black Bill. Maybe she hadn't been saved after all.

She scrambled out of the coach. A few yards away, Richard had gotten to his feet and was searching the brush at the side of the road, cursing a blue streak that shocked even her, a girl raised around coal miners. Black Bill approached him at a rapid pace, pistol at the ready.

"Raventhorpe!"

Richard whipped around. Hatred twisted his features. "Black Bill. Damn you!"

"Hands in the air. Step into the middle of the road."

"Will you murder me here?" Raventhorpe did as the highwayman bade him, then glanced at Annabelle. "In front of my fiancée?"

Black Bill never so much as glanced behind him. "Fiancée, is it? And here I thought she was another one of your victims."

"I am not betrothed to him," Annabelle called.

"Annabelle, do not lie simply because you are put out with me," Richard said, his voice taking on a persuasive tone. "Do you not realize this brigand is going to kill me with the slightest provocation?"

"Annabelle, is it?" Black Bill said. Again, he never looked away from Raventhorpe. "Annabelle Bailey? I had heard you were engaged to this poor excuse for a human being."

Annabelle lifted her chin and glared at Raventhorpe. "I broke the engagement only today, and that is when he kidnapped me."

Black Bill laughed. "Ah, now that sounds like the Raventhorpe I know. Jilted you, did she? A smart woman."

"What now?" Raventhorpe demanded. "Will you kill us both here in the middle of the road?"

"My dear Raventhorpe," Black Bill said with humor heavy in his voice. "With all the times I have intercepted your victims, have I ever killed anyone?"

"Actually no." A sly expression crossed Raventhorpe's face. His hands lowered an inch or so.

Black Bill tensed. "Do not try it. Just because I have not killed you yet does not mean I do not dream of doing so every day of my existence."

Raventhorpe froze. "What have I done to you that you would hate me so?"

"Someday I will tell you the tale. But not today. Miss Bailey?"

"Yes?"

"There should be some rope under the coachman's seat. Do you think you can fetch it and bring it here?"

Richard jerked his gaze to Annabelle, and she smiled. "Yes."

Raventhorpe's mouth fell open. Black Bill laughed as Annabelle hurried to do as he requested. "Do you think this girl is a fool, Raventhorpe? If so, then you are even more so."

"You speak like a gentleman," Raventhorpe said, his eyes narrowing.

"So do you, but we all know what you are, don't we?" Annabelle arrived with the rope. "Do you feel comfortable tying up His Lordship, Miss Bailey?"

"Absolutely." Annabelle marched forward. "Put your hands behind you, Richard."

Raventhorpe glared at her, and ice splintered through her as she caught a true glimpse of the evil that lurked behind his lordly demeanor.

"Do as she says," Black Bill said. He aimed at Raventhorpe's leg. "I am told a shattered kneecap is most painful."

Raventhorpe stiffened, then slowly complied.

"Have a care, Miss Bailey," Black Bill said. "He

would not be above trying to grab you and use you as a hostage."

"Thank you for the warning, sir," Annabelle said. She quickly wrapped the rope around the earl's wrists, then tied a knot and pulled the ends hard. The earl flinched. "Oh, did I hurt you, Richard? Good."

Black Bill chuckled as Annabelle moved away from the earl. "She's a feisty one, Raventhorpe. Too bad you did not realize the treasure you had in her while you had it. Now turn around."

Raventhorpe shuffled around so he faced away from the highwayman. "Will you shoot me in the back, coward that you are?"

"Only if you do something foolish." Black Bill examined Annabelle's handiwork, then cast her a smile. "An excellent knot, Miss Bailey. Where did you learn to tie so well?"

"I lived on a farm my whole life, and I was engaged to a sea captain."

"Excellent. Raventhorpe, down on your knees."

The earl obeyed with some awkwardness. "I will have the magistrate on you, you bastard. You have made a grave mistake treating me like this. Or perhaps you do not realize this is my land?"

"Of course I realize it is your land, my lord fool. I only work on your properties. That is the purpose of a vendetta."

"Vendetta? Damn you, what have I ever done to you? I do not even know who you are!"

"As I said, someday I will tell you the tale. Perhaps at your hanging." The highwayman approached Raventhorpe and put the barrel of his weapon against the earl's temple with one hand while he searched Raventhorpe's pockets with the other. "Let me see, where is it? Oh, I see. You're still wearing it." He slipped a ring from the earl's finger.

"Bloody thief!"

Black Bill laughed. "I *am* a highwayman, you know." Without turning away from his captive, he held up a ring. "Do you see this, Miss Bailey?"

"Yes."

"Taking a page from the Borgias, are you, Raventhorpe?" Black Bill pressed the ring against Raventhorpe's neck. A moment later the earl fell forward, unconscious.

"What have you done to him?" Annabelle cried.

Black Bill walked over to her and handed her the ring. "Have you seen this before?"

"Yes, it is Richard's family insignia. A dragon."

"He coats the claws of the dragon with a drug that induces sleep. It is how he takes his victims."

Annabelle jerked with shock and dropped the ring. "He did that to me. Something pricked my arm and then I awoke in the coach."

"The effects do not last long, apparently. Just long enough for him to transfer his captives." Mouth pressed in a grim line, Black Bill picked up the ring and wrapped it in his handkerchief. Tying it safely with a knot, he slipped the bundle into his pocket.

Annabelle folded her arms around herself, realizing suddenly that she stood in the middle of the road with a thief who a few moments ago had seemed a better alternative than Richard, but now . . . well, he *was* a highwayman. "What do you intend for me?"

Black Bill grinned. "I mean you no harm, Miss Bailey. Truth be told, I knew who you were when I came after you. Your father sent a note around to Captain Breedlove's inn to summon him, and word got back to me."

Relief shuddered through her. "Samuel is coming?"

"He was delayed, which is why I decided to intervene. Plus, I try never to miss an opportunity to serve a blow to Raventhorpe."

"You pretended not to know who I was. All that talk about slavery—"

"Is the truth." His jaw clenched. "My actions were intended to protect you and keep Raventhorpe guessing."

"But you shot our coachman."

The highwayman shook his head. "The fool fought me when I tried to shove him out of the driver's seat. He took a bullet in the arm. No doubt the captain will find him on his way here."

As if his words had summoned reality, the rumble of horses' hooves and coach wheels reached their ears.

"That is probably him now. Wait here. I will watch from nearby to assure you are safe in their care."

"You are a very strange highwayman."

"And you are a very brave woman. I will be watching, so have no fear."

Even though he dressed like a highwayman and had admitted to committing such crimes—if only for his own reasons—there was something in his eyes that reassured her. Something resembling honesty, strangely enough, that comforted her despite the circumstances. "Thank you."

He grinned and gave her a quick bow, then disappeared into the trees, leaving her standing at the side of the road beside Raventhorpe's unconscious body.

Chapter 21

"**A**re you certain you are going to be all right?" Cilla asked, casting a glance at the wounded man sitting on the seat next to Samuel.

"It's just a scratch, though you're a kind soul for asking," Tom Nethry said.

"So you're not the earl's normal driver?" Samuel said.

"No. He hires me once in a while when his other fellow is sick. Usually to take him down to Cornwall. This is the first time we went north."

"Didn't you realize that there might be something afoot when the earl carried Miss Bailey into the coach?" Samuel asked. "I would think you would be suspicious."

Nethry shrugged. "He said the lady fainted when he told her they were eloping, she was so excited. It's not my place to ask questions."

Cilla met Samuel's eyes, and he shrugged. Clearly the driver was a bit of a simpleton, hired by Raventhorpe only on occasion, and there was not much they could learn from him except their destination had indeed been Gretna Green.

The coach suddenly slowed. "Samuel!" John called.

Samuel glanced out the window, then shoved the door open and leaped out as the vehicle rocked to a halt. "Annabelle! Are you all right?"

Cilla scrambled to get out on the other side. She stumbled a bit as her feet hit the ground, and she looked up just in time to see Annabelle fling herself into Samuel's arms. Her chest tightened.

Mr. Nethry appeared in the doorway of the carriage. "That highwayman killed Lord Raventhorpe!"

"I do not believe so," Cilla said. "He is moving." *Raventhorpe was moving.* She took a step forward, then another. Raventhorpe's shoulders were definitely flexing, as if he fought against his bonds. Yet his eyes remained closed.

John took a moment to tie the reins, then jumped down from the coachman's box.

"Guess the lady tied up the earl real tight," Tom Nethry said. "He's squirming like a worm on a hook."

The earl gave a final jerk. His arms were free. His eyes opened, and he leaped to his feet. The light of the setting sun glinted off something in his hand. He braced his legs, drew back his arm, and fixed his gaze on Samuel's back.

"Samuel!" Cilla cried. She rushed forward.

The blade slammed into her shoulder. She staggered and fell to her knees.

"Cilla!" Samuel sprinted toward her.

In one smooth motion, John grabbed his rifle from the coachman's box and fired at the fleeing

Raventhorpe. The earl flinched and stumbled. Blood bloomed on the seat of his trousers. He took two more steps, then fell, gripping the wound.

Samuel reached Cilla's side, landing on his knees in the road. "Let me see. Damned clothes!" He cradled her in a sitting position with one arm and grabbed the hilt of the dagger with the other. He locked eyes with her, willing himself to be calm, willing his hands not to shake. "I have to take it out."

"All right." She bit her lip, her face pale with pain. "I am ready."

He rested his forehead against hers for a moment. "I'm sorry."

"Do it."

He tugged the knife out of the wound. She screamed and lolled in his arms.

"Is she all right?" Annabelle sank to her knees on Cilla's other side. "Oh, God, so much blood. What do you need?"

"Something to use as a bandage."

"Give me the knife. Might as well use all these petticoats for some good." She took the blade from his hand, then pulled up the edge of her dress and began to trim long strips from the edges of her underskirts.

Samuel cupped Cilla's face. "Stay with me, sweetheart." He realized what he'd said and glanced at Annabelle.

"Here." Solemn-faced, Annabelle handed over two long strips of snowy white cotton. "Fold these up and make a pad. I'll cut some more."

Samuel nodded and gently laid Cilla flat, then

ripped the edges of her dress around the tear left by the knife, exposing the injury. The wound oozed blood, a nasty insult to the creamy flesh. Annabelle handed him a folded strip of cloth, and he pressed it hard to try and stop the bleeding.

Cilla cried out, her eyes opening. She laid her hand over Samuel's.

"I'm sorry," he murmured. "We have to do it."

She nodded, then glanced at Annabelle.

"You're going to be fine," Annabelle said. She handed several more strips to Samuel, who began fashioning a bandage.

Each hiss of pain that escaped Cilla's lips made him wish the dagger had hit him instead. "Who tied up Raventhorpe?" he asked, trying to stay focused.

"I did," Annabelle said. "With the knot you showed me. I didn't figure he had a knife."

"You didn't search him first?"

"No, he didn't tell me to."

"Why would Raventhorpe tell you to search him?"

"Not him. Black Bill. He stopped the coach and saved me."

Samuel paused. "Black Bill?"

"He had me tie up Richard, then we heard you coming and he left."

"Samuel." Cilla's whisper grabbed their attention.

"What is it?" He leaned in as she gripped his hand.

"Raventhorpe?"

"We've got him," Samuel said.

"Yeah, don't worry about him," Annabelle said. "Samuel's coachman shot him in the backside."

Cilla smiled, then slipped back into oblivion.

The next hours passed in a blur. John summoned the magistrate and had that gentleman escort Raventhorpe to his private physician, while Samuel brought Cilla and Annabelle home to the Bailey house. A surgeon was summoned to see to Cilla's shoulder.

Samuel went outside to the garden, hoping the open space and foliage would soothe him. Unfortunately nothing was soothing him right now. Raventhorpe had tried to kill him—again. And Cilla had stepped in the way of the blade.

If he had not already realized how he felt about her, today would have brought it home like a cannon blast. He had been lying to himself for years, convincing himself and everyone else that he wasn't capable of love. Really, he was capable of too much, had been hurt too much in his early years, to chance it again. Saying it wasn't in him had kept him safe.

But had it? He'd fallen in love with Cilla. He'd gone along with her plan to learn about men knowing full well she was the romantic type who would naturally fall in love with her lover. But he had done it anyway; he wanted her any way he could get her. He had resigned himself to losing her, regretted the pain that would come for both of them.

But when he'd seen her step in the path of Raventhorpe's knife . . . when he'd held her in his arms while she bled . . . he knew he was fooling himself. He loved her, God help him.

"Samuel?" Annabelle came into the garden.

He turned to face her. "Did the surgeon leave?"

"Not yet." She walked over to him and laid a hand on his arm. "What are you doing out here?"

"I hate waiting, and I want to make sure Ci— Mrs. Burke is doing well before I return to the inn."

"That's kind of you. Would you sit with me?" She pointed to a nearby bench.

He nodded and accompanied her to the stone bench.

"Pa said that he told you what I decided."

"That you want to start courting again? Yes, he told me when we brought you home."

Annabelle twisted her fingers in her lap. "I had just told Richard the engagement was off, which was why he acted the way he did."

"Took it badly, did he?"

"Sure did." She grinned, then grew sober again. "Thank you for coming after me."

"Of course I came after you."

"I know Pa asked you to, and that's why you did it. That was really kind of you."

"It was the right thing to do."

"And you always do the right thing, don't you, Samuel?"

He almost looked away from the candor in those blue eyes. "I couldn't call myself a man if I didn't."

She nodded, then asked, "Do you love me?"

He hesitated. The moment of silence stretched into a whole minute while he sought the words.

"It's all right to tell me the truth."

He let out a breath. "All right then. I'll always look

after you, but no, I'm not in love with you, Annabelle. I don't want to start courting again. You and I can only ever be friends."

"That's what I thought. It's Mrs. Burke, isn't it?"

"What do you mean?"

"I'm not blind, Samuel." She laughed. "All right, maybe I was a little too preoccupied with my own concerns to see what was right under my nose. But when she stepped in front of that knife for you, I saw everything much more clearly. Especially when you were more concerned with her welfare than the fact that Richard was getting away."

"John had it under control."

"Oh, come on now. You've told me some of what Richard did to you, and I've heard rumors about other evil deeds to be laid at his door. The fact that you were more concerned with Mrs. Burke than catching the man who ruined your life speaks volumes to me. She was more important to you than your enemy."

"She'd just risked her life for me. What else was I supposed to do?"

"Yes, she had, and I find that very interesting. Clearly she returns your feelings."

He winced. "Neither one of us wanted to hurt you."

"Oh, I'm not hurt. I'm fond of you both. And goodness, you couldn't make it more clear to me that you were trying to protect me. And Mrs. Burke? She always told me that I should follow my heart. So that's what I'm going to do."

He frowned, puzzled. "Which means . . . ?"

"It means I don't want you to court me, Samuel.

I'd rather wait and marry a man for the right reasons than marry a fellow just to be married." She gave him a little shove. "Now go on upstairs and see how she's doing. I'll be all right."

Samuel jumped to his feet and nearly took off at a run, but he paused to take Annabelle's hand and press a hearty kiss to it. "You are wise beyond your years. Thank you."

"Go on. I just hope she'll let me be in the wedding."

"I'll make sure of it." He squeezed her hand, then hurried toward the house.

Left alone in the garden, Annabelle sighed. "I wonder how many girls have ever lost two suitors in one day?"

"Feeling sorry for yourself?"

She jumped, clapping a hand over her racing heart as Samuel's coachman appeared from around the hedges. "Heavens, what are you doing lurking around the shrubbery? John, isn't it?"

"They call me John Ready." He gave her a graceful bow that struck her as more courtier than coachman.

"Ready? Ready for what?"

He grinned, a wicked twinkle in his eye. "Anything."

She resisted the urge to flirt back. She was done with men, at least for the moment. "What are you doing here?"

"I was looking for Samuel to tell him the surgeon had left."

"And you decided to eavesdrop?"

"I decided not to interrupt. That was a nice thing you did just now."

"It was the right thing to do."

"It was a selfless thing, and you made two people very happy."

She shrugged, a bit embarrassed by his praise. "I'm sure anyone else would do the same thing."

"No," he said, turning away. "They would not."

Cilla's shoulder ached as if it were on fire, but the surgeon had bandaged the wound and proclaimed that she would be about her duties in a week or so.

Although now that there was no wedding, she didn't know what those duties would be.

Her future hung in uncertainty. Now that Annabelle had truly and permanently jilted Raventhorpe, what would happen with Annabelle and Samuel? Would he revisit an old love in hopes of recapturing what he had lost? Would they go back to America together?

Tears stung her eyes, and she turned her head away so the maid who was collecting her damaged clothing would not see. She had survived social ruin and near starvation; she would survive this.

A knock came at the door. Annabelle, no doubt. The girl had been haunting the hallway since the surgeon arrived. She heard the maid open the door and then the whisper of conversation. One of the voices was much lower than Annabelle's—a male rumble. She turned her head just as the maid darted out the door with her arms full of the torn dress, and Samuel entered, leaving the door ajar. Her stomach did that little flip of excitement that it always did when she saw him.

"How is the patient?" His cheerful tone raised her hopes and dashed them all at once. Certainly he must be pleased that Raventhorpe had been defeated. But did that mean that he intended to return to Annabelle?

What if she had taken the chance on trusting her judgment, only to have it prove to be the wrong decision once again?

"The surgeon has declared I shall be fit in a week." She sat up a bit more against the pillows, tugging her long braid over one shoulder and wishing she wore something more alluring than a nightdress. "It was kind of you to ask."

He frowned. "Kind? Cilla, you took a blade meant for me. It is more than kindness."

"Gratitude then. You are welcome." To her horror, the tears stung her eyes again. She glanced away, trying to blink them back. "How is Dolly?"

"Broken leg and a bump on her head. She'll be fine, though she won't be going anywhere for several weeks." He took her hand. "Look at me, sweetheart."

She tugged, but he would not release her until she met his gaze. Damn him for forcing her to show him her doubt. "And Raventhorpe?"

"John summoned the magistrate to take him to his private physician, but though what he did was reprehensible, the bastard may yet escape any legal action."

"But not the scandal. I imagine he will have to flee

the country, at least for a little while." She turned away again. She could barely keep up this polite conversation when her emotions were fighting to burst free in a torrent of tears.

He squeezed her hand. "Look at me, love. I have news."

Her heart clenched at the endearment. "What news?"

"Annabelle has finally given up on me. She knows I'm in love with someone else."

Her entire world flipped over, scattering her emotions like a broken strand of pearls. "She did? You are?"

He pressed a kiss to her palm. "I am. With you."

"Oh." Elation surged through her. She stared into his eyes, hardly able to comprehend the tenderness she saw there. "I thought you said you were not capable of love?"

"I lied. To myself and everyone else."

"Oh, thank heavens." She closed her eyes and took a deep breath to keep her overwhelming joy from reducing her to a blubbering watering pot. "How is Annabelle?"

"She's fine. Annabelle is a smart girl, if young. She wants what her parents have in a marriage, and once I told her that my heart was otherwise engaged, she agreed we should not court after all. She didn't want to live a lie."

"I can hardly credit it." Tears threatened her composure again. She struggled, but the betraying moisture welled in her eyes and began streaming down her cheeks. She sniffled. "I apologize."

"Don't." He handed her his handkerchief and dropped a kiss on her head. "Your soft heart is why I fell in love with you."

These words served to only make the tears come faster. She blotted her eyes and laughed at the mess she must appear. "I imagine I will lose my position here when Dolly finds out. I suppose I can make arrangements to move to my parents' house in London."

"I'm sure Dolly will be pleased for both of us, once she gets over her disappointment. After all, this was Annabelle's decision."

She crumpled the handkerchief in her hand and searched his eyes. "Are you sure this is what you want?"

"Are you crazy? Of course it is." He pressed her hand against his cheek. "You reminded me of what real love is, Priscilla Burke, and I'll be damned if I'll let you slip away from me."

"I never knew myself until I met you."

He cupped her cheek in his palm. "I want a family with you, so you have to marry me."

"Yes. Oh, God, yes." She rubbed her cheek against his hand. "My mother will be thrilled."

"My business is in America, but I imagine we will have to spend some time here in England as well so you can see your family."

"That would be wonderful."

"There is one last thing." Samuel looked down at her hand as he played with her fingers. "I have several more lessons for you. They are absolutely required for a wife."

"Oh? How many more?"

"A lifetime's worth."

She grinned at him. "I expect I will be a most eager student. When do we begin?"

"Now."

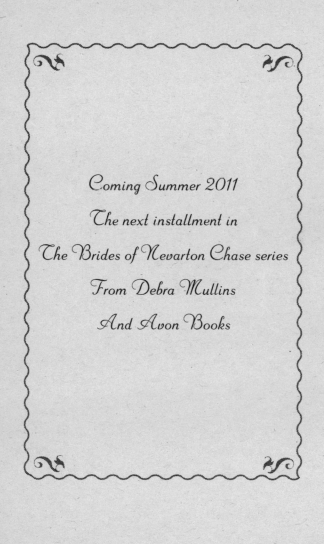

Coming Summer 2011

The next installment in

The Brides of Nevarton Chase series

From Debra Mullins

And Avon Books

At Avon Books, we know your passion for romance—once you finish one of our novels, you find yourself wanting more.

May we tempt you with . . .

- **Excerpts** from our upcoming releases.
- Entertaining **extras**, including authors' personal photo albums and book lists.
- Behind-the-scenes **scoop** on your favorite characters and series.
- **Sweepstakes** for the chance to win free books, romantic getaways, and other fun prizes.
- Writing **tips** from our authors and editors.
- **Blog** with our authors and find out why they love to write romance.
- **Exclusive content** that's not contained within the pages of our novels.

Join us at
www.avonbooks.com

AVON

An Imprint of HarperCollins Publishers
www.avonromance.com

Available wherever books are sold or please call 1-800-331-3761 to order.

FTH 0708